I0550552

BAD TASTE IN MEN

a novel by

Lana Cooper

Copyright © 2013 Lana Cooper
All rights reserved.

ISBN-13: 9780615899602
ISBN-10: 0615899609
Library of Congress Control Number: 2013954072
Delightfully Dysfunctional Books, Philadelphia, PA

For Mom and Dad: I hope I make you as proud of me as I still am of you. Thank you for being the best parents a goofy kid could ever hope for. You have always been and will always be my heroes. I love you and I miss you.

And for Emil: Thank you for showing me that happy endings are possible and for sticking with this tortoise throughout the race. I love you.

AUTHOR'S NOTE

This novel is a work of fiction. Names, characters, businesses, places, events and incidents are either the products of the author's warped imagination or used in a fictitious manner. Any resemblance to actual persons, living or dead, or actual events is one helluva coincidence.

CHAPTER ONE
FACETS

When I was eight years old, I thought I was a lesbian. In an era where prepubescent girls simultaneously played with Barbies and lusted after Garanimals-wearing boys whose testicles had yet to descend, I wondered why I didn't get hot for the jocks of my male playmates, failing to take our mutual affinity for G.I. Joe and wrestling at more than face value. Most girls my age talked constantly about boys they thought were cute. I didn't get it. Boys were my friends, not objects of lust.

The only guy whose name I ever scribbled on my notebook preceded by an "I heart" was Freddy Krueger. I didn't want to marry Freddy; I just admired his sense of humor and style.

I assumed since I wasn't boy-crazy like most of my female contemporaries, I must be gay.

AIDS had recently become a hot topic with the deaths of Liberace and Rock Hudson. On one of the rare occasions where my family and I went out to eat, I recalled overhearing another patron's conversation: "I never knew Rock Hudson was a faggot!"

Growing up in Fletcher, Pennsylvania – a backwards small town with about three black people, a handful of Latinos, and where being different in any way made you a target for abuse – I wondered if being gay was a bad thing.

During our formative years, my younger brother Orion and I could already attest to what it was like to be different. Amidst the bulk of Bobs and abundance of Amandas in Fletcher, being named "Orion" and "Nova" was the equivalent of walking around with a "kick me" sign.

Our parents were much more open-minded than your average Fletcherites. Mom spent her college years in Philadelphia. As a young woman, she sang at Atlantic City's Steel Pier and performed in Summer Stock theatre. After college, she moved back to Fletcher to teach high school English. She quit teaching after my brother was born and it wasn't until we were both in high school that Mom went back.

Dad grew up in Baltimore and spent much of his own youth as a touring musician before settling down in a factory job in Fletcher. The faint trace of Southern accent he harbored earned him the nickname "Grits" from his co-workers. Even after putting down stakes in Fletcher, Dad never totally lost his accent, or his love of music. He and Mom met playing in a local Top 40 / standards band that gigged at supper clubs in the area. Whether he was on the road or living in Fletcher, Dad marched beat of his own drum. Culturally, he identified as half-Jewish, one-quarter Cherokee, and 100% loud n' proud of his heritage. In terms of faith, Dad took the "super sampler" approach to religion, embracing Judaism, Wicca, Methodist Christianity and Catholicism all at once. "They're all the same thing," he opined. "Just different trimmings."

On the flipside, Mom was as die-hard Catholic as they come. Yet, despite her Catholic upbringing, nothing fazed her. An accomplished pianist herself, Mom's Holy Trinity consisted of Jerry Lee Lewis, Little Richard, and Liberace. While "The Killer"'s hetero-status was confirmed in spades, the jury was still out on Little Richard. The question of Liberace's sexuality wasn't answered until his untimely death. But did it matter who was gay or who was straight when you listened to any of these men play?

Our family lived in a two-bedroom rental home on the far edge of Fletcher. Growing up, there were very few kids in our neighborhood. Sharing a room and a mutual disdain for one another for the first ten years of our lives, my brother and I were still each other's only game in town. Like it or not, if I had a secret I absolutely needed to tell someone, that someone was Orion.

"Orion?" I whispered one night across the several foot divide between our twin beds. "Can I tell you a secret?" I paused for dramatic effect as my brother glanced over at me. "I think I'm gay."

My brother broke into a fit of convulsive laughter after promising he wouldn't tell Mom and Dad.

Orion usually blabbed anything I confided in him to Mom. I can chalk up my misplaced trust in him to an altruistic need to hope for the best in others, but I was probably only slightly less gullible as a kid than I am now as an adult.

While I wasn't present for the actual act of my brother diming my midnight confession to Mom, I can only imagine how it all went down: Orion, grinning like a bowl cut-wearing imp, tugging at the hem of Mom's skirt and lisping through a sparsely populated mouth of baby teeth: *"Mom! Guessth what? Nova told me she thinksth she'sth gay! Because she doesthn't like boysth! Justht as friendsth! Haaahaaaahaaa!"* As my brother cackled maniacally, I imagined Mom picking him up in a big hug, laughing along with her youngest child and applauding this resourcefulness that would provide her with solid entertainment at my expense and a reliable means of keeping tabs on her firstborn's antics.

One morning, as Mom was doing my hair, she broached the subject to me in a calm, pleasant, motherly manner. "So, you really think that you're gay?" I was too stunned to hear Mom ask that loaded question to realize that my brother had ratted me out.

I blurted it all out from there, telling Mom that I thought I might be gay because I didn't like boys. All the other girls at school talked about the boys they thought were cute and I didn't think any of them were cute. "Cute" was a term reserved for my stuffed animals, not my male classmates. Was there something wrong with me because I didn't like boys except as friends?

Mom asked me if I was attracted to girls, to which I replied, "No." I wasn't attracted to *anyone*. She laughed and asked me if I knew what being gay meant. I told her that I guessed that it meant when a girl likes girls instead of boys and boys like boys instead of liking girls. I also asked if this was a bad thing, judging by the tone in most Fletcherite's voices whenever they uttered the words "lezzie" or "faggot" – like when the news reported Liberace's death.

Mom explained that being gay was far from being a bad thing. Prompted by the slander hurled at her personal hero, the likeable Liberace who merged classical piano with boogie-woogie, Mom proceeded to give me the most beautiful lesson in tolerance and steering clear of bigotry.

She took off one of her rings and showed it to me. "See these little cuts across the surface of the jewel? Those are called 'facets.' Each gem is made up of hundreds of tiny facets that make it sparkle. Each is an important part of the whole gem, but one facet isn't the whole jewel. Liberace being gay was just one facet of who he was. He was also a great pianist, a decent enough actor, and a nice person who gave to many different charities. And that's what made him sparkle. Everyone is like a gem and has different facets that make us sparkle. You're a funny little girl with a bright imagination. That's part of what makes you sparkle. So, remember, it's all about 'facets'... not 'faggots.'"

Mom would later make fun of me mercilessly whenever she found out about any crushes I had later on in life, but I could forgive every minute she mocked me because she imparted such a wonderful, moving, life lesson that stuck with me ever since.

Even though I came away with a greater understanding of myself and people in general from our little heart-to-heart, I think Mom was relieved that I wasn't interested in dating just yet. She was happy that I was more interested in watching horror movies and playing with toys like a prepubescent kid should.

Mom's relief was short-lived. The following year, at the age of nine, it happened.

I came home from school, not looking any different than I did the day before. "Guess what I got today?"

"An 'A'?" Her tone lacked the excited surprise of a parent whose little underachiever was finally catapulted into the rarified stratosphere of third grade academia. This was more the nonchalance of a parent who expects nothing less from her child.

"Nope," I replied. "I got my period."

Ding, ding, ding! We have a winner! Mom certainly wasn't expecting to hear that. At worst, she may have anticipated that I had received a dreaded B-minus on a book report or test – not that her eldest child would be receiving a lifetime's worth of tickets to monthly gigs by Alexander's Rag Time Band at Snatch Stadium before she turned ten.

"Are you scared?" she asked me.

"Not really. I guess this just means I'm not a little girl anymore?" The words came out with mixed feelings, more sadness than any grain of fear, probably mirroring Mom's own feelings. If there was one thing I was grateful for, it was that my parents – for all their foul language, loud arguments, and crude humor – never talked down to me or my brother as kids.

Mom, in particular, spoke to my brother and me like we were "little adults." The fact that our parents ensured we were both capable of comprehending intellectual conversation as well as discussing the finer points of *Sesame Street* made us much more well-rounded and resilient individuals.

I had already been preconditioned to hearing the term "period." Mom explained that it was a girls-only thing that involved painless bleeding from the area where you pee and mild stomach cramps. Periods also involved these hilarious wads of cotton known as "Kotex" that strapped into your underpants so you didn't get gross blood stains all over your clothes.

Apparently, having one's period also involved a superhuman ability to excuse bitchy behavior, judging by the way that Dad would snarl, "What are you, on your period or something?" whenever Mom would issue one of her biting, sarcastic remarks in his direction.

Mom had already made me well-aware of the concept of "the period," although she had left out the more adult points regarding reproduction. Fortunately (or unfortunately, depending upon how you look at it), I had already been given some insight into the whole sordid process by a classmate.

At school, there was a slut that I was friends with who would describe her tawdry exploits in great detail. (Don't lie. You probably had at least one "slut friend" growing up, too.) I would get an earful from Slut Friend about her uber-romantic evenings with older boys, most of which involved getting felt up on hayrides. Although Slut Friend had already failed third grade twice before, she was still well beyond her years in terms of carnal knowledge.

Mom was relieved that she didn't have to explain the logistics of intercourse to me, since Slut Friend already did. Still, I sensed sadness in Mom's voice as she recounted the workings of the female reproduction system, that having a period meant that you could get pregnant. While I knew that babies didn't come from the stork, Mom dropped the bomb that they don't come out of the mother's stomach, either – unless they had a Cesarean section. When I found out the exact area that they squirmed out of, I confided in Mom, "That's alright; I didn't want to have babies anyway." Mom offered that the birthing process really wasn't as bad as many women make it out to be.

"It's like taking a really big, really hard shit... only from where you pee." And thus, that was how the miracle of childbirth was explained to me by my mother. Her frank, take-no-prisoners explanation was made even funnier when I considered Mom's typically ladylike demeanor and thin, blonde frame. Her take on childbirth didn't have quite the philosophical allure of her speech on facets, but achieved its aim as an adequate descriptor of labor without actually having to go through it.

The rest of puberty's accoutrements soon followed and I developed quite a set of hooters for a 10 year old. I was still "one of the guys," although a few scumbags would occasionally ask, "Can I see them?" to which I would immediately answer with a closed fist to the jaw.

It wasn't until two years later that my elementary school decided to bring in a so-called expert to lecture at an all-girls assembly about the "Wonders of Womanhood." My male friends encouraged me to go to the seminar to procure pamphlets and other "products" to be mined for comedic value and humiliation at the expense of some of the other girls in our class.

I didn't go. There was no need to. I already knew the score. Besides, no motivational menstruational speaker could ever explain it as well or as memorable as Mom did.

CHAPTER TWO
LOVE HURTS

I started developing an interest in boys during fifth grade. Although I was an early convert to puberty, I was a late bloomer in terms of lust. But when it happened, it took hold fast and furious.

The first tremblings of not-so-ladylike feelings below the belt struck while watching an episode of *Donahue* on male strippers. These weren't *any* sausage shakers, though. This episode featured the Chippendale dancers, the pinnacle of class at the top of Male Stripper Mountain.

Watching these chiseled, bronzed men rub themselves down with oil as they gyrated their bulging, leopard-clad crotches to '80s radio rock induced a pleasant tingling in my preteen nether regions. (To this day, I still get a raging girl-boner every time I see a man in leopard underwear or hear Bad Company's "Feel Like Makin' Love.")

To quell this tingling, I started grinding myself against the arm of the chair in as inconspicuous a manner as possible. Promptly after *Donahue*'s credits rolled, I went to my bedroom to rub one out under the pretense of taking a nap before dinner.

While a younger generation may credit Jerry Springer for their first trashy auto-erotic fantasies, I can thank Phil Donahue for mine. (Thanks, Phil!)

After my first magical masturbatory experience, I decided I had to be respectable about my urges and promptly developed my first real celebrity crush.

While most girls my age were pining after the members of New Kids on the Block (interpret that statement with or without a double entendre), I had set my sights on a rock n' roll bad boy. Long before the popular television commercial hawking power ballad compilations had declared it, I believed that "every bad boy has a soft side."

My man of choice was Mick Mars, the guitarist for Mötley Crüe.

I didn't go for blond, pretty boy lead singer Vince Neil or charismatic songwriter/bassist Nikki Sixx. Tommy Lee was married (at the time) to Heather Locklear and at the age of 11, having a crush on a guy who was married was just plain wrong. Besides, I grew up watching *Dynasty* and couldn't lust after Sammy Jo's real-life husband. It was just bad karma.

I picked Mick, "the quiet one." Mick, with his bright blue eyes, vampiric complexion, and long black hair was dubbed by critics as "the creepy one" of the group.

Conversely, *I* was known as "the creepy one" in my elementary school. The attraction was natural.

To glean granules of information about my favorite bands, I would shamelessly sprawl out at an empty checkout counter while my parents went grocery shopping. I faithfully read *Metal Edge*, *RIP*, *Circus* – metal music magazines that were the hard rock equivalent of *Tiger Beat*. In doing so, I learned that Mick loved horror movies, too. At last, a worldly man who could understand me! Someone else who thought Freddy Krueger was as cool as I did and wasn't in fifth grade!

I never wrote "Mrs. Mick Mars" on my spiral-bound notebooks the way other girls used to scrawl "Mrs. Joey McEntyre" or "I *heart* Jordan Knight" on theirs. I didn't want to be one of "those girls."

In my pre-teen fantasies, I'd be content to "live in sin" (like the Bon Jovi song!) or (to use Mom's terminology) "shack up" in blissful cohabitation with Mick when he wasn't touring. He was a man of the road whose guitar and music came first. Even though I was only eleven, I understood that. There would be plenty of time for us to debate bands and horror movies, go to the mall, or get Blizzards at Dairy Queen when he came off the road with the Crüe.

By the time sixth grade rolled around, I started looking for a crush my own age who didn't live thousands of miles away, who wouldn't get arrested if he took me on a (imaginary) date to Dairy Queen, and most importantly, who was actually aware of my existence.

That's when I started liking Frankie Gilroy, a boy in my grade.

Frankie and I had gone to the same elementary school before he transferred to St. Basil's, the local parochial school.

Back in third grade, I liked Frankie as nothing more than a friend.

Fast forward three years later and Mom decided to transfer me and Orion to Catholic school. The local public intermediate school was two steps above prison, and considering I could be a bit unruly, Mom figured it would be a bad influence on my already mischievous behavior. Mom, a product of Catholic schools herself, thought that I would benefit from what she dubbed "The Nun Experience."

Thanks to a parish scholarship fund, my parents were able to find it within their means to pay a fraction of the tuition costs to give me "The Nun Experience" I may not have otherwise had.

That said, there are two types of kids who attend Catholic school: The first being the kids whose parents are parish suck-ups and have money to burn.

The second classification includes the kids who aren't quite bad enough to land in a juvenile detention facility but still require a stronger strain of discipline – like rehab with knee socks.

You can guess which group I fell into.

Much like prison, Catholic school plants kids with a roguish streak among a population of like-minded individuals who thrive on a sense of chaos, enabling them to compare techniques for inducing mayhem and to learn new ones. Many of the boys attending St. Basil's came from my elementary school and were probably enrolled for the same reasons I was.

One of the guys I had rekindled a friendship with was Frankie Gilroy. He had grown a foot taller since I last saw him three years ago and looked like more of an adult than most of the guys in my grade. He was thin, pale, and gawky with wavy blond hair. He was also the only guy in my grade who had the capability of growing a mustache.

I thought he was hot stuff.

Even better, Frankie was... Weird.

One of the reasons I took such a liking to Frankie in "that way" was because I admired his blatant attempts at entertaining and attention whoring.

In hindsight, I was a bit of an attention whore myself.

Since there were very few kids in the neighborhood where my family lived, I spent a lot of time in front of the tube logging a ridiculous amount classic television and prime-time programming.

It was "Must See TV" that shaped my young consciousness and branded me with an impression of what impending adulthood could be like.

I wanted to enter a room like Norm from *Cheers* and deliver devastating one-liners like ALF, ready with a quick remark or hilarious catchphrase that would elicit laughter and applause from everyone in the room.

My favorite show was *The Golden Girls*. I couldn't get enough of those sassy seniors. Maybe it was because I grew up around adults and was treated as one, but I found myself identifying with Dorothy, Rose, Blanche, and Sophia more than any of the characters on *Blossom* or *Full House*. (That was probably a good thing, considering the life path I might have taken if I looked to Joey Gladstone as a role model. Then again, Dave Coulier *did* manage to get a hummer from Alanis Morisette in a theatre, so he must have been doing something right.)

Mom and my brother were big *Golden Girls* fans, too. Owing to my bookish nature – and deep voice for a twelve year old girl – Mom dubbed me the Dorothy of our family. Played by Bea Arthur, Dorothy was gifted with a sarcastic wit, often cutting down everyone else in the house with stinging one-liners. At the same time, Dorothy was also the brunt of nearly every one of her mother Sophia's jokes.

While I dug Dorothy, I would have preferred to have been Blanche.

As a 40-year-old trapped in the body of an overdeveloped, puberty-stricken 12-year-old, the character of Blanche Deveraux was the greatest possible example from which I could take notes on how to get guys.

I figured that my relatively deep voice for a girl would be off-putting to boys and negatively impact my chances of getting one to go out with me. That was when I decided to adopt a fake Southern accent. I used it to loudly announce my presence each morning to the rest of the class with a bold, "Hi, y'all!" If it worked for Blanche, it just might work for me in terms of attracting the opposite sex.

My teachers never inquired as to where this accent suddenly came from. Probably because they all knew I was slightly off my rocker to begin with. My fellow students thought nothing of it, either. As much of an attention whore that I was, I think they enjoyed being entertained by my pathetic attempts at creating a zany persona.

While I was acquiring my own set of preteen eccentricities, Frankie Gilroy was busy snapping up his.

One fine day, Gilroy announced that he brought a tin of Kiwi shoe polish with him to use as a lubricant to whack off in the school bathroom.

No one took Frankie seriously until he asked to be excused during fifth period. He returned ten minutes later in the middle of Sustained Silent Reading, showing a select group of friends the dark brown hue that had adhered to the crooks of his palm after having allegedly waxed his carrot in the crapper.

I thought that was *so* cool.

Looking back, I should have realized that if Frankie Gilroy really *did* whack off with shoe polish, he'd have ended up in the school nurse's office instead of returning to class. He was merely milking this stunt for comedic value and to shock our classmates.

I *still* thought he was beyond cool.

Adding to Gilroy's cool points was the fact that he wrote songs. This was obviously the musician mojo at work. Most chicks are susceptible to the potent power of guys who play music, only I was too young and to unsophisticated in the ways of love (or "like") to realize what strange magic was at work.

Writing assignments are a given in school, and as budding artists, Frankie Gilroy and I took it upon ourselves to use these educational experiences to turn our classmates into a captive audience. While I made up fanciful stories about my friends and me engaging in all manner of illegal activities and triumphing in the face of the establishment, Frankie would read aloud his own poetic creations, sans music, like a beat poet of yore. The one that brought it home for me was the underdog epic, "A Man Like Costanza," an eloquent metaphor for self-esteem issues utilizing *Seinfeld's* toady to illustrate these adolescent pangs. (Frankie and I also shared a common muse in primetime television.)

Frankie's words resonated with me. With a persistent sinus condition and glasses so thick they could burn ants on a summer sidewalk; I, too, had felt much like the ne'er-do-well nebbish, George Costanza. I was a dork, but like George, I aspired to be so much more.

In a school designed around the concept of routine and conformity – using bland, navy blue-and-white uniforms and First Friday Mass as its tools of orthodoxy – I had found a kindred spirit in Frankie.

Okay, let's not romance it up too much here. I found *many* kindred spirits at St. Basil's. However, I think Frankie's patent weirdness was the reason why he was the only guy in my class I had a crush on.

Most girls chuckled at Frankie's extrovert antics but didn't give him a second glance. They didn't dislike him, but it became pretty clear that (like me), Frankie was destined for that dread alternate dimension of junior high existence known as "The Friend Zone."

Unconsciously, I think it was my internal defense mechanism to go for the guys that no one else was interested in. I didn't want to be part of a competition that I knew I would lose if a guy was given another choice of female besides me.

This was when I decided that I would ask Frankie Gilroy if he wanted to go out.

Up until that point, I didn't tell anyone that I liked him. Whenever some girl went rogue, foaming at the mouth, professing her "love" for some boy or started scribbling his name on her note book, most of the girls I hung out with and *all* of the guys would roll their eyes.

There was no way I would let myself become one of *those* chicks.

Through the years, I worked hard to develop a reputation as a bad ass. Before developing this reputation, my coke bottle glasses, sinus condition, puberty-induced acne, dandruff, and huge boobs made me a target for bullies.

Despite my mother insisting that I was "the nicest little girl" when I was younger, she knew the day would come when I would snap like a rubber band and exact stern vengeance upon my elementary school classmates who dared make fun of me.

Fortunately, both of my parents believed that sometimes, the only thing some people understand is a good, hard rap in the mouth. Dad taught me to fight in case I ever had to match hurtful insults from classmates with physical blows.

My initiation into Club Bad Ass came in the third grade. It had been a long, torment-filled day at school. As I walked to the car where Mom was waiting, a girl in my grade started yelling that I stuffed my bra and that my boobs were actually two globules of snot suspended from my chest.

Her words were enough to make me literally see red and black out with rage. I heard Dad's voice in my head, sounding like a gravelly Obi-Wan Kenobi with a slight Southern accent: "If you control the head, you control the whole body."

In my Hulk-like rage, I wound the girl's hair around my fist and used it to commandeer her nose into the nearest brick wall. When I heard the girl screaming and crying, I realized what I had done and made a beeline for Mom's car.

I climbed into the familiar maroon '76 Charger Daytona and instructed my mother to "just drive" and get the hell out of there as fast as possible. Reluctantly, I told her what had happened. I was afraid I'd be punished for wailing away on my tormentor. Instead, Mom beamed with pride that I finally stood up for myself.

You know the old saying, "sticks and stones may break my bones, but names will never hurt me"? Well, names *do* hurt. They stick in your craw and come creeping back at inopportune moments to eat away at your self-esteem. Even if the person who says hurtful things to you isn't worth a damn, it's still something that takes a long time to get over. Usually, seeing that person 20 years later; fat, balding, and miserable in life is the best therapy ever.

However, when you're a kid, you live in the moment and don't have the benefit of that vindication until much later. You have no clue of what will happen to you in the future – or to anyone else, for that matter. You think the status quo may never change.

The best coping mechanism I could whip up at that time was cultivating a hard ass image. It deterred bullies who soon learned that I would put up a fight if provoked.

While this carefully built reputation afforded me more respect from my peers, a sense of sanity, and the ability to concentrate on my studies without being bullied; it was also one of the reasons why Mom put me in Catholic school.

There was no way I was going to ruin my rep by copping to a goofy schoolgirl crush. I would keep this info that I totally had a thing for Frankie Gilroy under my hat ... and five-inch, spray-mounted bangs that were oh-so-fashionable at the time.

And I sure as hell wasn't going to tell my brother. He would have a field day with the news that I actually liked a guy and blab to Mom and Dad.

As for the rest of my family, Dad was oblivious to either of his kid's crushes. I preferred to keep it this way. Although Dad was cool and the parent least likely to freak out about anything,

I still didn't want to spill the beans about having the hots for a guy to my Pops.

Telling Mom would be a very bad move. Although she could explain life's lessons with an unparalleled candor, Mom was still a kid at heart. The type of kid who would tease you mercilessly about liking someone. I knew that if she teamed up with my kid brother, they would make my life unbearable. I winced imagining their sing-song taunts of "Ooooooh! Nova likes Frankie Gilroy!" followed by a series of kissy faces and smooching noises.

I decided to take the direct route and ask Frankie out myself. There would be no passing of incriminating notes or recruiting a third-party classmate to find out if he liked me or not.

I would do this on my own.

I devised a plan to get Frankie alone in the hallway between classes. I shadowed him coming out of Social Studies and waited for an opportune moment when there were very few people around to hear what I had to say.

"Hey, Frank," I said in as nonchalant a manner as I could muster. For all he knew, I could have been ready to inquire what he brought for lunch.

I knew better, though. This was it. I was going to ask him out.

"Hey, Nova. What's up?" Frank was equally nonchalant.

I got right down to the nitty gritty. "Not much. I was wondering..." I paused, peering seductively from behind my coke-bottle glasses before bringing my gaze straight ahead to his. "You're not dating anyone. I'm not dating anyone. We have a lot in common and I think you're very attractive. Have you ever thought about... Maybe being more than just friends and going out sometime?"

There! I said it! I said I liked him without actually *saying* that I liked him!

Frankie stood quietly for a moment. The corner of his mouth twitched.

For a split second, I wondered if this cinematic pause would precede him sweeping me into his arms like in the final scene of *An Officer and A Gentleman*, carrying my chunky ass down the hall while we sucked face.

In my momentary reverie awaiting his response, I mused that perhaps he was at a loss for words and contemplating if it would be better to *show* me how he felt.

Oh, Frankie Gilroy showed me how he felt alright.

With a spit take.

The cough drop Frankie had been sucking on flew out of his mouth and onto the cold linoleum of St. Basil's hallowed hallway.

"Fuck no!" Gilroy exclaimed. "You're ugly!"

I knew I wasn't going to make the cover of *Maxim*, but a simple "no" would have sufficed. If he was feeling particularly wordy, he could have added that time-honored excuse (one that I would hear many times thereafter): "I don't want to ruin our friendship."

That was when all of my coquettish, Blanche Deveraux-esque charm dissipated.

At that moment, my real voice came through – loud, deep and booming. I decided it was time to man up and own my Bea Arthur-ness. Would Dorothy Zbornak take this shit?

To quote Frankie Gilroy's own words, "Fuck no!"

That's when I unleashed a torrent of insults in Frankie Gilroy's direction. I was hurt that someone I had considered a friend could be that harsh. Even if I *was* kind of, well... ugly, to put it mildly.

I was humiliated and had to save face. I couldn't let anyone see me in a fragile state, so I started saying the most insulting, horrible things I could think of in retaliation.

By this point, our little debacle had gathered an audience. And the attention whore that I was at the time craved nothing more than an audience to play to. If they wanted drama, I was only too happy to give them one hell of a show.

To his credit, Frankie fired back some good shots himself: "I never saw a pepperoni pizza wear glasses before" and "Some girls are built like a brick shithouse. You're just built like shit!"

However, I delivered the final, clinching blow right before the lunch bell rang:

"Why you gotta be so mean, sweet thang?! You weren't like that last night *at all!*"

The girls clutched their nameplate necklaces. The boys cheered me on with a stunned "Ohhhh!," rooting that I'd say something even more shocking to Gilroy.

It was obvious that Frankie and I hadn't so much as locked pinkies let alone plowed, but the implication of it was enough to make him feel disgusted, mentally violated, and publicly humiliated.

I had won.

It was a hollow victory, though. Irreparable damage had been done to our friendship in less than three minutes.

I kept it together until I went to bed that night and could safely wallow in my own self-pity.

Was I really that ugly? Sure, I was chunky, but there were girls who were a lot fatter than I was and who had more zits. I wasn't the only girl in my grade with glasses. Maybe it was my personality that was off-putting? I had tried to camouflage my faults with the saucy, pseudo-Southern belle routine, but obviously, that didn't work too well.

Moving forward, I decided to drop the pretense. I utilized the full, raspy quality of my real voice and became even more blunt and tactless than before.

Reveling in my darker side proved liberating. If people were going to like me or find me obnoxious, it would be because I'd given them the full dose of who I really was.

Even if Frankie Gilroy didn't like me, I liked me.

Sort of. Okay, not really.

Truthfully, I would have been more surprised if Frankie Gilroy had actually said, "Yes, Nova! You're the girl of my dreams! Let's go to Chez McDonald's this weekend and I'll let you Super-Size it, baby!"

I pretty much knew I was going to be turned down, but wanted to ask him out for my own peace of mind rather than wondering "what if." Despite the fact that the dude tore me a new one and expressed zero interest in being "a little more than friends," I still dug him.

Even worse, I thought that in time he'd change his mind and want to go out with me.

The smart thing to do would be to walk away entirely. But that's kind of hard to do when an assigned seating chart places you in a row across from him for six hours a day.

I reached out for help and made mention of the incident to my brother. Initially, Orion offered a supportive, "Wow. That sucks" followed promptly by fiendish laughter. It wouldn't be long before he blabbed this latest item to Mom. I should have known better.

Usually, Orion would have at least afforded me the dignity of telling Mom about some of the more unsavory aspects of my personal life without my actually being present.

As fate would have it, my wounds were still fresh when Mom, Orion, and I were shopping after school and we ran into Frankie and his mother. Mrs. Gilroy was always a nice lady and she and Mom were pretty chummy. They chatted for a while in the mall.

Neither Frankie nor I said a word to each other.

After his family and mine went our separate directions, Mom remarked that it was odd that Frankie and I didn't say anything to each other, especially since I talked about him a lot at home.

"That's because Frankie turned Nova down," Orion piped up excitedly.

He paused for dramatic effect and to allow my shock and awe to register. Once he was satisfied that it had sunken in, he emphatically re-stated the words with a knowing smirk: "Turned. Her. *Down*."

I was livid.

"I knew it! I knew you liked him!" Mom shouted, pointing a finger at me.

My jaw was still on the mall floor right outside of The Shoe Shack. Orion grinned, damn near turning a celebratory cartwheel.

"So, what happened?" There was a vague undercurrent of sympathy in Mom's voice, but her tone was far more like detective leading a line of questioning.

And my brother had a front row seat to my humiliation.

I recounted my tale of woe to Mom as we walked the length of the mall.

"He actually said that you?"

"Yep."

"Well, it serves you right. Girls shouldn't ask guys out. That's just not right."

Mom's proclamation was met with peals of Ed McMahon-like laughter from Orion. "Ha, ha, ha, ha... Yes!"

I trudged alongside my family. At Mom's behest, I continued the story.

"At least you redeemed yourself," Mom voiced her approval.

That made me feel a little better. From Mom, that was the closest you could get to an outpouring of emotion.

For the rest of sixth and seventh grade at St. Basil's, I remained an extroverted class clown, as did Frankie.

The guys in my class, most of whom I was good friends with, never let Frankie live that day down. Quite often, they'd either try to put in a good word for me or just tease Frankie about what happened. It was common knowledge that, in spite of everything, I still had a crush on him.

My crafty 12-going-on-40 brain kept trying to devise ways in which I could pull off the impossible and get him to like me back.

Years of watching soap operas and professional wrestling (virtually the same thing, at times) taught me that people always want the person they know they can't have. Something is infinitely more appealing when you know that there is no chance of obtaining it – or that it would be all the more satisfying to take it from a rival for your own.

That's when I hit upon an ingenious plan sure to catch Frankie's attention: I invented my own boyfriend.

His name was Bob... Just "Bob."

The impetus for Bob-Just-Bob came about thanks to a random pervert who called a pay phone outside a neighborhood supermarket where my friends and I used to hang out.

One sunny spring day, my friends (who still went to public school) and I were scoping out the parking lot of Price Chopper, looking for abandoned handicapped carts to race around the lot.

That's when the pay phone rang.

My friend Dave picked it up. On the other end was a voice saying things in hushed tones that would make even the most hardcore perv on *Dateline: To Catch a Predator* blush. It was hard to tell how old this dude was. Breathing heavily tends to do that. I thought I heard his voice crack a few times, so he may not have been much older than me and my friends.

We asked the goon what his name was. Between orgasmic grunts he replied, "Bob... Just 'Bob'."

As Bob-Just-Bob yelped in the heat of the moment that he liked to eat his own spooge, the idea hit me that Bob-Just-Bob would make the perfect boyfriend!

Wait a minute! Let me explain!

No, I wasn't such damaged goods from the Frankie Gilroy experience that I thought some unseen pervert beating his meat for a bunch of pre-teens on a supermarket pay phone was a prime piece of dating real estate. Instead, this bizarre display of vocal exhibitionism made me realize that if Bob-Just-Bob could pretend... So could I!

I perfected my plot over the weekend, concocting the perfect story of how my soon-to-be sweetie Bob-Just-Bob and I had met before divulging the details of my latest love interest to my classmates. Surely, this would make Frankie Gilroy jealous once he heard that some older boy had it bad for me.

I had to make this realistic. It was hard to tell just how old Bob-Just-Bob was over the phone. Judging by the Peter Brady-esque cracks in his voice, he couldn't have been more than 15. That would work perfectly. Saying that I was dating anyone older than 15 or 16 years old wouldn't be believable.

I left out the part where Bob-Just-Bob proclaimed his love of a high protein diet of the homemade variety. It didn't exactly scream "knight in shining armor."

When I returned to school on Monday, I made it my business to all but glow, overflowing with joy at my new (and completely fabricated) romance.

Spring was here. Love was in the air. And I was brimming with bullshit.

I dropped my bullshit bomb at lunch. Since St. Basil's was such a small school, you could still make out inklings of everyone else's conversations even if you sat at a table clear across the room. This would be the perfect vehicle for getting out the word about Bob-Just-Bob.

I covered the bases of how Bob-Just-Bob and I met:

"Well, I was standing outside of Price Chopper with my friends when he caught my attention."

It's not like it was a total lie.

"He's a little bit older than me."

Once again, I wasn't exactly lying. At the very least, the real Bob-Just-Bob had to be old enough to both manufacture and snack on his own boy batter.

That was where fact ended and the fiction began.

According to me, Bob-Just-Bob was tall, pale, had medium-length brown hair and went to public school. (Nine times out of ten, whenever a girl in Catholic school wants to make up a story that she has a boyfriend, this fictional creation usually attends public school.)

Bob-Just-Bob was also a big fan of Mötley Crüe. I was wearing one of my favorite band t-shirts, sparking our conversation outside of that temple of adolescent ardor, Price Chopper.

I explained that we exchanged phone numbers. (Pfft! That'd be the day! Imagine midnight calls from the *real* Bob-Just-Bob.)

Via our flurry of phone conversations, Bob-Just-Bob and I agreed we would meet up for a "date" at the mall the following Saturday afternoon.

Then, one of the girls asked the hard line question: "What's Bob's last name?"

Shit! I hadn't thought of that! Why didn't I think of a last name for Bob-Just-Bob!?

Thinking on my feet, I said that we had been having such a great conversation that I didn't even think to ask what his last name was. (Whew! Good answer!)

Other than that, I played it cool, not really making a big deal that I had a big (albeit fictitious) date with an older boy that weekend.

Maybe it was just my imagination, but although I never told him on a one-on-one basis, Frankie Gilroy seemed to be looking in my direction more often in the lunch room and in some of our classes where the alphabetical seating chart order didn't apply.

I knew my plan would work!

Fully committed to living the lie, I made sure I was at the mall, right on time for my two o'clock "date" with Bob-Just-Bob.

Just as I was making my entrance, I ran into two classmates who were leaving the mall.

Perfect! On Monday, they would be sure to leak back to the rest of the class that I was there for my big date!

I patrolled the mall for about an hour or so, checking out the book store and record shop before heading back home to formulate details of my rendezvous with Bob-Just-Bob.

Digging through my mental files for juicy tidbits from *Days of Our Lives* and professional wrestling plotlines to come up with just the right post-modern love story, I decided that this "date" had cemented our status as a couple. Bob-Just-Bob and I were now officially boyfriend and girlfriend. Eat that, Frankie Gilroy!

At school on Monday, I held court in the lunchroom, dishing the details of my "big date" with Bob-Just-Bob. I decided that his last name was "Kryznik," in case that question came at me again. It was so ethnic and completely unattractive-sounding that there was no way it could be a fake name.

The rest of the story was such a load of horseshit. I almost grossed myself out with syrupy details that we held hands in the mall and got pizza in the food court.

However revolting the details of my imaginary romance were, the plan seemed to be working. For the first time in months since "the incident," Frankie Gilroy was talking to me again.

I couldn't tell if it was because he figured that since I was so preoccupied with my new "boyfriend" that he was officially off my list and safe from my clutches. Or, maybe he was jealous because he had been replaced as the object of my affections. Nevertheless, I played it to the hilt.

Frankie never addressed the issue of my new "boyfriend," but it was apparent he knew. The story that "Nova Porter is dating an older boy!" was the talk of the seventh grade. Things between Frankie and I seemed to have gone back to the good ol' days when we'd laugh, joke, and try and out-do one another with shock tactics on our classmates and teachers.

A few weeks later, I had grown tired of maintaining the charade. I decided that my plan to catch the attention of Frankie Gilroy was working and that it was time to dissolve the faux courtship between Bob-Just-Bob and myself.

I made it a point to look depressed one Monday when I returned to school. I worked myself into the role, becoming an entirely different and downcast animal from my normally gregarious self. It was Oscar-worthy.

Oh-so-reluctantly, I told my classmates what had happened, claiming that things just weren't working out and the age difference was awkward. My parents were fine with it, but I just felt that "it wasn't our season" – or some crap like that. However, Bob-Just-Bob and I would remain friends.

The news got around to Frankie Gilroy, just like I knew it would.

Did he seize his opportunity, recognizing that I was "the one that got away" and that he now had a second chance? Did he sweep me off my feet and carry me off into the sunset?

Nope. In fact, Frankie Gilroy went back to being a total dick to me. So much for that brief period of détente.

Not even losing weight allowed me to ensnare the affections of Frankie Gilroy.

Between myself, Mom, and the family doctor noticing that I was a few pounds overweight, they put me on a strict 1,200 calorie a day diet. I lost twenty pounds safely over the course of eight months and was noticeably thinner by the summer before seventh grade.

Dieting didn't make Frankie Gilroy want to go out with me any more than he did before. If someone doesn't want to go out with you, it wouldn't make a difference if you surgically grafted a mask of Heidi Klum to your face if that other person just doesn't have a connection with you. (Furthermore, if you're enough of a whacko to actually go through the trouble of adhering a supermodel's face to your own, there's probably a damn good reason why no one wants to date you.) As far as Frankie Gilroy was concerned, I just happened to be creepy and off-putting enough on my very own.

Shortly before the start of eighth grade, in an act of mutual accordance with Sister Joan (my arch-nemesis, school principal, and overlord of the Order of the Immaculate Heart of Pure Evil), it was decided that it would be best that I no longer attend St. Basil's. My particular brand of humor and lifestyle choices were deemed inappropriate behavior for a 13-year-old girl attending parochial school.

Sister Joan took issue with my reading tabloid magazines during Sustained Silent Reading. And she *really* took issue with my offering a supplemental account of my hometown's history in class one day, citing Fletcher's past as both a prominent coal mining town and thriving red light district in the early 1900s.

And while it was perfectly okay for girls whose parents were major parish contributors to sport Lee Press-On Nails that could lance a boil from five feet away, it was deemed a major moral infraction if I wore purple glitter on my short, stubby nails.

Fortunately, Mom also felt that my time for "The Nun Experience" had passed and that it would be better for me to attend public school. It was cheaper and the faculty wouldn't be as uptight.

So, I left on the next train out of Dodge and headed for the local public junior high school. Unlike Pat Garrett – or even Mrs. Garrett (Tootie!), for that matter – I never got my man.

At least I never wrote "I *heart* Frankie Gilroy" – or "I *heart* Bob-Just-Bob" – on my notebooks. There's some small shred of dignity in that.

CHAPTER THREE
HOME ECCHH: A LEGEND IN MY OWN MIND

Fresh from "The Nun Experience," I was enrolled in a local public middle school at the start of eighth grade. While East Fletcher Junior High had some good teachers, the capacity for learning was pretty low considering that it was two steps above prison. Most of this could be attributed to the incompetence of the school's principal who allowed the inmates to run the asylum.

I had to suck it up and deal, however. I was stuck at this particular school thanks to town boundary jurisdictions. Since I lived in the northern part of town, I was condemned to a school on the east side. (When you consider the whole of Fletcher encompasses only 10 miles, the idea of boundary jurisdictions is even more ridiculous.)

East Fletcher Junior High – tersely referred to as "East" by students – resembled a prison with its high, grey walls and a large, wrought iron fence topped with spikes. There was very little natural light in the hallways and the classrooms were reminiscent of dank interrogation rooms.

Within my first few weeks at East, I was a hit with the teachers, racking up straight A's. The teachers liked me, but I didn't really fit in with the rest of the kids. Regularly getting hit with spitballs in home economics was my first clue.

In an attempt to entertain myself, I set my sights on another recent transfer, some kid named Bob Barlow. I decided he was the guy I would try to ensnare before I left East.

Maybe I was just stuck on the name "Bob" (what with my fictional romance with Bob-Just-Bob hovering in the not-so-distant past), but ironically, Bob Barlow looked a lot like my fictitious description of Bob-Just-Bob.

He was average height with peach fuzz on his upper lip standing out against his pale, acne-speckled skin. Adding to Bob's super-hot bad boy factor was his dark, flowing mullet with a heavy fringe of bangs that looked as if they were snipped by Moe from The Three Stooges himself.

I wanted to *nyuck-nyuck-nyuck* him in the worst way.

Bob and I were in the same gym class. He and I frequently forgot gym clothes or proper attire for what loosely passed for Phys. Ed.

The punishment for forgetting your gym clothes and not participating in P.E. was to write "lines" while sitting on the sidelines on the gym floor. (Bleachers? What are those?!) Students hurling dodgeballs at one another didn't create the most intimate atmosphere, but it didn't stop me from trying to strike up a conversation with the kid.

"So, what do they have you writing?"

"Lines," he mumbled.

"Yeah. Me, too. How many times do you have to write them?"

"100."

Bob was quite the sparkling conversationalist.

"I only had to do 50. I'm bored as shit now." I figured I'd throw in a "shit" to show him I was no square.

"Yeah," Bob grunted as he diligently continued scribbling his P.E. penance.

This was going to pose quite a challenge. It was evident that Bob lacked the charisma of Frankie Gilroy, nevertheless, he was still (pseudo) eye candy.

In a last-ditch effort that reeked of desperation, I blurted out, "Hey! If you want, I could finish those lines for you? I'm pretty good at forging handwriting. Besides, I'm bored."

"No," Bob replied. "That's okay."

Well, that was a riveting exchange.

I sat back against the wall and watched my classmates engage in sanctioned, ball-lobbing barbarism while I contemplated the deeper mysteries of the universe: *Will I ever get a date? Will Jay Leno ever live up to Johnny Carson? Will Vince Neil ever get back with Mötley Crüe? Can't we all just get along?* And the ever-popular: *How the hell am I going to make it out of this school alive?*

I was saved from the crashing waves of my inner thoughts by the dismissal bell and headed to my next class.

Little did I know that fate would have much more in store for me than baking zucchini bread in seventh period home ec(ch).

It was a Friday like any other. Students were restless and rambunctious, ready for the long Columbus Day weekend. Rodney Alberts, a student who I had been at odds with throughout my stay at East, was feeling more rambunctious than usual.

While I had my back turned, Alberts hocked a loogie at the back of my head. I whipped around to see a shit-eating grin on the little bastard's face.

In retaliation, I spat a similarly-sized lunger back at him before grabbing a paper towel and dabbing at the besmirched strands of my long, brown hair.

I turned around again, satisfied by the look of horror Alberts registered after being given taste of his own medicine.

When I got back to my seat, Alberts came over and said, "You made a big mistake, Porter. Big mistake."

I thought nothing of it. I figured if he attempted to retaliate, I could take him down. Alberts was only a few inches taller than me. A skinny, blonde runt with a bowl cut and glasses.

Alberts, however, was a skinny, *fast* runt and more disgusting than I had initially given him credit for.

Some of my classmates informed me that Alberts was planning on saving up a mouthful of spit for the remainder of the period – approximately 33 minutes and 27 seconds worth of saliva – and spewing it at me when the bell rang.

Pfft! No way! No one would be even remotely that gross to do that, I thought to myself.

I looked back over my shoulder and saw Alberts swishing a mouthful of spit around in his mouth, his eyes tinted with the maniacal glimmer of one who was amazed by his own vile capabilities.

I figured this was just for show. A mere scare tactic.

Boy, was I wrong.

After the bell rang, Alberts cut directly in front of me, unleashing a massive stream of spit directly in my face. The gooey mess splattered against my glasses, dripped down my chin and onto my shirt. If I didn't know any better, I'd have sworn I had just wandered off of the set of *Bukkake Bonanza 14* with the amount of bodily fluid dribbling from my face.

Alberts took off running.

I ran down the hallway after him, spit flying off of me as I unleashed a torrent of expletives:

"You fucking motherfucker! I'm going to beat your fucking ass, you piece of fucking shit! I'll rip your dick off and fuck you in the mouth with it, you fucking cum stain!"

My angry tirade echoed throughout the halls of East. As luck would have it, a teacher finally poked her head out of her classroom. With a pen and pink slip in hand, she wrote me up for foul language and sent me to the principal's office.

The teacher was oblivious to the fact that I was soaked in spit. I explained to her that there was a damn good reason for my flurry of "fucks," and that I was running after the person who slathered me in slobber.

Rolling her eyes, she also wrote up a ticket for Rodney Alberts, sending him to the principal's office, too.

I managed to convince her to let me go to the bathroom to wash my face and wipe my glasses off. She agreed on the condition that she accompany me to the bathroom, lest I take off on a wanton crime spree if left unattended. She hovered behind me as I washed my face, watching me like a prison warden ready to spring should I attempt to make a break for it.

A few minutes later, I made my way to the principal's office where I was joined by Rodney Alberts.

"You know we wouldn't be here right now if you didn't spit back at me," he whined.

"No, asshole. We wouldn't be here right now if *you* hadn't spit at me in the first place."

He stared stupidly at the floor. "You know we're *both* gonna be in big trouble now."

I rolled my eyes just as Principal Deskins burst into the room.

Deskins was in his mid-50s; tall and thin with even thinner hair. The harsh lighting of his office gleamed off of his balding scalp. One glance at the principal's bulbous, red nose and it was clear that gin was Deskins' beverage of choice. Probably Banker's Club, or some other bottom shelf blockbuster.

He sat down at his desk. "What happened?" he barked impatiently. "I don't have time for this bullshit. Nova, you tell your side of the story first."

"I was sitting in home ec and Alberts spit at the back of my head. It was gross and uncalled for. So, I spit back at him. Then he decided to save up a mouthful of spit for the rest of class and spewed it at me when the bell rang. Which is what all *this* is," I said, pointing to the spit stains covering the front of my shirt.

Shaking his head with disgust, Deskins leaned forward. "So, you spit back at him?"

"Yes. It was my first reaction. I mean, who the hell gets the bright idea to spit at someone else *in home ec*, of all places?"

"That's irrelevant," Deskins spoke. "Young ladies do not spit. That's disgusting. *You* disgust me."

I was flabbergasted. "*I* disgust *you*? *Alberts* was the one who spit first! At *me*! How am I the bad guy here?"

"That's not the point," he dismissed. "Young ladies don't spit back at someone. Didn't your parents teach you anything?"

I'd just been attacked by Rodney Alberts and his superlative spit-saving and spewing capabilities. Now the *school principal* was attacking me for defending myself?! Even better, this red-nosed imbecile was insinuating my parents' child-rearing skills were subpar!

Alberts sat in the seat next to me, grinning from ear to ear. Principal Deskins was all but giving him a free pass.

That was it. The floodgates were flung wide open and Alberts's shower of saliva would be just a mere drizzle by the time I was finished foaming at the mouth.

"So, I disgust you?" I said, channeling my best De Niro.

"Yes." Deskins's face contorted. "What you did was disgusting."

"So, *I* disgust *you*, for taking matters into my own hands? Obviously, you're not doing shit about it. I suppose you think I should have sat there and taken it?"

Deskins opened his mouth to speak. I cut him off. "You don't do *shit*! This school is a joke. It's the worst in the city. Because you don't do your job. And *I* disgust *you*?!"

"Now wait just a minute!" Deskins roared.

"No. *You* wait a minute. You are the most useless, fucking sexist asshole pig I have ever encountered in my short life."

"What!?" He was good and pissed now.

And so was I. "You didn't hear me the first time? Take the dick out of your ear, you fucking idiot! I *said*: "You are the biggest fucking sexist asshole pig I have ever met in my entire life!"

The school secretaries and the queue of students waiting to be reprimanded by Deskins had heard me loud and clear.

"You're out of here!" Deskins screamed.

He didn't mean that I was just out of his office. I was actually out of his *school*.

Within minutes, Principal Deskins's secretary dialed my father at work. Within a few more minutes, Dad was there to negotiate the terms of my release from East.

I was stunned. I had been given detention a few times at St. Basil's for forgetting my homework or talking in class, but this was *huge*. I had never even been *suspended* before! Now I was *expelled*.

Not just expelled. Expelled from the worst school in the city. A school that featured a minimum of three student altercations per period and school yard fights that made Chicago street brawls look like *Romper Room*.

This was awesome!

Technically, I wasn't formally expelled. That would have required far too much paperwork for Principal Deskins's liking. I'm sure having to explain to the district's superintendent that he had just been lit up by a student – one with potential grounds for a lawsuit – would severely cut into the amount of time Deskins could spend slugging bathtub gin over the three-day weekend.

As a result, my permanent record wasn't marred. Rather, it was agreed-upon by the principal and my very persuasive father that I'd be granted a boundary waiver to transfer to a different junior high school in the district.

I stood outside as Dad spoke with Principal Deskins. School had already let out. I waited, expecting the worst, in the school parking lot.

That was when Amy Quick, one of the baddest girls in school, came up to me. I was somewhat wary, considering she had glared at me several times before in the hallway.

"I heard what happened with Alberts and Deskins," she said. "That's fucked up. I'm glad you told Deskins off, though. He's an asshole."

"You heard I was kicked out already?!" Damn, word traveled fast.

"Yeah. It's all over the school. A few of my friends heard you give it to Deskins in his office. They said it was really cool."

Amy switched gears quickly. "Hey, you like Bob Barlow, right?"

And the shock just kept coming!

"Uhh, yeah? How did you know that?"

"Duh. It's pretty obvious. Hey, if you want, I could give your phone number to him. I don't know if he likes you back, or anything, but it's something. He's pretty quiet." She paused thoughtfully for a moment, pondering her next statement before granting me entry into the Hallowed Halls of Bad-Assery. "I'll take your phone number, too. Maybe we can hang out sometime."

I never did hang out with cool, bad ass Amy after that day, but I learned quite a few things from my brief stay at East:

I learned that the quickest way to get kicked out of a school is not to do bodily harm to another student, but to nail the principal with the most personal, foul-mouthed insult possible while simultaneously questioning his ability to perform his job.

The second thing I learned was that I really had to stop being so obvious about the guys I liked. The relatively safe world of Catholic school had made me too soft. Too complacent. I needed to sharpen my edges once more. I needed to decrease the transparency of my feelings and rip my heart off my sleeve again. If a dense, borderline mute with a mullet like Bob Barlow could figure out that I had the hots for him – and if a total stranger like Amy Quick, who I said barely two words to could see it, too – then I had to be more aggressive about keeping my guard up.

CHAPTER FOUR
AWKWARD AVOIDED

With my release from East Fletcher Junior High and my brand-spanking new boundary waiver in-hand, I enrolled in West Fletcher Intermediate, one of the best and most modern schools in the area.

To my surprise, neither Mom nor Dad wanted to strangle me for what took place in Principal Deskins' office. Apart from Amy Quick's public endorsement in the school parking lot, my folks were actually the first to congratulate me.

Mom wouldn't have to drive halfway across town to get me to school every day since West was much closer to Orion's school. And having deduced what a moron Principal Deskins was five minutes after meeting him, Dad was thrilled I was bounced from East.

It was like the universe was rewarding me for getting expelled! To top it all off, I'd be getting an above-boards education because I got myself ejected from the worst school in the city.

Man, did I hit the jackpot!

The Tuesday following the holiday was spent filling out paperwork at my new school with my parents. I was enrolled in the honors track and personally introduced to my new teachers by Ms. Miller, the school guidance counselor.

Although she had a penchant for polyester, Ms. Miller commanded respect from the student body and was on par with the school's principal in enforcing discipline and ensuring a quality curriculum. Despite her questionable fashion sense, she was actually a very nice lady with a good sense of humor.

While Ms. Miller could do no wrong in my eyes, she still stuck me at the worst lunch table in the whole school.

I was pretty low on the social totem pole but still managed to feel out of place among my new tablemates. There was a girl with scratches up and down her arms who frequently professed her love for sleeping with her pet rats.

There was another girl who had recurring dreams that she was from an alien planet – and that her dreams were reality.

The third girl at the table – apparently, the group's ringleader – had a combination speech impediment and lunch meat fetish that, frankly, I found disturbing. She would grill me regarding the contents of my brown bag, dismayed that I had chosen to consume yogurt instead of sliced deli offerings.

"How come you never bring luntsch meat? Don't you like luntsch meat?"

The "ch" somehow sprouted an "s" in front of it whenever she spoke rapturously about processed animal byproduct.

"I'm just not really a big fan," I replied.

"How can you not like luntsch meat!?" she slurped indignantly. "I love luntsch meat! My favorite is schalami, but I like baloney a lot, too. It'sch delishutsch!"

I was tempted to inquire about how she felt about "pastrami," but fought the urge.

My new lunch table didn't exactly put me in a prime spot to launch Clean Slate, Version 2.0.

On the flipside, I had little in common with the honor roll students I was grouped with in my classes, most of whom were jocks and preps.

All grousing aside, West was leaps above East on the junior high evolutionary scale. Even the worst of West's students were lot nicer compared to those at East.

That didn't stop some of them from tossing snide comments my way, however.

To say I had a unique look would be an understatement.

Convinced that blondes have more fun and in the hopes of upping my hot-stock with guys, I decided to lighten my dark auburn locks.

There was no way in hell my mother would allow her 13-year-old daughter to tart herself up like a bleached blonde floozy, so I had to be sly. Before my nightly shower, I would sneak some of Mom's peroxide in my shampoo bottle. The process was so gradual that my parents didn't notice my hair had turned blonde until Mom was organizing the family photo albums and realized that there was a distinct spectral discrepancy in the color of my hair between that year and the year before. After that, I didn't have to pay such strict attention to maintaining my roots to avoid suspicion.

Despite the new blonde hue to my 'do, I still had very thick, very dark eyebrows that were now even more prominent since I had yet to discover tweezers.

It could have been worse. At least I didn't have unibrow.

Things did get worse, however, when I got the brilliant idea to cut my long, all-one-length, blonde hair into layers. Instead of going to a professional, I decided I could do just as good a job on my own. I sliced one layer straight across at chin level, another at shoulder level, and left the rest elbow-length. Each "layer" became a descending shelf of hair.

I then proceeded to call attention to my "awesome" new layers by taking a crimping iron to everything but my bangs before spraying the whole thing upside down with half a can of Aqua Net.

I looked like a white, teenage, D-list Tina Turner.

Granted, big, bad hair was *en vogue* – but mine was a bit bigger and a lot badder than even the most destitute refugee from a Whitesnake concert.

This could have been almost forgivable in the eyes of my peers if it wasn't for one thing.

We were po'.

Not dirt poor, but certainly far from the middle class bracket. Thanks to scholarships, school lunch programs, and Mom's budgeting skills, things were made easier for our one-income family. Mom did a good job hiding this from me and Orion. Years later, I discovered that, at one point, we received food stamps during a six-month period when Dad's hours at the plant had been severely cut.

We managed to give the illusion of middle class status, living in a rental home on the outskirts of town and taking dance lessons thanks to the extra pin money Grandma forked over to Mom once a month. However, on paper (and in our refrigerator and closets), it was a whole other ball game.

My family's idea of spending like crazed Rockefellers was ordering from the dollar menu at McDonald's. Some folks dine *a la carte*. We dined *a la* car. Since Mickey D's frowned upon patrons bringing their own 25-cent cans of Shasta in lieu of coughing up $1.19 for a kiddie cup of cola, our family forays into fine dining were usually eaten in Mom's maroon '76 Charger Daytona.

We shopped exclusively at discount stores. Orion and I didn't wear the "designer" I.O.U. or Bum Equipment sweatshirts many of our schoolyard contemporaries sported. We were never poorly dressed, we just shopped on a budget.

The non-name brand clothes weren't an issue when my brother and I attended parochial school. However, the older we got and the more fashion-savvy our classmates got, they seized upon the fact that our clothes came from "United Colors of Bargain Basement" and not Benetton.

As if my crimped, peroxide-doused mane didn't already scream "Look at me!", I called even more attention to myself with long, dangling earrings and outfits in bright red, yellow, turquoise, and purple. I made use of my the oxford button-down holdovers from my Catholic school uniform and wore them with red-and-black tartan skirts, a faux leather vest with laces on the side, boots, and leggings. It was my symbolic mockery of the daily duds I used to sport at St. Basil's.

I thought I was cutting edge, but the jocks and preps would riddle me with ridicule on a daily basis:

"Where did you get that outfit? It looks so expensive!"

"Oh, my God! Who does your hair?! I love it!"

"You know, I should really stop shopping at The Gap and start shopping at Bargain Mart."

"Wow. You are so hot. Has anyone ever told you that you should be a model?"

Once, one of the school's biggest steroid abusers came up to me before class, sighing wistfully with a hand laid delicately across his Cro-Mag forehead, "Oh, Nova. You're as ugly as the day is long," followed by a frenzied round of high-fiving his buddies.

Hey, kids are cruel. Life is hard. Puppies die. It sucks, but it doesn't negate reality. It was still better than being at East.

Mom insisted that if people paid that much attention to what I was wearing, then my outfits must be pretty spectacular.

Dad interjected with his own stories of how he dressed in the 1950s: "My friends used to call me 'Christmas Tree.' I used to wear pegged pants in all different colors. I had an electric blue zoot suit. I wish I *still* had it!"

The snide comments from my peers really didn't matter to me. After two years of Catholic school repression, I snagged a page from Sammy Davis, Jr.'s book. I gotta be me, damnit!

While I was ridiculed for not being able to shop at the pricey shops where kids squandered their allowance money, I admittedly brought some of these comments upon myself with my outlandish hair, makeup, and clothes. I *could* have dressed more conservatively. Then again, the kids who dressed in five-dollar sweatshirts in the same muted earth tones as everyone else – minus the brand name splashed across the front – got made fun of just as much as I did for being poor. If I was going to be made fun of, I would at least be made fun of for dressing how I wanted to on the meager budget that I could afford.

Aside from a few douchebags, classes were great and so were my grades. However, I had been enrolled at West for over a month and didn't have any friends.

Something had to give.

One day, at the start of the second quarter, I sat in fourth period English, bummed out by the looming specter of lunch with the Whack Pack. I had already finished my assignment and was doodling band logos on my notebook. I was a big Kiss fan, which in a town like Fletcher, was not the most popular thing to be. My taste in hard rock and heavy metal added to the long list of reasons to make fun of me.

As I was doodling, a girl was collecting everyone's assignment folders to hand back to the teacher. The girl looked about two levels below earning her Tinkerbell badge and smiled constantly. She stood only a few inches taller than me and resembled a teenage Shirley Temple – dimples and all – with blonde, curly, waist-length hair.

The girl paused when she came to my desk to pick up my folder. I put down my pencil and handed her my assignment.

She looked down at my notebook, decorated with all four Kiss masks, the Kiss logo with thunderbolt "S"'s, and Mötley Crüe's *Theatre of Pain* masks.

"You like Kiss?"

I looked up and raised an eyebrow over the top of my glasses. *Here we go,* I thought. *Here comes the dumb ass "Are you, like, a headbanger or something?" question.*

"Yeah," I answered cautiously.

"Really!?" the girl squeaked. "Did you know that Gene Simmons' tongue is seven inches long and that he was born in Israel? And that Peter Criss' voice was dubbed in *Kiss Meets the Phantom of the Park?*"

My mouth dropped open. Someone else in eighth grade knew these random facts about Kiss, too?

I nodded excitedly as the girl rattled off several more facts about the band's short-term members like Vinnie Vincent and Mark St. John.

"Oh, my God!" I exclaimed, caught in a moment of revelation. "You have the *Metal Edge Kiss Fan Spectacular*, too!?"

"Yeah, but most of the pages are on my bedroom wall."

"Mine, too! I had to buy a second copy to read!" In my excitement, I sputtered out "Kiss was the first band I ever saw in concert!"

"No way! That's so cool!" She paused momentarily. "What are you doing for lunch? I don't think I've ever seen you in the cafeteria?"

I told her where I sat.

She made a face that reflected how I felt about my daily dining situation.

"Then it's settled! You're coming to eat lunch with us from now on!"

My jaw hit the floor. One minute, I was dreading lunch. The next, I had a new seat in the cafeteria and made a new friend!

Even better, I made a new friend who liked the same music as I did!

Offering her hand out to shake, the girl introduced herself as Samantha.

"But most people call me 'Sammi,'" she added.

I introduced myself, but Sammi already knew my name. Apparently, I was popular for all the wrong reasons.

Sammi waved the folders in one hand. "I gotta go hand these in, but I'll see you at lunch!"

When the bell rang, I raced to my locker to put my books away and grab my lunch. The cynical part of me wondered if I was being set up for a prank straight out of *Carrie*. Fortunately, that wasn't the case. Sammi introduced me to all of the girls at their table and the guys at the adjacent table.

For the first time since I arrived at West, I felt comfortable.

I knew a few of the kids at the tables from some of my other classes. There was the Cora Perez, who I recognized from several of my classes, and her boyfriend Ray Wilson. Ray and Cora epitomized the phrase "opposites attract." While Cora was a shy, pretty honors student, Ray was loud and funny with heavy acne.

I was also introduced to Ray's best friend, Royce Danielson, who also sat at the boys' table.

Only he wasn't sitting at the table. Instead, Royce was chasing Sam Lopez around the table, shrieking "I want your penis!" in a high pitched voice.

Suffice to say, I was enchanted.

When Royce finally sat down, Ray called him over to and introduced us. Royce was taller than average with sandy brown hair and a rat tail in the back. He wore baggy jeans and t-shirts that were likely hand-me-downs.

Even though I'd only known my new friends a short time, they made me a part of their group. We traded mix tapes and no one judged anyone on the basis of how they dressed or what their parents did for a living. It was like I had known them for years. Sammi and her friends clued me in to all of the cliques and the inside dirt on the students and teachers at West.

Another popular topic of conversation was sex and the pursuit of it.

The only one who was honest about her virginal status was Cora. The rest of us lied through our teeth about the extent of our sexual experience. Everyone's stories about what they did or didn't do varied from day to day.

I, for one, played it off like a grizzled veteran who had fought on many fronts of the wars of love and sex – a modern Mae West, if you will.

In reality, I hadn't even kissed a guy, let alone been plowed by one. I was clueless as to what to do with someone else's tongue in my mouth much less how to get one in there in the first place.

Like my friends and tablemates, I would construct elaborate stories designed to exhibit unparalleled carnal prowess. While these stories were entertaining, I figured that if I was talking out my ass, then mostly everyone else was probably full of shit, too.

Life at school got easier once I made friends. However, things began to get complicated when, once again, I developed feelings for a friend.

Cora, her boyfriend Ray, Royce, and I had the same eighth period social studies class. I think it was somewhere between General Cornwallis and the signing of the Declaration of Independence when I realized I liked Royce.

Royce was goofy and upbeat – like an overexcited puppy. He laughed at everything and enjoyed making others laugh with crazy sound effects or random observations. His wasn't an attention-seeking sort of humor, just a good-natured one. Everything about him radiated a genuine kindness.

Since Cora and I would help Ray and Royce with their homework at lunch, I talked with Royce a bit more than the other guys at the table. It wasn't until he broke up with his girlfriend that I started thinking of him as something more than a study buddy.

For the first time in my adolescent life, I felt comfortable enough with my friends to mention that I liked a guy. Normally, I kept these things to myself, not wanting to appear vulnerable or open myself up to ridicule. I knew that neither Sammi nor Cora would bust on me for digging a dude.

I wasn't counting on Cora spilling the beans to Ray, much less him pitching the idea to Royce that we should start dating. I preferred to do things myself and hear the verdict straight from the source.

Ray meant well when he took it upon himself to ask Royce out for me at the end of eighth period. That didn't stop me from turning several shades of crimson when Ray screamed across the room:

"Hey, Royce! You know who I think you would be good with? I think you should go out with Nova!"

Royce tilted his head to the side. "Nova? Really?"

"Yes! Really!" Ray continued. "Think about it! With her big lips and your little dick, it would be like Moby Dick sucking on a Tic Tac! It would be a thrill a minute for you! You should go out with her, man!"

My mouth hung open and my eyes bulged from their sockets. In a vain attempt to salvage what dignity I had left, I covered my face with my hand. Royce had also turned red with embarrassment and made a beeline for his locker.

The next day, Sammi and Cora decided to run damage control. I never would have asked them to speak to Royce on my behalf, but they insisted. Even though I wouldn't say it myself, my friends knew that I didn't want to alienate yet another friend who may not have been thrilled by the idea of becoming a couple.

"He's not mad at me, is he?" I asked Cora.

"No. Not at all."

I breathed an inward sigh of relief before curiosity got the better of me. "What did he say?"

"Oh, just that he didn't know you liked him."

"That was it?"

"Yeah, that was all."

My gut churned for an instant. "He wasn't pissed or anything that I liked him, though? Was he?"

"No," Sammi interjected. "Everything's cool. Don't worry about it!"

Okay. So he didn't like me back, but it could have been worse. I expected him to run screaming every time he saw me. Royce was cool about it, though. Before lunch, he came up to me in the locker corridor.

"Hey, Nova! What's up!?"

At that moment, I knew everything was fine. He acted as if the embarrassing exchange never happened.

I looked back at him and smiled perhaps the biggest smile of my life to that point. "Hey, Royce! You headed to lunch?"

"Yep. Thought I'd come by and talk to you before going to the caf."

The felt like I had a pebble lodged in the pit of my stomach. "I'm really sorry about yesterday. I had no idea Ray was going to say that."

Royce laughed."Don't worry about it! Ray pulls that shit all the time! You should hear what he says *without* any girls around."

He paused for a moment. "I just wanted you to know I was really flattered that you liked me."

I was so shocked that I almost fell through my locker. "Really? Wow. Thank you."

"Don't mention it!" he chirped.

After a few seconds of silence, I mustered enough courage to ask him the question I planned on asking him myself: "You wouldn't consider going out at any point, would you?"

"Not right now," he said. "I just broke up with my girlfriend a month ago. I don't think I'm ready to date anyone right now. And I really think we're better off as friends."

It wasn't the answer I wanted to hear, but I could accept that.

"That's cool," I said. "I really appreciate you taking the time to talk to me and make sure everything was cool."

"Aw, it's all good! No worries!"

It really *was* all good. Royce meant what he said and there was no awkwardness in our friendship from that point forward.

That didn't mean I stopped liking him, of course. At least knew where I stood, which was in the good graces of friendship.

Of all the guys who ever turned me down, Royce was one of the few who did it with kindness. He could have easily been a dick and acted differently towards me after he found out how I felt. But he didn't. Nothing changed. For a 14-year-old boy, he acted with more maturity than some guys twice his age.

The summer before high school, Royce's family moved. He ended up attending a different high school. The next time I saw him was during junior year. By then, I had dyed my blonde hair black and looked very different from the last time we saw each other. Royce still recognized me.

And he was still hot.

I walked up to him to say hello, and he gave me a big hug. He was as happy to see me as I was to see him. I asked him what he was up to these days. His mother had been in a car accident and he had dropped out of school to support his family. He had also been seeing a girl for over a year and was about to become a father. He was trying to get his G.E.D. and get into college. He told me that he wanted to make his mother proud and his family's life easier by getting a better job.

I didn't see Royce again until years later. He ended up doing alright for himself. He's still with the same girl he was with when I ran into him that last time and they now have three kids together.

Royce was one of those good guys who got the happy ending. It couldn't have happened to a nicer guy.

CHAPTER FIVE
WHEN LOVE AND HATE COLLIDE

This was it. I was finally a freshman at Thomas Jefferson High School. Other than the change of venue, it was mostly the same faces and the same routine. The only difference was that now students could eat lunch off-campus if they wanted to.

As happy as I was to be back at school with my friends, I was still bummed that Royce had transferred. For the first quarter of freshman year, I wandered around crushless. Not a single guy interested me.

For a split second, I had the hots for a senior with a long ponytail and an impressive collection of heavy metal t-shirts who went by the name "Fleck."

Despite his seemingly singular moniker, Fleck bore the distinction of being the only other honors student who wore a leather motorcycle jacket.

Fleck was friends with Sammi and she tried to hook us up, mentioning to him that I was in honors classes, too. Nevertheless, Fleck wasn't interested. Just a hunch, but it probably had more to do with my peroxide-blonde crimped hair and black eyebrows than my freshman status.

I bounced back quickly from Fleck's turndown service at the Heartbreak Hotel. It was just a fleeting attraction.

Jefferson High pulled in kids from all parts of the city and our group ended up initiating new people into our little clique. Sammi had a knack for taking in new strays and making them feel at home at our table.

That January, Sammi befriended a sophomore transfer named Rick Sanders in her math class. Rick was originally from West Virginia but came to Jefferson by way of a neighboring school district. He had a faint Southern drawl that sounded more like Larry the Cable Guy than Rhett Butler.

Initially, I found Rick to be completely repugnant and off-putting. The lone sophomore at our table, he branded us all "fuckin' freshman."

In terms of physical presence and persona, Rick was tall and lanky with a shaggy brown mullet and peach fuzz mustache. He had a collection of t-shirts that bore the names of bands like Entombed and Morbid Angel and wore tight, faded, grey jeans with holes at the knees. His sartorial staples were complimented by an assortment of cheap pewter skull jewelry scored from Heshers, a store in the mall where most of the stoners and metal kids shopped.

Rain, snow, or sunshine, Rick would strut down the hallway between classes wearing a hand-painted, acid-washed denim jacket that would have made Tim Gunn shit.

On the back of the jacket, Rick had painted the Slayer logo. Beneath it was a cartoon drawing of what was supposed to be a self-portrait of Rick's disembodied head – mullet and all – smoking a cigarette and wearing a pair of sunglasses. This bizarre, caricatured cranium floated in limbo against the backdrop of a crudely drawn brick wall that took up the back of his jean jacket.

When he wasn't hurling nasty comments at the rest of us "fuckin' freshmen," Rick (and his abomination of a jacket) frequently liked to whip out his sketchbook and work on more self-portraits inspired by bad death metal album covers.

Rick fancied himself something of a renaissance man. In addition to his art, he was also a self-proclaimed guitarist although the word "chord" was not in his vocabulary. The one instance where I actually did hear him play guitar involved a nearly unrecognizable rendering of Metallica's "One" on the sales floor of a local music store.

To hear Rick tell it, however, the only things hampering him from joining a real band were his own discriminating tastes in music and that no one else who wanted to play with him lived up to his standards. Rick had a wide array of bands and band names that annoyed him, thus prompting him to proclaim that "I would only be in a band if they had the word 'death' in their name. Anything else sounds stupid."

An arbiter of taste and proclaimer of all things "stupid," Rick also thought that guitar lessons were "for stupid people." He volunteered this information to me quite readily upon learning that I started taking guitar lessons that year.

It took awhile for Rick to grow on most of us. Sammi's boyfriend Chris wasn't too keen on him, although he posed no threat to their relationship. The other girls and guys at our table weren't too fond of his freshman hazing. On the rare occasions when he would subject them to his diatribes on how shitty any band not named Slayer, Death, Overkill, or Cornholed Cannibal Nun Holocaust was, the only reaction he received was silent eye-rolling.

The only other person besides Sammi who got along with Rick was Cora. Then again, Cora was the only other person who could possibly surpass Sammi on the fast track for teenage sainthood. In turn, Rick acted as a protective, big brother figure to both girls.

This sole, redeeming factor made me more inclined to give Rick the benefit of the doubt.

That didn't stop me from joining in on our lunchtime debates. More often than anyone else in our group, I was the target of Rick's sarcastic remarks. Much to the amusement of our gang, my love of hair metal combined with my love for a good verbal sparring match made for several noteworthy exchanges between Rick and myself.

Although we completely disagreed on the merits of hair metal vs. death metal, I was surprised to find that Rick and I shared some common musical ground.

One day at lunch, Rick mentioned his surprising love for Joan Jett and the Blackhearts. I had to toss a few more cool points his way since he admitted to having seen the woman herself live and in-concert.

"No shit!" I exclaimed. "You really saw Joan Jett?"

"Yeah. She kicked ass."

"Do you have any of her stuff with The Runaways? I have *Little Lost Girls* if you want to borrow it."

For an instant, Rick's face registered an actual expression. "Cool."

The next day, I let Rick borrow The Runaways cassette and was rather surprised to see that he had brought in Ozzy Osbourne's *No Rest For the Wicked* for me to borrow – an album I didn't have in my collection but really wanted to hear.

When Rick brought back my album in pristine condition the following Monday, something inside me clicked as I handed him back his Ozzy tape: Maybe Rick Sanders wasn't completely abhorrent.

While the bulk of our musical tastes didn't jive, Rick and I agreed to disagree regarding more contemporary bands. Having (sort of) bonded over tastes in classic rock, our discourse wasn't quite as venomous as it had once been.

As the school year progressed, I began noticing little things about Rick that were vaguely endearing. Like the way he would toss his mullet out of his eyes with a flip of his head instead of just using his hands.

Or how, when he'd pass the phone booth outside of the cafeteria, he'd dip his finger into the coin slot to pocket loose change. (I did that, too.)

Or the way he would stand with his hands crossed over his ridiculous jean jacket before either A.) issuing a swift kick to one of the guys for no real reason, or B.) reaching out and patting Sammi or Cora on top of the head in a grandfatherly manner.

Despite the hardcore brand of cool that Rick tried to peddle, he had a dorky laugh that sounded like the bastard offspring of Ernie from *Sesame Street* and a honking goose. I learned this along with the fact that we shared a warped, perverted sense of humor and a fondness for infantile jokes involving bodily fluids and sexual organs.

Rick and I bonded yet again when the ranks of our group were decimated by a fierce winter storm. Operating on a two-hour delay, most of the inhabitants of our lunch table failed to come to school that day.

Since Mom was a substitute teacher and was filling in for some of the teachers who were no-shows, I had no choice but to brave the cold and haul ass to class. On the other end of the spectrum, Rick had to attend school that day since he was treading a fine line of failure.

That afternoon, Rick and I were the only ones at the lunch table. Earlier that day, I found a stray cassette tape in the locker hall. It was Adam Sandler's debut comedy album, *They're All Gonna Laugh At You.*

I didn't have a Walkman with me, but Rick rarely came to school without his. Rather than face a one-on-one conversation with each other, I offered him the tape in exchange for sharing his headphones.

Despite having been sacked with the burden of scholastics on a day that rightfully belonged to snow, Rick and I both got an earful of raunchy comedy.

We howled with laughter listening to "At A Medium Pace," a song in which the *SNL* alum gave a heartfelt ode to rough, emasculating sex that involved cramming a shampoo bottle up the ol' poop chute and observing the act of masturbation under the pretense of being a pizza delivery guy.

It was cold outside, but thanks to a shared set of earbuds and Sandler's filthy comedic stylings, there was a bit of warmth in my heart. Suddenly, coming to school that frigid day was worth it.

I made Rick a copy of the album when I got home. Days later, Rick and I were quoting it extensively.

We were becoming friends and eventually exchanged phone numbers. One Friday night, I gave him a call. While I wasn't shocked that Rick was (like me) home with nothing to do, I was surprised that he sounded happy I called.

The surprises kept coming as our conversation segued between such topics as asshole preps at school, movies, and music.

That night, something had come over me, nudging me to unleash a revelation to Rick.

Rick admitted that he had been to Dollywood – a theme park built by the generous and generously endowed country singer Dolly Parton – on numerous occasions.

"My family lived in Tennessee for a little while," he explained. "When you live in Tennessee, it's like a law or something that you go to Dollywood at least 20 times."

Rick also copped to liking Dolly Parton's music. Short of taking a sledgehammer to the Berlin Wall, there was no greater instance of lowering one's defenses. Here was the guy who had dubbed Mötley Crüe "pussy metal" and revered Slayer as his own personal messiahs talking about how much he dug Dolly.

Overcome by this bold statement, I went out on a limb and decided to share a part of myself with Rick that I had never shared with anyone else before:

"*The Best Little Whorehouse in Texas* is one of only two movies that ever made me cry." "What?!"

"Yep. I don't know what it is, but for some reason, when Dolly sings 'Hard Candy Christmas' or 'I Will Always Love You' to Burt Reynolds, I cry like a bitch."

While lacking Whitney Houston's vocal pyrotechnics, Dolly Parton's version of "I Will Always Love You" encapsulated more raw emotion. Whitney's professing of on-screen love to Kevin Costner in *The Bodyguard* was more of a display of over-the-top diva vocalizing than genuine feeling. Multi-octave declarations were part and parcel of Whitney's rock star film character's everyday life.

On the flipside, the whispering quaver in Dolly's voice as she passionately stated that she "will always love" Burt Reynolds's Sheriff Earl had far more heart. Dolly's *Whorehouse* songs were more like Shakespearean soliloquies set to music. On a superficial level, her character is seen as something purely sexual. Yet, Mona (Dolly's character) batters down her own defenses when she needs them most and delivers an internal monologue with an unlikely sense of sweetness and sincerity. While Whitney plows her way through the song with F5 force, Dolly employs more subtle vocal dynamics before she belts it out in the final stretch.

I continued my dissertation to Rick on the other end of the phone.

"I mean, you just don't expect the madam of a whorehouse to get all heartfelt and choked up about the local sheriff she's been boning. And seriously, dude. Can you get a better, more appropriate name for a whorehouse madam than 'Mona'? Plus, most of the hookers at The Chicken Ranch are pretty much the only family she has and now she's being forced to close the place down. Everything good in her life is gone in one fell swoop. Bam. She loses a sweet job. She loses what is basically her family. And she can't be with the guy she loves. You can hear that sadness in those songs."

There was an awkward pause before Rick broke the silence. "Uh, Nova? You haven't been drinking, have you?"

"No. I haven't. And if you repeat one word of what I just told you to anyone else, I will kick your ass."

Rick agreed to keep quiet on the condition I tell him the other movie that made me cry. (*The Care Bears Movie.*)

Within a month or so, Rick became an accepted part of our lunch table and a better friend to everyone. He was still sarcastic and snide, but had grown less critical of others and began to really open up.

Like the day he decided to use a safety pin to pierce his nipple at the table in the lunchroom.

For no other reason that claiming to be bored, Rick unhinged a safety pin from his backpack and began unbuttoning his flannel shirt. I looked over at Sammi, Cora, and our friend Jenn. The four of us wore similar confused expressions as Rick poked the pin through his chest.

I was hoping that the dull look on my face was convincing enough of to mask my real feelings of titillation. Outside of the porno movies I'd occasionally sneak out of Dad's bathroom and the hot lifeguards who worked summers at the community pool, this was the longest flash of boy-flesh that I'd been given a chance to ogle.

Although I'm positive that Rick's display was intended to register more shock value than sensuality, I couldn't help but feel a fondue in my panties. I could not pry my eyes away from the sight of Rick's long fingers pressing the sharp, silver safety pin through his erect nipple. I watched him squeeze it, wincing slightly as the tip sunk inside the soft, pink flesh.

I could hear his sharp intake of breath and watched his lips move as he tried working it through the delicate bundle of nerves on his chest. I sat transfixed watching this display until finally, the tip poked through the other side of his nipple and Rick fastened the safety pin shut, moving it back and forth as he admired his handiwork.

If I was a smoker, I would have needed a cigarette.

I was pretty damn sure that I had a mad crush on Rick. The night of "The Great Dolly Parton Revelation" all but confirmed my feelings for him, but the sexual subtext of his public piercing nailed it home for me. The months of bickering back and forth were really just an outlet for my pent-up crush-stration. I hadn't had a good crush on someone since Royce.

I couldn't fathom my attraction to Rick. I hated his guts when I first met him. This guy had been on my case since Day One, busting on my taste in music, clothes, and makeup. And now I had the major hots for him!? I couldn't figure it out. Was there something wrong with me?

I watched with a twinge of disappointment as the expanse of milky white skin on Rick's hairless chest slowly disappeared with each button he redid. I sat back in my chair as the show – and my internal monologue – came to a close.

Regaining my composure, I conjured my gruffest tone and informed him that, "You better make sure you sterilize that when you get home. You don't want your nipple to get infected and rot off."

He looked back over at me and nodded. "Good point."

That night, I went home and diddled myself.

Twice.

I ended up rubbing one out again a few weeks later when Rick disclosed that he was wearing leopard print underwear.

It started innocently enough. One of the guys joked that his undies probably had brown spots on them after ingesting some of the cafeteria's biohazard buffet. Rick mentioned that his drawers did, in fact, have brown spots on them. He went as far as unzipping his jeans and hiking up his skimpy, animal print briefs to show everyone at the table.

I was instantly transported back to my first masturbatory experience courtesy of the *Phil Donohue Show* and his cortege of Chippendale dancer guests. Dozens of male strippers with their meat muffins and baloney ponies happily housed in leopard print G-strings gyrated in my mind's eye to the strains of a bump-n'-grind fueled Hallelujah Chorus.

Short of Rick busting some moves and grinding his jungle cat-clad pelvis like a fine Jamaican coffee, no pre-recorded male striptease could top this display.

And he was wearing *briefs*! No guys wore briefs anymore! This was the epoch when crotch-concealing boxers made their big comeback. Having been exposed to the likes of Vince Neil and David Lee Roth who proudly sported neon and zebra print briefs, this was the stuff my adolescent fantasies were made of!

This was fate! A true sign that Rick was the guy for me! What were the odds that, after months of intense dislike, some guy I was just starting to develop feelings for, would drop trou in the lunchroom, only to be wearing the same species of underpants that I harbored a particular fetish for?

I hid my arousal behind my usual veil of sarcasm. "Classy. Did your mom pick those out for you?"

Tucking his shirt back into his pants, Rick laughed. "Nah. She'd kill me if she saw these. She's almost as big a bitch as you are."

"Really?" I smirked, playing along. "You think I'm a bitch?"

"Yes. You can be a real bitch sometimes, Nova," he said with a smile.

Already amped up by the display of Rick's scanty manties mere moments ago, the deviant gears in my brain clicked. The dismissal bell rang, shooing us from the lunchroom towards class.

"Wow. I had no idea you thought I was that big of a bitch, Rick." I advanced towards him, ready to playfully pounce. "I mean, if I was a *real* bitch, then I would do something like *this*." Reaching for him, I lightly pulled at the safety pin piercing his nipple beneath his shirt fabric. Tweaking it between my thumb and index finger, I smiled with syrupy sweetness. "You don't *really* think I'm a bitch, now, do you?"

Rick's mouth dropped open in shock as I smiled even more. "No, ma'am! You're not a bitch at all! Nicest girl I know!"

I relinquished my hold and laughed as Rick and Sammi headed to their next class and Cora and I darted off to ours.

"I can't believe you did that!?" a stunned Cora cried.

"I can't believe I did that, either!" I replied, surprised myself.

I didn't know what came over me. Was I so emboldened by his leopard-clad loins that I went mad with lust and decided to prey upon his pierced nipple? Was I was mildly turned on by him recognizing that, yes, I was a bitch? My mind raced with possible explanations for my behavior before sanity settled back in.

"Whoa. Do you think he's pissed at me now?"

"I'm sure he knows you were joking around," Cora replied

"Yeah, but I never grabbed his nipple before. Now that I think about it, it was pretty out of line."

"You were just kidding around. I've seen you both say way worse to each other."

Cora had a point. Rick and I routinely said mean things to one another but it was always understood to be in jest.

"If you feel that bad about it, just apologize to him after class. I don't think you have anything to worry about."

I breathed a sigh of relief. "That makes sense. I don't see why I got so worked up about it."

"I think I know why," Cora teased. "You like him."

The jig was up. I'd been found out.

"You did the same thing with Royce when you liked him. You get worried about saying the same mean or perverted things you said to guys *before* you wanted to go out with them."

Shit. Cora knew me like a book.

Once I admitted to myself that I liked Rick, I let Sammi, Cora and Jenn in on the secret. It was liberating to get that out in the open. (I left out the part about Dolly Parton, though.)

Once you allow a secret like that to see the light of day, there's no turning back. You find yourself at a fork in the road with one path pointing towards silent, unrequited love and the other jutting out on a limb and trying to make those dreams a reality.

Until that point, I had *liked* guys. For some unexplainable reason, I really believed I was in love with Rick. I may have really *liked* Royce and Frankie Gilroy, but I never felt like this about them.

All sappy sentiments aside, I debated with myself and my girlfriends about how much I "really liked" Rick and whether or not I should ask him out.

The business of asking someone out in high school is complicated. You know you want to do it. You look for the perfect window of opportunity to present itself. Asking your friends if they think the object of your affection likes you back and if you really *should* ask them out is just an attempt at finding a channel of moral support in case you get turned down.

Buoyed by my friends' encouragement, I began plotting the perfect way to ask Rick if he wanted to be "more than friends." I'd already been down this road before and it wasn't pretty. Having already batted a big fat zero when it came to asking guys out, I realized that making your feelings known to a person involves a soul-crushing variety of heartbreak when you're turned down. It also puts a wedge of awkwardness into a friendship.

I had to handle this situation with an air of tact, grace, and vulnerability – three attributes that I did not possess. I scrambled for a way to weasel a prime opportunity to get Rick alone and tell him my feelings with a minimum of humiliation on my end.

One Friday in late March, spring was all around and love was in the air. The entire gang went outside for lunch to a wooded alleyway a block away from the high school. When the weather was nice, we would head to the alley and have lunch off-campus. Plus, it gave us a place to drink booze pilfered from our parents' liquor cabinets (or in my case, from the back of Mom's closet) during school hours.

Maybe it was the room temperature peppermint schnapps that I sucked back in the alley that day, but I found the (liquid) courage to ask Cora to tell Rick that I wanted to talk to him after eighth period by the lockers. She was a willing accomplice and relayed the message to him. I thought I had this one in the bag.

I thought wrong.

That afternoon, during seventh period, Rick got into a fight with a C-list preppy named Craig Hawkins. You know the type. They're not the most popular kids in the school, but achieve a modicum of popularity by being friends with *another* group of friends who pal around with the *really* popular kids.

Craig wasn't known for much besides being a troublemaker who came from a long line of functioning societal dregs. Craig's uncle was a local fixture known as "Whiz" who earned his nickname when, one enchanted evening, he got so drunk that he drank an entire Budweiser bottle filled with pee. In turn, Uncle

Whiz promptly followed this feat by passing out and pissing himself.

Although I wasn't present for the actual fight, Rick's throwdown with Craig was less than legendary. The only moment that merited it a footnote in the historical annals of high school fights was that Rick bit Craig's nipple while trying to get out of a headlock.

This little stunt landed them both in the Vice Principal's office and resulted in a three-day suspension for Rick.

I'd never really liked Craig much before, particularly since he had made some disparaging comments to me over the years. But now I had even more reason to hate him: Without knowing it, Craig Hawkins totally cock-blocked me.

I walked out of my eighth period class, armed with the news that my planned encounter had been scuttled. In a bizarre twist of fate, my foot kicked a small, silvery object. Looking down, I saw a pewter cross made out of skulls.

I recognized this piece of cheap jewelry. In fact, I was rather well-acquainted with it, having stared at it dangling between Rick's perky, pierced nipples when he flashed them at the lunch table.

This was fate! I may not have been able to ask Rick out that day, but damnit, I held the remains of his necklace! It must have gotten ripped off and booted down the hallway during the lame scuffle with Craig Hawkins. I immediately dropped it into my purse for safe keeping, like it was a sacred relic on par with the Holy Grail

This was a great excuse to give Rick a call that night and offer my support to him during his suspension. I'd get all the gory details of the fight, plus, I could slip in a mention that I found his necklace and would give it to him when he came back to school, thus painting myself in the light of the dutiful and caring friend.

It was all so cinematic. Like something out of a spaghetti western: The misunderstood gunslinger gets in a nasty brawl with the corrupt, drunken town official while the saloon gal with a heart of gold keeps the gunslinger's prized pistol safe from the sheriff desperate to incriminate him.

That night, I called Rick on the phone. His mother answered, sounding none too pleased that her son was receiving calls during his suspension. She put Rick on the phone and I asked him what happened, getting the Cliff's Notes version:

"Hawkins started some shit with me in biology. Throwing spitballs in my hair and flicking shit at me. So, I grabbed him and threw him into the wall."

"I heard you bit his nipple."

"Yeah. He probably liked it," Rick laughed. "It was the only way I could think of to get out of the headlock."

"Hey," I hedged. "Did Craig rip off your necklace, by any chance? I found a broken chain with a skull cross that looks like yours."

"Yeah, he did. You found it?"

Pay dirt! "Yeah. I'll see if I can fix the links on the chain, but the rest of it is in good condition. I'll give it to you next time I see you."

"Cool." Simple. Unemotional. Pretty much what I was expecting.

As I debated telling Rick why I wanted to talk to him after class, Rick's mother made that decision for me.

"Get off the damn phone!" she cawed in the background. "You're in deep shit enough right now."

"Thanks again," Rick said, cool as ever before hanging up. "I'll talk to ya next week."

I found myself searching for a sign, some hint at a resolution to my dating dilemma. On one hand, I had Rick's broken necklace as a portent that I could be fated to be with him. On the other, there was the reality that he was oblivious to my feelings. Or maybe he just didn't feel anything back – hence his lack of curiosity about what I wanted to talk to him about earlier that day.

I wondered how I would survive three whole days without seeing Rick at school and how I would deal with the gnawing feeling in the pit of my stomach that wouldn't go away. If all had gone according to plan, I would have known that night if Rick wanted to go out with me or if I would just have to move on.

What's that they say about "the best laid plans of mice and men"? Yeah. Well, guess who felt like the big, bunny-petting clod who had to be put out of his misery by the end of the book?

The thought of gushy, gooey, obsessive, girly feelings for a guy sickened me. But it didn't stop me from making pilgrimage to the mall that weekend and picking up a copy of Rick's necklace. I decided that I would keep the one he had ripped off in the fight so I could sleep with it under my pillow. (Please feel free to take a vomit break if the urge strikes you. I know I would.)

When Rick finally returned to school, I gave him the duplicate necklace. He was none the wiser, thinking I fixed the chain and that it was as good as new.

I was determined to give it another try and ask him out the day after he returned.

Once again, fate had other plans. The day after, as it turned out, was April 8th, 1994 – a significant date to any fan of rock music in the early '90s.

As I was planning, yet again, on how to corner Rick and ask him out, a news bulletin broke through on the TV in the cafeteria. Kurt Cobain, lead singer of the band Nirvana, had been found dead at his home, the victim of a self-inflicted gunshot.

Following the announcement of Cobain's death, Sammi completely fell apart. Kurt was her hero. She broke down crying in the lunchroom. A lot of other students, particularly the popular ones, laughed at her, making matters worse.

I was ambivalent towards Kurt Cobain and his music but could sympathize with Sammi. Had I been in her shoes and any member of Mötley Crüe had died (or in Nikki Sixx's case, died a second time and wasn't resurrected from his overdose) I would have been a basket case. Suddenly, asking Rick out that day didn't feel right. With Sammi distraught, there was no way I could divert my focus from consoling her.

Now it wasn't *just* Craig Hawkins putting the kibosh on my love life. Now dead celebrities were getting in on the act and Kurt Cobain just cock blocked me, too.

The day that Kurt Cobain died proved to be a bigger tragedy on several levels. Sammi was never quite the same and it sparked the beginning of a downward spiral for my friend. Her notebooks were covered in scribblings taken from Cobain's publicized suicide note. The notes she would pass to me, Cora, and Jenn were post-scripted with some of Nirvana's most desolate lyrics. I noticed deep welts and cuts that began appearing on her arms, crisscrossing them so badly that she started wearing long-sleeved flannel pajama tops – eerily similar to the ones Cobain used to wear – to cover them.

Sammi's well-being superseded any of our own personal dramas. Like each of us in our circle of friends, Rick was doing his best to attempt to bring Sammi out of her desperate state, too.

In the weeks following Cobain's suicide, I found myself worrying about Sammi, worrying about finals, and worrying about how to broach my feelings to Rick.

One Friday a few weeks later, I made a spur of the moment decision to bite the bullet and tell Rick how I felt. I didn't plan on asking him out that day, but for two weeks, I was experiencing so much anxiety, I could barely finish the eight ounces of lemon yogurt I would bring for lunch every day.

I had to rip the Band-Aid off and resolve this once and for all.

Forcing down my semi-solid lunch and chucking the container in the recyclable bin, I approached Rick and attempted to conceal my nervousness. "Hey, would you mind if I talked with you outside in the hallway?"

He paused for a second, looking confused. "Yeah, sure. When?"

It was too late to not seem obvious. Glancing at my watch with five minutes left of lunch period, it was now or never.

"Whenever." I tried to sound relaxed. "Now would be cool."

"Okay." Rick shrugged, following me out the doors of the lunch room and into the hallway.

I could feel my hands shaking as I pushed against the metal doors that led to the lockers.

This was it. We were alone. There were no lunch ladies. No students. No hall monitors or teachers on duty milling about.

"So, what did you want to talk to me about?"

For a split second, I thought about giving myself an out. I could blurt out that I was worried about Sammi in light of this whole Kurt Cobain thing. I really *was* worried about her, but it seemed shitty to use a friend's predicament as a means to save face.

I took a deep breath. "I'm sure you probably know what this is about."

"I think so."

My voice lowered. "Oh."

The jig was up. Rick certainly wasn't an honors student (in fact, his parents proudly sported a bumper sticker on their beat up van that said "My kid beat up your honor student"), but he was far from dense.

I took another deep breath through my nose, exhaling shakily before continuing. "Look, I don't know how you feel, but

I was wondering if you ever thought about being more than friends? You know, like maybe hanging out and going to the mall together, or shit like that?"

Reverting to my standard tactic, I threw a "shit" into my last sentence. A good "shit" always lightens the severity of any situation.

Despite the four-inch heels I was wearing that day, I found myself feeling very small, looking up at 6'5" Rick. I searched his blue eyes, hidden behind wisps of long, brown hair for some indication of what he might be thinking at that moment before I continued.

"The truth is... I really like you. A lot. And I was wondering if there was any chance that you might like me. Even a little." I was going for broke and a torrent of verbal and emotional diarrhea began flowing from my Bonne Bell lip gloss-coated mouth. "You don't even have to like me a lot. You could just hang out with me on a trial basis to see if you *might* like me."

Embarrassed by my own words, I could hardly look Rick in the eye anymore, opting to stare down at the dim, fluorescent bulbs reflected in my black patent high-heeled Mary Janes.

Taking in a shallow breath, still staring at the floor, I managed to murmur one final sentence. "I was just wondering if that was something you would want, too."

I stood rigid – petrified by my own truth that had sprung a leak like a faulty colostomy bag.

After what seemed like an eternity, Rick finally spoke. "I never really thought about it before." For a second, there was a glimmer of light at the end of my long, dateless tunnel. "But I really think that we're better off as friends."

As gently as Rick let me down, it would be a gross understatement to say I was bummed out by his answer. I had thought for sure that I had found someone else of a similar mindset. A soulmate (although I really hate that word). That maybe there was someone else out there capable of real, human emotion even though they put up a tough exterior.

I was crushed. I *really* liked this guy.

Which was why I did what I did next.

"Hey, that's cool! No biggie. I'm glad we're still friends. Everything's cool between us, right?"

Rick shrugged casually."Yeah."

"Cool." And in one of my most desperate acts ever, I decided to go where I had never gone before. I masked my grief behind an accepting, stoic façade."Would it be too much to ask for a hug?"

I saw a twinge of discomfort in Rick's eyes, but he was gentlemanly enough to concede to my request. Tentatively, I put my arms around his waist, underneath his denim jacket and over the warm flannel of his shirt. My head rested against the middle of his chest and I squeezed his slender frame close to me.

To my surprise, he hugged me back. I didn't want to let go. For a single moment that I tried to hang onto for as long as possible, I was happy. I didn't feel as ugly or unattractive as I had been told I was for years. For once, I got to touch another person that I really cared about.

It didn't mean that person felt anything back for me, but it was nice to hold onto that illusion, however brief.

Plus, I wanted to cop a cheap feel.

And then the bell rang.

Classroom doors flew open and students streamed into the hallway. The lunchroom let out, too. Our friends burst through the cafeteria door, catching a good eyeful of me and Rick hugging in the middle of the hallway.

Any sense of mortification I felt, Rick had to feel tenfold. He probably would have preferred to be anally raped with a wire brush than to have half the school see him locked in an embrace with the girl who would later be voted the "Scariest Girl in the

Graduating Class of 1997." Not that Rick ranked much higher on the social totem pole. but when you spend the bulk of your school career cultivating a certain image, the single worst thing that could happen is to have your classmates see you showing some flicker of emotion.

Hastily dropping my arms and extracting myself from Rick (much to his relief, I'm sure), I glanced over at our group of friends standing in the doorway. The guys' mouths hung open in shock. Cora flashed a demure smile. And for the first time in the weeks since Kurt Cobain went to that big, flannel warehouse in the sky, Sammi had a full-blown grin.

"Uh, see ya later," I called over my shoulder to Rick as I hurried down the stairs with Sammi and Cora to our next class.

"So, are you guys going out?" Cora asked excitedly. Sammi's eyes grew as wide as her smile while they anticipated my answer.

"Nope. We're just going to be friends."

That was it. All those weeks of balled-up feelings in my stomach had amounted to Rick dropping the worst f-bomb ever: "Friends." Not only was *Friends* a TV show about six pals who lived in the same building and eventually fucked their way through the ranks of nearly every opposite-sex member within their circle they weren't related to, but "friends" was also a way of life for me in regards to dating. The only difference was that the "friends" on the TV show had some promise of action. I didn't.

As I hid my disappointment, Sammi tried to interject a ray of hope. "That's cool. Who knows? Maybe down the line it might turn into something more."

For a moment, I believed her. A faint shimmer of a Camelot-like dream existed that someday I would share something more than just friendship with Rick.

As friends, we were closer than ever. There were no awkward feelings resulting from that conversation and we continued to trade good-natured barbs and debate music and pop culture. After that day, however, we were both a bit more mindful of each other's feelings, not really saying anything too mean to one another, even in jest.

I didn't know what was ahead or if Rick would ever feel the way I did about him, but I still had hope.

That hope, however, came to a screeching halt in the wake of a shadowy, corpulent, chain-smoking figure: Mrs. Sanders.

As luck would have it, Mom was late picking me up from school one day near the end of the year. I decided to hang out on the corner and wait for her. It was a warm day on the cusp of summer. Perfect weather for standing around outside with friends.

I wandered over to where my crew was huddled. Rick was standing next to a short, stout woman with long, frizzy red hair. She was complaining about some "swish-ass" in the grocery store checkout line, talking through the side of her mouth that wasn't occupied by a Marlboro.

Although I wasn't close enough to determine the particular brand of cigarette Mrs. Sanders favored, she made her preference loud and clear by the oversized, grey-that-used-to-be-black Marlboro t-shirt she was sporting.

She paused her tirade long enough to remove the cigarette from her mouth and flick its ashes onto the pavement. Her beady eyes scanned the collection of teenagers in front of her.

"Well, introduce me to your friends!" Rick winced as his mother gave him a hard swat on his arm. Maybe it was just my imagination, but I felt her give me the proverbial once-over, assessing me with a critical eye that may or may not have rolled in its socket as she took another drag off her cancer stick.

"Nice to meet you, Mrs. Sanders," I said

"Hi," she said disinterestedly before taking another puff.

The next day at lunch, I dropped a comment to Rick. "It was nice meeting your mom. She's pretty cool."

Rick's response was a non-verbal grunt. It didn't exactly leave me with a case of the warm-n'-fuzzies.

The following weekend, when I made my usual Friday night phone call to Rick, his mother picked up the phone.

"Hi. Is Rick there?"

"Who's this?" rasped the voice on the other end.

"It's his friend Nova from school"

"He can't talk now."

"Okay. No biggie. Just let him know I called. Have a good weekend."

I heard a pause on the other end before Rick's mom managed to caw out a monosyllabic "Yeah" before hanging up.

I was beginning to get the impression that Mrs. Sanders didn't like me very much.

My suspicions were given more credence when I called Rick a few weeks later. Before long, his mom asked who he was talking to. No less than two minutes after he dropped my name, Mrs. Sanders was telling him to get off the phone and wash the dishes.

Paranoia or no, it was pretty clear that Rick's mom did not want him to associate with me. I wracked my brain trying to figure out what it was that she disliked so much about me. She seemed alright with Rick hanging around with Sammi and Cora. Then again, they had boyfriends and Cora didn't hang out with anyone after school due to her parents' strict rules.

And neither Cora nor Sammi had asked Rick out.

I replayed the encounter in my head, struggling to come up with some reason why she seemed to have such a problem with me. The best I could come up with was my choice of attire.

That day, I happened to be wearing a knee-length denim skirt, a red tank top and cardigan with a pair of red heels. Perhaps, in her feeble mind, I had invoked the color traditionally favored by harlots.

Now I was pissed. Who the hell was this woman to judge me on my appearance when she walked around looking like something Joe Camel threw up?! I wasn't about to bust out a burqa to appease Mrs. Sanders.

Not that it would have made a difference. Rick began behaving differently towards me.

During the last week of school, Sammi, Cora, Rick, and I headed to a local café to bide our time between early morning and late afternoon finals. Some enterprising Fletcherite decided to capitalize on the Seattle coffee house trend and opened a café in town. Since there was nothing else to do, the four of us decided to check it out before heading back for exams.

Sammi had slowly begun to recover from Kurt Cobain's death. However, she still looked to the late Nirvana singer for inspiration, championing his personal philosophies in lieu of her old, loveable, shit-stirring ways.

Cora was relieved to have one last hurrah with friends before her strict parents put her on lockdown for the summer.

Since I lived across town from my friends, I wouldn't see them much over the summer aside from talking on the phone. I was grateful for this extra time before next school year to spend with my friends and Rick.

Or so I thought.

Rick and I didn't say much to each other on the walk downtown. At the café, Sammi made an offhanded comment to him: "So, how does it feel to be surrounded by three hot chicks all day? It's like you're our pimp!"

Rick responded with a laugh. "Make that *two* hot chicks. I don't think anyone would pay to sleep with Nova."

I was used to exchanging barbs with Rick, but he had never said anything that mean before. I mustered an eye-roll.

"Rick!" exclaimed Cora. "That's not nice! Tell Nova you're sorry!"

"Okay, okay!" he conceded with a smirk. "I'm sorry you're not getting laid, Nova."

"That's alright, Rick. I don't need an apology. I don't see the ladies lining up around the block to bang you, either."

I didn't know if my comment nailed him the way his had dented me, but Rick looked down, thumbing through the magazine in front of him. Satisfied with my rebuttal, I regally extended my pinky while taking a sip from my Styrofoam coffee cup.

An awkward silence hung in the air before the conversation rebooted itself.

I put my coffee down and cracked open my notebook to get in some last minute cramming for my final. I rummaged through my purse to find a highlighter. After emptying out half of my purse onto the table, I finally found one.

"What *don't* you have in your purse?" asked Sammi as I shoved makeup, pens, a notepad, paper clips, mace, some cassette tapes, and other assorted items back into my handbag.

"Pretty much my whole life is in this thing. I could *MacGyver* my way out of anything with what I've got in here."

"Do you ever *shut up*?!" Rick exclaimed, eyeing me with complete disgust. "Every time you open your mouth something stupid comes out."

Whoa! I wasn't even addressing Rick, let alone spouting off elaborate theories. His earlier remarks hurt, but his latest stung even worse. I couldn't care less if Rick found me attractive, but insinuating I was stupid made me livid. I couldn't stop myself from tearing into him.

"Hey, asshole! I don't know where this shit is coming from or what the fuck I did to piss you off, but you've got a lot of nerve calling *me* stupid."

Sammi and Cora looked on anxiously, not wanting to get involved on either friend's behalf.

Sammi eyed me imploringly as Rick grew red with rage.

I, on the other hand, was on a roll. "Have you listened to yourself talk? Have you heard your stupid *accent*, Cletus? Real stellar GPA you have, too. Oh! And let's not forget your dumb jacket, either. People can see you're a moron coming *and* going."

Rick just sat there and took it. Any other time that I hit someone with a low zinger, I felt pleased with myself. This time, it felt horrible.

An awkward silence hung in the air after I finally exhausted my insult tank. I couldn't bring myself to look at anyone, and stared down at the same textbook page for a good five minutes.

Mercifully, Sammi broke the silence and suggested we head back to school. Sammi walked ahead with Rick. I lagged several paces behind with Cora.

When we got back to school, I said goodbye to Sammi, wished her luck on her final, and told her I'd call her over the summer.

Cora and I headed to our history final. We finished the test in under an hour and she waited with me for Mom to come pick me up. Nothing was said regarding the verbal altercation between me and Rick, but I told her to give me a call during vacation if her parents allowed her.

I got in the car with Mom, pulling away from the building for the last time until September. My brother was in the car with her, having already completed his last day of school for the year. He eyed me suspiciously, wearing his usual shit-eating grin. He knew *something* had happened and that he would eventually pry it out of me.

CHAPTER SIX
THE SUMMER OF HATE

The first few weeks of summer were uneventful. I hadn't heard from my friends since school let out. As a result, Orion was experiencing a serious drought of phone-based entertainment. The kid was a one-man wiretap that could rival the C.I.A. He could pick up the other line without me or the unsuspecting party on the other end aware that he was listening in. This was how he kept himself entertained and supplied Mom with a steady stream of information on me and my friends.

The only time when I was ever able to discern when my brother was listening in was when he would grow bored with the phone conversation and begin pressing buttons, making a series of ear-splitting bleeps with the keypad on the other end. That was usually my cue to hang up the phone – whether I wanted to or not.

Despite my brother's douchery, his talent for listening in on my phone conversations came in handy a few times and helped strengthen our brotherly/sisterly bond.

Although I was now much closer with my brother, there were still certain things I was hesitant to tell him lest it get back to Mom. There was no way I was going to let Orion in on the details of my love life... Or lack thereof.

I knew better than to say anything to Mom about what happened with Rick. Not that she would have had any objections to me having the hots for somebody, nor would she impose any restrictions to prohibit me from going out on a date with a guy.

I just didn't want her to make fun of me.

My family was not an emotional lot. It was not within our genetic makeup to skip through the daisies and pirouette in the street, proclaiming to the world that you were "in love." In the Porter household, love – much less the high school variety – was something to be mocked.

While I still had "feelings" for Rick, I approached any type of vulnerability with a certain level of shame. And while Orion and I had formed a new alliance, his allegiance to Mom as her pet snitch was much stronger.

Nevertheless, I couldn't restrain myself from telling Orion the sordid details of my verbal throw-down with Rick. It was summer vacation and I didn't have anyone else around to talk to. Rather than agonize over the situation and stew in my own juices for the next three months, I broke down and told my brother what happened.

To my surprise, he only laughed at me for five straight minutes.

"Do you feel bad about what you said to him?"

"I'm not sure," I replied truthfully. "I mean, yeah, I *do* think he deserved the things I said to him. He was being a dick to me for no real reason."

"Then you have nothing to worry about!" my brother exclaimed.

"On the other hand, I feel bad that I said *so many* insulting things to him. I mean, dude... They just came pouring out."

Orion paused for a moment before eyeing me with keen disgust, as if someone just waved moldy cheese under his nose. "Ugh. You really like him, don't you?"

I didn't say a word. Admitting my feelings for Rick would show weakness and doom me to a summer of misery with Orion mocking me for the next three months.

Rather than say anything, I just rolled my eyes.

"Aaaaahaaahaa!" my brother burst out laughing. "That's 'The Horny Look'! Whenever you get horny for some guy and someone calls you out on it, you roll your eyes! Haha! You're fuckin' horny!"

I knew this was a bad idea.

I stood there and absorbed his juvenile taunts before Orion stopped laughing long enough to offer a suggestion.

"Have you thought about calling him to just say 'hi'?"

I raised an eyebrow. "Are you out of your fucking mind? I lit him up! Why the hell would he want to talk to me?"

"Hey, it's been a couple of weeks. Things blow over. He probably forgot about it. You know how things go at our house. We insult the shit out of each other. Five minutes later, everyone goes out and gets pizza like nothing ever happened."

He had a point. However, I suspected that my brother just wanted to listen in on the phone conversation.

It took me a few days to gather my thoughts and figure out what I wanted to say to Rick to rectify the situation. In keeping with tradition, I waited for a Friday night to call him. Orion was nice enough to not listen in on the conversation. That meant a lot to me.

I dialed the number and Rick answered. "Y'ello."

"Hey, Rick!" I said casually. "Just wanted to give ya a call and see how your summer's been going."

There was an awkward pause before he spoke again. "Eh. It's summer," he replied in his usual, nonplussed manner.

More awkward. More pause.

My carefully bullet-pointed plan was spiraling down the shitter fast. It was time to just blurt it out and get it over with.

"Yeah. Summer. Mine's been pretty good so far." It was cute how I was trying to make this sound like an actual conversation. "Uhh... Rick? I just wanted to call and say I'm sorry I flipped out at you that last day at school. I'm not sure what was up with you and – you know me – I'm not too good about keeping my mouth shut when I get pissed off. Anyway, I just wanted to tell you I'm sorry for being a bitch at the café and that I hope we're still cool as friends."

The awkward pauses just kept a-comin'. Ten seconds elapsed before Rick intoned that we were, indeed, "cool" and that there were no hard feelings. I heaved a sigh of relief before he said he had to go and take out the garbage.

"Alright," I said cheerily. "Gimme a buzz any time if you're bored. Have a good one!"

"You, too. See ya!" he replied before he hung up.

Orion opened the door to my room. "How'd it go?"

"Better than I expected," I shrugged. "He doesn't hate me."

My brother nodded intently, indicating that he wanted me to elaborate on anything potentially incriminating.

"Did he sound like he was glad to hear from you?" Orion prodded.

"Not really. It was a pretty cut-and-dry conversation. I apologized. He accepted my apology. Then he had to take out the garbage."

My brother was direct and to the point: "He's not interested in you. You guys are just friends. Deal with it."

As much as it hurt to hear, he was right. I didn't feel any sparks flying through the phone. Not even a warm, fuzzy feeling that we had repaired our friendship. We were well-acquainted acquaintances who were a part of the same social circle. I was kidding myself if I thought otherwise.

"Fuck it, man," my brother said. "It's summer! Have fun!"

He was right. And with that, I followed him out to the living room to watch the rest of ABC's T.G.I.F. lineup. Oh, that Urkel!

Urkel was a temporary panacea, however. No matter how many times I went for a swim at the community pool or shot hoops with my brother, I couldn't shake the feeling that if Rick and I were at least acquaintances, maybe something could be done to rebuild our friendship.

A few weeks had elapsed. I deemed a safe amount of time had passed and that I could call Rick again. Dialing the now-memorized seven digits (obsession and nothing else to do over the summer will do that), Rick's mother answered the phone.

"Hi. Is Rick around?"

"Who's this?" Her tone was more pointed than a '50s bra.

"It's Nova. His friend from school."

"He doesn't want to talk to you" she spat into the receiver and hung up the phone up with a slam.

My mouth dropped open in shock. I thought the slate had been cleaned.

One of two things must have happened: Either Rick had an ass full of me and told his mother how annoying I was. Or, Rick's mother (as I had assumed before) hated my guts and painted me as a Slattern Supreme and convinced her son of the same.

Just like that, my hopes for a closer bond with Rick Sanders dissipated into the air like vapors from the cigarette that was perpetually fixed to his mother's lower lip. Several miles across town, I could swear the old bag was chain smoking her way through a pack of Marlboros – probably diddling herself with nicotine-stained, sausage link fingers – satisfied that she had intercepted what she believed was the last phone call I would ever make to her son.

It's not going to be that easy, toots, I said to myself.

The mental image of that corpulent cow enraged me. I didn't know who I was more disgusted with: her or Rick. Up until that last day of school, I had never been anything but nice to him. Not knowing why Rick didn't want to talk to me hurt worse than a boot to the groin. What had I done to piss him off? *He* was the one who threw down the gauntlet and kicked off the verbal beat down. Apologizing to him had been a complete waste of time. It hurt even more that he couldn't tell me he hated me himself and just sicced his mother on me instead.

Rick's mother. Now, *there* was the problem. I did nothing to the woman, yet for some reason, she wanted me as far away from Rick as possible. Maybe she had a thing against chicks who wore denim skirts? Or maybe Mrs. Sanders had some weird, Mrs. Bates-like grasp her son and saw me as a potential threat? I leaned towards the latter theory. I certainly wasn't the only chick in school with a denim mini hanging in her closet, but I *was* the only girl in school who showed an interest in Rick.

"Why the hell does that twat-a-saurus hate me so much?" I asked my brother one day on the basketball court.

"Why do you care?" Orion retorted. "She's a fat, redheaded piece of hell. Why should you care what she thinks? That's Rick's problem if he's been brainwashed by her. Not yours." My twelve year old brother was, astoundingly, the voice of reason. "Even if you do end up going out with him – which is a really big 'if' – you'll have to deal with his mother. All the time."

"What if we date secretly?" I offered.

"Dude... He doesn't want to go out with you!" Brutal, yet to the point, Orion made a strong case. "And why do *you* still want to go out with *him*? Even if he wanted to go out with you, he's so whipped by his mother that he doesn't have the guts to stand up to her and tell her that you're not a skank."

Orion was right. Rick and I would never date. Anything I had previously found to be so attractive in Rick was now non-existent. The rebellious, "I don't give a shit" outsider and deeply buried intellect routine was a total sham.

To top it off, I was fairly disgusted with *myself* for falling for him.

I come from a family of puke-ers. We vomit when we're sick. We hurl when we're nervous. And we blow chunks when we're really upset.

In addition to being a puke-er himself, Orion always got a big kick out of watching others power vomit.

Not only had Orion hit the mother lode of love life gossip that he could carry back to Mom and curry favor, but he struck pay dirt in the puke department, too.

I had been in the throes of depression for a few days and was sick to my stomach. It felt similar to the churning feeling I got when I tried to wrangle the courage to ask Rick out several months before. Only this time, I felt nauseated for agonizing so much over someone who thought so little of me.

That's when I looked to my brother for help yet again.

Orion had a knack for coming up with the most disgusting shit you could think of. I vividly recall one morning when Orion said so many vile things that I relinquished a delicious blueberry muffin to him because I was too grossed out to eat it. Orion had a rare, God-given gift that came in handy during my time of need.

"Dude. I need you to help me puke," I said. "I feel really sick and nothing is coming out. I think if I vomit, I might feel better. My stomach is a mess and I can't take a dump or do anything."

"Maybe you should try picking your face up out of that bag of Cheezer Puffs," he offered. "Keep eating and no guy is going to want to go out with you. At the rate you're putting back the Razberry Rollz, you're going to end up looking like Rick's mother."

Orion agreed to help me puke on the condition that he was able to have unfettered reign to say whatever he wanted, no matter how disgusting. He also stipulated that he would be allowed to watch and laugh at me while I barfed.

I was desperate at this point and agreed to anything if it would help make me feel better.

I braced myself against the cold, white porcelain; kneeling on the bathroom tile as my head hovered over the bowl. Pulling my hair back with an elastic, I prepared for the torrent of raunch I was about to be hit with.

This was my therapy.

"Dirty pubes. Dirty, red pubes that look like filthy, little Cheezer Puffs. Filthy, *hairy* Cheezer Puffs."

In a span of seconds, my brother ruined one of my favorite snack foods for me. The assault on the crunchy, curly, cheese-flavored bites kept coming more vicious than ever: "Oh, shit! Mrs. Sanders just pulled down her pants and she's trying to shove her Cheezer Puff snatch in your face! Whatcha gonna do now?!"

I could feel the vomit charting its course up my esophagus.

"And then," he paused for dramatic effect. "Mrs. Sanders takes the cigarette out of her mouth and shoves it up her snatch." Taking it a step further, Orion began to imitate Mrs. Sanders, warping his voice into an exaggerated backwoods twang riddled with smoker's rasp: "I tol' you not to call mah boy, girl! You done keep callin' mah house! He's MAH son! I gits to fuck 'im! But I'll let you eat mah pussy! My nasty, Cheezer Puff pussy! Here! Puff on mah cigarette I got crammed in there for ya!"

That did it. That was the money shot right there.

Blurrrrgggghhh!

The mental image of Rick's mother with her pants down alone was bad enough, but combined with snack foods, cigarettes, and the offer of chowing down on her gross, yeasty box; it was enough to make me heave up the contents of my stomach.

My brother cackled like a mad man as I hurled into the bowl in front of me.

"That," I said, wiping my mouth with a piece of toilet paper. "Was disgusting. Nice job."

"I could say some more if you're not finished yet?" Orion offered, grinning impishly.

"Nah. That's okay. Save it for another time. That was really fucking disgusting."

"Yeah." He smiled proudly. "I know."

After mentally berating myself for a day or two on an emptied stomach, I decided I was letting the summer slip away from me and embarked on a course of self-improvement... and revenge. They say that hell hath no fury like a woman scorned, but that's not entirely true: Hell hath no fury like a *teenage girl* scorned.

Lacking in wisdom and maturity, I substituted those virtues with copious amounts of daytime television that I wasn't privy to during the school year. I formulated a plan to ruin the rest of Rick's summer and give him a taste of things to come in the school year ahead. My nefarious, genius plot revolved around that tried and true method of making someone's life miserable from a distance: the prank phone call.

In the days before cell phones and caller I.D., you didn't have to be quite as crafty about making crank calls and not getting caught. Thanks to *69, it was a bit more difficult – although not impossible – to prank someone undetected.

The mall was only a short distance from my house. I made my crank calls there. The mall had plenty of pay phones and, in those days, a simple quarter could buy you a nearly limitless amount of enjoyment and personal satisfaction.

I picked up the receiver and keyed in the numbers I had become so familiar with, only dialing them with a much different intent than all those times before.

After a few rings, someone picked up. "Yeah? Hello?" croaked the voice on the other end. It was the old buzzard. Mrs. Sanders herself.

I altered my voice with a faux-British accent and yelled into the receiver: "Ya got any fuckin' Slayer, maaaan!?!"

It took all of the restraint I could muster to refrain from laughing as the old bag angrily blasted me from the other end.

"Who the hell is this? This phone is tapped!"

Deepening my voice to sound like a pubescent male, I yelled "Fuck you, bitch!" into the receiver before slamming it down.

God, that felt good!

I mulled the moment over in my mind, savoring my victory.

I strode back into the house with a big, shit-eating grin on my face. Orion was playing basketball on the front porch. He looked at me and knew something was up.

"What happened?"

"I pranked Rick's mother. It was awesome!"

My brother listened intently as I recounted the epic thirty-second exchange.

"Oh! And the best part? The old twat starts yelling, 'This phone is taaa-aapped,'" I recalled, imitating Mrs. Sanders's hillbilly accent. "And then I screamed right back at her into the phone, 'Fuck you, bitch!' It was awesome!"

"Shit!" my brother exclaimed. "Why didn't you tell me you were pranking?! I wanna come next time!"

I paused for a moment. My brother said the magic words: *"Next time."*

Yes. There *would be* a next time. And the next time would be an even bigger, better, more vicious assault. This was all out war! I didn't care if Rick answered the phone. Truthfully, I didn't *want* him to answer the phone. I wanted to talk to that chain-smoking sack of crap and make her so shit-scared to answer the phone that the hairs on her fat, pimpled back would stand on end every time she heard it ring.

I smiled and nodded at my brother. If I had a mustache, damn skippy I would have twirled it.

For the remainder of the summer, we made it a point to ambush Mrs. Sanders on the phone at least once a week. When Orion and I were bored with the pool, playing basketball, or watching *Three's Company* reruns, we would venture to the frozen yogurt stand not far from our house to grab some creamy summertime refreshment and use our spare change to inflict torment upon Rick's big, red, nasty mother.

On the last day of summer vacation, Orion and I decided to take our crank calls to an unprecedented level. I wanted to set the tone for the new school year. I wanted Rick to feel as ill at ease as he and his mother had made me feel at the outset of summer break: We were going to threaten Rick with getting jumped on the first day of school.

Armed with a fistful of quarters, my brother and I made our way up the hill to the pay phone at the mini-mall up the street. We had a rough idea of what we were going to say in the event that Rick (highly unlikely) or his mother (the preferred candidate) answered the phone.

We huddled around the receiver, grinning like assholes and listening to the ring tone in anticipation of hearing a voice on the other end.

"Hello? Who's this?!" crackled a familiar, smoke-addled twang.

"Is Rick there?" Once again, I deepened my voice to a convincingly masculine level.

"Who's this?!" she squawked again.

She was already on the ropes. I had to work fast. She could hang up at any second and I would lose my chance to set the wheels of my plan in motion.

"Listen, bitch. You don't *need* to know who the fuck this is. I'm gonna give you a message to give to your boy, ya got me?"

I was in rare form. The voice on the other end was silent as I continued. "Tell your boy that we're gonna kick his ass all the way back to West Virginny where his bitch ass belongs... Know what I'm sayin'!? You tell Rick that when he comes to school tomorrow... He best come STRAPPED!"

Admittedly, I had been listening to a lot of Eazy-E that summer.

My brother put a hand over his mouth to stifle his laughter. His eyes widened and he nodded his head eagerly. The kid wanted his shot at Mrs. Sanders on the phone.

"Yo, I'm gonna put you on the phone with my associate... Bitch!"

Orion grabbed the receiver. "Take that to the bank, you fat fuck! Suck my balls!"

At that point, Rick's mother promptly hung up the phone, no doubt carrying the message that her son should "come strapped" on the first day of school.

Orion and I erupted in laughter, congratulating one another on the outstanding job of tele-terrorism we had enacted upon my arch nemesis. I couldn't wait to see the fruits of my labor tomorrow at school.

In acknowledgement that my transformation to the Dark Side had become complete, I decided to celebrate my new attitude with a new look. I examined my long, brassy blonde hair and realized that blondes *don't* have more fun. I was tired of being a mousy doormat.

I went to the drugstore up the street and bought a four-dollar box of black hair dye and set to work altering my locks to a darker hue.

The rationale for my transformation was simple. Cool people had black hair: Three-fourths of Mötley Crüe. Dracula. Elvira. Cher. Elvis.

Black hair suited my mood more than the blah shade of dirty blonde I had previously sported – which was now tinted a faint shade of chartreuse from frequent exposure to chlorine. Plus, black would be easier to maintain and would probably make my hair healthier.

I was mighty impressed with my handiwork after washing and drying my freshly-dyed hair. There were no blonde spots left. Even better, I didn't leave any stains on the bathroom — which would have incurred an ass-beating from Mom that would have made the one Rick may have been anticipating at school tomorrow look like a love tap.

Actually, Mom approved of the new 'do. "*Much* better! The blonde didn't do anything for you. This is much more flattering. I love it!"

When Dad came home from work and saw me sitting in the living room, I got a slightly different reaction: "Jesus Christ! If your mom didn't tell me you dyed your hair, I probably would have shot you! You don't even look like you.... It looks good!"

The backhanded compliments from both of my parents were just the thing I needed to hear! I had successfully turned myself into a brand new me with a brand new attitude.

I couldn't wait to go to school the next morning.

CHAPTER SEVEN
SOPHOMORE SLUMP

The sun was shining. The birds were singing. Rick was probably shitting bricks. And I was headed off to my first day of sophomore year. Oh, what a beautiful morning!

Climbing the stairs to the second floor and remembering the combination on my centrally located locker, I smiled to myself, thinking about the things that I hoped this year would bring – namely, Rick to his knees.

As I rummaged in my bag for my class schedule, I caught sight of my friend Jenn walking down the hallway. Over the summer, Jenn and I had grown pretty close. Sammi had been M.I.A. No one had heard from her. I tried calling her several times during the summer, but she never returned my calls – or anyone else's, for that matter.

Jenn and I started hanging out more often. An attractive girl with long, chestnut hair and mile-high mall bangs spray-mounted in place with a can of AquaNet, Jenn and I bonded that summer. We hung out at the mall and discussed the disappearing species of hot, hair metal males that had given way to crusty, grunge guys who had no interest in posing for photos with their shirts off.

Over the summer, I told Jenn about what happened with Rick and how his mother had it in for me. She was a little bummed out. While Jenn wasn't super closewith Rick (considering he used to lambaste her taste in music, too), she knew I liked him a lot.

I let Jenn in on the phone "conversation" I had yesterday with Rick's mother. We both wondered how Rick would react or if his mother even told him that an anonymous caller advised him to watch his back on the first day of class.

We would get our answer soon enough. Rick was walking down the hall. Staring straight ahead, with a jerk of his head, he flicked his long, brown bangs out of his eyes.

Then again, the head-jerk thing was sometimes Rick's way of saying "hi." It was hard to tell.

Rick walked directly to his locker, just a few doors down from mine. His mullet had grown out over the summer.

"What's up, dude?" I said absently as he began fiddling with his locker and loaded a large pile of CDs onto the top shelf.

"Nothing. Just trying to figure out my schedule this year. I'm already fuckin' pissed off."

I did a good job of concealing my Inner Snicker, wondering just what could have made Our Intrepid Zero so discombobulated.

"Why? What happened?"

"Some asshole called my house last night and told my mother that they were going to jump me at school today."

It took every fiber of self-control that I had to not bust out laughing.

"That's fucked up!" I exclaimed in mock outrage. "Yo, I have some pepper spray in my purse if you need to borrow it?" My offer was in keeping with the typical, desperate Nova that Rick had come to know and loathe. The sick, sad thing was if Rick actually *was* in trouble, I probably would have handed over my can of Mini Mace to him in a heartbeat.

"Nah. That's okay. I brought a couple knives with me. I'll take care of them if they try to fuck with me."

"Do you have any idea who called your house?" Jenn asked.

"Not sure. I think it was fuckin' Kevin Doherty."

I restrained myself, choking back on the knowledge that the dastardly deceiver was not "fuckin' Kevin Doherty," but that it was really me. I felt bad considering I knew Kevin and he was a nice kid with a good sense of humor. I wouldn't have expected Rick to think it was Kevin.

Then again, that spoke volumes about how many people and friends Rick – or his mother – had alienated.

"You think it was Kevin? Kev wouldn't pull that shit!"

"Nah," he said confidently. "I'm pretty damn sure it was fuckin' Doherty pulling a prank."

"Well, be careful just in case it was someone who was serious. And let me know if you need to borrow my mace."

Rick squinted in the dim light of the hallway, eyeing me curiously. "Did you dye your hair over the summer, Nova?"

As much as I enjoyed tormenting Rick, I secretly hoped he'd notice that I dyed my hair a radically different color over the summer. More so, I was hoping that he would compliment me on my new look.

"Yeah." For a second, those old butterflies crept back into my stomach.

"Huh." He paused thoughtfully for a moment. "It looks really fucking stupid on you."

And with that, he walked away.

"Wow. What an asshole," Jenn muttered under her breath.

"That fucking grease ball is going down," I said through gritted teeth. Any shred of guilt I had about pranking Rick had evaporated. In an instant, my resolve to turn him into a sniveling heap by the end of the school year had been strengthened.

I would have my chance since Rick and I ended up in the same, second period art class with Jenn. We sat at the same workbench table along with a few other students.

I had already come to grips with the fact that Rick would never take a romantic interest in me. That came right behind the realization that he and I weren't going to be friends, either. It was safe to say he was pretty repulsed by me.

One day in class, I asked him to pass me the tube of red acrylic paint. Handing it over, his fingertips accidentally brushed mine. Upon making contact, he pulled his hand away like he had just been burned with acid. Then he made a big production of wiping his fingers off on his pants.

Rick's reaction to touching "just the tip" of my fingers was one of those split-second moments that haunted me for a long time. For years after that incident, I didn't initiate shaking hands with people. I waited for them to do it first. Or I would politely nod in their direction rather than touch them. I'm a firm believer in not invading people's space unless they ask first, but that incident with Rick made me extremely self-conscious as to how someone else would perceive even my slightest touch.

Although Rick and I were at odds, I got along with the rest of the people at our art class table. At least *they* wouldn't freak out if I asked them to pass me a #5 Filbert.

I recognized Claire from my art class last year. Back in elementary school, Claire and I didn't like each other very much. We shared a few friends, but she always made snide comments about me behind my back. Claire was far more popular than me or Jenn, but relished her newfound status as "slumming it" among the freaks and geeks having recently adopted a much more *avant garde* wardrobe and grown out her perm into a long, straight, strawberry blonde, hippie princess style.

I ended up becoming good friends with Claire and learned that there was much more to her than she initially projected.

While capable of kindness, Claire still had this thing about being the Queen Bee of her social circle, adopting me and Jenn as her "ladies-in-waiting." Both Jenn and I were feisty enough to be entertaining, but still mild-mannered enough to humor Claire with very little argument.

The group dynamic was changing rapidly within my tight circle of friends from freshman year. As a result, I wound up spending more time with Claire and Jenn. The beginning of the end for our group came when Sammi's mother decided that Sammi should transfer schools midway through sophomore year.

Sammi's problems were escalating and her mother thought that a change of scenery would straighten her out.

Sammi was no longer just smoking pot and had graduated to using harder drugs. One day, she peaked on an acid trip during (ironically enough) health class. A friend and I had to physically carry her out of class and call her mother to pick her up and take her home. Sammi was spiraling downward fast. I knew she hit rock bottom when I saw her come out of a bathroom stall, completely fucked up on God knows what.

Cora and I tried to talk to her. To understand why she was doing this to herself. It was no use. Two 15-year-old girls are hardly qualified professionals.

You can care so much about the person mired in addiction, but once someone makes up their mind to start using, there is nothing you can do to pry them away from the thing that allows them to escape. And Sammi needed an escape. She was the *de facto* caretaker for her baby sister while her mother was off either working or dating. She was made fun of by bullies on a daily basis for her change in appearance. When she dyed her long blonde curls with colorful blue, red, and green streaks, she became a marked woman. Factor in Sammi's love of Kurt Cobain and baggy skater pants and it gave more fuel to the bullies' fire

– all for just being true to herself and not politely shutting it up inside. To top it all off, she had broken up with Chris, who was, at that point, the great love of her life. It's hard to point to just one thing that triggered it.

In less than a year, I saw an unbelievably good person with sparkling eyes turn into something that barely resembled my friend. I felt powerless that I couldn't rescue Sammi from her addiction the same way she rescued me from being lonely back in middle school. It's impossible to tell a person who has so much weight placed upon her shoulders that things will get better. The only immediate fix to dealing with her pain was shooting up.

After sending her daughter to dry out at an area rehab facility, Sammi's mother enrolled her in Catholic school. That lasted about a week. The only other option was to send her to another public school in the district which was actually a much bigger haven for drugs than Jefferson ever was.

I tried to keep in contact with Sammi. I called her a couple times each week to talk or see if she wanted to hang out. She was never around and had immersed herself in a new group of friends and more drugs. At one point, I tried calling and the number didn't work anymore. Her mother had changed their home number in a vain attempt to keep Sammi away from bad influences and old "friends," not realizing she was shutting out most of the good ones who cared about her daughter.

Occasionally, I would hear how Sammi was doing through friends on the local music scene who frequented the same clubs she did. Before the end of the school year, Cora, Jenn, and I paid her a visit at her house to say hello. Sammi would have long stretches of sobriety, then lapse back into using. Sober or high, I missed seeing Sammi every day. She was a great friend.

Cora and I were still very close. We ate lunch together every day and watched as our old gang was slowly breaking down or breaking away. We were in a lot of the same classes together but, because of her stern parents, we never got to hang out outside of school.

That didn't stop Cora from having a full social life at school, however. After she and Ray had (amicably) split, she started dating a freshman named Greg who she was madly in love with. Cora had always been the romantic of our group. Despite her parents putting her on lockdown, Cora had no shortage of guys who were interested in her and who she dated behind her parents' backs. During sophomore year, her parents started to loosen up a bit. At one point, I even hung out over at her house.

Jenn and I had also become closer – my reluctant ally in the war on Rick. Prior to dating a string of losers, Jenn finally hooked up with a good dude, Brian Weller. Brian was a shy, funny, artistic guy – who, incidentally, also sat at our table in art class that year. He was tall with jet black hair and a tendency to abstain from drama. They ended up bringing out the best in each other. Brian became more outgoing and vocal, while Jenn finally had someone who wasn't a douche and would treat her like a queen.

Rick and Brian were chummy, bonding over an interest in painting and drawing, but it didn't stop The Greaseball from flinging sarcastic comments Brian's way, too.

Nevertheless, Jenn and Brian didn't get nearly as much shit from Rick as I did on a daily basis. My clothes, hair, and makeup were Rick's favorite subjects of ridicule.

I may not have been an *actual* slut, but I *really* tried to look the part although there was more heavy-petting going on in a leper colony than there was in my bedroom.

Irony can be a real trip sometimes.

"Hey, Nova! How much do you charge?" Rick looked my hot pink mini dress and black fishnet tights up and down. "Did you steal that outfit from Kelly Bundy, or did you just walk off the set of a Slaughter video?"

My leopard print ensembles and black patent come-fuck-me boots did more to attract Rick's sarcastic comments than they did to attract *him*.

However, I relished the (negative) attention. It gave me an opportunity to interact with him even if it wasn't under the most congenial circumstances.

"Nice to see you wore clothes today, Nova," sneered Rick one day in art class when I switched things up a bit, wearing a black mock turtleneck with a leopard mini and boots.

My retort was icy. "Thank you, Rick Sanders: Fashion Consultant To No One."

By this point, I was used to Rick's snide comments. Actually, I found his mean-spirited sense of humor attractive. Maybe it was a bit masochistic – or even narcissistic – on my part since Rick's caustic barbs often mirrored my own sometimes-malicious humor.

Seeing our circle of friends crumble, Rick didn't have too many familiar faces to pal around with. He and Brian were friendly, but the only other guy Rick sort of hung around with was Kevin Doherty. And ever since he wrongly suspected that Kevin was pranking his house on a regular basis, things were somewhat tense between them. Instead of asking him directly, Rick just assumed that Kevin was harassing his mother. While I felt bad about the abuse Kevin was sitting back and taking, I sure as hell wasn't going to out myself as the culprit.

Tensions came to a head when the two of them came close to blows, meriting a trip to the vice principal's office.

I'm not quite sure what happened and who said what to whom, but at some point, I was called down to Vice Principal McWilliams' office, having somehow been implicated in the fracas. Unfortunately, I was in gym class at the time and wearing a dowdy pair of black sweatpants and a Marilyn Manson t-shirt.

It was hardly the type of look that would get me off the hook with the vice principal if I trotted into the office wearing that.

I headed back to the locker room to grab my books and get changed. If I was going to be cast in the role of the villainess, than I was going to look the part. And let's face it, sweat pants are not very *femme fatale*.

I changed back into my black ruffled long sleeved top, lime green skirt and matching shoes before reapplying a coat of fuchsia lip gloss. I was oh-so Sarah Michelle Gellar in *Cruel Intentions* before it ever saw wide release!

I felt an odd sense of dread en route to McWilliams' office. I had only been called to the vice principal's office once before due to a minor misunderstanding of having been mistakenly marked absent in study hall.

This, however, was a bit bigger than a case of mistaken absence. To my advantage, I had a pretty good repartee with the vice principal. To boot, I was an honors student without a blemish on my record. (Well, at least at *this* school.) Rick, on the other hand, was such a regular in McWilliams' office that he practically shared a nameplate on the desk.

I walked up to the secretary and, using my politest tone, asked why I had been summoned.

The secretary looked at her memo and asked me to take a seat with Rick and Kevin.

I didn't even have to sit down. No sooner than I poked my head in the door, McWilliams spoke: "Miss Porter, Mr. Sanders and Mr. Doherty just got into a fight today. Mr. Sanders said that you had something to do with it."

I wrinkled my nose. It was important to look shocked, but not too shocked. Subtlety was the key. "What was the fight about?" I asked, innocent as a stuffed animal.

Rick barked that I was turning everyone against him.

I rolled my eyes and shook my head, saying "That's ridiculous. Why would I do that, Rick? You're more than capable of turning people against you without any help."

McWilliams waved me off in the doorway. "That will be all, Miss Porter. You can leave now." He turned his gaze back to the two boys seated in front of him. "And I suggest that you two learn to get along with each other."

I didn't hear the rest of the conversation and missed a big chunk of what happened in the beginning. All I knew was that I was off the hook after putting in a cameo appearance.

A small speck of vanity glimmered through my usually low self-esteem. On the surface, it looked like two guys were fighting over me. *Yeah,* I said to myself. *That'd be the day.* I was still tickled that Rick had to make a trip to the office.

In hindsight, my war with Rick really had very little to do with Rick himself. I was carrying out a vendetta against his mother. Unfortunately, Rick and Kevin were getting hurt in the process. As angry as I was with Rick, what I was doing was wrong and just plain mean. However, a hurt animal has little regard for anyone or anything else except its own survival. It doesn't make what I did any less wrong, but that was my rationale at the time.

Following Doherty-gate, there had been something of a *détente* between Rick and me. However, a frosty front still existed between us even though we sat at the same table in second period.

While Jenn grew friendlier with Rick due to him being pals with her boyfriend Brian, Claire didn't particularly like Rick. She would hurl insulting comments at him similar to the way he would criticize me.

Usually, Claire targeted her comments at the thing Rick took the most pride in: his art. Claire enjoyed picking apart Rick's photos and paintings in a way that made Don Rickles look downright sensitive.

Rick would either smirk out of self-preservation or seques-ter himself at a large table near the sinks to work on his projects out of reach of her barbs.

It felt like karmic justice to see Rick tuck his tail between his legs and have to deal with the same sort of comments he directed at me.

Claire snickering to Jenn and I about Rick's paintings and his limited wardrobe (flannel and metal t-shirts) constituted a large part of our daily art classes.

Which was why it came as a shock when I found out Rick and Claire were dating.

Neither of them told me they were dating. They hadn't told Jenn or Brian, either. Cora was the one let me know what was going on.

"What!? That's impossible! Claire *hates* Rick. She's *repulsed* by him!"

Denial is always the first stage.

When I stopped to think about it, it made perfect sense in a fucked-up flow chart kind of way: Rick made fun of me because he didn't want to date me. I made fun of Rick because I wanted to date him. Rick liked when Claire made fun of him because he liked her. And Claire made fun of Rick because she was a bitch.

"Don't let Rick or Claire know that I told you," Cora pleaded. "He wanted to tell you himself."

"Oh," I said quietly. I could feel warm tears beginning to well behind my eyes.

"The only reason I found out was because someone came up and asked me if Nova Porter was going to kick Claire McNamara's ass for going out with her boyfriend," explained Cora. "When I heard that, I went and asked Rick myself if he was going out with Claire."

"Wait a minute," I said, putting the brakes on any sort of emotional outburst. "People think Rick is *my boyfriend*?"

"Yeah. A lot of people thought you two were going out."

"Where the hell would they get that idea?!" Rick and I never strolled the hallways hand-in-hand. We didn't act like we even *liked* each other, much less like we were *in love* with one another. Maybe people saw us hugging that one time and got the wrong impression.

Quick! Send in the clowns.

Don't bother... They're here.

Sure enough, Rick and Claire strode towards me as I stood at my locker. The scene played out in slow motion when I noticed they were holding hands.

I wanted to vomit.

I glanced backwards at my locker. My heart raced as I desperately tried to open it, hoping that I could crawl inside and die with dignity.

"Hey, Nova," called Rick. "Can we talk to you for a minute?"

We. He used the word "we." Rick and Claire were now a singular entity known as "we."

So this was what the Ninth Circle of Hell felt like.

"Sure." I blinked back the tears that tried to make a break for it from their ducts.

"Yeah, Claire and I started dating a week ago. We didn't want to tell you because, well, I know you still like me and we didn't want to hurt your feelings."

While I appreciated that Rick wanted to spare my feelings, his tone was cocky. Like he thought he was a hot commodity because he had not *one*, but *two* girls that wanted to date him.

I realized that *this* was *my* karma for Rick and Kevin Doherty getting sent to the vice principal's office.

Claire chimed in. "I didn't want you to be mad at either of us. You're a really good friend and I don't want me and Rick dating to strain that friendship."

I noticed Claire did not use the dread "we" when stating that "she" thought of me as a "really good friend."

Because "really good friends" always go out with guys other "really good friends" have liked for a long time. Especially when they spend the bulk of their time in class making fun of the guys their "really good friends" happen to like.

My basest instinct would have been to swipe Rick's leg out from under him and kick him in the balls before grabbing Claire by her mane of strawberry blonde hair and slamming her willowy frame into a locker.

Instead, I decided to be as mature as possible about this. Smoothing out the folds of my black sweater dress and standing as tall as I possibly could in my gold high heels, I took a deep breath, sucking back any rogue tears that tried to escape. "I understand," I said calmly. "Rick, I asked you out before and obviously, you didn't want to date me. Why should I be angry if you like someone else and they want to go out with you? That's your decision and I want you both to be happy." My voice cracked as I looked at the two of them.

"Are you okay?" asked Claire. "You're okay with us dating?"

"Yeah," I said dismissively. "You didn't have to keep it a secret from me. What the hell did you think I was going to do?"

"I didn't know if you would freak out and maybe try to beat me up." Which confirmed what Cora had said about everyone in school wrongly assuming that Rick and I had been an item.

"I would never beat either of you up," I said, just moments after having contemplated going all UFC on both of them. "I just wish you would have told me. You didn't have to sneak around behind my back. If you like each other, you should have just come out and said it." I stared down at my shiny, shiny shoes again as tears started forming.

"Okay, then," said Rick quickly. "Glad you're not mad. See ya in second period."

The two walked off, their hands mercifully unclasped, leaving me alone by my locker. I was somewhat grateful to Rick for rushing away. It gave me a chance to slam my books into my bag and make a beeline for the bathroom stall. I closed the door and sat down on the crapper and bawled my eyes out into a handful of wadded up toilet paper to stifle the sound. I stayed in the bathroom, sobbing silently for several minutes before finally exiting the stall to splash cold water on my face and reapply my makeup. I figured if I trowelled on enough black eyeliner, it would hide how red and swollen my eyes had become from crying.

The bell rang and I headed to first period Geometry. I sat there for a full 45 minutes, sick to my stomach and dreading having to sit at the same table as Rick and Claire next period.

That's when I decided to take matters into my own hands: I was going to fake sick. It wasn't *exactly* faking sick since I already wanted to heave my guts up. However, I'd never pretended to be sick before as an excuse to bail on going to class. I figured that given my track record, this could work in my favor.

I approached the teacher's desk and quietly asked if I could go to the nurse's office. I half-lied when I said I wasn't feeling well. I'd never been so grateful to use a hall pass in my life. Even if I didn't get sent home, it was still a legal excuse to suck up an hour in the school nurse's office so I wouldn't have to go to second period, look at the lovebirds, and feel the knife twist a few more times. The way my luck was running, I'd have probably vomited on the spot and killed any tough-girl credibility I had left.

The nurse bought my excuse. Despite taking my temperature and coming up with a balmy 98.6, she called Mom to come pick me up after I complained of stomach pains and nausea. Maybe she thought I had a case of that teen pregnancy thing that was going around.

Mom signed me out and once we were safely in her car – a cream-colored behemoth of pure American metal (none of that fiberglass crap) known as the Oldsmobile Delta 88 – she asked me what was wrong.

I sighed heavily before answering with the truth. "I just don't feel good and didn't feel like dealing with people's bullshit today."

Most parents would have sent their kids marching straight back to class. Mom just gripped the steering wheel and sighed. "I know what you mean. Sometimes I don't feel like dealing with people, either."

I didn't want to tell Mom the real reason why I wanted to stay home. If she knew I was upset over Claire dating Rick, she'd make fun of me.

And rightly so.

As much as I'm sure Mom would have snapped me back to reality, I decided to keep this information to myself. The best "therapy" would be to sit in my room and get out all of my emotions in private. Sure, I punked out on seeing them face-to-face, but I was entitled to stage a little drama of my own every so often.

When we got home, I told Mom I wanted to take a nap. Actually, I just wanted to listen to music and have a good cry. But a nap seemed to be a convincing enough excuse to be left to my own devices for a while.

"I'll wake you up in time for some lunch and *Days of Our Lives,*" Mom offered.

I thanked her before closing the door to my room and turning down my bed. I closed the blinds and grabbed my Walkman, popping in Counting Crows' *August and Everything After.* If Jack Kevorkian had ever conceived an assisted suicide soundtrack, *August and Everything After* would be it. The band never replicated the same incredibly beautiful, incredibly depressing quality of their debut (which may or may not be attributed to lead singer Adam Duritz focusing more on boning his way through the female members of the cast of *Friends* than writing more maudlin lyrics), but that album remains mandatory listening for anyone who wants to sob themselves into a stupor – which was exactly what I did with the covers pulled up over my head.

After that rollicking joyride, I put in a mix tape I had specifically crafted for times like these. It was an All-You-Can-Weep buffet of depressing songs. Dire Straits brought some misery to the table with their eight-minute opus of longing, "Tunnel of Love."

From "depressed," I shifted gears to "fucking furious." Type O Negative's "Unsuccessfully Coping With the Natural Beauty of Infidelity" provided 12-minutes of pure, unadulterated anger with a wronged Peter Steele repeatedly bellowing, "I know you're fucking someone else." Sadness glimmered through Steele's righteous anger. I could sympathize. Granted, it wasn't like Rick was cheating on me. We'd never actually dated, but I still felt like something had been taken from me and it just wasn't fair, damnit!

I started to feel better by the time Air Supply's "Makin' Love Out of Nothing At All" queued up. In fact, I was feeling downright spunky! I put a pair of socks on my hands to assist me in providing a pantomime of the backup singers' voices on the chorus.

This was the opposite of a pep rally. Only no one was cheering me on in my misery. It was pretty pathetic.

It's one thing to cry over some dude, but it's a whole other drawer of dildos when you're alone in your room, playing cheesy '80s arena rock, and tearfully enlisting sock puppets to join you on the chorus.

Before I could sink any lower into the depths of my despair, Mom burst into the room. Thankfully, she didn't notice the socks on my hands. (I hoped.)

"Get up! *Days of Our Lives* is on in 15 minutes! Vivian's crazy and Stefano DiMera is back!" Mom's excitement made me smile.

"I'll be right out!" It was enough to snap me out of my miserable mood. When Mom left, I hastily discarded my makeshift sock backup singers into the hamper. After helping Mom throw in a few loads of laundry, we sat down on the couch to watch our soap, each with a bowl of tomato rice soup and a grilled cheese sandwich.

I felt safe with Mom. Watching our show together made me feel like I was a little kid again and removed from all of those icky, adolescent feelings that only made for pain and heartbreak. It reminded me of the times we'd watch *Sesame Street* and *Days of Our Lives* together in the years before I went off to kindergarten.

For an hour, nothing else mattered but sitting on the couch with Mom and laughing as the dimwitted, sanctimonious residents of Salem fell victim to the schemes of our favorite characters.

It was good to be home.

But as much as campy daytime television and Mom's homemade grilled cheese had lifted my spirits, I still had to go back to school tomorrow and face the music.

The next day in art class, I took my usual seat. Brian was nowhere to be found and Jenn was strangely silent. I sat down next to Claire and noticed that Rick had decided to sit by himself at the table near the sinks.

"You know, you guys don't have to sit separately from each other around me," I said to Claire. "If you want to sit next to each other, do it. It's not going to bother me."

My voice began to crack as the words fell out of my mouth. I attempted to continue, fighting back tears: "I want you guys to be happy. I know Rick didn't want me." Voicing that realization was the final crack in the dam.

I was a sobbing wreck at this point, pulling my long black hair over my face to hide the tears. I may have lost Rick to Claire, but I'd be damned if I'd be caught crying in public.

"Obviously, you're not okay with me and Rick dating. Is that why you disappeared yesterday?" probed Claire. "Are you jealous?"

I was angry and sad all at once. "I just don't understand. You always went on and on about how disgusting you found Rick. I thought you were still hung up on Jim?" (Jim was this kid Claire had been pining after for years. Basically, Jim was to Claire what Rick was to me.)

In a hushed whisper, Claire admitted, "Well... I still have feelings for Jim. I don't even know why I'm going out with Rick. He just asked me out one day after school and I didn't know what to say."

"So you said '*yes*'?!' You knew how much I liked him! And it's not like *you* even like him! I don't get it!"

"I didn't want to hurt his feelings."

"So you go and hurt mine instead?" My voice rose with more anger than pain.

"You said yourself that Rick would probably never go out with you. Besides, I'm going to break up with him soon." She paused for a second, looking disgusted. "Relax. It's not like I ever kissed him. I don't even like holding hands with him."

My mouth hung open. On one hand, I was relieved that Rick and Claire hadn't "sealed the deal." On the other, I was taken aback at how callous Claire was in toying with Rick's emotions.

"Yeah, but why would you lead him on? Don't you think that's going to hurt him more when you break up with him?"

"He'll get over it."

By that point, I had stopped sobbing like a sideshow freak. Which was fortunate since Rick decided to meander over to our table.

"Hey, ladies," he said with a smirk. "You up to no good?"

"What's it to you, fuck face?" I replied, returning his smirk.

Rick laughed and things were back to "normal." I felt a little better knowing there was a pre-determined shelf life on Claire and Rick's sham of a relationship.

That shelf life hit its expiration a couple weeks later. Claire broke it off with Rick after he took her out for ice cream with his mother, the always-charming Mrs. Sanders. I had to give Claire credit for being able to stomach eating with Mrs. Sanders. I'd have lost my appetite if I had to look at Big Red lapping at a cone of ice cream. On second thought, maybe she ate it out of a trough.

The most Rick ever got for those dollar menu food court dates at the mall was a begrudging peck on the cheek from Claire. Astonishingly, Rick was too much of a gentleman and would never force the issue of asking Cold Fish Claire to kiss him.

Once they were no longer a (pfft!) couple, Rick retreated to his side table yet again to work on his projects in relative solitude. Occasionally, he would visit our table and try to make small talk. I made an effort to be nicer to him. Not because I thought it would land me a walk-on role as his girlfriend, but more out of sympathy. I knew his breakup with Claire was inevitable. As predicted, it hurt him much more that she gave him false hope than turning him down outright. Having been down that road myself, I didn't have the heart to be as mean to Rick as I used to be – even though he still bombarded me with insults on a daily basis.

"Nice makeup, Nova. You thinking of applying to clown college?"

It was this comment that prompted Claire to give me a "make-under." Well...that comment and guilt.

"I hate to admit it, but Rick has a point. You would look so much better with less makeup."

"Really," Jenn chimed in. "You have pretty eyes, but you can't tell with all the eyeliner you wear."

It was true. I wore so much liquid black eyeliner that even Robert Smith would have slapped me.

"And you know that cheap dollar store lipstick you wear is actually orange and not red, right?" Claire continued. "You need to get rid of it. It keeps sticking to your teeth."

She was right. At least three times a day, someone would tell me to "Go like this," motioning for me to scrape off the orange-red blotches of lipstick that clung to my teeth.

The next morning, Claire instructed me to come in without wearing any makeup. My orders were to bring in my makeup case, focusing on soft pastels and neutral tones.

It felt weird going to school without my usual amount of makeup spackled on. The upside, however, was that I saved myself at least thirty minutes in the bathroom without having to do and re-do my liquid eyeliner.

I packed the little makeup kit that Mom had bought me for Christmas into my school bag. Glancing at the palate of dusty rose hues in the sleek, black compact, I think Mom was hinting that my cosmetic artistry sucked and was implying I should go with something more subtle.

When I got to second period, Claire and Jenn had their own little art project in store for me.

"You don't need foundation or powder," explained Claire. "You have good skin. Powder only makes it look flakey. Just moisturize."

Next, it was Jenn's turn to attack me with a brush, asking me to smile. "You've been using peach blush which is way too harsh. You have pink undertones to your skin, not yellow. Just apply this little bit of pink to the apples of your cheeks."

Claire then applied a small bit of rose shadow to my eyelids, directly under the crease. It created this shimmering effect that made my eyes appear a brighter shade of blue.

Jenn stood back and frowned. I raised my eyebrows suspiciously, wondering what was next.

"Do we have any eyebrow pencil?" Jenn asked.

"I don't think so," I said. "I don't really need it. My eyebrows are too thick."

"I *know* they are," replied Claire. "But you shouldn't have bleached them."

"Well how the hell was I supposed to make them less prominent?" I demanded. "I want them to look like yours." I motioned towards the perfectly sculpted arches perched above Claire's hazel eyes.

"Then you're going to have to pluck them," Claire said.

"Pluck them?" Until this point, I didn't realize that girls weren't always naturally gifted with thin, feminine eyebrows. Apparently, they plucked them into submission.

This was an epiphany! It was like Prometheus bringing fire to man! And much like Prometheus did for mankind, this revelation would help to make me hot!

I never saw Mom pluck her eyebrows before, however, she was a natural blonde and had light eyebrows to begin with. In fact, she'd lightly pencil them in with a tan powder to give them more definition.

I, on the other hand, thought that if I made my eyebrows lighter, they'd be less noticeable. Suffice to say, it wasn't one of my better ideas when I decided to dab cotton balls loaded with peroxide over the top of my dark brown eyebrows, turning them bright orange.

Let's face it; orange eyebrows and black hair are not a winning combination.

Claire produced a small pair of tweezers that came with my makeup kit and started plucking away at stray hairs, depleting their vast expanse of real estate.

Dipping a sponge-tipped applicator into a deep brown eyeshadow, Claire used short strokes to go over my newly-groomed eyebrows, making them match my dark hair.

Standing back to admire her handiwork, Claire forbade me look in the mirror just yet. She asked me to dab on a bit of the pretty, dusty mauve lipstick on my mouth before gently blotting at it with one of the brown industrial paper towels in the art room.

"Okay! You can look!"

I held up the mirror and was pleasantly surprised. I loved my new eyebrows.

My eyes, as promised, looked bluer and my mouth looked less clownish with a natural hint of pink accenting my lips.

"Wow," I said, shaking my head in disbelief. "You made me look pretty! Thank you!"

I gave Claire and Jenn a rather atypical round of hugs. I was still in shock that I actually liked my new look.

To my surprise, Rick seemed to like it, too, wandering over from his self-imposed exile to give me a verbal thumbs up.

"Wow. Your makeup looks really good. You don't look like that much of a hooker anymore."

"Thanks, Rick. Your hair looks really good today, too. Was this your month to wash it?"

He laughed, running a hand through his long, brown hair before congratulating Claire and Jenn on remaking the Bride of Frankenstein into something that could pass as human. I wondered about the sincerity of his words or if it was just an opening for him to compliment Claire in a roundabout way on her make-under skills.

I didn't care. After school, Mom complimented me on my new look and was ecstatic that I used the makeup kit she got me. I also set to work at pulling out even more of my eyebrows and vowed to try to get them back to their natural color instead of the bizarre shade of orange that they were now.

I was making progress.

While I had improved my image for the better, Rick had decided to try out a new look himself – with disastrous results.

The next morning, I was late to homeroom. As I rushed down the locker corridor to get my books, I saw a tall, thin figure that looked vaguely familiar. I recognized the slouched posture and the copious amounts of flannel. When I saw the familiar blood red backpack covered in band patches, I did a double take.

It was Rick. Minus most of his hair.

It looked like he had tried to give himself a Mohawk – if you could call it that. The flaccid, stumpy strip of hair was confined to just the top of his head and didn't extend all the way down the back down his neck. It looked more like a porn star's landing strip than a bad ass punk 'do.

"Rick?" I called down the hallway. "Is that you?"

He stared ahead silently, racing to homeroom himself.

"What the hell did you do to your head?!" I asked in disbelief.

Suddenly, a tsunami of bitch-dom washed over me as I remembered that first day of sophomore year when Rick told me how "stupid" my hair looked after I dyed it black. In that moment, I recalled every single derogatory comment he had ever made about my physical appearance, attire, or makeup.

Payback was going to be a bitch.

"This is *not* a good look for you, buddy," I called down the hallway.

I stashed my jacket in my locker and grabbed my books, damn near bum rushing my homeroom door. I sat down at my desk and opened my notebook. Fast and furious, I started scribbling down insults I planned to hurl at Rick come second period. Sure, I could wing it, but opportunities like this didn't happen very often.

By the time second period rolled around, Rick was late to class – as usual. I anticipated this and decided to ambush him upon his entrance, taking up a rousing chant of: "Hare Krishna! Hare Krishna!" clapping and pounding on the table like Bill Murray in *Stripes*. Several classmates joined me.

Rick pulled the hood of his sweatshirt over his head and retreated to his Fortress / Table of Solitude, out of range of my jeering commentary.

"Oh, my God," said Claire under her breath. "I didn't think it was possible for him to look any worse. What the hell was he thinking?"

Jenn and Brian glanced sympathetically at Rick from our table, too kind to kick the guy when he was down.

I felt a little twinge of sympathy. Horrendous haircut or no, I still had feelings for Rick. Divided in my loyalties, I felt bad about teasing him about shaving his head, yet at the same time, I didn't think he felt the same level of remorse for some of the things he had said to me over the years.

Which was why I felt compelled to sneak over to his table under the guise of washing my brushes at the sink.

"Hey, Rick!" I said brightly. "You're not Susan Powter. Stop the insanity!" I giggled at my own joke, likening Rick's new 'do to that of the bleached blonde buzz cut sported by the then-popular fitness guru and talk show host.

Rick pulled the drawstring of his hoodie tighter beneath his chin in a vain attempt to cover his head or disappear altogether.

But I couldn't let well enough alone.

I still had a lot more material to use. Regardless of whether or not I had an audience, I was determined to unleash my arsenal of insults on Rick that morning. I struck gold again, enlisting the films of one of America's most beloved actors to rank on Rick's new look.

I pulled up a chair next to Rick and sat down, inquiring quite conversationally, "Is Tom Hanks your hero or something? First you sound like him in *Forest Gump*. Now you want to look like him in *Philadelphia*. What gives, dude?"

Rick stared at his project, dabbing paint on his canvas in a futile attempt to ignore my relentless assault. He was stonewalling me.

Not receiving the outburst or effect I desired, I sat back down, leaving him to his work.

Later that day in the cafeteria, I made it a point to run up behind Rick and slapped him across the back of his bald head on my way to the bathroom.

I glanced over my shoulder to see Rick rubbing his scalp and shaking his head with a slight chuckle.

As bad as Rick's hair – or lack thereof – looked, I didn't have the heart to keep chipping away at his self-confidence after that day. In that 24-hour window, I managed to channel all of the anger, pain, and disappointment I had been harboring for two years and hurled it at him like Zeus pitching lightning bolts.

I was mad at him for shaving his head. Partly because I liked his hair. But mostly because I was angry that he now resembled even less of the person I remembered who gave me a hug and showed that he could be a really nice guy despite his smart ass exterior.

That day, I realized that things were never going to be the same. In the span of a year, Rick changed his appearance. I changed my appearance. And the small circle of friends that comprised our group from freshman year had changed, too.

I didn't like these changes. And I worried that the bonds of any friendships I might forge in the future wouldn't be as strong as the friends I was losing to drugs, relocation, or just overall changing circumstances.

It scared me. Many of the things I loved about my life were changing. I was growing older and college was in the not-so-distant future. College meant moving away, which meant I might not be with my family as much as I wanted to be. I wasn't a little girl anymore and at some point, I wouldn't have the luxury of watching soaps and eating grilled cheese on the couch with Mom whenever I wanted to.

And as quickly as I was "growing up," I didn't have any of the things I wanted that "grown-ups" were supposed to have: a circle of friends I knew would always be there or a boyfriend. I vented my frustrations on Rick, not really caring if *he* was hurt or about any of the problems or issues *he* may have been dealing with.

As pleased as I was with my torrential blast of insults, I decided to try to be nicer to Rick the next day in class.

I sat down next to him at his table. "Hey, dude. What's up?"

"Not much," he grunted, avoiding eye contact.

I paused for a moment. I didn't exactly want to apologize to him. I had too much fun busting his chops and, to tell the truth, he had it coming for all the times he hurt my feelings. However, I didn't want Rick to feel like a *complete* bag of shit.

"You know, the hair doesn't look that bad. It's kind of Maynard James Keenan. Are you going to grow it back?"

He gave a deep sigh. "I don't know."

"It would probably work better if you grew a goatee with it. That might actually look pretty cool."

Rick tilted his head to the side, pondering my suggestion. "Yeah," he mused. "That *would* be cool. I don't know if my mom will let me grow one, though."

"Did she let you shave your head?"

"Not really. She kicked my ass and hid my clippers when she saw it," he laughed. "She said once I turned 18, I could do whatever I wanted. I turn 18 in six months, so I figured I'd start now with giving myself a 'hawk and then work up to getting a tattoo on my eighteenth birthday."

"Sweet! What do you want to get done?"

"A design I'm working on. It'll probably be the beginning of a half-sleeve."

"Cool," I said sincerely. "I'd like to see the design sometime."

"I'll show it to you once I'm done drawing it up."

I smiled and nodded. "You know, you don't have to sit here by yourself all the time. Why don't you sit with Claire, Brian, Jenn and me?"

"I might."

"Cool," I replied, heading back to the table to work on my own painting.

"Maynard, huh?" he called after me.

"Yeah. Definitely Maynard."

That was the longest, most civil conversation Rick and I had in months. It was kind of nice to treat each other like human beings.

While I had stood down, Claire, on the other hand, had become more relentless with her caustic remarks. She had taken to referring to Rick as "The Head" and reverted back to critiquing his artwork in the meanest way possible.

Rick had been absent from class for a few days, but not before he began work on a large, three-foot high self-portrait of just his head. It was a morbid affair with swirls of black, grey, and murky red in the background. On top of all that, the portrait featured two, milky white eyes devoid of irises. In a further attempt to create some sort of a macabre masterpiece, Rick had painted a swirling, grey infinity symbol on his self-portrait's gigantic forehead.

How very Aleister Crowley of him.

I'll admit, it wasn't the most pleasant *objet d'art* to look at. However, Rick was pretty proud of it. He placed the painting at the front of the class to dry until the next time he was able to work on it.

During Rick's absence, Claire expressed her loathing of the painting.

"I can't stand looking at it! It's his big, stupid head and it keeps staring at me! It's like he's trying to say 'Look at me! I'm all deep! Here's my big, infinity symbol head!' It's like he put it here in front of our table on purpose!"

"I don't think if he did it on purpose," I said. "After all, he sits at this table...Sometimes."

"I don't care. I can't look at it anymore! It's annoying me," sputtered Claire, getting up to turn the portrait towards the wall.

To a degree, I was kind of relieved. I didn't want to say it myself, but Claire was spot-on in her analysis of the portrait – even though Rick intended the piece to be on the disturbing side. He was trying his damnedest to reinvent himself as some scene kid.

In addition to his new haircut, Rick traded in his tight, shredded jeans and flannels for baggy pants and an omnipresent wallet chain that whacked against his leg whenever he lurched down the hallway.

He was scrambling for a new identity. He had struck out with the ladies as an old-school metalhead. Now he was now trying to get in with the hardcore punk kids. Not that he didn't like that music to begin with. Rick extolled the virtues of Avail and Madball as much as he did Slayer, but his change in appearance was so drastic that it seemed like a frantic attempt to change who he was from the outside in.

Rick was none too pleased when he came back to class and saw that his portrait was now facing the wall. Of course, he thought *I* was the one who did it and our Cold War began all over again.

Much like how I gave Rick a free pass for douchebag behavior because I still had feelings for him, Rick refused to believe that Claire could be as cruel as she was because *he* still had feelings for *her*.

It was a vicious cycle. I wondered if it would ever end.

CHAPTER EIGHT
LOWERED EXPECTATIONS

Around the time that Rick started to change, I discovered that it was possible to like two people at the same time.

There was this guy named Wendell who took dance lessons at the same studio as my brother and I that I had locked in my dating crosshairs and attempted to attract his attention.

For years, my brother and I had taken dance lessons. Orion was an *extremely* talented dancer. He had trained in classical ballet, jazz, and tap since he was three. As a male, he was a rare commodity and numerous dance studios in the area offered him scholarships.

As Orion's older sister, I was the Charlie Murphy of dance. I wasn't great, but I wasn't terrible, either. It was good exercise and I enjoyed the performance aspect. I knew my shortcomings and worked at them.

Even though Orion was three years younger and in more advanced classes, he helped me improve by trying to teach me more advanced combinations.

Dance was another way in which my brother and I had bonded. It was something he was serious about and a potential career path for him. Truthfully, it was his dedication to dance that made *me* so interested in the art. Orion made it look effortless and I admired him for being able to do it so well. I wanted to be like him in that respect even though I knew I wasn't nearly as good as he was. At the same time, Mom was also big into the performing arts – particularly theatre and dance – so it was a way to bond with *her*, as well.

Mom and Dad would take turns carting Orion and I to our lessons three times a week. We spent a lot of time at the Fletcher Dance Academy, sometimes doing our homework in the lobby while waiting for the other to get out of class.

The studio had a family-like atmosphere. My brother's teacher and the studio's co-owner, Gregory Lindstrom, was like a big brother figure to him. As far as ballet instructors went, Gregory was pretty unorthodox. He was in his early 40s with unruly brown hair that peeked from beneath a weathered baseball cap with a broken brim. He was a habitual gum-chewer who taught class wearing jeans and sneakers despite having studied with some of the finest Russian ballet instructors of all time. In turn, Gregory had danced with major companies throughout the U.S. and even taught classes to NFL football players as part of their training program.

Gregory co-owned the studio with his wife Elisa who was more of a traditional ballet instructor – all leotards, tights, and pulled back hair. They believed in giving girls who weren't your typical ballerinas a chance to shine, valuing dedication and talent over a visible ribcage – which was fortunate for me.

Like most ballet schools, the Fletcher Dance Academy put on an annual winter production of *The Nutcracker*. That year, Orion was cast in the role of the Nutcracker Prince. I danced as part of the corps in "Waltz of the Flowers" and as part of the army of mice in the climactic battle sequence between the Nutcracker and the Mouse King.

One Saturday afternoon, I showed up to rehearsals for the battle scene and spotted guy with long red hair (like Axl Rose!) wearing a black t-shirt with a grim reaper on it.

Suffice to say, there aren't too many guys with long hair wearing shirts with grim reapers on them in a ballet studio.

I sat in the corner with the rest of my fellow mice, observing.

A few minutes later, I learned that the hot Metal Ballet Dude and I would be working together. He was cast as the Mouse King and I was to be one of his minions. It dawned on me that I would soon be sporting a baggy grey bodysuit with mouse ears and a tail in front of this dude. Since that look didn't exactly translate into instant sex appeal, I decided I should work fast and introduce myself to him before that image was burned into his brain.

"Isn't it weird being the old people?" Metal Ballet Dude and I were slightly older than most of the kids in the scene, which called for a variety of sizes – and ages – of mice.

"A little awkward," he agreed. "I haven't seen you at the U. Do you take classes there?" In addition to owning their own studio, Gregory and Elisa were affiliated with Fletcher University's dance department. Their college students were required to take part in one of the company's productions and perform alongside students at Gregory and Elisa's studio.

"I'm not in college yet. I've got another two years. I take class with Gregory and Elisa here during the week."

As it turned out, Hot Metal Ballet Dude disclosed that he was a college sophomore whereas I was a high school sophomore. Oh, the irony!

He paused for a moment as I laughed and shook my head. "Please allow me to introduce myself. My name's Wendell."

"Nice to meet you, Wendell," I replied, prepared to offer a firm handshake. Instead, Wendell took my hand and bowed a low, old fashioned gentleman's bow, tipping his forehead towards my downturned palm.

I laughed nervously. I wasn't used to a guy showing me this sort of attention, much less appearing to reciprocate some level of attraction.

I introduced myself to Wendell and mentioned Orion was my brother. They would be dancing opposite each other as the Nutcracker and Mouse King. He seemed impressed that my brother was the dancer that everyone had been raving about and was relieved to have an "in" with the only other male dancer in the room that day – even if he happened to be seven years older than Orion.

As luck would have it, I ended up in more scenes with Wendell. In addition to being one of the mice in the scene, being one of the older girls who had a more "mature" build, I was lumped in with the college students dancing as parents in the party scene.

Not only was my brother playing the Nutcracker Prince, but Orion was reprising the role of the female lead Clara's bratty brother Fritz. Not just reprising it, but playing the role for seven consecutive years. At this point, Orion was going through puberty and the lederhosen-and-blouse combo he sported for the costume looked ridiculous. His version of Fritz looked less like a destructive little brat and more like Clara's "special" older brother on holiday leave from "the home."

Nevertheless, Orion relished this role and the opportunity it afforded him to play it completely over-the-top. He even went so far as to rip off the wooden stunt Nutcracker's head with his teeth, dangling it from his jaws like he was Ozzy Osbourne.

Even more hilarious, Gregory decided to cast me as my own brother's mother in the party scene. I was pretty excited. The role of Frau Silberhaus, Clara and Fritz's mother, would give me a chance to ham it up and play comedy on stage. Plus, I'd get to be in yet another scene with my brother.

I mean, how often do you get to be your own brother's mother and *not* be a resident of Pennsyltucky!? This was pretty cool!

As an added bonus, Gregory cast Wendell in the role of my "husband," Herr Silberhaus.

This was the perfect opportunity for me to get more face time with Wendell!

Behind the scenes, my brother chatted with Wendell who was not well-liked by the studio's predominately female populace. Wendell wore the same grim reaper shirt every day and smelled a bit rank. However, Orion and I maintained that he was a good guy despite his stench.

"Yo," Orion said to me one day after rehearsal. "Wendell said to me 'Your sister's cute.'" He grinned like an idiot, reverting back to the brother who would make fun of me every time he found out I liked a guy. "Dude. I think Wendell wants to do you!" He punctuated the word "do" with an exaggerated gesture of pelvic thrusting, just in case I didn't know what he meant.

"You're a sick little shit," I said, raising an eyebrow. It did nothing to stop his relentless needling.

"So, you're ditching Sanders and now it's 'Go 'head, Mr. Wendell'?"

It was ironic that Orion earmarked Arrested Development's ode to a homeless man name "Mr. Wendell" as his song of choice to harass me with given that Wendell was, in fact, homeless.

Unless living out of your car counted as having a "home."

The year before, Wendell was kicked out of his house by his mother. Orion heard a rumor from some of the other college kids that Wendell was homeless. He didn't readily tell people he lived out of his car but admitted to it when Orion asked him about it.

Due to Wendell's special circumstances, Gregory granted him a scholarship to the Fletcher Dance Academy in addition to the college dance course he was taking.

By day, Wendell used Fletcher University's facilities to work on his studies as a computer programmer and occasionally bathe. By night, he delivered pizzas in his car/house. Boxes of cassettes, books, and piles of clothes were visible through the hatchback of his grey Chevette.

While Orion was friendly with Wendell, it didn't stop him from cracking jokes at his expense... or mine, for that matter.

"So, are you going to try to have sex with Wendell?" asked my brother, wearing a shit-eating smirk along with his dance leotard and tights. "It might be hard to bang him in his car with all of his stuff in there. The seats probably won't go back all the way, so you might have to fuck him with your ass on the steering wheel."

"You're disgusting," I replied.

"Are you excited that you might lose your virginity to a pizza delivery guy?" Orion queried, brimming with overly exaggerated enthusiasm. "Are you going to let him give you the extra pepperoni and scream out 'Pizza man delivers!' after he's done?"

"Dude," I said, losing patience. "You're *really* fucking disgusting."

My brother stood there, smiling until it seemed like the corners of his mouth would extend past the given borders of his face. I could hear the wheels of perversion clicking in his head, attempting to come up with something that would garner a volatile reaction out of me. Orion decided the best way to do that would to scream out in a mock-orgasm:

"Oh, Wendell! Give it to me hot in the box!"

Although my brother and I had become the best of friends and his relentless teasing was all in good fun, Orion couldn't resist telling Mom that I had a crush on Wendell. To my surprise, Mom didn't make fun of me.

"I think Wendell is a nice boy," she said on the car ride home from rehearsal one evening.

I wondered if Mom had been taken over by Pod People. It was so unlike her *not* to mock my choice in guys.

"He doesn't come from the greatest home situation, but he tries his best. He's hard-working, he's getting an education, and he's interested in the arts." As a former speech and drama teacher, this put Wendell high on Mom's list.

"I think Wendell would be a good match for Nova." Mom diplomatically kept my brother's jabs at bay while simultaneously acting as a campaign manager, endorsing Wendell as my potential boyfriend.

I don't know who was more shocked, me or my brother.

In all his years of diming me out to Mom and the two of them acting as a tag team to wring droplets of humiliation from me, Orion never encountered the problem of Mom supporting any of my crushes.

Dumbstruck, Orion attempted to counter Mom, going for a two-point jump shot on my self-esteem by tossing out yet another of his song parodies. This time, he reshaped TLC's hit single "Waterfalls" into a taunting imperative: *"Don't go chasing Wendell's balls / Please stick to the Sanders and Gilroys you're used to!"*

He sang it on repeat several times throughout the journey home. Mom thought it was pretty funny. Hell, I thought it was pretty funny, too. At this point, I didn't care what my brother sang. The odds were looking pretty good that I was going to have a boyfriend sometime in the near future.

For once, I had a ray of hope. Before, whenever I liked a guy or planned to ask him out, in the back of my mind I knew it was all an exercise in futility. I *knew* they would say no. This time, I honestly believed that if I asked Wendell on a date, there was a good shot he would agree to it.

This newfound hope gave me a glow that I couldn't hide. At school, I told Cora, Jenn, and Claire about Wendell.

Rick got wind of the news of my new crush and was treating me nicer than ever. Either he was genuinely happy for me as a friend or he was relieved that he didn't have to worry about fending off my advances.

I didn't want to jump the gun and ask Wendell out immediately. I wanted to wait until after *The Nutcracker*. If he ended up turning me down, it would have made for a big batch of awkward when we had to dance together as Herr and Frau Silberhaus.

As dumpy as I knew I would look in my mouse costume, my Frau Silberhaus costume more than made up for it. I got to wear a regal, turn-of-the-century gown and extravagant costume jewelry that Mom let me borrow from her limited-edition J.C. Penney *Dynasty* collection. If a touch of Joan Collins-by-way-of-Alexis Carrington doesn't give a gal confidence, nothing will!

The Nutcracker ran for three consecutive nights with two matinee shows on the weekends. Since Wendell and I were in two scenes together, it gave me plenty of time to interact with him. I took the initiative to come up with some funny schtick to incorporate into the party scene with Wendell flirting with one of the other guests and my character whacking him in the arm to knock it off. The bit was a hit with the audience and added some more comedy to the opening scene. Wendell and I came up with several other improv bits that Gregory approved to punch up the first act.

On rehearsal breaks, Wendell and I chatted often. He promised to loan me one of his GWAR cassettes after I had loaned him Butt Trumpet and made him a mix of a few of my Sam Kinison albums. Wendell didn't really have the disposable income to blow on albums. I figured it would be a thoughtful gesture to give him some new listening material.

Things were going really well. Mom approved of my crush and Orion kept putting in a good word for me whenever he rehearsed with Wendell.

While Wendell and I were certainly friends, he was slightly flirty with me. I started to believe that maybe I wouldn't relegated to the dread outer limits known as "The Friend Zone."

I decided not to ask Wendell out after *The Nutcracker* wrapped. I told myself that I wanted to take things slow and see if maybe *he* would ask me out, instead.

Rehearsals for the company's spring performance of *Coppelia* began that January after winter break.

Once again, I found myself in the same scene as Wendell, dancing as part of the peasant corps in the town dance scene. I didn't have much of a chance to talk with him a since he was dancing with a different group, but he and I still chatted during breaks.

I made up my mind to ask Wendell out after the production of *Coppelia* wrapped. Classes would soon be over, barring a few summer sessions that Wendell may or may not have ended up attending.

I had to make my move.

After Wendell and I finished our parts onstage, we hung around in the wings to watch the rest of the show. I wondered if I should take a more seductive route than I had in the past. Should I reach over and start giving him a back rub or play with his hair? My Holden Caulfield complex kicked in and I thought better of it, considering a bunch of ten-year-olds in tutus were afoot.

While I hadn't taken up Orion on his offer to snap semi-nudies of Wendell while he was getting changed in the dressing room they shared, I decided that this time I would do things differently. I would not take the direct route that had failed me so many times before: I enlisted my brother in asking Wendell out for me.

Orion already relayed the news that Wendell thought I was "cute" and "hot" and had continued to hint to him that I was interested. I figured since Orion had so successfully managed my campaign to this point, he would be the one to call the final, most crucial play of the season.

There was a cast party following the show. If all went according to plan, Wendell and I would make our first official public appearance as a couple at this little fete. I had already picked out a black-and-white dress to wear to the shindig and shook my long black hair out of the tight ballerina bun into a more fetching, flowing style.

I waited backstage for the verdict to arrive, pacing back and forth. Suddenly, I spotted my brother walking down the hallway, ready to go to the cast party and wearing a purple suit.

From several yards away, I could see he was also wearing an expression that said, *"Well...I tried."*

I was hoping this was Vintage Orion attempting to fake me out. No such luck.

"He said 'no,' didn't he?"

"Yep." He wasn't deriving as much amusement from this as I thought he would.

"Did he say why?"

"He said that he thinks you're too young for him."

"Did you tell him I'm going to be 16 next month?" It was a desperate, but valid point.

"I mentioned that," Orion said, sounding like an agent trying to negotiate a contract for his client. "He countered it by saying he would be 21 the month after that."

Seeing the look of disgust on my face, my brother tried to smooth the rejection over. "He still wants to be friends with you, though. He thinks you're a really nice girl."

There it was. The sign up ahead in blazing, neon letters marking familiar territory: Friends Zone ahead!

At least there would be no awkward meetings with Wendell at the cast party. He had excused himself from the festivities by saying that he had work that night and would be using his car/ house to deliver pizzas that evening.

"Hey," Orion interjected. "Don't be sad about this. Wendell lives in his fucking car. You can do better! Think about it. Do you *really* want to be 'That Girl Who Dates The Guy Who Lives In His Car'?"

"Fuck no!" I replied, amped up by my brother's pep talk.

"See! That wasn't so bad! Now let's get to the party before everyone picks over all the good appetizers!"

My 12-year-old brother had more sense than I did.

Hanging around with him and the rest of the dance troupe perked me up, as did the delicious spread of cheeses and *hors d'oeuvres*. Mom had bought me a bouquet of beautiful wildflowers wrapped in shimmering paper and snapped a photo of me with them. I was just in the chorus and didn't have a starring role like my brother did, but my parents made me feel like a star. Dad even managed to sneak me a glass of wine. It was Lambrusco – his favorite, not mine – but I appreciated the fact that he thought enough of his little girl to bring her some hooch.

That night, unlike most of the other times after I'd been rejected by a guy I liked, I didn't cry. I went to sleep with a smile on my face. I had a wonderful evening despite it not turning out exactly as I had planned.

The worst part of the entire experience came when I returned to school on Monday.

My friends all knew about my plans to ask out Wendell and were eager to know how things went.

"So, how did it go?" asked Jenn.

"He turned me down," I said plainly. The anticipatory smiles on the faces of Claire and Jenn had disappeared, giving way to more sympathetic expressions. At the far end of the table, however, Rick's smile had grown even bigger.

"Smart man!" exclaimed Rick, laughing as he laid out his materials for his next heinously self-aggrandizing disasterpiece.

It was Bob-Just-Bob all over again. The second my *faux-mance* with Bob-Just-Bob fizzled, Frankie Gilroy went right back to hating my guts. And now, no sooner than Rick found out Wendell rejected me, he reverted back to his usual routine of nailing me with douchebag comments.

Neither Rick nor I had made any jokes at the others' expense for months. Did he assume since Wendell was off the menu that I'd resume throwing myself at him or I'd attempt to rekindle the non-existent spark between us?

I honestly didn't know, but the last thing I needed to hear were the comments coming from Rick's peanut gallery. I refused to let him see me sweat and fired a round back at him:

"Don't you have something hideous to paint? Another self-portrait, perhaps?"

Rick just smiled to himself, filling his palate with paint while I seethed internally.

I kept to myself after his comment. We sat at the same table, but said nothing to one another.

In fact, Rick's haggard Weeble of a mother had more to say to me than he did.

That afternoon after school, Mom, Orion and I went grocery shopping. Mom parked her Delta '88 Oldsmobile in the lot and we went to grab a shopping cart.

When what to my wondering eyes should appear, but a fat, redheaded cow wearing sweatpants and a sneer.

Outside the grocery store, Mrs. Sanders supervised as Rick unloaded the grocery bags from their cart and piled them into his family's rusted out shitwagon.

Rick acknowledged my presence with his usual curt head-nod in my direction. It was as pleasant as he got. On the other hand, Rick's mother eyed me up and down, surveying my ensemble with a sadistic smirk on her face.

"Her stockings are sagging," cawed Mrs. Sanders in a clearly audible voice. It was the type of comment that was meant to sound like an aside, but said loud enough to make sure everyone in the vicinity heard her.

Mom heard Rick's mother's comment and knew exactly what the old bag was trying to do. "What are you looking at, Tarzan?" she asked pointedly.

Mrs. Sanders's mouth opened so wide that her cigarette would have fallen out had it not already been surgically grafted to the corner of her lip.

I laughed out loud, shooting a grateful glance at my mother. Orion got in on the action, too, pointing out that he saw several bags of Cheezer Puffs sticking out of the bags that remained in the cart.

It was a small victory. However, it was just one link in a chain of unfortunate events that started to come together.

Dance classes were still in effect although Wendell wasn't around as often. He only came in on weekends since there were no more rehearsals for upcoming shows. Word on the street was that he had other things to occupy his time.

Mandy, one of the girls in my brother's dance class, had a juicy tidbit of gossip that she was all too willing to broadcast to the rest of the dance academy.

"Ew!" Mandy exclaimed. "You will never guess what that scumbag Wendell is doing! Or more like *who* he's doing!"

One month after Wendell turned me down because he thought I was "too young," he started dating a girl who was only 14 and attended the same school as Mandy.

One Friday, Mandy saw Wendell arrive in his hooptie to pick his girlfriend up from school. He proceeded to suck face with the girl in front of an appalled student body before opening the door for her in an oh-so-chivalrous manner, granting her access to the passenger side of his hatchback chariot before driving into the sunset to play "Pizza Man: He Delivers."

I was dumbstruck. Once again, my low self-esteem kicked in and my imagination went wild. I imagined Wendell's new piece of jailbait as a tall, blonde Lolita with full lips and a dumper that wouldn't quit.

That, however, was the exact opposite description of Wendell's new girlfriend.

"Are you fucking kidding me?!" I shouted.

"Nope," chirped Mandy with a laugh. "Those two deserve each other. His girlfriend's nickname at school is 'Beavis.' Total freakshow. Hangs out with another winner that everyone calls 'Butt-head.'"

I wanted to puke. What the hell did I do wrong!? Wendell and I got along great. He thought I was "hot." Then again, he thought a chick whose nickname was "Beavis" was "hot," too.

"I don't know why you wanted to go out with that loser," Mandy said, wrinkling her nose. While Mandy viewed Wendell as a lower life form, she and I always got along. She never held held it against me that I was interested in Wendell. Everyone's entitled to a character flaw. Mine just happened to be bad taste in men.

That summer, our instructors Gregory and Elisa were running a summer dance camp in conjunction with Fletcher University. My brother was awarded a full scholarship and Mom and I drove him to campus every day for classes and practice.

Wendell was also awarded a full scholarship, as was Mandy.

Mandy was a year younger than me and two years older than my brother. Orion had a huge crush on her. Mandy was thin, petite, and pretty. She was also a complete wiseass with the ability to level cutting remarks at people twice her age despite being only 14-years-old. No student or instructor – not even Gregory and Elisa – were safe from Mandy's zingers.

Orion had asked her out – twice – and she turned him down. However, they stayed close friends, mostly because they both loved to antagonize others.

That summer, Orion and Mandy teamed up to bust Wendell's balls non-stop. Before, during, and after classes, it was open season on Wendell.

"Splish-splash you should be taking a bath," sniped Mandy, catching a whiff of Wendell who was on his third consecutive day without showering. Summer heat, living in a car, and working in a pizza shop doesn't exactly make for the greatest aroma. Nor does dancing in the same grim reaper t-shirt for days on end.

Working as a team, Mandy shamed Wendell into bathing and Orion commented on his (slightly) improved odor.

When Wendell came out of the shower with his long red hair wrapped in a towel turban atop his head, Orion called out: "Hi, Mom! Oh, wait! It's just Wendell!"

The rest of the dancers erupted in laughter and an embarrassed Wendell took off after my brother, chasing him into one of the stairwells. When he finally caught up with him, he pinned Orion to the wall. Despite being seven years younger and 50 pounds lighter, Orion wasn't intimidated by Wendell and continued to giggle hysterically.

"I'll let you go," Wendell said through clenched teeth. "But you better stop trying to make an ass out of me with your little friend Mandy."

"Okay, okay," panted Orion. He stood there for a moment, catching his breath and cowering in the corner after Wendell unwrapped his hands from around my brother's bony wrists.

"I'm sorry," Orion said, still trying to catch his breath.

"You should be," sniffed Wendell.

"I'm sorry... Sorry your girlfriend's a *whore!*"

Laughing, Orion jumped down the stairwell and landed on his feet like a cat. He gained a substantial head start on Wendell who was unbalanced by the sopping towel turban atop his head. Orion's laughter bounced off of the spiral staircase with a maniacal flourish as he made his escape.

I appreciated this show of solidarity from my brother. He didn't have to lob the whore grenade at Wendell, particularly under penalty of peril to himself.

For me, the incident solidified that there comes a time when siblings stop beating the ever-loving shit out of each other and start helping one another out. My brother and I were tight before this incident, but afterwards, we rarely fought and always had each other's back.

Orion and I made a great team. Our Good Cop / Bad Cop routine bordered on genius. Harassing Wendell scored Orion serious points with Mandy, one-upping her in their pissing contest to see who could be the bigger ballet bully.

Meanwhile, I would still pop up at dance camp with Mom to pick up Orion. Not having had the face-to-face indignity of Wendell turning me down made the incident seem less like it ever happened. I still chatted with Wendell when I saw him, listening to him complain about Orion harassing him.

"Can you *please* tell your brother to stop picking on me? He can be such a little jerk sometimes!"

"I'll see what I can do," I said, attempting to sound sincere.

Truthfully, I lost a lot of respect for Wendell and had no interest in dating him. I attributed any lingering interest in him to my curiosity about what his girlfriend looked like and why he picked her over me when I had been getting such strong signals from him. I think I liked the challenge of having a mystery to unravel more than I liked him.

Long before Orion started mocking him on a daily basis, Wendell had been mooching food and money from my little brother. He'd ask for spare change so he could make a run for the border (or at least the township bridge) and snap up some items from the Taco Bell Value Menu. Another time, he ganked a few Little Debbie snack cakes that Mom had packed in Orion's lunch bag, laughing as he opened the wrapper in front of my brother and taking a gigantic bite out of it.

I think Wendell nabbing the Little Debbie Oatmeal Crème Pie was what pushed Orion over the edge. Stealing another man's snack cakes means war.

It wasn't until the end of the summer that I finally got a gander at "Beavis" herself. Wendell brought her to the final performance of the summer dance camp. I learned of my rival's presence thanks to a loud guffaw from Mandy: "Oh, God! Beavis is here!"

When Mom and I went backstage to pick up Orion, I caught a glimpse of Wendell and his jailbait girlfriend canoodling. How lovely.

She fit the description of a "Beavis." Melissa (her real name) was short with no boobs. She had large eyes and bee-stung lips that accentuated her overbite. Her heavily-permed blonde hair was cut to chin length. It gave her head an odd, triangular shape. Despite it being summer, she wore a sleeveless leotard beneath a pair of carpenter jeans and an open flannel shirt.

Nice to see she dressed for the occasion.

Orion and I walked past the two of them and Wendell stopped cramming his tongue down Beavis's throat long enough to introduce us to his girlfriend.

I was polite, although I worried I would blurt out "Nice to meet you, Beavis...I mean, 'Melissa'" thanks to Mandy continually likening her to the dimwitted cartoon character.

Wendell and Melissa made quite a display of rubbing up against one another like they were trying to create atomic-level friction.

I'd already been down this path before, having seen a guy I had feelings for holding hands with another girl – a girl I had considered a friend, no less. Maybe that was why Wendell getting all grope-y with his girlfriend didn't really bother me as much as it disgusted me.

I didn't let it show, however. Then again, I didn't have to since Orion showed more than enough contempt for the both of us.

Wendell and Melissa continued to publicly paw at each other while I attempted to engage them in small talk.

"How did you two meet?" I asked. (I'll admit it. I was curious.)

"Melissa came into the pizza shop one day while I was working the counter."

"And it was love at first sight," Melissa interjected.

How cute. They were already finishing one another's sentences.

"Wow," said my brother, looking at Melissa with wide-eyed wonder. "You really *do* have low self-esteem."

"Yeah," she replied, not missing a beat. "I know." With that, she leaned in and full-on tongue-blasted Wendell.

I think I threw up in my mouth a little as they jumped into an impromptu make out session, complete with Wendell struggling to run his fingers through Beavis's badly-permed hair.

I glanced at Orion. He looked like he was ready to heave a quart of vom, too.

In an attempt to be polite, I managed to squeeze out a "Nice to meet you" before my brother and I made a hasty – and thoroughly disgusted – retreat.

Before we took off to try to find Mom backstage and head to Friendly's to get something to eat, I needed a bit of therapy. I needed to prank call Rick's house again.

It wasn't like I was angry at Rick. We were civil with each other even if we weren't best buds. Pranking Rick was just a summer tradition and some opportunities are too good to pass up. There were a ton of available pay phones on campus that would not be able to be traced.

Besides, it wasn't so much Rick that my brother and I enjoyed pranking. It was his mother.

True to form, Mrs. Sanders picked up the phone. Orion and I covered the receiver, trying hard not to laugh.

"Who's this?" she crackled into the phone.

Our silence disturbed Mrs. Sanders as we tried to compose ourselves.

"Who the hell is this?!" she demanded.

"You know who this is, you human fart mark!" Orion added a maniacal laugh for good measure.

"I know exactly who this is!" replied Mrs. Sanders.

"Yeah? Who?!"

I hoped Mrs. Sanders had already deduced that it wasn't The Big Bopper. Nonetheless, you could practically hear crickets chirping on the other end.

In desperation, she croaked out her go-to catchphrase: "This phone is tapped!"

I fired back, just waiting to coin a catchphrase of my own. "Tap-schmap my ass, bitch!"

Not to be outdone, Orion encouraged Mrs. Sanders to "Have a nice summer, ya fucking pig!" before slamming the receiver down.

We erupted in laughter, high-fiving each other before tracking down our parents to head to a late night dinner at Friendly's.

Before departing to that mecca of family dining and ice cream, my brother and I saw Wendell and Beavis yet again before we left.

There they were. Entwined in each other's arms and staring doe-eyed at each other. They were sharing one of those moments in coupledom that exists as a dream between soulmates, a wish that would never end that they could cherish forever.

Orion killed their moment as we passed by, blasting them with a snippet of yet another of his song parodies, loudly singing to the tune of David Lee Roth's "Just Like Paradise": *"This must be just like living in Wendell's car / 'Cause he don't have a home!"*

Wendell looked absolutely disgusted. His jailbait girlfriend looked equally violated. That night at Friendly's, I recalled their exact expressions and smiled heartily as I took the first spoonful of my Happy Ending Sundae across the table from my family.

CHAPTER NINE
CROSSROADS

One short month later and I was a high school junior. Once again, Claire, Jenn, Brian, Rick and I were in the same art class. Occasionally, a skinny blonde named Jill joined us.

Jill was one of those girls who never lingered at any one table for too long. She liked to mine one table for gossip before flitting to the next in search of more juicy items. Jill was also one of those girls who never learned the importance of blending her foundation. As a result, it looked as if she was wearing a very tan mask suspended above a pasty, heavily-freckled neck.

Aside from the infrequent presence of Jill, it was business as usual in first period art. Jenn and I were still close, Brian was still the buffer of tensions, and Claire reveled in her status as our group's chief Mean Girl.

The only difference was that Rick and I were getting along better.

School wasn't back in session an entire month before a bomb threat was called in early one morning.

Everyone was accounted for except Rick who was serving an in-school suspension that day. I chatted with him briefly in the locker hall before homeroom, learning he'd be confined to the school's basement that day because he showed up late to homeroom three times that month.

Jenn, Brian, Claire and I sat in class, wondering what was going on.

The police – complete with a K9 unit – requested that everyone stay in their classrooms, ensuring no one would interfere with their search.

Some kids thought it was a drug bust. Another student said he heard that we were being kept in class because of a bomb threat.

I was nervous but not really afraid of a bomb threat. Usually, these things were bullshit. Truthfully, I was more worried about Rick serving hard time in the basement with his in-school suspension.

On the other hand, I wondered if Rick was the one who called in the bomb threat himself. He seemed to enjoy pilfering hairspray cans from me and Jenn to construct makeshift blowtorches with his lighter at lunch.

Nevertheless, it was an extended, two-and-a-half hour long art class. We sat around gossiping and working on our projects as the teacher kept calling the principal's office every 15 minutes for an update.

Not knowing why we were encamped in a seemingly endless first period, the natives started to get restless. (I was just grateful we were in art class and not Algebra II / Trig.)

Finally, Principal Giannelli's voice sounded over the loudspeaker, instructing our teachers to evacuate us from the building in an orderly manner.

Owing to my natural, go-to defense mechanism of laughing at inappropriate moments (or making shit jokes), I broke into nervous laughter at Mrs. Medibi as her voice quavered in an unintentional rhyme, urging us to "walk in pairs down the stairs."

Yeah. Right around now, I was pretty shit-scared.

The principal's announcement sent chills down my spine, as did the sight of yellow caution tape strung across several third floor lockers. Catching a glimpse of flack jacket-wearing bomb squad personnel accompanied by a pack of German Shepherds made the threat even more real.

Claire and I exchanged glances as we paired up and followed the teacher. My legs felt like Jell-O as we walked down three flights of stairs to the ground floor. Once we were outside the building and found an unoccupied payphone, Jenn, Brian, and I waited with Claire before her mother came to pick her up.

While we were waiting, we saw Cora and her boyfriend Steve. They decided to hang around the school for a while, grateful that they had some time to spend together. Cora's father had no idea she was dating Steve and would have hit the roof if he found out. This non-publicized bomb threat gave them an opportunity to walk around and hit the mall for as close to a real "date" as they would get for some time.

I was relieved that all of my friends were accounted for – except Rick. I had a sick feeling in the pit of my stomach and wanted to head back to the school to see if I could find him.

"We'll go with you," offered Brian. Jenn nodded in agreement with her boyfriend and the three of us headed back to school grounds.

Normally, bomb threats are cause for celebration. It means you have most of the day to fritter away, free of school obligations. For me, it was agony. I was worried sick about whether or not Rick was still in the school basement. He had been acting weird lately and seemed very down in the dumps. I worried that he was depressed or even suicidal. He exhibited a lot of the signs: Drastic change in appearance. Becoming more withdrawn from friends and social activities. Mood swings. Some days he'd be cracking jokes. Other days, he'd barely say a word.

It was pretty far-fetched to think that Rick had chained himself to a one-armed desk in the boiler room in an attempt to ride out the bomb blast while attached to it like Slim Pickens in *Dr. Strangelove*. Nevertheless, it didn't stop me and my overactive imagination from constructing an elaborate scenario in which I would somehow gain Hulk-like strength and carry Rick (and his desk) to safety before the building exploded.

No one was allowed back in the building, but I spoke with the security guards stationed outside the school. I told him that one of my friends was in the basement serving in-school suspension and wanted to make sure he was out.

"Trust me," the guard said. "Unless they walk on four legs or have Kevlar on, no one's in the building. You have nothing to worry about. Your friend is fine."

It was mildly reassuring but I needed tangible proof that Rick was safe.

I was a nervous wreck but Jenn and Brian figured it would be best if we all headed back to her house. Jenn's mother was nice enough to make us some iced tea and let me use her phone to call Mom.

Within half an hour, Mom picked me up from Jenn's house. By then, it was about noon and I had a nice chunk of free time on my hands. I wanted to call Rick's house to see if he made it home. However, if he was running around town having a good time and was perfectly safe, I didn't want to risk calling the house and landing him in hot water with Big Red.

I passed the time hanging out on the couch with Mom, watching *Days of Our Lives* and sharing leftover Chinese while filling her in on the details of the bomb threat.

A few hours later, we picked Orion up from school.

"A bomb threat? Cool! We never get bomb threats!"

When we got home, Orion and I decided to play some basketball at the neighborhood playground. I told him about my dilemma.

"Wow. You're fucking stupid."

"What the fuck, dude?! Why?!"

"I can't believe you actually went back to the school! What if there really *was* a bomb there? Rick wasn't trying to find *you*. What the hell were you thinking!?" Orion raised his voice several octaves higher in an attempt to mock me. *"I'll find you Rick! I'll save you! And if not, we can die together!"*

"I don't sound anything like that," I spat.

"You're right." He repeated what he said about Rick and I getting obliterated together but dropped his voice several octaves lower to Bea Arthur levels.

"Seriously, dude. I just want to know if he made it home okay."

"Alright," Orion conceded. "Grab some change and let's head to the pay phone. He should be home by now."

In exchange for his silence after I called Rick, I promised Orion I we'd stop off for frozen yogurt on the way back. My treat.

Dropping my quarter into the slot, I felt that familiar feeling in the pit of my stomach that I always got every time I called Rick. Praying that his mother wasn't the one to pick up, I heaved a sigh of relief when Rick answered the phone.

"Y'ello," he said in his usual tone, brimming with ennui.

"Hey, Rick! Just wanted to see if you made it back in one piece," I said with a laugh and realizing how stupid I sounded as the words fell out of my mouth. Orion confirmed my stupidity by rolling his eyes and shaking his head.

"I'm fine," replied Rick. "No big thing. We used to have bomb threats like this all the time at my old school."

"Lucky," I quipped, attempting to recover some shred of cool. "Yeah, Brian, Jenn, and I were trying to find you after they let us out."

"Yeah? I ended up going to the mall. Ran into Cora and her new boyfriend. Seems like a good guy."

"Yeah. I like the kid. Don't know how much Cora's parents will like him, but he treats her right."

"He better," Rick retorted. "Or I'll kick his ass."

I laughed. "You'll have company kicking his ass if he breaks Cora's heart!" Both Rick and I were fiercely protective of Cora, viewing her as our little sister.

"Cool," he replied. "I've seen you in fights. He *should* be afraid."

"No slouch yourself, chief." Before the conversation dragged on too long or Rick's mother figured out who he was talking to on the phone, I decided to cut it short. "Anyway, dude, have a good night. You going to be in-class tomorrow or is in-school suspension cancelled?"

"Don't know yet. Guess I'll find out when I get there."

"Cool. See ya then. Have a good one!"

"You, too" Rick said, hanging up the phone.

"Nice save, Porter," my brother grinned, raising an eyebrow. "You pulled it out of the toilet and managed to sound cool at the end."

My brother was actually being sincere. To my own surprise, I didn't sound like a complete tool on the phone. I was definitely in the mood for some frozen yogurt now!

If only things continued down that path. As usual, I never learn when to keep my big mouth shut.

A few weeks later, Rick was absent again. Something was up with him that I couldn't put my finger on. He seemed more down than usual and from what I could pry out of him in his typically terse state, his mother had been getting on his case more often.

Ever since Rick turned 18 and had developed a new look for himself, his mother was harder on him than ever. Claire, Jenn, and I were discussing what a headcase Rick's mother was when Jill started grilling us about Rick and his family.

"What's his deal?" she asked. "What's with the tattoos and the weird hair? He's clearly got issues." Although she had sat at our table off and on for several months, Jill was still an outsider, continually trying to wring the gossip out of every situation. Initially, I thought Jill might have had a thing for Rick but he wasn't her type. Jill preferred preppy guys but she took her gossip any way she could get it.

"Rick's not a bad guy at all," I said. "He's just experimenting with his look. Most of Rick's problems stem from his mother."

Claire and Jenn nodded in agreement.

"Why? What's so bad about his mother?"

Overcome by my utter loathing of Mrs. Sanders, I played right into Jill's hands.

Without hesitation, I gave her my unbridled opinion. "Rick's mother is a vile, redheaded, chain-smoking dung heap who is quite possibly one of the most manipulative bitches I have ever met. She keeps her husband's balls in her purse and Rick lives in fear of her mood swings. I've never heard Rick or his father utter a single word whenever she starts spewing out crazy, ignorant shit in between puffs on her cigarette."

"So, I guess she doesn't like that you're going out with her son?" Jill asked.

"Rick and I never went out," I said curtly. "Rick and Claire did, though."

"Only for a week or two!" Claire exclaimed, defending herself with a disgusted look on her face.

Jill turned her interrogative gaze to Claire. "Did his mother hate you?"

"Not at first," she replied. "Eventually, she comes to hate everyone. But I think she knew that I wasn't going to be dating him for any length of time."

Jill turned back towards me.

"But *you* like, Rick, don't you?" Jill plunked down her Barbara Walters card. I wasn't used to having someone ask me so many questions – particularly about a subject that I had strong feelings about.

"As a friend," I denied. I didn't know why I refused admit that I cared about Rick when it seemed so obvious to everyone else.

"So, you two never went out?" she pushed.

"No. We never went out. He didn't want to go out with me and even if he did, I'm sure his mother probably would have packed up the family and moved."

I was on a roll and my mouth could not be stopped.

"This is the longest they've stayed in one town. Maybe because his mother pushes all his friends away."

"Umm... Rick's father used to be in the military," offered Jenn softly.

"Okay, so maybe that's why they move. But I'm sure some of that moving shit has to do with his mother. Mrs. Sanders flipped out on me one time when I called Rick. I swear, that bitch reminds me of the mother from Stephen King's *Carrie*. The bitch is *fucking creepy*. "

I sealed my fate with those words. Rick sought me out in the locker hall the next morning.

"You should think the next time before you open your mouth," he snarled.

"What the hell are you talking about?" I asked.

"You know damn well what I'm talking about," he replied. "You fucking crossed the line yesterday talking shit about my family."

"I didn't say anything about *you*." I was actually telling the truth.

"Yes, you did. You said I have 'mommy issues'."

"Those weren't my exact words, Rick. But yeah, I think your mother is a giant, fucking bitch. She hates my guts and has no problem making snide comments about me or your other friends. So why the hell *shouldn't* I say what I really think about *her*?"

"Because you're supposed to be my friend. I don't need you talking shit about my family to anyone who will listen."

"The only person I said this to was Jill and only because she kept pressing the issue and asking me about you and your family."

"Then you could have just shut the fuck up," Rick fired back. "She told me exactly what you said. Which makes her more of a friend than you are."

"That's fucking bullshit, Rick," I spat. "I've been a damn good friend to you, even after you've said some really fucked up shit to me."

He stood silent for a moment, glaring angrily. "I don't need you talking shit about me and my family, got it? From now on, just stay the fuck away from me."

"Seriously, dude?" My voice rose. "You're going to take Jill's word over mine? You hardly know her! I *never* talked shit about you. I said you were a good guy, but your mother is a fucking asshole. I'm entitled to my opinion the same way she's entitled to hers."

"Yeah? Well, you could have shut your fucking mouth for once and not embarrassed me. I don't need a friend who talks shit behind my back. Just leave me alone. I'm done with you.

Just fuck off." He turned away from me and walked down the hallway.

I ran after him. "Okay, Rick. Fuck it. You're pissed. I'm pissed. Let's throw down right here. I'll let you have the first punch. Get it out of your system and we move on as friends."

Rick looked at me in disgust. "I would never hit a woman. Not even one like you." He continued walking while I stood stunned and alone in the locker hall.

"Look. I'm sorry," I called after him. I meant it, but the words just bounced off the lockers, echoing into nothingness.

There was no turning back from this. I had screwed things up beyond repair.

Rick was right. You don't talk shit about your friends behind their back. I could have used some discretion and kept my mouth shut but I let my anger get the best of me and kept right on going.

The worst part was, I didn't mean to say anything bad about Rick. He didn't know the depth of my feelings for him. He knew I liked him but didn't know that I would have done anything for him – even run back into a building to try to save him from a (non-existent) bomb.

I wanted to make things right with Rick but, ironically, a few weeks later, he and his family moved to a nearby town. He finished his senior year at another school.

I found out that Rick ended up getting a girlfriend at his new school and made some good friends there. He actually got to go to his prom that year and I was glad that he was able to have some sort of a normal, happy high school experience, however brief.

I really missed Rick, but I had to move on. Which was why I decided to focus on trying to break up Wendell and his jailbait girlfriend.

It's not the most feminist thing to admit, but in hindsight, but I always needed to have a crush on *someone*. It was a challenge. It gave me something to build a fantasy off of. With Rick completely gone from my life, I needed someone else who was familiar territory for me to throw my energies into and someone to throw myself at.

Unfortunately, Wendell fit the bill.

"Jesus Christ! It smells like a cat pissed under his armpits!" exclaimed Will Olsen. He was damn near a folk hero to me and Orion. "Wild" Will Olsen was the stuff of legend. He was also one of those guys consistently referred to by both his first and last name.

In his early 30s, Will Olsen was easily the oldest dancer in the company who took classes at the Academy. He wasn't that much younger than Gregory and made no bones about the fact that, two years ago, he had fallen prey to male pattern baldness, prompting him to have new hair woven into his scalp. Will Olsen rocked a weave and didn't care who knew it. Hell yeah.

He also didn't care that everyone knew he culled his dating prospects through personals ads. Will Olsen would often regale me and Orion with tales of blind dates which often resulted in unintentional hilarity. Like the time he found himself at a Bob's Big Boy with a woman who, on their first (and last) date, admitted she had multiple personality disorder. That episode paled in comparison to the time he wound up on a blind date with a woman who neglected to mention she was a double amputee.

It was pretty telling for Will Olsen, the man who had scraped the bottom of the dating barrel and answered largely unanswerable personals ads, to say that Wendell was a scumbag who smelled worse than a litter box.

As for Wendell, he had already made quite an impression on Melissa's parents. According to Mandy, word around her school was that Melissa's father walked in on the two of them banging and he threw Wendell out of the house.

It sure wasn't the first house Wendell had been thrown out of and it probably wouldn't be the last. He was still living out of his car that year when Gregory's mentor invited the Academy to perform *The Nutcracker* in West Virginia during Christmas break. Suffice to say, Wendell jumped at the chance to spend some time in a hotel room on someone else's dime.

Orion would be reprising his role as the Nutcracker Prince. Since he was only 13, Mom and Dad would be accompanying him on the trip. I got roped into going, too, since my parents didn't want to leave me with the house to myself for four days.

Unfortunately, I wasn't chosen to perform in the show. I was at least hoping I'd get to reprise the role of Frau Silberhaus in the opening party scene. Instead, I was drafted to help to load mats, scenery flats, and backdrops onto the bus.

Even though I didn't have a glamorous role in the ballet production, at least I'd be excused from school for a few days under the premise that this was an educational trip. I took it as a good omen that Mae West – one of my heroes – had once played the venue where the company would be performing. It had a history as an old vaudeville theatre and the dressing rooms were scrawled with signatures of stars who had also shared that stage – including Yul Brynner and Ozzy Osbourne.

With the possibility of sex goddess Mae West's good juju hanging in the air of that West Virginia theatre, there was no way I could strike out with my plan to seduce Wendell!

As a backup, Orion helped plot my strategy.

The day of our departure, after the bus was loaded, Orion and I configured our seating arrangements. Mom and Dad sat near the front of the bus and Orion and I sat further back. He wanted to sit with Mandy, who he still had a major crush on.

Mandy, however, had a crush on this kid named Paul that went to her school.

Orion was as determined as I was to pry the eyes of his own crush away from another and I fully supported him in it.

Before the bus took off, my brother spotted Wendell sitting by himself, gazing out the window.

"Hey, Wendell," my brother taunted. "You look like the dude from that Goo Goo Dolls video that stares out the bus window." Orion arched an eyebrow and smirked. "Don't worry, Wendell. 'I won't tell no one your name.'"

Wendell pursed his lips and squinted his eyes in an attempt to be menacing. Orion, of course, remained undaunted.

"Why don't you go sit with my sister?" he offered. "She's sitting by herself and probably has some books you can read." Orion played Wendell like a violin. Within seconds, he went from being a complete ball buster to the dude's best friend. The kid was a genius.

"Fine," sniffed Wendell. "I think I will."

Wendell asked if the seat next to me was taken before sitting down. He took me up on my offer of *Rolling Stone* and we read silently for a long while before eventually engaging in a half-hour long discussion on the merits of GWAR.

By then, we had pulled into a rest stop. Everyone swarmed off of the bus to get some food from Wendy's.

"You getting anything?" I asked.

"No," sighed Wendell. "It's not really within my budget."

I decided I'd bring him back a burger or some chicken nuggets. As a dollar menu aficionado, I figured a buck was a small price to pay to sweeten the deal with Wendell. Besides, I had been working for several months at Burger Land and squirreled away some pocket money for precisely this sort of opportunity.

While we were in line, Orion asked me how it was going.

"Not bad. I figured I'd get Wendell something from the dollar menu."

"Did he give you money for anything?" my brother asked.

"Nope."

"Dude. Don't be a chump. He's a bum. I can't believe you're buying him food."

"He didn't ask me for anything," I said, defending Wendell. "I just asked him if he wanted anything and he said he had no money."

Overhearing our conversation, Will Olsen chimed in to impart his vast wisdom acquired through thirty-odd years of hair weaves and personals ads gone awry:

"I can't believe you want to date that guy. He smells like a roving garbage scow. Trust me, kid. Your brother's right. He's a bum. He may not have asked you to get some food for him, but he's milking that 'Wah! I live out of my car!' shit for all its worth. You're playing right into it. He probably feeds his girlfriend the same sob story and she foots the bill for their dates. Either that, or the asshole takes her out to dinner at the pizza parlor where he works."

Will Olsen raised an eyebrow before delivering his final verdict: "He's a scam artist. I've seen lots of guys like him and they never change. Their life is one, big grift."

Will Olsen made sense. That didn't stop me from buying Wendell a junior bacon cheeseburger, though. My plan hinged on Wendell being lured in with the promise of food. Feed a cat and it'll hang around.

Later during the six-hour bus ride, I swapped seats and sat with Orion and Will Olsen for the remainder of the trip. I didn't want to wear out my welcome with Wendell (who, truth be told, smelled a bit ripe). I figured it would be best to leave him wanting more.

More chicken nuggets.

"So, if you had to pick between Rick or Wendell," Orion asked as we continued towards West Virginia, "who would you pick?"

"I don't know."

"You have to pick one," my brother insisted. Orion was a big fan of the game "You Have To Pick One." Normally, the options were completely disgusting, but this time he opted for a more serious round of questioning.

Knowing my brother, he wouldn't let up until I gave him a straight answer.

"Fine," I said. "I'd go with Rick."

"Really?" Orion asked, sounding surprised. "Then why the hell are you going after Wendell?"

"Honestly?" I breathed deeply, pondering the question myself as I exhaled. "I guess it's because he's available."

"But he's not," Orion said. "He already has a girlfriend."

"Yeah, but I saw him first. I think it's because I thought he liked me, then gave me some lame-ass excuse that I was too young. And then he took up with Beavis McJailbait. It's not that I don't like Wendell – I do. But at this point, I think I'm more interested in the challenge of getting him to want me than actually wanting to date him."

"You know that's kind of sick, right?" Orion queried with a smirk.

"Oh, yeah," I replied emphatically. "I know it is. The worst part is, after he turned me down for this chick and then started bumming money off of you to pay for his Taco Bell lunches, I lost a lot of respect for the guy. Part of me thinks that he's a person who's had some tough breaks. The other part of me thinks maybe he's just a scumbag opportunist. I'd like to see him do better for himself, but I really felt betrayed by his lack of honesty."

Orion nodded, taking in my assessment of the situation before we traded cassettes to listen to on the rest of the journey.

A few hours later, we reached our destination. The first order of business was unloading all the scenery flats and props from the bus. From there, it was off to the hotel where the entire troupe was staying. Mom, Dad, Orion, and I had our own room with two double beds and a futon.

Even better, the hotel room had cable, which played into my plan perfectly. I did what any teenage Lolita without an ounce of self-respect and bent on wanton seduction would do: I invited Wendell to my hotel room to watch *Highlander: The Series*...with my parents in the room.

As Orion and I explored the hotel to find out which room Mandy was in, we ran into Wendell and invited him back to our room. He seemed grateful for the company. He said he would be over around five o'clock after he found a pay phone to call his girlfriend – collect, of course – to let her know that he'd arrived safely.

I looked at the chain around Wendell's neck and noticed a dainty class ring suspended from it. I recognized the school colors and realized it was Beavis's class ring. How cute.

It didn't matter. I had a plan.

Wendell appeared at our door as soon as Queen's "Princes of the Universe" kicked off the credits to *Highlander*. He sat down on the floor with me and Dad, debating whether Connor or Duncan was the superior McLeod. Dad and Wendell fell squarely in the camp of Duncan while I declared myself a member of Clan Connor on the basis that Connor lived longer and was more focused while Duncan was a manwhore who didn't "noble up" until the 20th century.

Dad seemed to like Wendell and Mom invited him to partake of our bucket of KFC that Dad picked up while Mom and Orion were unpacking.

After *Highlander* was over and he had finished eating, Wendell headed back to his room to get an early night's sleep. Fondling the class ring around his neck, he made it a point to mention that he was going to call Melissa and wish her a good night.

So much for my plan.

I didn't interact much with Wendell throughout the rest of the trip. He, my brother, and the rest of the troupe were practicing in the theatre most of the time. Mom sat in one of the many empty seats to watch the dancers rehearse.

Since I didn't have anything else to do besides load and unload the bus when it pulled in, I hung out with Dad and watched cable TV back in the hotel.

Dad and I bought some ice cream in the hotel lobby and sat in front of the tube, sharing a carton of Chocolate Marshmallow Swirl while watching *Kung Fu: The Legend Continues*.

"Where's your friend?" asked Dad.

"Who?" I asked, slightly confused.

"That kid Wendell."

"He's practicing for the show."

"I'm surprised he's not here. Whenever there's free food, the guy shows up."

I laughed. Dad made a very valid point.

"He's a nice kid," Dad started. "I feel bad for him. Your mother feels bad for him. But in the end, he's a bum and won't amount to anything."

"He's trying," I offered. "He just didn't have the money to go back to school." It was true. Wendell had dropped out of college because he could no longer afford tuition and missed financial aid application deadlines. On top of that, his grades had slipped, due in-part to living out of his car.

"Maybe," said Dad. "But there's always a way if you want something bad enough. He wants people to do everything for him. I feel bad for the kid, but he's still a mooch."

A former touring musician fast-approaching his 60s, Dad had seen his share of guys who always had a scam. Hell, Dad would even admit that at one time or another, he *was* one of those guys pulling a scam. This sage advice from Dad gave me a clearer, more honest picture of the situation.

Coupled with not really being interested in Wendell anyway beyond the challenge he posed, Dad's commentary was impetus enough to abort the mission and quit pursuing Wendell.

We continued our father-daughter bonding which consisted of eating ice cream straight from the carton and watching David Carradine kick some ass. Following some quality, syndicated television, Dad and I put on our best duds to check out the show that night.

The rest of the trip was uneventful. Highlights included the continental breakfast and chowing down on KFC takeout with Dad while watching reruns. The time I spent with Dad and spent alone on the trip gave me some time to re-evaluate my priorities and where my life was headed.

On the bus ride home, I sat with Orion and Will Olsen, laughing and joking the whole way. Wendell slept on the bus, taking up two seats. I didn't plan on sitting next to him anyway.

In the weeks after the West Virginia excursion, I noticed Wendell was spending less and less time at the studio, too, which was just as well.

As it turns out, Wendell's girlfriend was a dancer, too. Melissa/Beavis, however, danced with a rival studio where Wendell was *also* accepting free lessons and double-dipping. Gregory and Elisa didn't find out about it until some time later and Wendell had been poached by the rival studio, leaving their company short one male ballet dancer.

I didn't really care that Wendell was gone. I was over him and not seeing him around the studio was one less thing I had to deal with. I wasn't angry with him. In fact, I wished the guy well. He hadn't been dealt the best hand and was working with what he had. I don't think he was entirely truthful with me, but nonetheless, he still treated me like a friend and a gentleman – and didn't make me feel awkward about hanging out with him on the few occasions we did after knowing I had feelings for him.

It was on to the next chapter of my life.

CHAPTER TEN
MALL WHORES, EPISODE IV: A NEW LOW

Growing up in a small town like Fletcher, there wasn't a lot to do on a Friday night – regardless of whether you had a boyfriend or if you were swingin' single. If you weren't of legal drinking age, your options involved either the mall, a bowling alley, or the dollar movie theatre downtown.

Occasionally, a decent band would play the local dive that held hardcore and metal all-ages shows, but those events were few and far between.

For the most part, it was free to walk around the mall and people-watch. Plus, there was always the chance you would run into more friends.

On the Fridays when I wasn't holding down my big-time job at Burger Land, I would hit the mall with Jenn and Brian who were nice enough to tolerate a third wheel. We would walk around the mall on a Friday night, talking about life in general and our rapidly shrinking circle of friends from freshman year. A few months back, Cora's father's job transferred him to a different state and she moved to Florida.

The summer before our senior year, with just the three of us remaining from the original gang, it became a Friday night ritual for Jenn and Brian to watch me desperately scour the mall for guys to throw myself at. The pickings were slim at school and in my other social circles, so I hit upon the brilliant idea to expand my dating pool to include random dudes I would scope out at the mall.

As desperate as I was, I was still kind of picky. I went for a certain type – any guy who had long hair, a band t-shirt, and ripped jeans.

My first attempt at trying to snare a mallrat came in the form of a tall, blonde, Nordic looking fellow with glasses. I spotted his long blonde hair and Aerosmith shirt outside of Radio Shack and pointed him out to Jenn.

I quickened my pace and began walking towards my intended victim sitting on the edge of the coin fountain in the middle of the mall. I'm not sure where I found this sudden burst of confidence. Maybe it was because I recently traded in my Coke bottle glasses for contact lenses. Still, a voice inside my head said, "You can do this!"

While confidence was never my strong suit, I had always been pretty shameless. Throw in a dash of desperation and you'd be surprised at what new lows you can reach.

"Hi," I said. "Are you waiting for someone?"

Blondie looked up, startled by my question. "No."

Emboldened by his response, I got down to the nitty gritty:

"So," I began, cocking my head to the side. "Do you have a girlfriend?"

Blondie looked even more surprised at this question than he did the first. "No," he replied, somewhat bewildered.

Pay dirt! He was single!

"You look bored sitting here by yourself," I suggested. "How about walking around the mall with me and my friends?"

He considered my proposition and accompanied me around the mall. After introducing him to Jenn and Brian, I discovered that Blondie's name was Matt. He was 19 and attending culinary school. Matt was pretty quiet during our stroll around the mall.

I gave him my phone number and wasn't too surprised – or bummed out – when he never called.

That didn't deter me from attempting to hit on other guys at the mall.

One Friday, Jenn, Claire and I got together for a girl's night out shopping. We swung by the food court to get something to eat. After picking up some chicken nuggets, I also decided to pick up a guy I spotted from a distance. Claire and Jenn looked on as I closed in on the guy without a shred of shame.

There he was. Picking at a slice of pizza by himself. His exotic, Native American looks caught my eye while I was standing in line at Wendy's. He had olive skin and long, dark hair. His prominent nose made him look like one of the hot, young braves in Disney's *Pocohontas*. He didn't notice as I approached his table and inquired "Is this seat taken?"

He looked up at me and I realized why he hadn't seen me approach.

He only had one eye.

That tends to mess with the old peripheral vision.

I played it calm and cool, not focusing on his lack of eye. His right eye was brown, normal, and unremarkable. His other orbit, however, was fringed by an otherwise normal looking eyelid but had no iris or pigmentation whatsoever. It was just pure white in its socket.

The guy said that the seat wasn't taken and motioned towards me to sit in the empty chair.

I sat down and introduced myself and shook his hand.

"What's your name?"

"Jack," he replied.

Oh, Christ. Of course it was.

One-Eyed Jack's nose was a bit beaky for my tastes, but aside from that, he wasn't bad. He seemed like a nice enough person and, at this point, it would be hypocritical of me to run away screaming like I just saw Frankenstein. After all, I was the one who approached *him* in the first place and I didn't exactly have guys beating down my door, either. Apart from having only one eye, Jack was kinda hot.

"Nice to meet you, Jack," I said smiling. "What brings you here on a Friday night?"

"There's not much else to do," he said with a laugh.

"Did you come here by yourself?"

"Yep," he replied, telling me that he had driven up from Mt. Chicamacomico, an even smaller, more rural town about 45 minutes away that made Fletcher look like a thriving metropolis by comparison. It was known for being home to either farmers or the very wealthy who preferred to live in seclusion.

We chatted for a while and I discovered that Jack was 19 and had a black belt in karate. He lived at home and was still in the process of "finding himself," pondering whether he wanted to go to college or what to study.

We talked for a bit and I gave him my phone number. To my surprise, he gave me his in return. I told him that I had to get back to my friends, motioning to Jenn and Claire who were watching with great amusement from a nearby table.

After bidding him a good evening, Claire, Jenn, and I exited the food court and continued to walk around the mall.

"Nova?" asked Jenn softly.

I kept walking briskly.

"Uh, Nova?"

"Yeah. I know," I said in a monotone voice.

"He's got one eye. You *do* know that he's only got one eye, right?" ventured Claire.

"Yep," I replied curtly, the humor of my situation sinking in. "One fucking eye."

"He seems nice, otherwise," offered Jenn.

"Seriously, though," said Claire. "He's got one eye. Didn't you see that from across the mall?!"

"No," I replied. "I didn't! Okay!? Why should I hold it against him that he's got one eye? He's probably a nice person. And he seemed interested in me. Hell, he gave me his phone number."

"No offense, but how many girls do you really think approach him?" asked Claire. "And how do you know he didn't give you a fake number?"

As it turned out, Jack called my house a few nights later while I was at work. Much to my chagrin, Mom took a message for me.

"Who's Jack?" she asked.

"Some guy I met at the mall," I responded, knowing this would open up a huge can of worms. The second Mom knew either of her kids liked someone or had someone interested in them, she would pounce with the jokes.

Knowing full well what I was getting myself into, I told Mom about Jack... and his one eye.

To my surprise, Mom was unfazed. "If he's from Mt. Chicamacomico, has no career goals, and is still living with his parents, he's probably got money. Who gives a shit if he's only got one eye?!"

Somehow, I had once again managed to escape being the brunt of Mom's jokes. Things were looking up!

That night, I called Jack back and we talked for nearly an hour. I learned more about the movies and music he enjoyed and how he had taken up karate to protect himself from the kids at school who made fun of him.

I still couldn't muster the courage to ask him about his eye or how he made the 45 minute drive from Mt. Chicamacomico to Fletcher by himself. While he didn't see me approach him in the food court, I wondered how he had managed to obtain a driver's license if he was legally blind in one eye. I also assumed (but didn't have the guts to ask) that he was born with just one eye and that it wasn't the result of an accident.

We talked about our common Native American heritage. I was one-eighth Cherokee while he was more than a quarter Native American. He told me that he had thought about living on a reservation to discover more about his roots. He was quite a fascinating guy.

After talking to each other nearly every night for a week, Jack agreed to meet up that Friday and catch a movie.

My first date! I was so excited!

In preparation for our date, I made sure I had the night off from work. As soon as I came home from school, I jumped in the shower and did my hair and makeup.

Dad planned to drop me off at the movies at around 6:30 P.M. He was actually pretty excited for me. Jack and I would be meeting up with Jenn and Brian at the movie theatre so Dad was definitely cool with the idea of it being a double date. I didn't tell Mom I was going on a date figuring she'd use it as an opportunity to bust my balls.

At around 5:30 P.M., roughly 45 minutes before Dad and I planned to leave the house, Jack called to cancel.

"I'm so sorry," he said. "I've been feeling under the weather all day. I just wanted to see how I was feeling before I knew for sure I couldn't make it."

"I'm glad you called." I was disappointed, but concerned. "I hope you feel better soon."

"Thank you. How about we make plans for next Friday instead?"

I perked up. "Sounds awesome! Looking forward to it."

"Great. I'm going to go get some rest, but I'll call you during the week?"

"I'd like that," I replied before hanging up.

I told Dad that I would be hanging at home that night, slightly bummed out by the rescheduled date. From there, I called Jenn and Brian to tell them that Jack had cancelled our date and that I was going to spend Friday night in. I figured they would probably appreciate some alone time.

Sunday night, Jack was feeling better and gave me a call. We talked for a while and he apologized for backing out on our date. I told him it was no problem and that I was really excited about seeing him that Friday.

Throughout the week, we took turns calling one another, spending 45 minutes at a clip on the phone each night.

By the time Friday rolled around, I was walking on air. This was it! I was finally going on my first date! Nothing was going to stop me! In a repeat performance of the previous Friday, I ran to the shower, picked out the perfect outfit and carefully did my hair and makeup.

And in yet another repeat performance, Jack called once again to cancel.

At first I thought it was a joke and laughed it off. Jack apologized profusely and clarified that he really couldn't make it to the movies that night.

"My friend Shannon is coming into town and I haven't seen her in a long time," he explained. "Shannon is a very *special* friend. That's the only reason why I can't make it out tonight. I'm really sorry."

I stood dumbfounded on the other end of the receiver. "Yeah. Okay," I deadpanned before hanging up.

I wasn't a total moron. I could read between the lines. Shannon was a "special friend." One of those "special friends" you only see from time to time. One of those "special friends" that you can't take on a date with the person you've been talking to on the phone for two weeks. One of those "special friends" you take to Walgreens to pick up a dozen condoms.

Yeah. I knew what sort of "special friend" Shannon was.

I was pissed. I'd been stood up by a guy with one eye...Twice!

"Fuck him!" said Dad. "The guy's a freak. He's only got one eye in his damn head! You can do better than him anyway. I don't know why you're always so down on yourself, kid. You gotta stop chasing these losers."

I nodded sadly to the sounds of Dad's sage wisdom. He made sense, but I was so disappointed. I had been talking to this guy for two weeks. *Two whole weeks!* I thought he liked me! Okay, there was never anything romantic or anything beyond pleasant, 45-minute conversations between us. He never called me any pet names or said he had feelings for me. Nevertheless, I had assumed the guy liked me by virtue of the fact that he continued to call and wanted to take a rain check on a trip to the movies.

I felt like a complete dumbass.

I wish I could say The Ballad of One-Eyed Jack ended there, but it didn't.

Two days later, Mom came strolling into my room with the monthly phone bill in her hand. In my blissful state, I didn't realize that Mt. Chicamacomico – the home of One-Eyed Jack – was a long-distance call zone.

"All those calls you made to your one-eyed lover boy just cost you $80," said Mom with a smirk, handing me the itemized bill with all of the calls made to Mt. Chicamacomico circled in red along with their respective charges.

There I was. Brokenhearted with a share of the phone bill that just ate two week's pay from my afterschool job. I stared at the long list of calls and minutes wasted talking to a guy that stood me up twice. A guy with one fucking eye.

Jack never called me after breaking our date to spend quality time with "Special Friend Shannon." And truthfully, after seeing how much it cost to dial 1-900-DEAD-EYE, I sure as hell wasn't going to call him, either.

I learned my lesson the hard way that no good comes from trying to pick up guys in the food court at the mall. From that point on, my Friday night excursions to the mall were reserved for shopping or social time with friends.

Two weeks later, I was back in Friday night action with Jenn and Claire, when lo and behold, who should I see walking around the mall with a roly poly male companion.

It was painfully obvious from the looks of this little sausage-fest-for-two that One-Eyed Jack and his pudgy pal were trolling the food court for poonani on an otherwise lonely Friday night. You could practically smell the "single" rolling off of them.

Guess things didn't work out with "Special Friend Shannon."

I tried to avoid being seen, but it was no use. Even with one eye, Jack had spotted me and was walking towards me.

"Hi, Nova," Jack exclaimed. "It's good to see you again!"

I resolved to be polite, even though I wanted to vomit on his shoes. "Good to see you, too, Jack."

"I haven't heard from you in a while." His voice was far too chipper.

"That's a two-way street, pal," I replied, failing at being polite.

He laughed nervously and asked if the girls and I would like to grab a bite to eat with him and his friend.

"Thanks for the offer, but we're actually meeting up with a few more people later and are going out for pizza afterwards."

"That's cool. Maybe we'll catch up with you later. Or maybe we could go see a movie next week," he offered.

"Yeah," I said evenly. "We'll see." I exhaled quickly before telling him I'd see him around in as nonplussed a voice as possible. With that, Claire, Jenn, and I made our way to the bookstore downstairs.

I made a beeline for the back of the store where the children's books lived. I needed something to cheer me up and with the exception of a few extremely depressing children's books (go read *Love You Forever* and learn just how depressing kiddie lit can be), the kids' section of the bookstore was my go-to place for emotional uplifting.

As I thumbed through the pages of a *Sesame Street* book with Cookie Monster on the cover, I felt my anger begin to dissipate.

"Wow, that was weird running into that guy," spoke Jenn. "What was his name again?"

"Jack," I retorted quickly, the corner of my mouth twitching as I was snapped from my pleasant, children's book-induced reverie by the thought of the man who had stood me up and left me with nothing but an $80 phone bill and a broken heart.

I put the *Sesame Street* book down so as not to taint it with my rising ire.

"Can you believe the nerve of that prick?!" I spat before raising my voice in a high-pitched, mocking tone. 'Maybe we can see a movie sometime?' Yeah, buddy. Let's make plans to see a movie so you can stand me up again."

I was on a roll. The floodgates had opened and there was no stopping the torrent of tirade rolling off my tongue.

"Uh, Nova?" nudged Jenn, attempting to staunch the flow.

I was in a different world. I had been beamed down to Planet Go Fuck Yourself, completely oblivious to what my friends were trying to say or anything else going on around me.

"Gee, I guess things didn't work out with 'Shannon,'" I snarked.

"Nova?" ventured Claire, her eyes growing wide as Jenna Jamison's love canal as my voice got louder.

"Yeah. Guess 'Shannon' sent his ass packing. I mean, did you see his friend he was roaming the mall with? Those two clowns are poster boys for single. Probably running around trying to find chicks desperate enough to hook up with them tonight. Or maybe Jack just wants to find someone else he can stand up, too? Yeah, like I really want to go out and get pizza with you or go see a movie, you asshole! Fuck you, One-Eyed Jack!"

"Uhhh..... Nova?" spoke Jenn as I just finished my scathing monologue. "You might want to turn around."

I noticed the horrified looks on my friends' faces before I whirled around to find One-Eyed Jack and his portly pal standing less than five feet behind me.

Shit.

Jack's mouth hung wide open while his friend's face was blank and expressionless.

I wasn't even going to attempt to offer an explanation. It was just as well since Jack and his buddy turned on their heels and exited the store.

"Wow!" exclaimed Claire. "That was harsh!"

I nodded in agreement, but didn't really think it was that big of a deal. Come to think of it, this was the best possible ending to The Ballad of One-Eyed Jack. Sure, I could have went out like a sucker and apologized to him. But his whole schpiel was just so insincere it was hard to take him seriously. It reeked of desperation – and coming from the chick who tried to pick him up in a food court at the mall – that was pretty damn desperate.

I felt bad that he heard my tirade. Particularly the part where I referred to him as "One-Eyed Jack." It wasn't like I *intended* to say it to his face. I would have been perfectly content to have left our conversation on an icy, open-ended note when I departed the food court.

It wasn't even his one eye that bothered me. The $80 phone bill and the fact that the douchebag led me on bugged me a lot more. The one-eyed leading the blind.

I tried to take the high road, but ended up on a surprise detour to the low road.

And it felt pretty damn good.

Jack really was an asshole. If he hadn't run into me, I probably never would have spoken with him again. If he really wanted to apologize for breaking our dates, he would have grew a pair and called or asked to meet in-person. He didn't trail me downstairs to the book store with the intent to apologize. Things probably bottomed out with Special Friend Shannon and One-Eyed Jack probably wanted to get his One-Eyed Willy wet. It was as simple as that.

All things considered, I'm glad he heard what I had to say, even if it was pretty mean. Sometimes, when you least expect it, the universe aligns itself in a way that allows you to have your revenge without even trying.

CHAPTER ELEVEN
WHORIN' HANK

With the food court off the menu, my field of options had narrowed. I had to find more creative ways to go man hunting. Summer was fast approaching and I was hurtling towards my senior year in high school.

Not only were my days as a junior numbered, but so were my days at Burger Land. After having done hard time behind the broiler for a year, I decided I wanted a job that didn't leave my skin saturated with a semi-permanent film of grease.

I had put in applications to a few stores in the mall. Finally, that summer before senior year, I landed the gig I really wanted: sales associate at Heshers – a store that specialized in heavy metal t-shirts and apparel, black light posters, and other random items.

I was hired a week after I applied. I guess it helped fulfill their goth chick quota.

I had been working at the store for nearly a month before I ended up sharing a shift with Hank. Hank was a tall, toned, confident 19-year-old with a heavy curtain of light brown hair that matched his complexion and intense hazel eyes. Hank had a natural way with customers. During my first shift with him, I'd seen him get several chicks' phone numbers.

At closing time, while the Assistant Manager Eileen and Hank counted out the register, I was responsible for vacuuming the store and bringing in the displays before we brought down the metal safety gate for the night.

Eileen and Hank had finished counting out the cash and preparing the night's deposit so Hank decided to "help" me bring in some of the display items.

Upon seeing a large, stuffed panda that would have otherwise been smooshed by the metal gate, Hank picked him up in a fireman's carry and spun him around before crashing the bear to the floor inside the store.

"Hank does it again!" he declared. "Another win for Handsome Hank! Wooo!!!" And with that, Hank proceeded to strut across the floor in an imitation of wrestler Hulk Hogan, raising a hand to his ear and throwing muscle man poses.

I laughed out loud at Hank's display. In a rare moment of cool, I deadpanned that "Sometimes, when I'm alone in my room, I like to pretend I'm Goldust," referring to a wrestler whose heavily made-up, gold glitter-loving character was that of an androgynous film buff.

Hank looked intrigued. "Really!?"

"No. But Ric Flair and Goldust are two of my favorites."

"So, you watch wrestling?"

After confirming I was the rare, female wrestling fan weaned on Hulkamania and Macho Madness during my formative years, Hank proclaimed: "You're okay, kid. You're gonna be alright here." He smiled as he walked towards the time clock to punch out for the night.

Beyond wrestling, Hank and I liked a lot of the same things: metal, hardcore, and an appreciation of fine cinema – namely, *Pee Wee's Big Adventure*. When we weren't talking wrestling, Hank and I were talking music.

Actually, we talked music when he wasn't busy being a total man whore. Hank was a shameless flirt. He was ridiculously hot and he knew it, often using it to his advantage.

He would openly try to pick up girls in front of our manager Eileen. When she'd warn him to back off, he'd flirt with *her*. Flinging an arm around her shoulder, he'd cajole, "Come on, Eileen! Don't deny the ladies a chance with destiny!" In turn, our manager would giggle like a schoolgirl.

The truth was, I was starting to fall for Hank's charms, too. Hell, he'd even flirt with *me* – something I was completely unaccustomed to. What the hell was a good looking dude like Hank doing flirting with me?!

My own low self-esteem made me believe that no one could ever find me attractive. When you're told day in and day out that you're ugly, you start to believe it. Sure, my parents told me that I was pretty, but they were my parents. No parent tells their kid to put a bag over their head before leaving the house.

I wasn't as unattractive as I had been during freshman year. Since then, I had "grown into myself." Thanks to contact lenses, I no longer had to wear glasses that could burn ants on a summer sidewalk in order to correct my vision. My zits had cleared up. Dying my hair black had made it shinier and it had grown longer and thicker over the years. Plus, I had lost weight.

I wasn't pageant material, but I wasn't completely hideous.

This realization hit me one night at Heshers.

It was my job that night to "man the perimeter" of the store and stay alert for any thieves or weirdoes. The kids who'd come in and try to steal cheap jewelry or a vibrator for shits and giggles. Or the Friday night drunks who would stumble into the store and try to hit on some of the girls I worked with.

As I walked past the storefront windows, I caught a glimpse of an attractive woman with long, dark hair and pale skin.

Wow! She's striking, I said to myself. For a second, I believed that the girl I had seen was just another mall patron, rushing off to Macy's and browsing in Heshers' window. Looking again, I realized that girl was *me* and that I was staring at my own reflection. Within seconds, the girl I had perceived as attractive had turned plain...and then ugly.

At that moment, I realized that I was my own biggest detriment to my self-esteem. Proof of my own self-loathing had manifested itself in that store window. I had it beaten into my head for years that I was ugly, mostly because I was "different." Once I looked at myself with my own eyes and not through the eyes of others, I realized that I wasn't a half-bad looking chick.

It's hard to make that disconnect when "ugly" is all you hear. That's the thing about school – and school in a small town, in particular: You can change your appearance. You can change who you *are*, but no one ever lets you forget what you *were*.

Once you've been marked as a nerd or an outcast, as long as you stay in that school, you'll always *be* that same outcast or nerd. Conversely, if you're pretty and popular when you're younger, even if you pack on a few pounds, you're still part of the in-crowd and no one sees you as anything less than gorgeous. The hierarchy has already been established.

My experience with seeing my own reflection and being on the receiving end of Hank's flirtations worked wonders for my self-esteem (even though he would flirt with anything with a ham wallet between her legs). His more sexually charged comments were nothing more than "Hank being Hank," but I relished the fact that he had thrown some attention my way.

"Nova being Nova," that translated into me developing a crush on Hank. Even though I stopped believing the negative things that others said about me, once again, I was not immune to the power of suggestion. Hank had painted himself as a true ladies' man and bolstered his own reputation as a dashing

Lothario. He was his own best public relations advocate and I had totally bought into the hype.

My years of watching wrestling had trained me well in the art of strategy. Much like the training I had received watching the daytime machinations of the villainous Stefano DiMera on *Days of Our Lives*, I picked up several pointers from watching professional wrestling – essentially a soap opera with big, beefy, sweaty dudes.

Like the great 16-time champion, Ric Flair always said, "To be The Man, you've got to beat The Man." Warping his words to fit my own situation, I figured to get The Man, you have to *become* The Man. You need to get inside their brain and see what it is that makes them tick.

I admired Hank's staggering bravado and began to adopt it myself. Some animals – and a lot of humans – will mimic the body language or even the mannerisms of who they are trying to attract.

Having seen the ease with which Hank would chat up members of the opposite sex, I decided that I would emulate some of his own tactics and use them on him.

Knowing that Eileen was planning to reprimand Hank for flirting with customers, I took it upon myself to give him a heads-up.

At the time, I was hanging out with Claire and her new boyfriend, Austin, reprising my role as third wheel.

Austin was a year older than Claire and went to a nearby public high school. I wasn't quite sure how they met, but after graduation, Austin decided to stay in Fletcher to help run his family's restaurant and work on a computer programming degree at the local community college.

Claire and I were now high school seniors. Austin's influence had done wonders to mellow her. With Claire in a happier state, she had become a better person and a better friend. I started hanging out with her and Austin more often outside of school and on the weekends. I even wound up playing *Dungeons and Dragons* with Austin and his cousin Chris on the weekends. I had a strong circle of friends that could count on each other and felt that they really understood me.

Which was why I balked when Austin and Claire shook their heads at me the night that I called Hank to warn him about Eileen's "come to Jesus" talk.

Hank had given me his number some time ago, telling me to give him a call if I ever needed a ride to one of the local metal club's all-ages shows. Even though I wasn't headed to a show, I figured this was a good time to call Hank. It was the perfect opportunity to talk to him and demonstrate my worth as a friend and potential love interest.

"Hey, baby cakes!" Hank said, picking up. "What's going on?"

"Not much, dude. Just a heads up, but you might want to take it easy with talking to some of the female customers on the clock. I overheard Eileen saying that she was going to have a little talk with you next time you're in."

He brushed it off casually. "I'm not worried. I've got Eileen wrapped around my finger."

"Maybe. But she sounded pretty pissed. All I'm saying is watch yourself."

"Relax, doll face! Nothing's going to happen!"

"Okay," I sighed. "Just wanted to let you know what's up so you don't get railroaded when you come in."

"It's cool. Everything's under control."

"Alright. But remember who gave your sexy ass a heads up if shit goes down. I got your back."

"And I've got your back," replied Hank. "Baby got back!"

Reveling in the attention, I purred seductively – or at least as seductively as I could muster: "You know you want it."

Hank laughed on the other end and said he'd see me at work later that weekend. I hung up the phone in a serious state of swoon.

Claire stood in the doorway, rolling her eyes as I hung up the phone. Austin just shook his head.

"Really?" asked Claire. "'Sexy ass'? 'You know you want it'?! You should *really* be ashamed of yourself."

Austin laughed and pointed at me, still shaking his head. "You sounded like you were doing a commercial for yourself. It was like a cross between a bad political ad and a 1-900 number."

My mouth hung open in disgust. Did I really sound like that much of a jackass?

"Yes," insisted Claire. "I'm not liking this whole Blatantly Self-Promoting Nova that you're turning into. It's kind of sleazy."

She was right. I was taking this "method acting" approach to dating too far. I was thinking too much like Hank. My personality had taken a bizarre, 180-degree turn. I went from having zero self-esteem to shifting into the egomaniacal fast lane. It wasn't me.

I decided to abandon the Used Car Saleswoman of Love approach.

It was just as well. As Hank predicted, he dodged a severe reprimand from our manager and held back on flirting with the customers for awhile.

Halloween was just around the corner and as part of Heshers' seasonal sales push, employees were expected to wear costumes from the store's stock to help move merchandise during their shifts.

Halloween had always been my favorite holiday and I loved this part of the job. I chose a Morticia Addams costume to wear around the store.

I loved that costume. For one, I didn't need to wear a wig or makeup to make a convincing Morticia. Secondly, the clingy material of the dress showed no cleavage or leg whatsoever but it made my ass look borderline fabulous and less like the cellulite-riddled bowl of cottage cheese it really was.

In a bizarre, self-fulfilling prophecy, my ass became the object of Hank's attention. Since Eileen put the kibosh on Hank hitting up the female clientele for their phone numbers, he hit on me instead.

During Halloween season, business was booming. One night, I was re-stocking the selection of pewter skull and dragon jewelry and there were no step ladders in sight. Being 5'1", there wasn't much hope of being able to reach the top of the display rack. To boot, I was wearing my Morticia costume which wasn't exactly conducive to climbing around on things.

Hank offered his help. "Looks like you're having a problem with your rack, Nova," he said with a smirk.

I half-smiled and rolled my eyes at him. "Yes, actually," I admitted. "Would you mind helping me out?"

Hank was well over six feet tall and could easily reach the top. "No problem, Nova-Bendova," he said taking some of the pieces of jewelry from my hands and grinning. "Where do you want it?"

Marveling at how well Hank had mastered the single entendre, I pointed out the shelves I couldn't reach. Hank situated himself right behind me and reached overhead, hanging the necklaces on the top two rows. He braced his hands on the display case on either side of me, grazing the front of his pants against my behind.

"Ooops!" he laughed.

I stood there in a state of disbelief, not moving or rubbing back up against him. I wasn't offended. Just shocked.

Holy shit! A hot guy just brushed his pecker against my ass! This is the best job ever!

So what if we were both fully clothed! A hot dude touched my ass!

The whole encounter lasted all of two seconds. Certainly not long enough for Whorin' Hank to get his rocks off. I think he meant it in more of a humorous way than anything since he was laughing the whole time. Plus, it didn't feel like there was any wood in the shed back there.

I didn't care if Hank's pelvic region stayed in a dormant, gummy worm-like state. I just got my ass touched on the clock! By a hot dude! It was the most awesome two seconds I had ever been paid for and could declare on a W-2!

CHAPTER TWELVE
SOPHOMORE STALKING

After the kinda-sorta ass touching incident, it looked like I was ready to reel Hank in. Then again, it wouldn't be the first time that I thought a guy was interested in me and came up empty. Whorin' Hank liked a variety of girls. Any perceived interest he showed in me was attributed to his nature as an incorrigible flirt. What seemed like a big deal to me, was actually no more routine to Hank than brushing his teeth or changing his underwear. (If he even wore underwear.)

I decided I should keep my options open.

Having struck out with homeless dudes and one-eyed guys, I decided to take a more scientific approach. I realized that the last four guys I had pursued were all older than me: Rick was a year older than me, Wendell was five years older, and One-Eyed Jack was three years older.

Since I struck out with the older ones, I wondered if I should start aiming for the youngins.

As a high school senior, younger guys were pretty much the default choice.

The perfect opportunity manifested itself when a sophomore named Elijah arrived at school. With his long, multi-colored dreadlocks, Elijah was the newfound eye-candy of every female freak in the school.

As a senior, I was now "Head Freak." At Jefferson High, you were either a prep, a wallflower, or a freak. With my leather motorcycle jacket, long black hair, and locker full of heavy metal posters, I was not just "a" freak, but "The" Freak.

As Head Freak, it was my duty to look after underclassmen freaks and protect them from bullying jocks and preps. It was a proud tradition amongst freaks to look out for our own and make sure everyone got out of high school with as little pain as possible. You know the drill: With great power comes great responsibility.

I loved all the underclassmen "freaks." We were bonded through shared misery and a common goal of getting out of Jefferson High alive. It was almost impossible to do it alone. With the exception of a few, good-hearted members of the faculty; our school was rife with authority figures who were largely unsupportive of demonstrations of individuality. You had to find some sort of an internal support system in the school to help get you through.

My fellow upperclassmen freaks and I would frequently intervene on behalf of younger outcasts who were being harassed or pushed around (sometimes literally) by the jocks and preps.

One of these underclassmen was Elijah. His colorful dreads, all-black wardrobe and backpack laden with band patches made him a marked man.

"Fag!"

"Freak!"

"I'm gonna kick your ass!"

One of the things I admired about Elijah was that he was one of the few freaks who would give it right back. He didn't need anyone to "come to his rescue." Pretty impressive for a kid who had transferred from Vermont.

One afternoon, en route to English class, I spotted Elijah being hassled by my least favorite duo: Derek Marcus and Eric Stanton.

Eric and Derek were two large, red-faced, 'roid-packing meatheads. They were inseparable and indistinguishable from each other except for the numbers on their football jerseys.

We had a history. Back in middle school, Eric enjoyed reminding me on a daily basis that I was "as ugly as the day is long." Derek's claim to fame was pushing me and Sammi down the stairs back in freshman year. Sammi injured her arm and in a 'roid-fueled rage, Derek grabbed me by the back of my neck. Scraping the heel of my shoe against his shin, I broke free from his grip and punched him square in the eye. I grabbed Sammi from where she fell and we ran to Mom's car. Derek found himself sporting a black eye for the next few days.

Seeing these two no-necks attempting to shake down a new kid in school boiled my blood. I was prepared to jump into the fray, but, to my surprise, Elijah bit back.

"Hey, does your boyfriend like your pretty colored braids?" taunted Derek

"I don't know," responded Elijah. "How does *your* boyfriend feel about you two wearing matching jerseys?"

"What the fuck did you say?" said a stunned Eric

"Does it bother you that you're both wearing the same thing? Or do you like to match so everyone knows you're a couple?"

"I'm gonna kick your fucking ass!" exclaimed Derek ....or Eric. It was hard to tell them apart, especially when they were angry. Derek made a lunge for the sophomore just as I arrived.

"Eric! Derek! Nice to see you managed to stop jamming needles in each other's asses long enough to make new friends!"

Eric whipped his head around, making it seem like he almost had a neck for a split second. "Did I *ask* you to say something, you fucking skank?"

Just then, one of the hall monitors saw the four of us standing in the hall. "Get back to class!" she called, jerking her thumb behind her.

Derek glared at Elijah. "Next time I see you, you're dead fucking meat."

"I'll start making plans with the undertaker," he deadpanned, raising an eyebrow.

As Derek and Eric went their way, I offered to escort Elijah to his class.

"You're Nova Porter, aren't you?"

I was surprised he knew who I was. "Yeah," I laughed. "You're new here. It's Elijah, right?"

"That's me. How did you know?"

"I'm friends with Dave King and Brianne Stark. They said you were in some of their honors classes and seemed like a nice kid."

"Thanks. That's pretty cool. Good to meet you," he said, extending his hand.

I shook it and he asked how I knew the two guys who had been hassling him.

"That was Derek Marcus and Eric Stanton. Total douchebags. They're seniors. I've had several run-ins with them, too."

"They're pretty obsessed with calling everyone 'gay.' I mean, I'm not a homophobe or anything, but they seem kind of repressed. I grew up in Vermont. They're a lot more open-minded than they are here."

"Yeah," I nodded wryly. "Welcome to Fletcher."

We arrived at the first floor where his eighth period class was located several doors down from mine. "Looks like this is my stop."

"Cool. See ya around."

"Nice meeting you."

"You, too," I said, turning down the hall and into A.P. English.

After that, I ran into Elijah in the hallways a few times each day. When I was coming out of my second period computer class, he was leaving honors Geometry. Sometimes we'd run into one another during lunch and then again heading to our respective eighth period English classes.

Elijah was a really nice kid. He was intelligent and unafraid to be an individual – even in a school like Jefferson. I admired his spunk.

One day, I asked him what his parents were thinking when they moved from Vermont to Fletcher. He had told me that his father was a minister and was moving to a different parish. I was intrigued. The kid was smart, well-adjusted, well-mannered, an individual... and the son of a preacher man! It was all so Dusty Springfield!

Despite being two years older than Elijah, I had developed a small crush on him. It was almost verboten for seniors to even think of dating anyone as young as a sophomore. Then again, I was only thinking.

While I had a bit of a lust thing going for Whorin' Hank, Elijah was dating material. He was smart, witty, and a good kid. Elijah was relationship caliber.

It was tempting to use my powers as Head Freak for personal gain. Waging a Shakespearean battle within, like a cross between Hamlet and Lady MacBeth, I was torn between upholding my sacred duty to protect underclassmen outcasts and attempting to use my miniscule bit of authority to enrich my (seriously lacking) love life. I pondered whether I could protect Elijah and his magical, super-awesome rainbow dreads from the slurs and arrows of outrageous morons and somehow parlay that protection into affection for me.

I rationalized that I wouldn't be using my powers for evil. To borrow *Dungeons & Dragons* terminology, it would be more like Chaotic Neutrality.

By chatting with Elijah on a regular basis between classes, I had pretty much figured out his schedule. As a result, I made a handy-dandy stalker chart in the back of my notebook that allowed me to take the most efficient route through the hallways and allow me to cross paths with Elijah, thereby maximizing my time with him between classes.

This was brick-and-mortar stalking before things got all high-tech with Facebook or electronically posted class schedules. It was an art I was well-versed in, having made similar charts of Rick's class schedules years before.

I was either a master strategist or a complete sicko. (I vote for the latter.)

The challenge of stalking him aside, I really liked Elijah as a person. Granted, I didn't have the depth of feelings for him that I once held for Rick, but he was a really nice kid. I don't think he saw me as anything more than a protective "big sister," nor did he have any indication that I had a slight crush on him.

That was probably why one Friday, when we were discussing our weekend plans, he mentioned he would be hanging out with his girlfriend who was visiting from Vermont.

It figured.

He was a nice, smart, cool guy. *Of course* he would have a girlfriend!

There was no way in good conscience that I would try to warp Elijah's feelings of friendship for me into something more – especially since he had maintained a long-distance relationship with his girlfriend.

Truth be told, I wasn't even sure I had a chance.

Elijah and I stayed friends until I graduated. However, he was off the dating menu from that point forward. It was back to the drawing board.

CHAPTER THIRTEEN
THE RETURN

With Elijah off-limits, I devoted my efforts towards trying to throw myself at Hank. We usually worked the same shift. When we weren't, I worked with Hank's friend Bill who had just started at Heshers.

Bill was the exact opposite of Hank in nearly every way: Hank was tall and Bill was short. Hank had long, light brown hair while Bill's was dark and close-cropped. Bill had a monogamous relationship with the same girl since middle school and Hank would try to nail anything with a whisker biscuit. The biggest difference, however, was that Bill was quiet and lacked the bombastic bravado that Hank possessed.

Yet, the two guys were best friends. Go figure.

Bill was also the guitarist in Last Bastion, a local hardcore band that Hank fronted.

Speaking objectively, Last Bastion was a good band. Even if I didn't have the hots for Hank and wasn't friends with Bill, I would have gone to see them play anyway.

"We'll be playing again in a couple weeks. We're trying to put a demo tape together and sell it at a few shows," said Bill during one of our shifts at Heshers.

"Dude! That's awesome. I'll definitely pick up a copy. Just let me know for sure when you guys are playing next. I'm there."

Little did I know that the next time Last Bastion played, it would be an even bigger event than I expected.

The night of the show, Claire and Austin called to say that they would be coming to the show, too. This was a surprise. Austin was a fan of classic rock like Zeppelin, Queen, and The Beatles while Claire's taste in music ran towards girly pop and country. Why the hell did they suddenly want to see a metal band?

"It'll be a fun night out for the four of us," said Austin.

"The four of us?" I ventured.

"My friend Rick Sanders is home from college for the weekend. He really wanted to see Last Bastion play. He knows a couple of the guys in the band."

I went numb.

"Rick Sanders?" My mouth was barely able to form the words. "How do you know Rick Sanders?"

As it turned out, Austin and Rick graduated from the same high school. They became good friends the year that Rick transferred from Jefferson.

I listened quietly as Claire filled me in on the oh-so-ironic details she had neglected to mention before of how she and Austin began dating.

Several months ago, Rick and Austin were hanging out together in Claire's neighborhood. Rick decided to bring Austin with him to pay a visit to his "ex-girlfriend" and say hi. Austin and Claire were instantly attracted to each other and Rick proudly proclaimed that he was responsible for bringing the couple together.

While I was really happy to hear that Rick had dramatically turned things around for himself in his senior year, improving his grades to the point that he was able to attend Parsons in New York, I still felt very uneasy about hanging out with him. It had been over a year since I last saw him – not to mention that we parted ways on bad terms.

"Guys," my voice was tinged with trepidation. "This is going to be extremely weird. I really don't want to hang out with Rick. I think I'll sit this one out."

"Nova," said Claire calmly. "Rick said he has no problem with you. When he said that he was coming in and wanted to check out the Last Bastion show, we told him that you were planning on seeing them, too. He said he would really like to catch up with you."

"Seriously?" I wasn't buying it.

Just then, I heard a familiar voice pick up the phone from the other end: "Tell that bitch that she's going to the show and she's going to have a good time!"

It was Rick. I'd know that voice anywhere with its faint, West Virginia twang. Oddly enough, his jovial tone put me completely at ease. This was Rick's usual way of speaking and there wasn't a trace of animosity or anger in his voice.

"Alright! Alright!" I laughed. "But we're *not* taking the Pinto. There's no way in hell we're driving to the show in your shit box." Rick had an old, beat up Ford Pinto that had been Frankensteined back to life on more than one occasion. The interior was adorned with duct tape and its doors were covered in dings thanks to a few years of Rick's "defensive" driving.

I hung up the phone and busied myself with getting ready for the show, deciding what outfit to wear. I was going for Hank. I didn't care what Rick thought I looked like, although, if he was still the same old Rick, he would have a smart ass comment no matter what I wore.

I was over Rick and hadn't given him a romantic thought in nearly a year. I had resigned myself that I would never see him again and put him out of my mind. I was focused on the future and Hank.

Half an hour later, Austin, Claire, and Rick arrived at my house to pick me up in Austin's Volkswagen Beetle. Austin had been trying to restore an old VW Bug with money from slinging pizza at his family's restaurant. It was a pretty sweet ride.

Claire got out of the car and pulled her seat forward so I could get in the backseat. With Rick.

Jesus Christ! Were they *trying* to torture me?

"Aww, man!" exclaimed Rick with a laugh. "I have to sit in the back with *her*?!"

I raised my eyebrow and smirked at Rick as I climbed into the back, duly noting the irony of the situation. For years, I'd have given my right eye to be that close to Rick, let alone share the backseat of a car with him. Right now, the backseat of a car with Rick was last place on the planet that I wanted to be.

Attempting to diffuse the tension, I joked that Rick had cooties and that I wasn't thrilled to be sharing the backseat of a car with him, either.

I tend to make lame jokes when I'm nervous, although this was a completely different variety of nervous than the *"I-can't-finish-my-yogurt"* nervousness I experienced right before I asked Rick out years ago. This was the "I-know-you-probably-hate-me-and-this-is-so-awkward" brand of nervous. I had said some really mean things to Rick the last time I saw him. Sure, he said some pretty mean things to me, too, but I really raised the bar.

Taking a cue, Austin and Claire asked if we wanted to grab some fast food before headed to the club. Both Rick and I were game.

"It's good to see you again, Nova," spoke Rick between bites of burger. "What the hell have you been up to?"

I studied him for a second. His hair had grown out and he had dyed the tips dark blue to match his new lip ring. "Who are you and what have you done with Rick Sanders?"

"Aww," he sighed, grinning sarcastically. "I missed you, too!"

What the hell was wrong with me? Why was I being so defensive? He was obviously trying to make an effort to be nice and for whatever reason, I was determined to be a bitch. I decided that if he could make the effort to be nice, I would, too.

"Things are alright. It's senior year, so there's all that S.A.T. fun and applying to schools stuff."

"Where are you applying?"

"Temple, Paley, Penn State, Fordham, and NYU," I said, counting out the schools on my fingers.

"Not bad choices," he replied.

"You're at Parsons now, right? Do you like it?"

"I love it," he replied earnestly. He was studying photography, fine arts, and technology — three things that were right up his alley.

"Dude, that's awesome! I'm really glad you got your shit together and got into a good school."

"Yeah. Me, too. It's a different world than Fletcher. People are a lot more open-minded. Lots of things to do in the city. Classes are interesting. I'm lucky that financial aid covers most of my tuition."

"I've been looking into a lot of grants and loans myself. I'm hoping that I can get a scholarship, too. That's pretty much the deciding factor. Which school offers the most financial aid and scholarships."

"You'll get something," Rick said confidently. "I wish I'd done better in school. They probably would have given me more money if I did. You've got nothing to worry about, though. You always got good grades and were pretty smart."

I was flabbergasted. Rick actually paid me a compliment?!

"Thanks," I said, feeling somewhat honored. "You're no slouch yourself. It's about time good things started happening for you."

It was a nice, normal conversation that reminded me of the old days when Rick and I weren't just civil with one another, but when we were actually friends.

Before long, everyone finished their food and loaded back into Austin's car. By the time we arrived at the club, none of the bands scheduled had taken the stage just yet. The four of us milled about, saying hi to a few people we recognized and with Rick getting a warm reception from some old friends – including Bill.

"How the hell are ya?" asked Rick, clapping Bill on the back.

"Man, I haven't seen you in a while."

"Yeah," Rick replied. "I'm on break from school for the next month."

"We should definitely get together. You've got my number, right?"

"I do, sir," replied Rick as Bill noticed me standing next to him and waved.

"Hey, Nova!" exclaimed Bill. "Have you met Rick before?"

I smiled. "Rick and I go waaay, back."

"That's crazy! Small world, isn't it?" he mused before turning to head backstage. "I'll see you guys around. I gotta get ready for the show."

Just then, Hank appeared out of nowhere. "Nova Bendova!" he screamed. "You actually showed up! Hot damn!" Hank picked me up off the ground and spun me around.

"You know *him*, too?!" asked Rick as Hank planted my feet back down on the club's sticky floor.

"I work with him and Bill at Heshers."

"Wait," said Hank to Rick. "How do you and Nova know each other?"

"We were friends back when I went to Jefferson."

"This bitch is fuckin' crazy." Hank draped an arm around my shoulder and gave me a friendly squeeze.

"Yeah," nodded Rick. "She's out there, alright."

I laughed nervously. This was making for an even more awkward of a night than I'd imagined.

"So you're back in town from New York on break?" asked Hank.

"Yep. I'll be here about a month."

"Still doing photography?"

"Yeah. I'm pulling a double major in photography and technology."

"Cool," said Hank, thinking for a moment. "Hey, maybe we could get you to take a few pictures for our demo. We're recording a few songs and need some band photos and a group shot for the cover. Do you think you might be able to do us a solid? Don't know if we can pay you, though."

"That's cool," replied Rick. "I brought most of my cameras home with me, so maybe we can meet up sometime this month and get something going."

"Righteous, my brother. Righteous," he said before turning to me with a wink. "And I'll see *you* later. Stay out of trouble!"

With that, Hank pranced away to prepare for his set.

"Dude," I said. "That's pretty sweet. You'll get to add to your portfolio while you're on break. Not bad."

"Yeah," Rick nodded. "Hank's a pretty cool guy."

"He is. He's fun to work with."

"Yep. He'll flirt with anything in a skirt," Rick remarked. "Speaking of which, I'm surprised you didn't wear one. Your taste in clothing seems to have improved since I last saw you."

I rolled my eyes and smiled at Rick's comment. "Same ol' Sanders." He paid me a backhanded compliment, but a compliment no less. I wondered if he was jealous of the attention that Hank had shown me a few minutes ago, feeling compelled to remark about his notorious nature with the ladies. Or if he was pointing out that Hank would flirt with just about anyone, even me.

Maybe this would prove to Rick, once and for all, that guys *did* find me attractive, regardless of how he felt about me and that maybe he had been wrong.

Not that I had feelings for Rick anymore, but he and I had a history. And what were the odds that Whorin' Hank knew Rick Sanders?

As much as this scenario made me smile with satisfaction, I paused for a moment: Why did I always have to make everything a competition? Why did I always have to overanalyze everything and read things into a situation that may not have been there in the first place?

For all I knew, Rick was just being Rick, opening his mouth without thinking. There may not have been anything to what he said beyond face value. That was one of the personality traits we shared – besides checking pay phones for loose change. We both lacked the internal censor buttons most people possessed and said things without realizing how incorrectly they might be perceived.

Rick could very well have just been paying me a compliment, trying to be a friend and warn me that Hank was a bit of a man whore. I decided to stop being so defensive and lighten up as far as Rick was concerned.

Initially, I thought the night was going to be a bust, having to prove to Rick that I was over him and endure awkward conversation. Instead, it ended up being a lot of fun. The band sounded great and the four of us hung around afterwards so Rick could chat with some of his old friends before we went all headed home. Rick was spending the night at Austin's place.

I later learned Rick hung out at Austin's a lot when they were in high school together. Austin's house was something of a hub for all of his friends and his mother, Patty, loved having a house full of her son's friends to feed.

Considering what a wing nut Rick's own mother was, it was no wonder he spent so much time at Austin's house. I wondered if Austin's family's influence played a factor in Rick getting his life in order and applying to a school that would get him out of his crazy mother's clutches.

"I'm starving," said Claire suddenly, leaping up from the couch to see what was in the fridge. Discerning that it contained nothing she wanted, Claire suggested to Austin that they go downstairs to the restaurant kitchen.

"You two stay here. We'll bring back some food," said Austin. "Chili dogs okay?"

"Sounds good to me! You sure you don't need any help?"

"Nope," replied Claire hurriedly. "You guys just hang out here. We'll be back."

Fifteen minutes passed. Austin and Claire didn't come back yet.

"Where the hell are they?" I sputtered.

"I know," said Rick. "I'm starting to get hungry. I might just check out the fridge myself to see what I can cook up."

"Hell, it's just hot dogs. It's not like they're preparing fillet mignon or anything. What's taking them so long?"

Rick got up from his post on the couch and headed for the fridge. "I'm at least going to grab a soda. You want one?"

"Sure," I said, joining him in the kitchen.

"You still drinking that diet shit?" Rick smirked.

"Yep," I replied, thanking him before cracking it open and taking a quick chug.

I let the carbonated beverage restore some sort of moisture to my throat before speaking again.

"I'm sorry, Rick."

"Huh? For what?"

"For being a bitch."

"You're always a bitch. No reason to apologize now."

"No. I'm talking about the last time I saw you. Before tonight. I never had the chance to apologize to you for what I said and what I did. I was a real asshole and I never meant to overstep my bounds and hurt you. I was a really shitty friend to do that and I never got the chance to tell you how sorry I was before you moved."

"Don't worry about it," said Rick casually. "That happened a long time ago."

"Yeah, but it doesn't make what I did right and it's definitely something I should apologize for."

"It's no big deal. I know you weren't trying to hurt me. And my mother *is* a fucking nut. I know it. Austin knows it. Claire knows it. At the time, I just didn't want a lot of other people to know it."

"Still, you trusted me and I said some shit I shouldn't have. The last thing I wanted was to hurt you."

"It's no big deal," he said. "So we're friends?"

"Hell yeah!"

"Cool," replied Rick in his usual, blasé sort of way before taking a sip of soda. "So, I hear you like Hank." There was a wicked gleam in his eye.

"Who told you!?" I said in mock anger.

"Who do you think?"

"Those bastards. Speaking of, wanna go downstairs and see what's keeping them? I'm starving already."

Rick and I were just about to make our way downstairs to find Austin and Claire when they arrived bearing food items.

"What took you so long?" demanded Rick, snatching the bag of Texas Wieners from Austin's hands.

"We were just sitting outside on the porch swing," he replied happily. Their timing was impeccable. Claire later told me they orchestrated the whole thing so that Rick and I could make our truce official.

It was good to finally have that weight lifted. I felt guilty for so long and wanted to clear the air with a person who had meant a lot to me. Not that I'd be seeing him around with any sort of regularity like back in high school.

Or so I thought.

Two months after winter break, Rick found himself back in Fletcher thanks to his parents. As it turned out, the illustrious Sanders clan had found a way to throw the kibosh on Rick's schooling. Unbeknownst to him, Rick's parents had used his Social Security number to their own benefit. Their little stunt impacted the amount of financial aid Rick was able to receive. Without a full time job or any real means to pay the hefty tuition price tag, Rick was booted from Parsons. He drove the Pinto from New York back to Fletcher where it promptly crapped out in front of Austin's house upon his return.

Rick's luck couldn't get much worse than that.

Actually, it could. His parents decided to move yet again, uprooting stakes from Fletcher to an even more Bumblefuck town within the tri-state area. It was like they were trying to separate Rick from everything and everyone that had been a positive influence on his life.

Thoroughly disgusted with his parents, Rick decided to live with Austin for the time being. Austin's mother was more than happy to take in another stray while Rick figured out what he was going to do next.

"I'm thinking of joining the Marines."

"Are you fucking crazy?!"

"Yeah," he replied. "That's why I'd probably do alright in the Marines."

"The Marines require discipline, Rick," said Austin.

"I could do it. I'd try to get stationed in Okinawa. Maybe study Karate over there. Then maybe I could get my college education paid for on the G.I. Bill."

He made several good points. However, I didn't like the idea of Rick potentially putting himself in harm's way, particularly in a foreign country.

"Hey," I offered. "How about I bring over my financial aid packet and we can see if you're eligible for any grants? Dad and I have to fill out a bunch of paperwork. There's bound to be something in there that could apply to you."

I had just been accepted to Paley University on a partial academic scholarship. What the scholarship didn't cover, I hoped state and federal financial aid would before I had to take on some student loans.

"Thanks, but I can't get PA state aid for a school in New York."

"Have you thought about going to a school here in Pennsylvania? Being a resident, tuition would probably be a lot cheaper."

"Thought about that, too. There just aren't schools here that have the courses I'm looking for. I think the Marines might be the way to go."

"You're being ridiculous," exclaimed Claire, who had recently proclaimed herself a pacifist and "neo-hippie."

Rick shrugged before Austin wisely decided to change the subject.

A few days later at school, Claire and I discussed Rick's predicament.

"I can't believe he's seriously considering joining the Marines. It's not what he really wants to do."

"It's his decision, though," replied Claire. "I don't agree with it, but from what Austin said, he thinks he doesn't have any other options."

"Yeah," I said bitterly. "Basically, his credit's been ruined right out of the gate thanks to his fucking parents. I wish that old bag would just die already."

"You're a little riled up over this, don't you think?" Claire sat quietly for a moment before it dawned on her. "Oh, no! You like him *again*, don't you?"

"No," I lied defensively. "I'm just worried that he's making a mistake. I don't think he's fully exploring his options."

"Whatever. I think you still like him. I haven't even heard you mention Hank that much this past month. The only thing that's changed is that Rick's been back in town for the past three months. Coincidence?"

"Yeah. It is," I said indignantly. "I mean, I just haven't wanted to push the issue with Hank. Besides, I haven't worked too many shifts with him lately."

"I'm not buying it. This is the same way you used to act when Rick was in school with us. You were always overly concerned and constantly worrying about him. Do I have to remind you that you went back to the damn school to make sure he didn't get blown up by the imaginary bomb?"

"Dude. Just drop it. I'm not interested in him. I would be just as pissed if you or Austin got screwed out of a college education by your parents."

"I know," Claire replied. "I just find it funny that four months ago, you didn't even want to be in the same room with him and now you're worried that he's going to ship himself off to Abu Dhabi or wherever..."

"Okinawa," I corrected her.

"See!" Claire exclaimed. "You know exactly where he was trying to get himself stationed!"

"No. I just pay attention to details."

"Trust me," she said in a less accusatory tone. "None of us want to see Rick do something rash without thinking it through. I'm just saying, I don't think you're admitting to yourself that you still have feelings for him. There's nothing *wrong* with it if you do. You just need to admit that you're not as over him as you thought you were."

I considered her words carefully for a moment. The worst thing that could happen if I admitted to having feelings for Rick would be him finding out. If that were the case, he might dismiss any argument I had for him to stay on the grounds that I was some silly chick with an ulterior motive.

On the other hand, considering we had become much better friends and put the past behind us, there was a chance Rick might consider dating me. Maybe him finding out that I cared about him would be the push he needed to stick around and apply to a school in Pennsylvania.

I admitted to Claire that maybe I wasn't quite "over" him and that these past couple months had rekindled the old feelings I had for Rick.

Claire wasn't shocked, however, her boyfriend was greatly amused by this revelation.

Austin danced around, hopping from foot to foot, laughing and pointing at me like a demented toddler, singing: "Ah-ha! Nova likes Rick! Nova likes Rick!"

Yeah. This was a great idea.

With Claire and Austin in-the-know, it was only fitting that Orion should also hear about my current conundrum and have a crack at mocking me, too. (Who says I'm not a masochist at heart?)

"I knew it," Orion said, shaking his head back and forth. "It was only a matter of time before you started getting hot for Rick's jock again after he moved back."

"Why the hell did I even tell you this?"

"Because I would have found out anyway. And when I did, I'd say something in front of Mom so she could make fun of you, too. Since you came out and told me, I'll just say something to

Mom in private and we'll make fun of you behind your back instead. It'll be slightly less embarrassing for you."

"Thanks," I said, rolling my eyes.

"Keep rolling your eyes," he cautioned. "I may change my mind."

"Just stop being an asshole for a second and tell me what you think I should do."

"You still like Hank, too?"

"Yeah," I said. "Not as much. They're different types, but yeah. Hank's cool."

"You fucking pig," he kidded. "That's like cheating on Rick."

"It would be if I were going out with him. I'm just keeping my options open. Maybe I'll ask one of them to prom."

"I thought you said you didn't want to go to the prom?"

"I don't," I lied again. "It's more of an excuse to ask either of them out than anything. Otherwise, why the hell would I want to pay money to hang around with dipshits I can't stand to be around for free? Besides, I'd be all dressed up and doing nothing but standing around by the punch bowl, looking like an asshole. No thanks."

"But you'd want to go to prom with either Rick or Hank?" my brother needled.

"Sort of. Like I said, it would be an excuse to ask either of them out. Like a test run to see if they had a good time with me that night and if maybe they wanted to do a permanent dating type thing. I mean, I'd pay for them, so it wouldn't be like it'd be coming out of their pocket."

"God, you're desperate!" Orion exclaimed before leaving me to contemplate my fate on the Tree of Woe.

After much deliberation, I decided I wouldn't ask either of them to prom. As previously concluded during the Elijah vs. Hank debate, Hank just wasn't relationship material and he certainly wasn't prom material. Prom was kind of a big deal. Hank was certainly charming, but he wasn't Prince Charming – or the type to go for going to prom.

As for Rick, I didn't feel the timing was right to ask him out. I knew he had already gone to his prom, so the allure of attending someone else's prom would most likely not exist for him. With graduation approaching and anticipating going away to school and away from my family, it was just one more thing I didn't want to deal with directly. I ended up sitting out prom and spending the night grocery shopping with my parents.

It wasn't until that summer, a month after I graduated, that I decided that I was going to finally ask Rick out. Again. I was slightly more confident he would say "yes" than when I asked him out back in freshman year.

Then again, I once had confidence in a fart and ended up shitting myself.

I planned on asking Rick out at a party Austin was throwing in a few weeks. It was like freshman year all over again with my stomach in knots, worrying about each aspect of my plan.

With a shortage of females to talk to, I had to rely on my brother for a last-minute pep talk and advice. He was the Mickey to my Rocky – minus the knitted skullcap.

"What outfit should I wear tonight? Jeans or black hip-huggers?"

"Go with the black ones," he suggested. "They're classier."

"Okay. Now how about which shirt? I'm going to wear the black long-sleeved top but should I go with the green camo tank over it or the rainbow-striped tube top?"

"I'd say the rainbow tube top. You'll want more color in your outfit. The camo's too drab. You want to stand out."

I nodded, taking his opinion to heart.

"Do you know what you're going to say to him?"

"I'm just going to play it by ear, dude. See when there's an opportunity to get him alone and then spring it on him."

"Alright," Orion said pensively, mulling over my strategy before granting his approval. "Just remember: You're going away to school in another month. No matter what he says, don't let this throw you off your game. You've got a big year ahead of you, regardless of what his answer is. Worst case scenario, you're still going to be friends with him. In the best possible case, even if you do end up dating, you won't be seeing him every day. Just keep these things in mind."

I took heed of Orion's advice, enjoying the party that night and not worrying about when and how to ask Rick out.

My opportunity came when the party ended and it was time for everyone to head home. Austin and Claire, who weren't entirely aware of my plan, decided they wanted some alone time with Rick out of the house. In turn, Rick offered to drive me and another girl home. I lived further out of the way than the other girl and he had no problem with going for a longer-than-usual drive in the Pinto, which had subsequently been brought back to muffler-rattling life shortly after it croaked on Austin's lawn upon Rick's return from Parsons.

After dropping off the other girl at her house, Rick and I sped down the highway, blasting one of my Marilyn Manson cassettes that he'd borrowed and was still holding hostage in his car.

Rick missed the turn into the hidden driveway in front of my house.

"Whoops!" he said.

Before I could suggest that he could just make a right in the mall parking lot to get back on the highway, Rick decided that it would be much quicker to make a U-turn on the highway.

I grabbed one of the "Oh, Shit!" handles above the passenger window and braced myself for the possibility of being sandwiched between a steel divider and the side of a small mountain as Rick made a three-point turn. Suddenly, asking him out wasn't the most pressing thing on my mind as my life flashed before my eyes. That song lyric about a ten-ton truck killing Morrissey and the object of his affection in "There Is a Light That Never Goes Out" popped into my head.

Fortunately, it was one o'clock in the morning and there weren't any other cars on the usually heavily-trafficked highway. I crossed myself and said a silent prayer, relieved that I had survived the three-second ordeal and Rick's driving.

He pulled into the driveway and made a left, parking in front of the lone house at the end of the block where my family lived.

"Here's your stop."

"Thanks, Rick." The sky was velvet black with just a few visible stars and a sliver of a moon. This was my final stand. "I've been doing a bit of thinking lately. Would you mind if we hung out here for a few minutes and talked?"

Stupid, stupid, stupid! I thought, berating myself for the words that just farted out of my mouth.

"Sure." He cut the Pinto's engine and put the car in park. "About what?"

I took a deep breath. "I'm going to Philadelphia for school next month. You're not sure where you'll end up next. We're both heading into these unknown situations. I was thinking that maybe it would be cool if there was at least one thing that was still familiar for both of us."

Rick looked at me like I was speaking Sudanese.

"I don't know how you feel about long-distance relationships," I started. "But if you wanted to go out with me, I would really like to give it a shot. I know we've finally gotten to be friends – again – in the past few months. You have no idea how grateful I am for that and I don't want to fuck anything up. And I know you've gone through a lot of shit lately, so, I don't know if you'd even want to go out with me. I just thought, maybe it would be kind of cool for both of us to know we have someone, no matter where either of us ends up."

Rick removed his hands from the steering wheel of the now-parked Pinto and twisted himself around in his seat to face me, leaning against the car door. He nodded silently and contemplatively, taking in what I had to say before speaking himself.

"You're a really nice girl, Nova. And you're really pretty..."

Pretty? Really?! Holy shit! This was it!

"...but right now, I just can't feel anything for anyone. I don't want you to think that it has anything to do with you or that I don't like you as a friend. It's just that I don't know what the future holds for me and I don't want to drag anyone else into it. I'm still trying to figure things out. And until I can do that, I have this block on my feelings. I'm numb. I'm not the type of person that can feel something strong or be a good boyfriend right now."

I swallowed hard, not out of disappointment, but because I could tell how lost Rick felt. The guy had tried to get his life on track and then, through no fault of his own, had the rug ripped out from under him.

"Dude," I said quietly. "I understand. If you ever need a friend to talk to – no weirdness intended – I'm always here. Even when I'm in Philly. Give me a call if you ever need someone to listen."

"Thanks," Rick said stoically before saying that he had better get going.

"Anytime. Thanks for the ride home. And thanks for not getting us killed on the highway."

"Cool," he smirked. "See ya tomorrow."

I got out of the car and unlocked the door to my house. Mom and Dad were both asleep, knowing I'd be out late. However, Orion had waited up for me.

"How did it go?"

"Well, it wasn't as long, drawn-out, or embarrassing as it was the first time I asked him out. He still turned me down but was really nice about it."

"What excuse did he give you this time?"

"He said I was pretty." My voice registered the shock my brain still had yet to comprehend. "But he said that right now, he can't feel anything. He's kind of at a crossroads and not sure where he's headed or where his head is at. I don't think he's interested in me at all. And honestly? I can't blame him. He's been through a lot and maybe this came at the wrong time. The way he was talking, it didn't sound like there *couldn't* be a possibility that we date in the future... Distant future. But, he was cool about the whole thing"

"You didn't try to hug him again like you did before, did you?"

"Nah. This was pretty anticlimactic. It felt more grown-up and less awkward. I don't think I came across like the tool I was back in freshman year. Maybe because I knew what to expect."

"That's cool. At least you two are still friends. Did you have a good time at the party?"

"I did!" I gave him the lowdown on the party hijinks that had ensued before we headed back to our rooms to get some sleep.

The next day, Rick called my house. I was hoping it was because he changed his mind.

"Hey, Nova!" Rick said in a tone of voice I'd never heard him use before. He sounded chipper. It was disturbing. "How the hell are ya?"

"I'm good, Rick. What's going on?"

"Do you remember that kid Fuji that I introduced you to at the party last night?" The chipper still permeated his voice in an almost maniacal sort of way.

"Yeah," I said, remembering a short, Asian kid with shoulder length black hair and a skateboard. "Nice guy."

"He's right here with me and he said he thought you were hot and wants to go out with you."

"What?!?!" I exploded.

"Yeah," said Rick, brimming with cheer. "The little guy wants to go out with you."

"Rick," I said, still in shock. "I don't think I can do that."

"Why not?" he encouraged. "He's short. You're short. He's a nice guy. You should go out with him."

Did Rick forget that I had just asked him out last night? Was he completely oblivious to the fact that you just don't stop feeling something for someone less than 24 hours later and decide to date someone you just met at a party the night before?! Did he forget that I would be going away to school in less than a month?!

It wasn't that I didn't think Fuji was cute. He was. And he seemed like a nice kid, too. If I wasn't going away to school in less than a month, I probably would have taken a chance on him. However, there was no time to build a relationship with someone who I didn't know outside of a five-minute introduction at a party. I had no clue what bands he liked, what he liked to do for fun (besides skateboarding thanks to the ubiquitous prop), or anything else. Beyond that, I still had feelings for Rick and wasn't ready to close the door on them by dating someone I didn't know.

"He seems like a really nice guy, Rick. But I'm leaving for school in less than a month. I just can't get into a long-distance relationship with someone I don't really know. It's not really fair to him, either."

What I really wanted to say was: "Are you a fucking *idiot*?! I just asked *you* out last night! Now you're trying to pawn me off on your friend?!"

Remembering that my lack of verbal restraint landed me in hot water with Rick before, I kept those thoughts to myself.

"No problem," Rick, chipper firmly intact. "If you change your mind, let me know. I'll hook you two up. Look how good my matchmaking skills were with Claire and Austin."

"Thanks, Rick. I appreciate it. Please tell Fuji that I'm flattered. But it's just the wrong time since I'm leaving in less than a month. Tell him I'm really sorry."

"Don't worry about it. I think I might try to hook him up with Becky since you're leaving town."

It was a bizarre conversation. I wondered if this was Rick offering some sort of a consolation prize since he had turned me down yet again. Or did he think I was just some dumb slut looking to date anyone whether I knew them or not?

I didn't have a lot of time to be confused or to think about much of anything besides preparing for my move to Philadelphia and college. Two weeks later, I attended a three-day orientation at Paley University's campus. It was my first real taste of college life and the big city.

After planning my first semester course load, I rode the subway for the first time and hung out on South Street with a few new friends I made. Oddly enough, the people I gravitated towards were fellow misfits and refugees from Fletcher and other small towns. The lone exception was a kid named Dylan, a film major who was transferring to Paley from Virginia. One night during orientation, I ended up hanging out with Dylan until 2am, shooting pool and chatting about movies and life in general. He had a girlfriend back home that he wasn't too keen on leaving and I told him about my own dilemma with Rick.

Before orientation ended, I traded phone numbers with the new friends I had met so we could all find each other once the semester started. Safety in numbers.

I made more friends in three days at college orientation than I did in four years of high school For once, I didn't feel like an outsider. There were kids from all different racial and social backgrounds and everyone got along. No one was singled out for being different because *everyone* was different.

As excited as I was about the new experience that awaited me in Philly, I was glad to come home and tell my family and friends about my adventures. I left out the part about smoking a joint, but my parents were thrilled that I had already made friends. They were worried about shipping me off to school over 100 miles away and wanted to be sure I had people I could rely on.

After spending time with my family, I caught up with Claire and Austin, telling them all about my Philly adventure. They were pretty excited for me.

Midway through telling them about this cool, old, philosophical bum that my new friends Jerry, Boone, and I met on South Street, I heard the front door slam.

"Hey! Where the hell have you been?" asked Rick, strolling into the living room with a scantily clad female who I had never seen before.

"At orientation in Philly. I was just telling Austin and Claire about it."

"I know a few people out in Philly," spoke the girl who had walked in with Rick. "I lived there for a little while. I've lived all over."

"This is Candy," Rick interjected, clearing up part of the mystery of his new friend. I noticed Claire and Austin exchange uneasy looks.

"Nice to meet you, Candy," extending my hand in greeting.

She delivered a limp-wristed handshake before running a hand through her short shock of highlighted blonde hair. Her hand settled back on her jutting hip which was barely covered by a flouncy denim mini – more of a Band-Aid for her ass than an item of apparel. It still offered more coverage than her string bikini top leant to her prominently displayed B-cups.

"Candy, this is my friend Nova."

"I've heard a lot about you," Candy replied with a snort.

I bet you have, I thought to myself, still unsure what was going on.

I gave a slight laugh and asked how the two of them met.

"Brad introduced us last week," he explained. "We were hanging out at the mall."

"Brad and I used to go to school together," breathed Candy airily. "So, he hooked us up!"

"Awesome!" I said, trying to sound happy.

The high I was riding from my trip to Philly had just crashed and burned. I leave town for three days and Rick gets a girl-friend? Even worse, Austin and Claire didn't see fit to tell me? What the hell was going on?!

"Hey!" said Claire. "We're running low on food. How about we take a trip to the store?"

"Yeah," replied Austin. "You two lovebirds can stay here, though. Don't know if there's enough room for everyone in the car plus the food. We'll be right back."

With that neat little segue, Claire, Austin, and I made a beeline for Austin's Volkswagen. As soon as the car door shut, words began tumbling from my mouth.

"Okay. What just happened and why didn't anyone tell me?!"

"We didn't want to tell you because we wanted you to have a good time and enjoy yourself in Philly," Claire declared honestly.

"We didn't even think they'd be dating that long," said Austin.

"Dude. Where the fuck did he dig *her* up? For years, I hear all this shit from Rick about how *I* dress like a hooker... and then *this* bitch bounces in with more meat hanging out of her top than a deli case!"

Austin nodded, clearly not having warmed up to Candy in a way that extended beyond the solidarity of friendship.

"Don't worry," soothed Claire. "You won't see them together after tonight. You'll be away at school and you've already started making new friends. You'll meet someone new that'll be better for you than Rick ever would have been."

She was absolutely right, but at that moment, all I could do was see red. Less than two weeks ago, Rick fed me his sob story that he "just couldn't *feel* anything" for anyone. Fast forward two weeks later and here he was, right in front of me, feelin' on Candy's booty like R. Kelly. If he didn't want to go out with me, why couldn't he have spared me the line of bullshit and come right out and said it?

When we got back to the house with our grocery bags in-tow, Rick took it upon himself to show us the new "trick" he had taught Candy.

"Stop that!" she squealed as Rick pitched quarters at her, asking her to bend over and pick them up, exposing her pink-and-yellow striped panties to everyone in the room.

I wanted to vomit. Could he be any more tasteless? Not that I was a paragon of taste by any means, but I would never make such a flagrant display around someone who I knew had feelings for me, much less one that I considered as a friend. I could handle them holding hands. It may have been a hard pill to swallow, but it wasn't anywhere near the slap n' tickle shenanigans that Rick was perpetrating and that Whore *du Jour* was all too happy to oblige.

"Rick always makes me do that trick for people," she giggled.

"I'm sure you don't mind turning tricks for people," I deadpanned.

That felt good. Claire and Austin looked like smirking book-ends as Candy's mouth hung open. Shortly afterwards, she and Rick left for the evening.

Speaking of slutting it up, I still had a few weeks of the summer left at home and decided I did not want to go off to college as a virgin. I was determined to lose my virginity – or at least kiss a guy – before I scampered down the college trail.

I didn't want to lose it to just anyone. It had to be someone I knew and at least cared about a little. I thought of the biggest manwhore I knew lying dormant in my stable of dudes that I dug. This was a job for Whorin' Hank!

While Hank had no problem being forward with me (you don't get much more "forward" than grazing your junk against your co-worker's ass while tending stock), I was a little nervous to proposition him to do the deed.

I had to act fast since I would be leaving town in a little more than two weeks.

I decided to approach Hank's friend, our co-worker Bill to act as the go-between. I was friendly with both Bill and his girlfriend and they were always talking about how he wished Hank would stop dipping his stick into a variety of girls and get involved in a real relationship.

One afternoon at work, I told Bill about my plight.

"Wait," he said. "Rick Sanders turned you down? And he's dating Candy Wallace? Oh, man! That's hilarious!"

"Dude." My voice was stern. "It's not funny."

"No," he said apologetically. "What he did to *you* wasn't funny. But him dating Candy Wallace is! She's the biggest whore on the local metal scene! And a total whack job. I mean, she's hot. Hank banged her. But she'll screw anyone. The saying is 'Everybody gets a piece of Candy.'

"She makes up stories to get people to think she's rich," Bill chuckled. "She tried telling me, Hank, and Chelsea that her father was a porno producer."

"Classic," I said wryly before not-so-subtly switching gears. "So, Rick's hooked up with this chick and I really want to do something with someone before I go away to school. Do you think Hank would want to do something?"

"Like what?" he asked.

"Like be the guy to take my virginity?"

"Are you serious?" Bill replied, his jaw on the floor. "Do you *really* want to lose your virginity to someone you're not in love with?"

"I like Hank. He's a cool guy. I like him as a person. And he'll pretty much bang anything."

"True," said Bill. "If you really want me to, I'll ask him for you. But if you want my honest opinion, I think it's a bad idea."

"I know what you're saying, Bill. And I really appreciate it. But it's easy for you to say. You're 'The Relationship Guy.' You're a good dude, chicks dig you, and you're with someone you really care about. I don't have that luxury."

"You're going away to school," he reasoned. "In Philadelphia. There are tons of guys out there. And probably a lot who would love to go out with you and have a *real* relationship with you."

"Yeah," I said skeptically. "There *are* a lot of guys out there and with my luck, they'll all be assholes. At least with Hank, I know him. We're friends. We find each other attractive... At least I *think* he finds me attractive. I just want it done and over with and to close a chapter on my life before I start over."

"Okay," he hesitated. "I'll chat with him and see if he's interested."

A week later, I hadn't heard anything from Bill or Hank about my indecent proposal. I was getting desperate.

"Did you get a chance to ask him?"

Bill grimaced. "I did. But I think you might want to talk to him yourself."

"Uh-oh." This wasn't good.

"He thinks you're joking."

"Are you kidding me?! Why would he think that?"

"I don't know," he shrugged. "He just thinks you were kidding. Maybe you should talk to him about it. He didn't believe me when I said you were serious."

"Okay. I think he's on next shift. I'll talk to him around closing time. Thanks for going to bat for me, though. I mean, it was awkward and I didn't want to put you in a weird position, but I really appreciate it."

"Don't worry about it!" Bill waved it off with a laugh. "Everything's cool. Just talk with Hank and see what he says."

At the end of our shift, I steeled myself for my conversation with Hank. I had to be flirty, yet firm.

"Nova-Bendova!" Hank announced as I walked towards him in the abandoned back room near the time clock. "What can I do for ya?"

I laughed at his customary greeting. "I think you know," I said in a futile attempt at being seductive. "Did Bill talk to you?"

He looked like he was about to shit himself. I'd never seen the usually suave Hank caught so off guard. "About what?"

"About me losing my virginity to you."

"Oh. That. I thought you were kidding."

"No," I said matter-of-factly. "I wasn't kidding. I'm going away to school in a week and I really wanted to lose my virginity before I got to college. I figure you're the guy I know with the most experience, you know what you're doing, and you're hot. At least it'll be memorable and it won't be with some random guy."

Hank was clearly taken aback. "Whoa. I had no idea you were serious. I mean, that's cool. But...." He breathed deeply, taking both of my hands in his. "I know you love wrestling and I love wrestling, so I'm gonna break it down for you like this, baby doll: I know you want to get in the ring with the champ. Everybody does. But I don't think you're ready for it yet. You've gotta get some experience in the ring."

"But I don't *have* experience, Hank," I whined. "That's why I wanted you to be the one to show me the ropes."

"Nova," he said, still holding my hands in his. "Someday, you're going to find a guy that you're going to want to be tag team partners with. And it's going to be awesome. You might go through a few jobbers, but I know you've got it in you to be a champ like me someday and rule the ring. But until you find that tag team partner that you're meant to go off and be The Rockers with – the Marty Jannetty to your Shawn Michaels – I can't let you get in the ring with the champ. I'm sorry, doll face, but that's just the way it is."

It was the most bizarre way I've ever been turned down in my entire life. On one hand, I was crushed. Hank was supposed to be my sexual Obi-Wan Kenobi. He was my only hope! Hank was a carnal god who prided himself on banging anything. Instead, the plan to make *Star Whores* a reality was scuttled. I wasn't Princess Lay-A-Me. There was no Luke Thighwalker in my future. My sexual future was now in a galaxy far, far away. Very far away.

Once again, there was a Prohibition in my pants and I was resigned to the role of Agent Elliot Ness of *The Unfuckables*. Great.

On the other hand, he had a point. I shouldn't just slam down my V-card for anyone to take off the table. Maybe Bill had talked to him beforehand, putting his own moral spin on the situation. Or maybe Hank, despite being a total man-slut, really *did* have a heart of gold.

"I got a couple things that might make you feel better, though," Hank said, reaching into the front pocket of his black jeans.

Oh, Christ. Don't tell me after all this, he's going to whip out his pisser right here in the stock room.

He didn't. Instead, Hank produced a cassette tape with a bright orange cover from his pocket. "It's Last Bastion's demo tape!" he declared proudly, handing it to me. "Play it for all your new little friends in Philly and show them what real metal is."

"Sweet!" I looked it over and recognized a lot of the songs.

"There's some good pics of me on the interior, too, so you can show some of your new pals what a real man looks like, too."

All of a sudden, I felt like shit again.

"What's wrong?"

"Rick took a bunch of the pictures for the album. I remember you coming up to him in the club and asking him if he'd take some photos for the demo."

"Yeah," replied Hank. "He did. But I got some news about Rick that I think you're going to enjoy just as much as that demo."

I cocked an eyebrow.

"Here's a little tip. Candy dumped Rick a couple days ago."

"No way!"

"Way," he grinned. "Dumped him. Cold. She left with another dude at the club. I mean, it was inevitable. Almost all of us have banged her. She's a complete slut. Not a bad lay, but nothing mind-blowing."

"Yeah," I retorted grimly. "From what I understand, Rick lost his virginity to her."

"Probably," Hank breezed. "She'll fuck just about anyone. She's one of those girls who tries too hard to fit in on the scene. Only she doesn't have any talent besides her twat. Sex is her way of trying to fit in."

I stared at the floor, not wanting to think about the particulars of Rick getting a piece of Candy. *He* got to lose his virginity. Why not me?

On the other hand, Rick lost it to someone who dumped him less than a week later. *And* had his heart broken *and* was publicly humiliated the same way he tried to publicly torment me with his whorish hijinks at Austin's house. Served the fucker right.

"Do yourself a favor. Don't try to make a play for him now that he's broken up with her. You're headed to Philly. You might not get a guy who's as good in the ring or as naturally gorgeous as I am," said Hank without a trace of facetiousness in his voice. He meant that shit. "But you'll find someone who will treat you right and won't go after the first thing that flashes her cooze at him.... Remember: Philly, baby!"

I laughed and managed to muster a smile as Hank pulled me in for a goodbye hug.

And then he grabbed my ass.

That night, as I was clocking out, the gears in my brain started to turn. I replayed Hank's words in my head again, thinking of the adventure that lay ahead of me and all that I was leaving behind. I placed a quick call to Claire and Austin, telling them about my conversation with Hank and asked them to pick me up.

There was one last thing I had to do before I left for Philly while I still had the courage.

Minutes later, Austin's Beetle pulled up in front of the mall. Claire got out of the car and pushed the seat back, letting me squeeze into the backseat.

"I'm glad Hank made the decision for you," she said. "That would have been a huge mistake."

"I know." My voice was somber with the realization that I escaped the same fate that befell Rick. "How is he?"

"Hasn't come out of his room except to sneak a few slices of lunchmeat from the fridge," said Austin.

"Damn. That's bad."

On the drive to Austin's house, I sat silently in the backseat, mulling over what might be the last words I'd ever say to Rick. I remembered the year I sat on those unresolved issues, not having had a chance to clear the air with Rick before he moved. There was no way I was going to let things just lay there on a bad note for a second time.

Claire and Austin waited in the car as I climbed the stairs to Austin's house and let myself inside. Taking a deep breath, I knocked on the door to the guest room where Rick was staying.

"Come in."

"Hey," I said, opening the door.

"Hey."

"So, what's up?"

"Same shit, different day."

I could see we were off to a fine start. "I'm sorry."

"For what?"

"Well... The obvious. But I'm sorry I made that comment the last time I saw you with her, too."

"Nah. You were right. She was a big slut."

I snorted, trying to stifle a laugh. "Sorry. Not laughing at you. Just laughing at the slut thing."

"Who told you?"

"Hank."

"Shit. Everyone knows, don't they?"

"Kinda," I hedged. "Yeah. I think I was the last to know."

"I feel pretty fucking stupid. You know, I owe you an apology, too. I didn't need to parade her around, flashing her panties and everything in front of you. You didn't deserve that."

"No. I didn't. But I don't blame you. I was a dick to you a lot of times for no good reason."

"True," Rick replied. Half smiling, half serious. "You know, I never really had girls interested in me. You were the first. I'm not really good with the idea of someone having feelings for me and I'm sorry if I hurt you."

"All things considered, you were really nice about it. For the most part. I mean, what were you supposed to do? Go out with me when you'd rather chew glass?"

"Claire went out with me and she really didn't want to."

"Yeah. That didn't work out too well. False hope is worse than no hope."

"You know, I did the same shit to you when I was going out with Claire that I did with Candy. I think I rubbed it in more than I should have."

"It happens," I shrugged.

"Guess I got paid back in the end, huh?"

"No. You didn't deserve that."

Rick was quiet for a moment before he spoke again. "Last year. During senior year, I had a really good girl. We dated for about six months. Went to the prom. We decided we'd just go our separate ways after graduation. I was going to Parsons and she was going to U of Maryland. I kick myself that I didn't lose it to her before we split. Instead, I waited. Then I went and did this stupid shit."

I didn't know what to say to Rick. Here he was, spilling his guts to me and all I could think of was how glad I was that I didn't make the same mistake and lose my virginity to Hank.

"I'm sorry it didn't work out."

"Not your fault," he laughed ruefully, shaking his head.

I gave his hand a squeeze. To my surprise, he squeezed back.

There was nothing sexual or romantic behind the shared gesture. Rick was my friend. It took me four long years to realize we'd never be anything more than friends and I was more than okay with that.

CHAPTER FOURTEEN
MIXED SIGNALS

The week after I got closure on things with Rick and Hank, I packed my bags, some family photos, several new notebooks and pens, and my favorite stuffed animal and headed off to college.

Orion and my parents loaded my things into our car, making the trek with me to Philadelphia. In a rare display of emotion, tears welled in Mom's eyes as she gave me a big hug and told me she loved me. Dad wasn't quite as emotional, but told me that he would pick me up in two weeks for a visit back home. I shook hands with my brother and told him to call me if he needed anything – or just to shoot the shit for a good laugh.

It was strange to be this far from my family. Barring three days on a school-sponsored seventh grade camping trip during The Frankie Gilroy Years, I'd never been away from home for this long. At least with the camping trip and freshman orientation, there was a definite return home in sight. Now it would be weeks before I would see my family again.

I remembered a time when I wanted nothing more than to get the hell out of Fletcher and out of my parents' house. I wanted to be on my own. Now that I really *was* on my own, I was more homesick than I ever could have imagined.

That first night on campus, I went outside to the courtyard to think. I sat down on a bench and started writing down everything I was feeling and everything I had gone through in the last year of high school and what I hoped to accomplish in college. I wanted to find out who I really was.

For years, I felt constrained by my surroundings. Here, in a city as large as Philadelphia, there were a lot more people like myself who wouldn't bat an eyelash over what type of music I listened to or what I dressed like. I'd have a chance to discover a whole new life for myself and find someplace where I could freely be who I was without being condemned for it.

And, as Hank suggested, I might even find a boyfriend while I was out here.

I looked forward to heading to my new classes in a few days and learning new things.

I missed my family, but I had a lot of new friends who I clicked with almost instantly. We called each other once we received our room assignments in the mail to let each other know where we would be dorming.

The day my parents dropped me off, none of my friends had moved in yet.

Jerry and his family arrived early that Sunday. He had already unpacked, set up his computer, and hung several black-light Sublime posters on his side of the dorm room.

Jerry and I grabbed lunch in the cafeteria before we decided to check out where everyone else was.

"Let's go see where that skinny little shit Boone is," grinned Jerry. "If the gang's all here, we should start the school year off right." He mimed smoking a joint and instantaneously getting high off of the hit. Jerry was majoring in Pharmacy.

After a surprisingly decent cafeteria lunch, Jerry and I ambled over to the third floor of the dorms. Sure enough, the door to room 304 was propped open. Judging by the lava lamp on the desk and Dropkick Murphys poster already on the wall, it was a safe bet that Boone was in the process of moving in.

Boone and his parents came through the door, each carrying boxes of various sizes. Jerry and I offered to help them unpack and find places for things as Boone introduced us.

Mrs. Santini extended her hand to me in a warm, friendly greeting. She was a short, thin woman with long, curly hair and glasses, dressed in a brightly-colored peasant dress.

"It's so nice to meet you!"

Boone's equally cheerful father also shook my hand and issued a very pleasant hello.

By the time we'd helped them carry up several milk crates of CDs and a large suitcase of clothes, we were all chatting like old friends. Mrs. Santini and I began arranging some of the décor in Boone's room while Mr. Santini went downstairs to bring up his son's computer monitor.

She placed a large, framed photograph of the family on his desk along with a smaller, but substantially-sized photo of a fuzzy, grey cat.

"That's Boone's little brother, Bits," she said with a wink.

"Oh, God," muttered Boone in embarrassment.

"Well, he may as well be!" she exclaimed as Jerry raised an eyebrow.

"Awww!" I examined the picture of the mellow looking cat with one white paw raised in the air. "He's really cute."

"He just turned three," Boone's mother replied, beaming.

"Thank God you have Bits," Boone interjected. "With me out of the house, I don't know what you two would do."

"Oh," exclaimed Mrs. Santini. "You'll always be my baby boy! No matter where you go!" She took off his baseball cap and ruffled Boone's dark, wavy hair.

Boone had turned bright red. Jerry and I snickered. To Boone's relief, his father had just come through the door and asked him to help set up the computer and printer.

After everything had been put in its place, we walked Boone's parents back downstairs to their car. By then, the dorm was bustling with students with boxes and handcarts, moving their belongings in.

Boone's parents gave their son a goodbye hug and promised they would call him every night. "It was nice meeting you," said Mrs. Santini. "Look after my little boy when we're not here!"

"Don't worry, Mrs. S.," replied Jerry. "He's safe with us!"

Climbing back into their car, the Santinis drove away, waving from the window until they were out of sight.

"Dude! Your parents are awesome!" I exclaimed.

"Your parents are fucking crazy!" said Jerry.

"What's that supposed to mean?" asked Boone defensively.

"They're cool people, but *man*. You have a brother who's a *cat*? I like your folks, but they're just *wild*, man!"

"You have *no* idea how much they love Bits," Boone said, shaking his head back and forth, his dark curls swinging. "Mom dresses him up for holidays."

After hearing more about the further adventures of Bits the Cat, the three of us decided to head to the cafeteria to get dinner, possibly followed by a trip to the courtyard to smoke up.

Jerry, Boone, and I were an odd sight together. Jerry was a towering, hefty kid with white blonde hair, blue eyes, and a ruddy complexion. He was from Huntington, a town just 20 minutes outside of Fletcher. He had multiple piercings and a wardrobe that consisted of a seemingly unlimited supply of Adidas track pants and stoner band t-shirts.

Boone, on the other hand, was tall and lanky with curly, chin-length hair that hung from beneath a weathered baseball cap or knit beanie. He favored baggy skater pants and Vans.

And then, there was me: Short and pale with long black hair and a wardrobe best described as a cross between "Whitesnake Video Reject" and "Bargain Basement Stevie Nicks."

Jerry, Boone, and I took the stairs from Boone's third-floor dorm to my ninth-floor digs. Nearly everyone's doors were open and the girls on my all-female floor were mingling. That's how we met and became friends with my next-dorm neighbors, Carla and Liz.

Carla was a perky blonde with perfect hair, bright blue eyes, and a constant smile. She was so perennially perky that most people assumed she was full of shit. In reality, Carla was as genuinely nice as she seemed.

Her roommate, Liz, was a short, outgoing brunette with chin-length hair, a wide grin, and a sarcastic sense of humor evident within seconds of meeting her.

As I opened the door to my room to grab my purse, Carla and Liz appeared in the doorway.

"Hey!" said Carla brightly, waving at us. "I thought we heard some new voices over here!"

"Hi! I'm Liz and this is my roommate Carla We live next door in 914. Nice to meet you!"

Upon introductions, we learned Carla was majoring in Elementary Education and Liz was a Political Science major.

Somehow, something just clicked and the five of us became a tight-knit circle of friends. We were a melting pot of musical styles and academic disciplines, but somehow, we managed to find a few common threads. Of course, there was also the common bond you feel with people you party with, whether you're splitting a 40 with them or passing a joint around.

Jerry, Boone, Liz, Carla, and I spent a lot of time between classes together: grabbing lunch in the cafeteria, studying in one another's rooms, the occasional class with one another and finally, getting work study jobs together at Paley's library – which soon became our home away from the dorms.

The library was a great way to meet people on campus. The five of us – and about 30 other students ranging from freshmen to grad students – worked in the stacks. It was a pretty sweet deal. You'd walk around with your book truck, re-stocking the books that had just been checked back into the library, listening to your Walkman or Discman. The boss was flexible with hours and you could tailor them to accommodate your class schedule.

Plus, it was easy to get lost in the library and stand around talking with your coworkers.

The semester was rolling along nicely. I was really enjoying Philly and my new group of friends. My classes were interesting, I was getting good grades and having a lot of fun on top of it. At the same time, I would visit Fletcher every other weekend to hang out with my family and friends back home. It was the best of both worlds.

It was like, somehow, moving out of Fletcher had lifted a black cloud that had been hanging over my head. I felt at home. I finally fit in somewhere. The one thing that was missing was a guy. Once again, I found myself looking at one of my friends with new eyes.

I spent a lot of time with Boone and Jerry. We were like the Three Stooges and would hang out and smoke up quite a bit. There was no sexual tension between the three of us. I was, as always, "one of the guys."

Case in point: One night, Jerry, Boone, and I were toking up in the courtyard.

"You're like a guy with tits, Nova!" Jerry declared, high as a kite. "No offense. That's pretty fuckin' awesome. Most bitches piss me off when I smoke with them, but you're cool. You're like a dude."

I didn't take offense to Jerry's comment at all. It was just nice to have a bunch of friends that I felt comfortable with. I'm sure the fact that I loved weed and was always more than happy to share my stash made me more popular than I had any right to be.

Jerry and I were close friends, but I was closer with Boone. We shared the same major and were in most of each other's classes. Given the similarity of our class schedules, we ended up working matching shifts at the library. Factor in eating lunch and dinner together with our group every night, then hanging out and drinking and smoking up, Boone and I spent a lot of time together.

"Want to come over and study for the Communication Theory midterm in my room later?" he offered one afternoon in the library. "Your notes are better than mine and I want to make sure I'm not mixing up some theories."

"Sure," I said, secretly excited that he had asked me to hang out and study. When I arrived at his dorm later that afternoon, Boone was already spread out on the floor surrounded by piles of books. His hair flopped over one of his eyes as he looked up and waved at me, beckoning me to sit on the ground next to him.

I took my spiral notebook out of my backpack along with a couple granola bars and bag of yogurt raisins for us to snack on while studying.

"Nice," he replied, taking a handful of yogurt raisins.

We cracked open our books and I looked over at some of Boone's notes. His notebook was filled with band art and hand-drawn logos for bands like the Dropkick Murphys and Rancid.

"You were right," I laughed. "Your notes suck. But your artwork is pretty awesome."

"Thanks... I think."

"No. Seriously. I didn't know you had an artistic flair."

"Maybe a little," he replied sheepishly.

I noticed he also had done a logo art drawing of The Misfits amidst the plethora of new school punk and ska bands on his wall. It seemed curiously out of place.

"I didn't know you were a Misfits fan."

"Yeah. I was really into them in high school. I even quoted them in my yearbook... Do you wanna see my yearbook?"

"Hell yeah!" He made a beeline for his bottom desk drawer, taking out a blue leather tome with gold foil script on its spine.

"Were your school colors blue and white?" I asked, enraptured with discovering miniscule factoids.

"Yep."

"Mine, too!" I said it perhaps a bit too excitedly before examining his yearbook photo.

"Dude! You're wearing a suit! And no hat!"

"I know. I felt like such a dork. I felt all 'professional' and shit."

"It's not a bad look for you. Not what I'm used to, but you clean up alright." Seeing he seemed slightly embarrassed by my comment, I decided I would use my own humiliation as a buffer while bracing him for the coming unattraction. "Trust me. It's a lot better than my yearbook photo."

I proceeded to tell him about Mom's accidental yearbook substitution of a photo of me from pre-makeover sophomore year – complete with black hair, liquid eyeliner, and un-plucked orange eyebrows.

"Mom thought we had to submit black and white photos to the yearbook. The good photos – the ones where I look like I do now – were in color, so Mom swapped in a black and white one of me from sophomore year. Turns out, my photo was the only one in black and white which made it stand out even more. Great, huh?"

"Now you *have to* bring your yearbook in!" Boone urged. "I want to see this!"

After a brief interlude of yearbook-gazing, we went back to studying. An hour later, Jerry and the rest of the gang knocked at the door, ready to grab some dinner before more midterm cramming. We had already established a rule that no one was allowed to drink or smoke up until all tests had been taken and term papers written.

Following midterms, all bets were off. We planned a huge party right before mid-semester break. The afternoon of the party, Jerry, Boone and I made a massive beer run, smuggling our malt liquor contraband into the dorms.

We decided to have the party in Carla and Liz's room, which had become our group's designated hangout. Everyone else had a roommate who either A.) didn't party or B.) they couldn't stand. Carla and Liz being friends and roommates made their room the most logical place to hang out – plus, it was right next door to my room and one floor beneath Jerry's room.

That night, I got bombed and experienced The Four Stages of Drunkenness.

Sure, my future was my priority and I wanted to learn as much as possible, but I also wanted to enjoy myself as much as I could.

I was "responsible," to a degree, with my partying. In order to maintain my scholarship, I had to pull at least a 3.0 every semester. I knew that if I still wanted to drink and smoke up and have access to all these things, I needed to keep my scholarship.

My grades were high. And so was I.

That semester, I had been suppressing a lot. I was happy to have new friends and begin a new chapter of my life. Yet, at the same time, I was homesick and missed my parents and brother. While I was starting to develop feelings for Boone, I couldn't help but remember how fresh my wounds still were from everything that went down with Rick. I couldn't help but think about how I spent nearly four years throwing myself at a guy who wasn't interested in the slightest.

As if all that wasn't occupying enough space in my brain, I kept hearing that that "if you don't get laid by freshman year in college, there's no hope for you." That sentence danced around inside my head constantly. It made perfect sense. Seeing how busy I was with juggling a full class schedule, maintaining a 3.0 average, and holding down a job at the library, I could only imagine that things would get busier when I had an internship and even more intense courses within my major.

It was a lot of pressure all at once. Although I was doing well in my classes and had new, close friends on campus, I was scared, nervous, and even a little depressed.

What I liked about having such easy access to booze and weed was that it had a calming, numbing effect on me. Depending on your body chemistry, drinking and smoking pot can mask your pain and allow you to push it back so that it can't be felt – or it can bring that pain right up to the surface.

That night, I pounded back a few St. Ides Special Brews and a 40 or two of Olde E. Before I could begin skipping down the merry Blackout Drunk Trail, the Four Stages of Drunkenness kicked in.

As par for the course of Stage 1, I was a giddy, happy drunk. I was in a good mood, hanging out and laughing with everyone.

Then, the second stage – better known as "feelin' it" – reared its head. The room started to spin and I realized I probably drank more than I should have. When you're drunk, "feelin' it" is the last lucid stage where you are still reasonably in control.

By the time Stage 3 set in, I had already sat down on the floor in the corner of the room. Stage 3 varies for everyone, depending on one's own unique body chemistry and frame of mind at that point. You can either turn into an angry drunk or find yourself hit with a case of the crying jags, sobbing in the corner.

Suffice to say, I was balled up in a fetal position on Liz's bed, rocking myself back and forth.

Carla noticed me sitting in the corner, wondering if I had fallen asleep. She was pretty tanked herself but was sweet enough to ask me what was wrong.

"I'm okay," I sniffed, trying to bury my head in the pillow.

"Something's obviously wrong," she said reaching over and giving me a hug.

That was all it took to for the dam to burst and the water-works to come flooding. In a sober state, I would have never cried in public, let alone around a guy that I had a crush on. I'd have sooner embraced the angry drunk stage than show vulnerability.

I wasn't used to people hugging me. I hugged her back as I embarked upon a blathering torrent about how worried I was that I'd never get a boyfriend.

"Having a boyfriend is overrated!" said Liz, waving her hand and laughing. It was easy for her to say. Liz had been with the same guy since high school. Her boyfriend was so madly in love with her that he was transferring to Paley from a school where he had a full scholarship just to be with her. It was also easier for Liz to say since she hardly had anything to drink and was the only sober one in the bunch that night. I appreciated her gesture, but I don't think she quite understood.

"You're still thinking about all these fucking dudes from back home?" asked Jerry. "Fuck that!"

"You can do a lot better," said Boone quietly, sitting down on the bed and putting an arm around me. "That's in the past now. You're here now."

"I know. It's over and done." I felt my voice quavering. "I can't do it all over again, but sometimes, I really miss home."

"So do I," interjected Jerry. "But it's still there. You can go back and visit whenever you want on weekends. I miss my girlfriend, but this is where I gotta be to do something with my life."

"I'm so embarrassed," I said. "I hate being like this in public. I hate crying." It was true. Normally, I would drink alone and spare myself from putting on a shit show like this. I liked to keep up that tough broad façade. If I was in my right mind, I never would have allowed myself to have a meltdown of this caliber in front of people.

"Don't be embarrassed," said Carla in a soothing voice. Now I understood why she wanted to go into elementary education. She was so good at being calm and comforting. "Everyone has to cry sometime."

"Fuck," I slurred, finally snapping out of it. "I promise I won't puke on your bed, Liz."

She laughed and gave me a hug. I perked up, my mood lifted by all of the people who were around me at this point.

This was when the Fourth Stage of Drunkenness took hold.

The fabled Fourth Stage is the point when you realize that you've either been assaulting people physically and/or verbally or that you've just bawled your eyes out, soliciting unwarranted amounts of sympathy from everyone in the room. This stage is consistently accompanied by a profound sense of shame and the possession of a preternaturally heightened sense of social consciousness. You realize just what a fuck up you've been scant moments ago and desperately want to encourage everyone else around you to avoid fucking up on a similar level.

In some cases, when you're alone and not surrounded by other people, Stage Four is the point where you start drunk dialing friends and family members to tell them how much you love them and how badly you want them to succeed at whatever it is they want to do. When you're not alone, you go around hugging everyone, telling them how much you love them and how grateful you are to have them in your life.

Following a serious round of group hugging that would have put *The Golden Girls* to shame, we headed to the courtyard to smoke up before migrating back to Liz and Carla's, where we all wound up falling asleep on the floor of their room.

When I woke up, I found myself curled up in a comfortable spot on the girls' purple shag area rug.

Looking around at my equally inebriated compatriots, I realized that, for some strange reason, they still liked me after seeing me at my worst. Boone, curled up on the other end of the shag rug, opened one eye and waved to me.

It was a good feeling.

I wasn't sure if Boone liked me in a "boyfriend-girlfriend" way, but I felt very comfortable around him. I never had a male friend before who was that kind and affectionate towards me, much less one who I enjoyed spending so much time and didn't grate on my nerves.

I really wanted to ask him out, to see if he was as interested in turning our friendship into something else. However, from past experience, I was afraid that I would ruin our friendship if he didn't feel the same way.

After midterms, Jerry's girlfriend from back home in Huntington paid him a visit. She hung out with us quite a bit the weekend she was in town. She liked her a lot and she was cool to Boone – but she seemed to love bossing Jerry around.

Jerry's girlfriend smoked up with us, but complained about the quality of the weed that he had picked up. It was cool to have another person to smoke up with and show around campus, but something felt off. For someone who hadn't seen her boyfriend in a few weeks, you would have thought she'd act happier to see him.

After his girlfriend left, Jerry broached this subject to Boone, asking him what he thought of her and of them as a couple.

"She's got attitude," he replied. "I love a girl with attitude. I think girls who say what they mean are cool."

"Yeah," said Jerry slowly. "I love attitude on a chick."

"It really is hot," Boone said. "I kind of like being bossed around."

Hearing this, the gears began to click in my head: *Guys liked girls with attitude? Really? They like being told what to do?*

Now I was confused. I always showed "attitude" around Rick and he wouldn't touch me with his mom's dick. Then again, I was nice to him, too, so maybe that was my problem?

I made a mental note that instead of being Boone's buddy or being "a guy with tits," I would show him some more "attitude" – whatever that was.

That didn't work out too well.

There was this guy named Lou who sat in front of me and Boone in the lecture hall for our Communication Theory class. Emptying out my backpack in search of a pen, I placed a bunch of CDs on the seat next to me that I had been carting around to listen to during my shift at the library. Spying my copy of Kiss's *Revenge* album, he immediately jumped on it.

"You know," Lou said, cocking a lascivious eyebrow, "people tell me I look a lot like Gene Simmons." In an effort to further that connection, he stuck out his long tongue in emulation of Kiss's "demon," wiggling it back and forth.

He actually did look a bit like Gene Simmons. Lou was tall and solid with long, curly black hair that he wore pulled into a topknot. As evidenced by his stripe of light brown roots, the black hair was a dye job.

"I can see the resemblance," I replied, refraining from rolling my eyes.

"I'm Jewish, too," he said. "You know what that means, right? I'm circumcised."

"So, that means you don't have any problems with smegma?" I offered, not really getting the gist of what he was saying.

He laughed slightly before informing me that it meant that his junk was cut and, therefore, more enjoyable for women.

"My band is playing in town in a couple weeks. I sing and play bass... Like Gene Simmons. Let me know if you're going to come down and I'll make sure to tell some of my other groupies to stay home that night."

I smiled one of those non-committal half-smiles that barely veiled that I had just thrown up a little in my mouth. Lou sat back down in his chair, pulling up the arm rest and flipping to a clean page in his notebook. He turned around to wiggle his tongue at me.

"What the fuck was that?!" asked Boone, clearly as dumb-struck as I was.

"That," I replied. "Is a man who thinks he's a rock star."

"So you're his 'groupie,' now?" teased Boone.

"In order to be a groupie, you need to actually like a guy's band. I don't even *know* this guy's band."

"Would you?" he asked, still trying to bust my balls. "You wanna hook up with Lou the Jew?"

"No way," I said. "He's not a bad looking guy. But the dude isn't even subtle! He doesn't even know me, yet comes right up and propositions me? Shady!"

In the weeks that followed, Lou the Jew enacted several variations of this schpiel. I tried to be as polite as possible in declining his invitations. Either I was either too stupefied by his come-on tactics or too gutless to tell him to fuck off outright.

One day in class, Lou struck up a similar conversation with another girl, undoubtedly making her day. As he reiterated his bit about his anteater-like tongue and his kosher salami, Lou bent over the desk in front of me, making sure that his ample bottom jutted directly in my face.

I wondered if his attempt at giving me the stink face was purely accidental. I got my answer when he turned around mid-sentence and wiggled his tongue at me again.

Finished conversing with his latest victim, Lou sat back down in his chair

"So, Nova," he purred, stroking his goatee. "How are you today?"

Given how hard Lou was trying to copy his vocal inflections and mannerisms, I wondered if this guy had an identity outside of trying to be a pale imitation of the Kiss frontman, minus the finesse, talent, and business acumen. If I wasn't so disgusted, this would have been hilarious.

I looked anxiously at Boone, doodling away in his notebook. His face was hidden, but I could still see him smirking underneath his ballcap.

Desperate, I kicked Boone lightly under our adjacent desks, trying to get him to save me.

Boone looked over at me, narrowing his eyes as I widened mine in panic, attempting to send a telepathic message begging for help.

Instead, Boone looked back down and continued drawing on his notebook.

Across from me, Lou cleared his throat. "I said, 'How are you today?'"

"Oh! Sorry, Lou. I didn't hear you. I'm a little under the weather," I lied.

"Hmmm," he mused. "Maybe you just need a back rub?" Once again, he stuck his tongue out and wiggled it, to and fro. This dude was straight out of a cartoon.

"Nah," I replied. "I'm good. Just my sinuses acting up. I've been a veritable fountain of phlegm the past few days." Short of whipping out a picture of Lemon Party, nothing could be a bigger boner-killer than the mention of snot.

My ploy worked. "Good luck with that," smirked Lou before pivoting back on his seat.

Boone remained silent throughout the rest of the class. He didn't pass me any notes or make any comments as the professor lectured. Instead, he stared straight ahead at the podium, avoiding eye-contact with me during the hour-and-twenty minute class.

Leaving class, Boone walked briskly, his long legs carrying him a solid five paces ahead of me as I raced to catch up to him. We were headed in the same direction towards our shift at the library.

"Wait up, Boone!" I called, managing to finally catch up with him. "Are you mad at me or something?"

"No," he responded curtly.

"Are you sure?" I prodded. "I'm sorry I kicked you under the desk. I didn't hurt you or anything, did I?"

"No. I just know what you were trying to do when you kicked me."

"Huh? What do you mean" I asked, trying to play dumb. I was pretty sure I knew what he meant.

"Yeah. You wanted me to get involved when Lou the Jew was hitting on you."

"So? I was kinda hoping you'd play wingman and help bail me out on this one. He's been pretty persistent and really obnoxious with his overtures lately."

"Aww, did Nova want me to put my arm around her?" he intoned mockingly. "I'm not your boyfriend. You need to learn how to bail yourself out of these situations on your own."

"I did," I replied adamantly, recalling the oh-so-classy mention of my lung cheese to Lou.

"Whatever," Boone said dismissively. "I think you just wanted me to pretend to be your boyfriend."

"No, I didn't. But it would have been cool if you stepped in and tried to change the subject. I'm not saying you had to pretend you were my boyfriend or anything. But you could have been a better friend and said *something* instead of sitting there and watching me squirm."

"Oh," said Boone condescendingly. "I'm a bad friend because I wouldn't put my arm around you or lie and tell this guy I'm going out with you."

"I didn't say that," I snapped. "All I'm saying is you could have helped me out instead of thinking it was hilarious to watch this guy hit on me all the time. Just maybe ask me a question or something class-related. I'm not saying you had to pretend we're dating or anything."

"Whatever. It's not my fault you're not getting laid."

"Whoa! What the fuck crawled up your ass, dude?"

"You're being a spoiled bitch and expecting people – specifically, me – to bail you out whenever something bad happens."

"You know what?" I said with disgust. "Fuck you."

The corners of Boone's mouth twisted angrily as he flipped me the bird and walked in the opposite direction.

"Hey, genius," I called after him. "The library is that way."

"Tell John I don't feel like working with a bitch today." With that, Boone slammed the exit door of Masterson Hall behind him.

"Who's the bitch now," I muttered under my breath. "Fucking pussy. Calling out of work."

Nevertheless, I made up a story and told John, our boss, that Boone wasn't feeling well and called out sick today.

I figured Boone was just man-strating and would snap out of it soon enough.

That didn't happen. When Jerry, Carla, Liz and I showed up at Boone's door to pick him up for dinner that night, he cautiously peered out his door. Seeing me, he insisted he had some other things to do and wouldn't be coming.

In the cafeteria, I told everyone what happened earlier. Following dinner, Jerry, bearing some Thai bud, visited Boone in his room in an effort to try to make peace between us.

"You're being a real drama queen about this," he said. "Everything's cool. She's not pissed at you."

"Well, I'm pissed at her. She said 'fuck you' to me."

Jerry laughed. "That's it? You missed work today because she told you 'fuck you'? You need to calm down, dude. It's not that deep."

By contrast, while Jerry had tried to run interference for me, Liz was acting as Boone's ambassador.

"You really shouldn't have said 'fuck you' to him, Nova," she chided gently. "People tend to get upset when the f-bomb gets dropped."

"I feel bad, but he said a lot worse. This whole thing is just stupid. I want things to go back to normal and be friends, but he's the one who's calling off work and avoiding being around everyone if I happen to be around. He's on his period or something."

"I've talked to him. He was really offended that you said that to him"

So much for Boone liking "a girl with attitude."

"He felt like you were being really unfair to him and putting him on the spot to make him pretend he was your boyfriend."

"I didn't say he had to," I defended myself. "I was just looking for some help in fending off this goon who kept macking on me."

"He mentioned something about that."

"I didn't mean to put him in an awkward position, but he just sat there laughing at me while I was being treated like a dumb whore by some douchebag."

You should have told Lou the Jew to fuck off instead of Boone."

She was right. Liz and Boone were really close friends. Jerry and I were the "brutes" of our circle of friends. Liz was still fun and spontaneous, but was a bit more diplomatic in her dealings with people. Typical Poly-Sci major.

"I'll try to talk with him tomorrow," I said. "If you see him before that, tell him I really am sorry."

"I will. He's a sensitive kid. He's an only child, so that's where a lot of it comes from. He's not used to people being that blunt with him."

"I had no idea he would react that way. I don't like him being mad at me."

"You know what I think," said Liz with a slight smile. "I think you like Boone."

Carla's ears perked up. "Really?!"

"No," I denied the allegations although they were true. "He's just a good friend and I hate having a good friend mad at me."

"I don't know," teased Liz. "You said the other night that you're completely over Rick and we haven't seen you checking out anyone at the library. I think you have a crush on Boone!"

"Honestly, I really don't. We're just friends."

"Aww!" exclaimed Carla, ever-willing to play Cupid. "I think they'd make a cute couple!"

"I don't know," replied Liz, mulling over the thought of Boone and I. "I don't see you guys clicking in the long haul. No offense or anything. You have a lot in common, but I think your temperaments are too different to really work out relationship-wise."

I understood what Liz was saying and there was some validity to her theory. However, I was expecting a bit more support from her.

"It's a moot point," I interjected. "I'm not interested in him as anything more than a friend. And I just want us to be friends again."

I was overcome with a strange sense of déjà vu that I had experienced with the brief, shining turd of a moment that was Rick and Claire dating.

Sure, Liz already had a boyfriend – one who had been camping out on the sly in her room until he was formally enrolled at Paley – but she and Boone were pretty close and spent a lot of time together, too. I wondered if maybe she had a thing for Boone herself.

I brushed the feeling off. I already had enough to worry about. Instead, I chalked her verdict on Boone and I as a potential couple as Liz being totally honest, trying to spare everyone undue grief down the road.

The next day, I trudged to the lecture hall for Communication Theory. I sat down in my usual seat. So far, Boone hadn't shown up. Thankfully, neither had Lou the Jew.

When Boone finally did materialize, he put his backpack on one of the seats before sitting two seats away from me. Normally, we would sit right next to each other. He stared straight ahead, making a big production of getting a pen out of his backpack and turning to a fresh page in his spiral-bound notebook.

How passive-aggressive of you. Rather than saying it aloud, I moved over one more seat, allowing Boone's backpack on the chair between us to act as a Berlin Wall-like barrier.

"Are we really going to do this again?" I asked quietly. "I don't want to fight with you, Boone."

He kept staring forward, tilting his head towards me in a vague sense of acknowledgement.

"Look," I continued. "I'm sorry I said that to you and I'm really sorry if I made you uncomfortable. That was not my intent. I'm going to go back to my chair, but if you want to grab a coffee or something after class, maybe we can talk about this."

I moved back to my seat, attempting to pay attention for the full, agonizing hour and twenty minutes.

After class, Boone walked out slowly, allowing me to catch up to him before he finally turned and looked at me.

"Did you want to talk to me about something?" His tone was flat.

""I'm sorry I told you 'fuck you.' I was just really angry and hurt and blurted out the first thing that came to mind. I didn't think you would be so upset about it. To me, saying 'fuck you' is nothing. I figured we were good enough friends that it would roll off your back and things would go back to normal."

"Well, most people don't go around saying 'fuck you' to their friends."

"No. They don't. It doesn't make what I said right, but I was really upset myself and I'm sorry if I hurt your feelings. Where I'm from, you say 'fuck you' to someone and a half hour later, you knock on the door to their room and go pick up a pizza together. You don't dwell on it. I didn't think it would be a big deal."

"Look, I know that you and Jerry are from the same Bumblefuck area. He didn't seem to think it was such a big deal, either, but *I* do. That shit might be fine in Fletcher or Huntington, but where I'm from, it's a fucked up thing to say to your friends."

"For what it's worth, I'm sorry and I hope you can accept my apology."

"In all honesty, Nova, I don't know. There are a lot of issues tied into this."

"Seriously? So you chose to fly off the handle because I said 'fuck you' and use that as a springboard? Do you have a problem with me that you haven't told me about?"

"It's not really a problem. I'm just tired of you complaining that you're single. You bring it on yourself. You're too picky."

I was ready to explode. Here I was apologizing to him and then he turns around and throws this shit in my face. "Dude. If you're referring to Lou the Jew, it's not a matter of being picky.

Lou is a total manwhore. I'm pretty hard to offend – obviously, if I'm the type of person who doesn't get all butt hurt for days if I hear 'fuck you'. But this guy was pretty fucking offensive, as far as I'm concerned."

"So, you think Lou is a manwhore?" Boone replied with a snarl. "Oh. Okay. How is he different from Hank? That guy you used to work with that you wanted to hook up with? *He* was a manwhore, too and you wanted to have sex with him. You have a double standard. It was okay for Hank to grind on you, but Lou saying things to you is inappropriate? Is that because you don't find him attractive?"

"That's different," I said. "I actually knew Hank and was friends with him. And I found him attractive. Yeah, maybe that does factor into it. But so what?! That's *my* decision. Why would I want to lose my virginity or randomly hook up with someone I don't even know just because they want to pork me? I don't see why *my* being selective should be such a huge problem with *you*."

"You could get laid or have a boyfriend if you weren't so picky. Whenever we would get really drunk or high, you'd talk about Rick or One-Eyed Jack or any of the other guys who turned you down. I'm just tired of the whining."

I was fuming. "Look, I'm over this whole thing with Rick. It's not even on my radar anymore. I'm fine. I'm over it. I haven't mentioned him in a long time. And the only reason I told the story about One-Eyed Jack was because it was funny. People do that when they get drunk! Tell funny, fucked up stories. And for the record, some of the shit *you've* said to me over the past couple days is way worse than me simply telling you 'fuck you.'"

"Whatever."

"Whatever. Whatever," I replied, mocking him. "That's all you say. You know, we can't all be like you, Boone. You've never talked about anyone you used to date, just girls you've screwed. Not everyone can be a cold, unfeeling fish like you."

"I'm not a cold fish at all. *You're* the one who has all these little nicknames for people. *'One-Eyed Jack'? 'Lou the Jew'?* That's so racist."

"Are you kidding me? Fine. Since you're throwing shit in my face that I said when I was drunk, let's toss out some of the things *you* say, too. This is coming from the guy who would talk shit about his friend's fat mother, saying when she bent over she had an 'ass nut.' And for the record, *you're* the one who came up with 'Lou the Jew'!

"Yeah, but you keep referring to him as that!"

"Please," I replied. "I'm half Jewish. My dad is Jewish. That gives me a free pass."

"Oh," he replied quietly. "I didn't know that."

"Yeah, dude. Jew-ish."

"That's cool. Didn't realize it, with your last name and all."

"Yeah. Dad's mom was Jewish and his dad was Cherokee. Crazy mix, huh?"

"That's bizarre! But cool." I took this as a sign that our Cold War was beginning to thaw.

"You know, dude," I said. "I understand why you were so upset. You think I put you on the spot to pretend to be my boyfriend. I know I've complained a lot about being single. But, I think you were thinking I was expecting you to step up and pretend to be something you're not. That was *so* not my intent. The last thing I wanted to do was make you uncomfortable. The thing that hurt me the most was that you sat there and laughed while Lou was being a total pig. You didn't have to pretend to be my boyfriend, but maybe just asked me to look over something with you to get me away from the guy."

"No," Boone said, his tone much more even. "I understand. I know you've dealt with a lot of assholes, so maybe I misread you on that. And I'm sorry for some of the mean things I said. I was upset and hurt, too." He looked down at his olive green Vans sneakers before looking back up at me. "But I still think you're too picky about guys."

"Maybe I am," I laughed. "But I don't want to date anyone just to *say* I dated *someone*. I can't see dropping my v-card to someone I don't care about. I almost did and was lucky it didn't turn out that way."

"I understand," Boone replied. "I wish I lost mine to someone I cared about. It was more or less something to just get it over with."

"Wow. I'm really sorry." I said, somewhat shocked. "So, I guess you can bear with me if I whine sometimes that I'm single?" I added with a smirk.

Boone cracked a smile. "Yeah. I'll put up with your shit."

"Cool. And I owe you a coffee. If we go now, we can still get to the library on time."

"I could really go for a cappuccino," Boone agreed, the two of us walking together at a steady pace towards the lunch trucks.

I was relieved to have my friend back. At the same time, I was more confused than a vegan at KFC about how Boone felt about me. Did he see me as nothing more than a friend, the proverbial "guy with tits"? Did he know I liked him? If so, was he repulsed by the mere thought of having to pretend to be my boyfriend? Was he insisting that I was "too picky" so that I would hop on Lou the Jew's hamentashen and get off his back?

Or, did he have feelings for me and regret that he had lost his virginity to someone he didn't care about because he finally found someone he *did* care for? Was that person me? Maybe he was pissed because I was complaining about all the guys I couldn't have when he was right under my nose and I was too wrapped up in my past to see it?

I decided to tell someone how I felt about Boone so I could get some feedback on the situation. During our shift at the library, I told Carla. Carla was always telling me about her latest crushes and was one of those people who was in love with the idea of love.

"Really? I knew it!" Her blue eyes lit up. "I knew you liked Boone!"

"I wanted to tell someone. I know you and Liz already figured it out, so..."

"Aww!" Carla sighed. "This is so cool! I think you guys would be so cute together! He's tall, you're short. You both like to smoke weed. You both have the same major, which means you can get jobs together someday."

"That's a long way off."

"That doesn't matter!" Carla exclaimed cheerily. "All that matters is that you're in love. That's so adorable!"

"I don't want to jump the gun. I don't know if he likes me back in that way."

"I don't know." Carla's voice rose an octave higher thanks to her bubbling excitement. "You two spend a lot of time together. You spend a lot of time together with Jerry, too, but I don't see that sort of closeness or relationship-y thing between you and Jerry as much as I see it with you and Boone."

Just then, Liz came around the corner with her cart of books.

"Psst!" called Carla, motioning her towards us, hidden deep in the east wing of the second floor stacks.

Liz smiled and waved, abandoning her book truck and joining us.

"What are you two up to?" she asked in a playful, conspiratorial way.

"Nova likes Boone," Carla said in a hushed voice, her eyes wide and twinkling.

"I knew it!" cackled Liz, cracking a wide smile. "Did you guys finally make up?"

"Yeah. Thanks for the talking-to the other day. That helped."

"I'm glad you two are friends again. I couldn't take much more of either of you looking pissy 24-7."

"So," said Carla. "How are we going to fix these two up together?"

"Let's just see what happens," said Liz matter-of-factly. "These things take time. Whenever Nova's ready to ask him out, she'll ask him out. Or if Boone is ready to ask her out, he'll ask her out."

"Do you think there's a chance he might like me?"

"Maybe," replied Liz. "It's hard to tell. We all spend so much time with one another that anything is possible."

She had a point. Anything was possible. I just had to wait for the right time.

A few weeks later, Boone got his eyebrow pierced at a local tattoo parlor. In typical Boone fashion, he kept fiddling with his piercing. Whenever his hands weren't otherwise occupied, Boone would doodle in his notebook or chew on his pen. His latest accoutrement gave him a new toy to play with.

A couple days after he got his piercing, Boone called my room.

"Bring your emergency kit. I think we might need a flash-light, antiseptic, alcohol, and some tweezers."

This didn't sound good.

I made sure I had everything in my bag before hauling ass to the third floor. When I reached his room, I could already hear Jerry's voice.

"I told you to stop fiddling with it!"

That's not something you want to hear when you walk into a room.

"I wasn't fiddling with it, Jerry!" Boone protested. "I was just cleaning it and the ball fell out. Now I can't find it." He held the ring part of his piercing in place and looked at me with a mixture of desperation and exasperation.

"Thank God! You brought the MacGyver purse! My eyebrow ring fell out when I was cleaning it..."

"No. I bet he was playing with it and lost the ball. I told him this would happen."

"As I said," Boone continued. "I was cleaning my piercing and the ball fell out of the ring when I was trying to put it back in. Can you two help me find it?"

"Okay," I said calmly. "Any idea where it went?"

"Nope. It pinged across the room. I heard it roll somewhere."

Jerry and I began crawling around on our hands and knees. I took my flashlight out of my bag, shining it in the corners of the room and up against the baseboards.

"You know," said Jerry. "If this thing fell into your bed sheets, you're totally fucked."

"Thanks for the public service announcement," responded Boone witheringly.

"Chill! I'm just busting your balls. We'll find it."

Sure enough, we did find Boone's ball. Err... piercing ball.

"Alright," Jerry instructed. "First we've got to sterilize everything." He plucked the ring out of Boone's eyebrow. We let the ring soak for a few minutes before Jerry looped it back through the hole.

"Ow!" yelped Boone. "Take it easy, Jerry!"

"Stop being such a pussy and hold still. We have to put your ball back in."

The double-entendres were flying fast and furious. Just as Jerry, armed with my rubber tipped tweezers, was about to shove the ball back into the hoop, Boone protested.

"I want Nova to put my ball back in."

Gulp.

Jerry raised an eyebrow at Boone, sitting panicked on his bed.

"I just think Nova would be more gentle doing this. She has smaller hands can probably work it in better without stabbing my eye out."

"That's cool." Jerry sounded slightly hurt.

"I'm still going to need Jerry to hold your ring in place. I'll need two hands to make sure it doesn't slip out."

"I've heard that one before," said Boone with a wink.

"You wish," said Jerry.

"Pecker checker," Boone kidded. "Didn't think you swung that way!"

"Alright. Just chill, breathe, and don't freak out," I said, metal ball in one hand and tweezers in the other. Jerry held the eyebrow ring in place as I stood directly in front of a seated Boone.

"Jesus, Nova," Boone said. "Your boobs are right in my face! Are you going to pop my ball back in or breast feed me?"

"Just fuckin' relax," said Jerry. "You probably have a fetish for that shit, too!"

"Hey! I didn't say I was complaining!" laughed Boone.

"Bear with the tits for a minute," I said, maneuvering the ball into place with the tweezers and cupping it with my hand so that it didn't shoot out onto the floor. (There's another double entendre for yo' ass!)

"It's in!" I cheered. "You're set!"

"And stop fiddling with it!" barked Jerry.

"Thanks, guys," Boone said appreciatively, examining his piercing in the mirror.

"Just be glad you didn't get a Prince Albert. No fucking way would I help you with that," remarked Jerry.

Soon after, we picked up the rest of the gang and headed to the cafeteria. I thought about what Boone said during the eyebrow ring debacle. He wanted *me* to put his eyebrow ring in and didn't mind Muffy and Buffy spending some quality time in his face.

He trusted me. Hell, he even seemed somewhat flirty with me! I had never experienced that with any guy before. I wondered if this was what it felt like when someone liked you back.

I made up my mind that I would ask Boone out after finals and before everyone went their separate ways for Winter Break. If things went well, maybe Boone and I would be able to spend some time together during the break. We didn't live all that far from each other. And unlike Rick's family, Boone's parents really liked me.

Carla and Liz gave my plot their blessings. I planned to ask Boone out the night after a big post-finals party in my room.

My three roommates had already left early and were gone for the rest of the semester. Since I had a suite to myself – complete with a bathroom – we decided to forgo Liz and Carla's room as our go-to pad in case anyone had to vomit. Barfing in the community bathrooms on our floor ran the risk of being policed by an over-eager R.A. raring to write up a resident for telltale signs of underage drinking.

Jerry, Boone, and I made a major Stab n' Grab run that afternoon. We wound up filling a giant, leather duffel bag full of 40s and St. Ides Special Brews. Carla contributed a bottle of Rumplemintz for shots – a delicacy to underage college kids.

Some of Carla's off-campus friends attending brought the *really* good shit: bottles of vodka and Peach Schnapps to mix with orange juice and fifths of Jack Daniels.

At one point during the party, Boone and Carla stepped outside for a smoke.

"Don't go outside and freeze your asses off! Stay here!" I exclaimed. "We're going to open up the window to smoke some bud anyway!"

"Nah," protested Boone. "I don't want your room to reek of cigarette smoke. Besides, it's nice out."

"Hold up," said Jerry, still clutching a nearly-decimated 40 of Olde E. "I'll go with you guys."

Boone and Carla exchanged looks. "You stay here, Jerry," she replied. "You're in no condition to go outside."

"Okay," slurred Jerry, resigned to hanging upstairs. "I'm going to smoke some weed anyway. Have fun freezing your tits off, kids!"

I wondered why Carla and Boone were being so secretive as I ran around the room, frantically mopping up booze that Jerry had spilled on my evil roommate's area rug and detoxifying the puddle with Windex.

Jerry, either eager to toke up or sensing my unease, tipped his bottle in my direction and proffered some words of wisdom: "Nova, you need to relax, man! Smoke some weed! Everything's going to be alright! Stop cleaning and start smoking!"

Ten minutes later, Carla and Boone came back just as we started passing around the sweet sticky-icky. Boone had a blissful look on his face. Carla, however, thanks to the amount of alcohol she had already sucked back that night, was having a hard time hiding her "I have a secret" look.

"Come on, guys!" I said, motioning them forward and laughing. "You gotta do a hit! This is some strong shit!"

Carla was all too willing to accept the pink, jewel-encrusted pipe from my fingertips, taking a deep drag. "You have no idea how bad I need this. Can you mix me a Fuzzy Navel, too? Please?!"

She sounded desperate. This was unlike the normally bubbly Carla who was fun at parties.

"Sure. Let me grab the vodka out of the fridge in the other room." Red plastic party cup in tow, Carla offered to come with me.

She took me by surprise when she grabbed my arm in the other room, her eyes wide.

"Ohhhhhhh, my God!" The drama of her tone was greatly increased, if not exaggerated by the effects of the hooch.

"Are you okay, kiddo?" I asked, genuinely worried. "What's wrong? You look all weird after you came back from outside with Boone."

"I'm okay. I'm fine! I just don't know whether to laugh or cry."

"Can you de-vague that statement? Does this have anything to do with what you two were talking about outside?"

"Yes," she said slowly, cracking a big smile. "This whole thing is crazy!"

"What whole thing is crazy?" I was trying to pry it out of her. "What were you guys talking about?"

"You," she giggled.

"Me?! Oh, shit. He knows, doesn't he? He knows I like him and he knows I'm going to ask him out. I am *so* fucked."

"No! Not at all!" exclaimed Carla. I motioned to her to keep her voice down so that Boone wouldn't hear in the other room. "No. Really. We were talking about you and he only had good things to say about you. He wants to talk to you. That's all I can say. I don't want to say anything either way because he wants to tell you some things himself."

"Oh, my God! Really!? He wants to talk to me?" I had to remind myself to keep my own voice down.

"Yep. In private. But you can't tell him I told you this. I think he knows you like him. And I know you were planning on asking him out this weekend before everyone goes home. I told him you two would talk tomorrow."

"Okay," I smiled. I was high as shit from the weed but Carla's news only intensified my buzz.

By 2 A.M., everyone had dispersed from my room. After cleaning up and stashing empty, contraband bottles in Jerry's giant duffel bag hidden in my closet, I performed my usual post-bender ritual, following Dad's sage advice to always blow my groceries before bedtime after boozing to avoid pulling a Bon Scott.

Nervousness and what Carla said earlier were taking a toll on my stomach, making the quarts of alcohol come up all the easier. Holding my hair back and vomiting my worries to the porcelain confessor before me, I let it all out. Literally.

Why should I be nervous? I thought as I basted the bowl with barf. *This is as close to a sure thing as you can get.*

In hindsight, I think because I had been "The Dateless Wonder" for so long, I worried about how my life and my self-identity would change once I *did* have a boyfriend. And the para-noiac in me – well-aided by the weed – was thinking about the worst case scenario: *What if he just wants to be friends? What if he likes me, but is afraid of ruining our friendship if things don't work out?*

And then I heaved again and flushed.

The next morning, Boone knocked on my door. "Hey! Do you want to get some breakfast? I haven't eaten since last night and I'm starving!"

"Me, too." I was in dire need of hangover food.

I grabbed my jacket and backpack and we headed to the cafeteria.

"Let me know if you need help disposing of last night's evi-dence," Boone offered. "Jerry's leaving today and needs his duf-fel bag back. And you're leaving tomorrow, so we should prob-ably get rid of all of those bottles before the R.A. inspects the room."

"Awesome." I crammed my mouth full of cheese omelet and took a swig of orange juice.

We chatted about last night's party and the three classes we would be taking together next semester at the start of sophomore year. Soon after, we headed back to my room, refreshed from our hangover breakfast.

"Hey! Let's pick up Jerry," I suggested. "The more people we have looking out or dumping the bottles, the faster this will go. Besides, it's his duffel bag."

We swung by Jerry's room. Jerry was still hung over. Big time.

"You two dump the bottles," he said groggily. "Just bring me back my bag when you're done. I gotta sober up before I pack." He shut his door, retiring like a bear back to his cave to hibernate, leaving me and Boone to unload the stash ourselves.

Boone stood near the door, peering into the hallway as I grabbed the first armful of bottles that had been languishing on the floor of my closet. I hurried down the hall, ditching the evidence as quickly as possible before scurrying back to my room. Boone kept watch to make sure no one poked their heads out their doors as I scrambled to distribute the bottles among several trash cans on the floor. Boone took a few runs, too, emptying them in the lounge adjacent to my room.

Within 20 minutes, all the bottles were gone. We dropped the bag off at Jerry's and helped him pack before his parents picked him up later that afternoon.

We each hugged Jerry goodbye and told him to call during the break. Carla still had to pack and was planning on hanging out with some of her friends from home that night. Liz and her boyfriend Matt invited Boone and I to get pizza with them later.

Carla, Liz, and Matt knew I planned on asking Boone out that night. I could feel my stomach doing flips as I munched on a delicious slice of mushroom pizza, wondering exactly what I would say and when.

"We're going to go back to our room and ... ahem... 'hang out' while Carla's out with her friends... If you know what I mean," said Liz with a wink. "We'll see you guys tomorrow before everyone disperses!"

"Sounds good! Have a fun night, guys," I called as they went back to their room.

"Well," Boone turned to me. "I'm wide awake. You still wanna hang?"

"Hell yeah, I'm not quite ready to sleep yet, either."

"It's kind of nice out for December. Maybe we could chill out outside for now? I could really go for a cigarette."

"Cool." I wasn't a smoker myself. Just a sympathizer. Since the dorms didn't allow smoking, I'd usually accompany my friends outside just to chat.

Boone and I sat down on the bench as he lit up. I decided now was probably the best time to talk to him.

"So," I said more awkwardly than I'd have liked. "Carla said you wanted to talk to me. That's why you two went off last night?"

"What did she say to you? She didn't tell you anything, did she?" Panic lurked in his voice.

"No," I said quickly. "She just said you had something that you told her that you wanted to tell me and that you wanted to tell me yourself. She didn't say it was anything bad, but...."

He exhaled, releasing a puff of smoke along with what I interpreted as jitters. "Wow. I mean, it seemed like a good idea last night when I was drunk, but I'm really afraid to tell you all of this right now."

I felt a chill wash over me that had nothing to do with the December night air. What if I was wrong? What if he didn't like me? What if he liked Liz – or Carla, which would have explained why she was so freaked out by what Boone said to her last night?

Regardless of who he liked – even if it wasn't me – I knew I would regret it if I didn't at least say what I felt.

"Trust me," I said. "I there is nothing you could say that would upset me or any reason why you should be afraid to tell me anything. I really like you a lot. It's not like a 'rebound like' after everything that went down with Rick or even Whorin' Hank. I just really like *you*. I've never felt so comfortable around someone in my entire life. I like that we have classes together. That we laugh together. That we smoke up together. You're a really cool guy and I've never met anyone like you.

"The truth is, I was terrified about tonight. I wanted to tell you how much I like you and how much I care about you for a long time, but I was so afraid I would fuck up our friendship. Within the span of a few months, you've become one of my best friends. When we were fighting during midterms, it killed me that you were pissed at me. I hated having you angry with me. I didn't think I'd be able to recover from all of the shit that had gone down with guys back in high school, but you made things better. I can be myself around you and know you won't judge me.

"I don't know if you'd want to go out with me – or if you think this might mess up our friendship – but I would really like to try it out and see where this goes."

There. I said it. Sure, it was rambling, but at least it was coherent. I braced myself for his answer.

"When I talked to Carla last night," he started. "I kind of knew you liked me. She didn't say anything until I asked her, but I guessed it. I really wanted you to be the first person I told this to. But I just couldn't contain myself. I had to tell someone. And as close as I am to Jerry, there's *no way* I could have told him this yet. I told Carla because she's a good friend and she's sweet and nice and wouldn't judge. I told her I really wanted to tell you, but I was so afraid I would break your heart."

What was he talking about? Was he transferring schools next semester? Did he have a girlfriend? Did he get back with one of the exes that he insisted he had but never talked about?

And why was he worried he might break my heart? I sat there, biting at the flaky, dead skin on my lower lip and steeling myself to hear that he picked another girl over me and that I was too late.

"I'm gay," Boone said softly.

"What!?!?" I exclaimed, completely blindsided by his revelation.

"I'm gay," he said affirmatively. "I wasn't sure for a long time. I mean, I had a few girlfriends, but they didn't 'do it' for me. And I've been with guys and get *so* turned on by some guys. I've known this in my heart for years, but I was afraid to say anything while I was still in high school."

I sat in shock. No wonder why we got along so great. We both played for the same team.

"Oh, my God," Boone said. "Please say something. You're not mad at me, are you?"

"No way!" I said truthfully. "I'm honored that you wanted to tell me."

"I wanted you to be the first, but I told Carla this last night because I was drunk and I wanted to make sure that you and I had time alone together so I could tell you. I didn't want you to leave for the semester and not tell you," he said. "I don't know when I want to tell my parents yet and I'm a little afraid to tell Jerry since he's a guy. I know we're really good friends, but I just don't want him to think I'm, like, gay for *him*. He's totally not my type, but I don't want him to feel uncomfortable or for this to change our friendship."

"Dude," I said. "Jerry's a lot more open-minded than you think. I know he'll be cool with this. You don't stop being friends with someone just because they're gay. That's your decision, though. I won't say anything to him. You tell him whenever you feel you're ready."

Boone took yet another drag off of his cigarette. "I really wanted you to be the first person I told, though," he said. "Even more than some of my friends from high school back home. I knew you liked me and I know how shitty guys treated you in the past. I didn't want you to think that there was something wrong with *you* because I didn't like you back."

"It's not like there's something wrong with *you*, either," I said. "We have one more thing in common. We both like dick."

"You know, I don't even really like dick. I mean, I like having my dick sucked and I like giving anal sex, but I don't really like receiving," replied Boone thoughtfully. "I found out these things have names, too! Guys who like to give are called 'tops' and dudes who like to receive are 'bottoms'... I'm a top!"

This was a whole new world to me! It was like Candy Land with peppermint-striped dongs of all sizes and gumdrop anuses! Sure, I couldn't play in Candy Land, but I was enjoying my walk through the Peppermint Dick Forest and learning all sorts of fun, new, gay terminology.

"Yeah!" he said. "I've been learning all of these terms from a group I met here in the city. I saw a flyer on campus and went one night. I feel like there's a lot of things I can talk about now that I couldn't before. Things make so much more sense now!"

I was really excited for Boone. While I was a little disappointed that my bubble of an idea of an awesome relationship with someone I had a lot in common with was punctured, I still had my friend.

It was the least painful rejection I had ever experienced. I knew "it wasn't me" and that there wasn't any flaw that Boone may have perceived in me that would have turned him off. It was just that he didn't swing that way.

Better yet, there was no open-ended false hope that someday he would change his mind. There wouldn't be any of the plotting or planning that there had been with guys in the past because there was no door to be left open. Any of the sadness I may have felt about still being dateless had dissipated. I was so happy and excited for my friend that he was finally able to come out and honored that he chose me as one of the first people to tell.

We went back inside and picked up a couple pints of ice cream to eat in the lounge. We talked until about 3 A.M., comparing notes on guys around campus.

"Remember that raver kid I pointed out to you awhile back?"

"The one you thought looked cool and you said you wanted to hang out with?"

"Yeah. I've had the hugest crush on him since last semester. I think he might be gay, too."

It made sense now. Most straight guys don't point out other dudes they think it would be cool to be friends with. Suddenly, some of Boone's mannerisms – the things I thought that meant he "liked" me – were big clues I should have picked up on had my gaydar been more finely tuned.

I may have lost a potential boyfriend, but I strengthened a friendship in a way I never would have thought possible.

CHAPTER FIFTEEN
BE CAREFUL WHAT YOU WISH FOR

The semester after winter break, Boone formally came out. Jerry was totally cool with it, but just didn't want Boone talking about dudes in front of him. He had no problem with him being gay, he just didn't want the mental image of his buddy sword-fighting with other guys stuck in his head every time they smoked up together. It wasn't an issue of Jerry being a homophobe. He pretty much told everyone to shut up regarding their own personal sexual exploits. I couldn't even joke about my excessive masturbation habits around Jerry without him bellowing "Shut up! I don't need to hear this!"

After discovering he and I had one more thing in common, Boone and I grew closer as friends. It seemed that the tide was beginning to turn in terms of guys who were interested in me. There was that Fuji kid back home that Rick tried to fix me up with before I left, and Lou the Jew last semester.

Granted, I wasn't interested in these guys, but at least there were some dudes out there who found me attractive.

At the start of the semester, I found out that Dylan – the kid from Virginia that Jerry, Boone, and I met at orientation – straightened out his financial aid and was now enrolled as a junior. Dylan emailed me to let me know and he soon ended up hanging out with us, grabbing dinner with the gang on a nightly basis. He wasn't a pot smoker, so he never joined Jerry, Boone, and I in the courtyard, but he did hang out with us quite a bit.

Of everyone in the group, Dylan was closest with me. He was a film major and even though I was studying journalism and advertising, I had a keen appreciation for film.

Dylan was short and thin with dark shoulder-length hair and a goatee. His personal style was somewhere between "Redneck Goth" and Christian Slater's look in *Heathers*.

Dylan seemed homesick and constantly talked about his girlfriend back home in Virginia. At first, I thought it was kind of sweet. However, I got the feeling that something was a little off when Dylan kept trying to get me to come up to his room to look at the photos he and his girlfriend took before he left for Philadelphia.

I had never seen a picture of his girlfriend before, and he never mentioned her by name. Usually, a guy who mentions his special lady friend so frequently would have a picture of her in his wallet. Not the case with Dylan.

I wondered if I was being paranoid. Was I reading the guy wrong? My freak-o-meter went off, however, when Dylan decided to pay me a visit at the library one afternoon.

While working, I saw him out of the corner of my eye, weaving through the stacks. He would walk down one series of shelves, then crisscross through another, snaking a path between the tall spires of books from the back to the front of each case.

Liz and Carla saw him, too, and came back to tell me about Dylan's weird behavior. We agreed it seemed odd, him wandering around in such a methodical manner. In turn, we decided to get out of his range of sight and stay as close to the back of the stacks as possible.

Inevitably, we finished our cart and had to go back up front to grab another cart of books to re-shelve. When we got there, Dylan was waiting for us.

"Hey." He stood uncomfortably close to me. "I thought you might be working right now. Figured I'd stop by and say 'hi.'"

"Hi," I said, not letting on that I had seen him looking for me in the stacks. "How was class?"

"Not bad. It let out early and I wanted to see what you were up to after you got out."

"I've got a two-hour lab after I get out of here, but I'll see you at dinner," I replied.

"Wow," he said out of the blue. "You're wearing a skirt today."

"Yeah," I said, looking down at the black mini-skirt and heavy black tights I was sporting that day with a grey sweater. "I tend to do that sometimes."

"I mean, wow," he said yet again with a grin that bothered me. "You're wearing a skirt."

"Yeah," I repeated sternly. "I'm a girl. Sometimes girls wear these things called skirts. It's not all that remarkable."

I noticed Carla and Liz exchanging looks as Dylan said, "You should blow off lab next period and get lunch with me. I can hang out with you here until you get off of work."

My skin started to crawl. Dylan had never been this pushy before. Things had always been pretty friendly between us, but his behavior was really strange and overly insistent.

Carla, Liz, and I weren't the only ones who were a little freaked out. My supervisor, Tom – a big, burly bald dude who was into horror movies and knew nearly everything about old school ska and punk – thought something weird was going on, having seen Dylan weaving his serpentine path through the stacks.

"Hey, Nova!" Tom yelled. "Didn't I tell you about hanging out and talking to your friends before? Get back to work. You need to get that cart done before 2:30? Got it? Tell your friend you'll talk to him later."

I immediately started pushing my cart towards its designated aisle, telling Dylan, "You should probably go now. I'll see you at dinner."

"Okay," he said reluctantly, making a beeline for the elevators as Tom stood nearby, arms folded.

After Dylan was gone, Tom found me in the stacks, shelving books.

"Hey," he said. "I don't want you to think I was yelling at you. I didn't know if that guy was a friend of yours or not, but I saw him walking through the stacks before and thought he seemed weird. And I noticed you, Carla, and Liz looking at each other like something was up."

"Thanks. I'm actually glad you did say that. I'm friends with the guy, but he's been acting weird lately."

"Yeah. I heard the 'skirt' comment and it made me think twice about this cat."

"I figured you were trying to be nice and step in without having to physically escort the guy out of the library. Seriously, though... Thank you."

"Anytime," he said cheerfully. "Just watch yourself. And let me know if you see him around again or if he's bothering you or anyone else."

"Will do. Thanks, Tom."

Dylan never hunted for me in the stacks again, but it didn't stop him from tracking me down elsewhere in the library.

The biggest computer lab on campus was located in the library. When I didn't have class, I would head to the computer lab to work on papers after my shift. As much of a stoner as I was, I still liked to have all of my schoolwork done so I could party without a deadline hanging over my head.

In between working on papers, I would email my friends back home. One afternoon, I was emailing Jenn and Claire. I typed away, oblivious to the fact that Dylan was right behind me.

I had no idea he had been so intently reading what I wrote until I felt his arms wrap around my shoulders and his chin rest on top of my head, squeezing me from behind as he read my words off of the computer screen.

"'Things are going good here. Jerry, Boone, and I hang out and smoke up all the time. Nothing's changed since Boone told me he was gay. I was worried he'd feel weird around me, knowing I liked him, but honestly, we're better friends now than we ever were.'... Wow. I didn't know Boone was a fag," Dylan remarked. "I thought you two might have been a couple until I asked him if you two were dating. He said you were just friends, but I had no idea he was queer."

As if I didn't already want to gutterball Dylan for violating my personal space with his impromptu "hug" from behind, it took every ounce of personal restraint I had to not make a Dylan-sized stain on the wall behind me for referring to my friend as a "fag" and a "queer."

My blood ran cold. This creep had been behind me the entire time. While Boone wasn't in the closet anymore, he hadn't come out to Dylan for a reason. They weren't close friends and it was none of his business – nor should it have mattered to him.

I sat mortified, not knowing what to say. I was paralyzed with disgust and couldn't find the words to tell this guy what I should have at that moment: "Fuck off."

Instead I said, "Seriously, dude? He's not a 'fag.' He's gay. That shouldn't be a big deal to you. You seem to have no problem hanging out with him otherwise."

"Oh, it's not a big deal!" Dylan backpedaled. "I just had no idea he was gay. I was pretty surprised reading that."

"Well, you shouldn't have been reading that. Unless your name is 'Claire' or 'Jenn,' that email wasn't meant for your eyes, which seemed to have been perched over my shoulder for quite some time."

"I'm sorry. I didn't mean anything by it. I was just surprised that Boone was gay, is all."

I nodded, not really knowing what to say until Dylan spoke again: "I'll see you at dinner. I'll stop by and pick you up around 6:30!"

I waited 15 minutes, typing up the rest of my email and ran back upstairs to the stacks to track down Boone, Jerry, and the rest of the gang to tell them what happened.

"I am so sorry," I said to Boone. "That should have been your choice to tell Dylan if you wanted to. I didn't realize he was standing over my shoulder, reading everything I wrote. It was so creepy!"

"It's not your fault," he replied calmly. "You had no idea he was being a fucking stalker."

"You're not mad at me, are you?"

"No way! I'm not mad at you. I'm mad at *him*! He violated your privacy – and *mine*. He has the nerve to sit at the same table with me, pretend to be my friend and then call me a 'fag' and a 'queer' behind my back? It was never his damn business in the first place! No. *He's* the asshole here."

"Seriously, dude. I honestly don't want to eat dinner with Dylan. If that's how he feels about you – and judging by the creepy, stalker-ish way he's been acting lately – I really don't want him to be a part of our group."

"He's a fucking little shitbag," said Jerry. "Tom and Carla were telling me that he was walking around the whole damn library trying to find you the one day. He's a fucking homophobic piece of shit and he's trolling for pussy. Fuck him. We're not eating with him anymore. From now on, we're all going to go to dinner at 5:30 until the little shit gets the hint we don't want to look at him again."

We successfully dodged Dylan at dinner, although he left several messages on my answering machine when I got back to my room, saying that he dropped by a few times and must have missed me. Later that night, I learned that I was the only one from our group he had called.

Dylan, however, did not get the hint. He was like Jim Carey's character in *The Cable Guy*. I'd be in my room less than a half an hour before Dylan would knock on the door to make small talk or try to invite me up to his room to watch a movie or show me some pictures or letters that his "girlfriend" sent to him. That struck me as fishy. If he wanted me to see them so bad, why wouldn't he have brought the letters and pictures to my room instead of asking me to go visit him in his?

Whenever Dylan would turn up at my door, I'd grab my backpack and make up some lame excuse that I was pulling an extra shift at the library. Ever since Tom glared him out of the stacks, Dylan got the hint that the library was off-limits. It was the best excuse I could muster to shake the proverbial booger off my finger.

That week, I ended up spending a lot of time in the library – which just goes to show that passive-aggressive tactics don't work nearly as well as a direct approach. Dylan only half-got the hint that he wasn't welcome at our table, however, he figured out that we all hung out in Carla and Liz's room and started inviting himself over there.

As part of our weekly "girl time" ritual, Carla, Liz and I would hang out, chat and watch *Dawson's Creek* on Wednesday nights. One night, Dylan dropped by the girls' room, correct in his assumption that I would be there.

It was awkward and uncomfortable having him sit there. He didn't have anything in common with either Carla or Liz and neither liked Dylan very much, either. He just sat there, in the middle of the floor with his omnipresent black trench coat splayed out around him as he stared at the ceiling and stared at me.

"Hey, Dylan," said Liz. "We're getting ready to head to the sorority and help decorate for the fundraiser this weekend. We'll see you later."

"I didn't know you were in a sorority, Nova." he questioned.

"I'm not," I said. "I just offered to help them out and get things ready."

"Oh," he said. "Then maybe I could help out, too."

"No," said Liz pointedly. "It's all girls there. You wouldn't feel very comfortable."

It was the most polite way possible to tell him to get the hell out of their room. I was grateful to Liz for making up that cover story, but this passive-aggressive shtick could only go on for so long. I had to cowboy the fuck up and tell him to piss off myself.

I fully intended on telling Dylan to go to hell (or at least someplace a safe distance away from me) when I came back from a weekend visit back home.

When I arrived back on campus, Carla gave me a call and asked if I wanted to come over and watch the Super Bowl in her room with a few friends. Jerry and Boone were both back home to attending Super Bowl parties, and Liz and Matt were hanging at her father's house that weekend and would be back the next morning

There were only a few girls in Carla's room, but we all kicked back with some food and drinks with the odd occurrence of someone cracking open a book to study. I took notes on some of the commercials for an advertising and media studies assignment.

After a few commercial breaks, I had to "break the seal" and headed to the dorm's community bathroom.

While I was taking a whiz, Dylan dropped by Carla's room and asked where I was. He went by my room and no one answered and wondered if I was back from my weekend trip to Fletcher. Thankfully, I had to take a really long pee and missed out my stalker's impromptu visit. Carla told me what happened and lied that I hadn't come back home yet and that she hadn't heard from me.

I thanked Carla, but I was pretty spooked. "This shit is getting really weird. What a fucking nut job. I have seriously *got* tell this dude to piss off tomorrow."

Resolved to tell Dylan to leave me and my friends alone, I sat back down on the floor to watch the game.

Just then, there was a knock at the door. Carla peered out the peephole and turned white.

"Oh, my God," she gasped. "It's him again! Go hide in the closet, Nova!"

She hauled me up by my arm and shut me in the closet. Through the door, I could hear Carla telling Dylan that she hadn't seen or heard from me yet.

"Well, she must be coming back sometime tonight," he insisted.

"Maybe she's at a Super Bowl party back home?" offered Carla.

"I checked her room and she's still not there," he said, his voice rising.

"Don't worry about it. I'm sure she'll be back tomorrow."

She closed the door, but I opted to stay in the closet for a few more minutes. Alone in the dark, I thought about what a total, fucking wing nut this clown was. Was he planning on giving me a Super Bowl of roofies? Was that why he was so eager to get me to come up to his room by myself?

I thought about what Boone had said last semester when the Lou the Jew debacle went down. Why did I need other people to cover for me? Why couldn't I just rip into them on my own? I was more than capable of verbally decimating someone and speaking my mind. Why was it that I could say "fuck you" to a friend like Boone and not tell a shit-weasel stalker like Dylan to fuck off? I wasn't afraid of Dylan physically. I was only a few inches shorter than him and probably had a good ten pounds on the scrawny little prick.

It was imperative that I tell Dylan to leave me and my friends alone.

I had my chance less than 30 minutes later when, once again, Dylan came knock-knock-knockin' on Carla's door.

"Fuck this," I said. "I'm answering the fucking door this time."

"Are you crazy?!" Carla's eyes grew wide. "He's off his rocker!"

I didn't care. I was fired up. "No fucking way am I letting this asshole come here and bother everyone all fucking night with his bullshit. He's a creepy little bastard and needs to be told off."

I flung open the door to see Dylan and his black trench coat standing in the doorway.

"You just came back?" he inquired. "I've been looking for you all night."

"Oh, yeah," I sneered. "I'm well aware that you've been ping-ponging between my room and Carla's. You came by no less than three times."

"Yeah," he said with a shrug. "So?"

"So," I said. "It's creepy and it's stalkerish. Haven't you gotten the hint that I don't want to hang out with you? Have you not gotten a fucking clue that none of my friends want to hang out with you, either?"

"What are you talking about?"

"Well, first of all, you're a two-faced homophobe. You act all nice to Boone to his face and then call him a 'fag' and a 'queer' behind his back. You sneak up behind me and read my emails and you're constantly trying to get me to come up to your room – alone – to see pictures of your girlfriend. Not to mention bothering me when I'm at work after you've thoroughly inspected the stacks to see which one I might be stationed at.

That's a little fucking weird and *a lot* fucking creepy. I've been dodging you like a bad fart and you *still* haven't taken the hint. You need to fuck off and leave me alone."

"Fine," replied Dylan. "Whatever." He turned on his heel and strode down the hall, his long, black coat trailing behind him.

I was a little worried that maybe he'd retaliate and I'd come back to my room to find one of my stuffed animals in a pot of boiling water. Thankfully, there wasn't a stove in my dorm

Dylan never bothered me again. In a twist of irony, he ended up going out with my friend and library co-worker Eric's former stalker – a girl who had tried to break up Eric and his girlfriend.

It was kind of sweet that two creepy stalkers found each other and hooked up.

Okay, not really. But at least they weren't stalking anyone else anymore.

A month or so had passed and the weather began to get warmer. Spring was in the air and love was all around. Carla had a new crush and she and Jerry – who had broken up with his girlfriend with "attitude" – were flirting with each another. Boone had a new man. Liz and Matt were still together. And, one fine evening, some random chick on my dormitory floor dropped to her knees and gave some dude head in the hallway.

Things looked promising for me in the romance department, too. One day, when I was coming out of my Ancient Greek and Roman History class, a tall, skinny guy with long blonde hair and glasses approached me.

"I've seen you around on campus before and we always come out of class at the same time. I just wanted to say that if you're as interesting as you are beautiful, I would love to hang out with you sometime."

I was taken aback by how genuinely sweet this stranger's comment was. It was a pleasant contrast to Lou the Jew's tongue waggling and references to his circumcised He-blew National trouser snake.

While this random guy's comment could have come across as stalker-y, he lacked the creepy "I wanna roofie you" vibe that Dylan possessed.

"Thank you," I replied sincerely.

"Would you mind if I asked for your phone number?"

"Not at all." Taking a pen out of the front pouch of my backpack, I quickly jotted down my name and number and handed it to him, my hand poised over yet another fresh page in my spiral bound to take down his number.

"Nova?" he mused. "That's an interesting name. And very pretty, by the way." He paused for a moment before extending his hand. "My name's 'Sky.' It's an unusual one, but easy to remember. Nice to meet you, Nova."

I shook his hand and told him I would definitely give him a call.

I made a beeline for Carla and Liz's room to tell them what just transpired. I gave the girls a physical description of Sky, adding that I thought he seemed like kind of a hippie.

"That means he probably likes weed," offered Liz. "You two could smoke up together!"

Sky called the next night and we had one of those awkward-but-cool "getting to know you" phone conversations. He was a history major in his junior year and lived off campus with a roommate. He didn't watch television, but liked movies, citing horror and foreign films as his favorites. When the subject of music came up, he mentioned Dave Matthews and Phish along with some obscure, indie or folk artists I'd never heard of.

Taste in music aside, he seemed like a nice enough guy, which was why I agreed to hang out with him during my free period on the quad. Carla and Liz volunteered to go with me to help broaden the scope of conversation – and to make sure he wasn't a nut like Dylan.

We sat on one of the benches before Sky arrived, acoustic guitar in-hand and wearing a shirt that appeared to have been borrowed from the *Three's Company* Mr. Furley Collection.

Sky walked up to us and sat down on the grass.

"You girls should sit down on the grass instead," he suggested. "You can feel the Earth better that way."

Hesitating, I sat down on the expanse of green sprawling out from under the bench. Carla and Liz followed suit.

I introduced Sky to my friends. He was very polite and seemed pleased to meet them, but somewhat disappointed that I didn't arrive by myself.

"So," I said tentatively. "How was class today?"

"Not bad," he said, strumming a few chords on his guitar before asking: "Do you know what song I'm playing?"

"Nope," I laughed.

"Really?" He sounded surprised and blurted out the song's name, informing me that it was by a local indie-folk band that he was really into. "I write some music myself, too."

"No way!" I exclaimed. "Play something! I'd like to hear it."

Without any prompting, he launched into this mellow folk ditty about skipping down the street and eating ice cream cones – Chocolate, strawberry, and vanilla – Oh! What a beautiful day.

I found it hard to keep a straight face, not daring to look at either Carla or Liz for fear that their expressions mirrored what I was thinking.

He finished his song with a flourish, marking the final chords with a ridiculous facial expression executed with zero irony and meant to signal my approval of his disasterpiece.

Images of John Belushi pulling an El Kabong in *Animal House* danced in my head as I choked back laughter and bile. "That was pretty cool," I lied.

"No," he said. "It's *'groovy.'* You have to say *'groovy!'"*

I laughed, still managing not to look at my friends – both of whom I could feel exchanging uneasy glances.

"No. Really," Sky insisted. "You have to say the song was *'groovy.'* Say *'groovy.'"*

My mouth hung open in astonishment. This dude wasn't kidding.

"That was groovy, Sky," I said, totally hating myself at that moment. Self-loathing and I had been well-acquainted for some time, but this was a new low.

"Thanks!" he said, smiling and making the same weird, semi "o-face" he finished his song with.

Mercifully, the half hour on the quad was over and my friends and I had to head to the library. I bid Sky farewell, giving him a hug and was overcome by the stench of hoagie-like B.O. poorly masked by a shitload of patchouli.

"I'll call you tonight," he said.

"Groovy," I said, barely concealing the sarcasm in my voice.

"You're getting the hang of it!" he exclaimed, full of vim before walking towards Anderson Hall.

When he was safely out of earshot, Carla and Liz heaved a collective "Ooooookaaaay."

I arched an eyebrow at my compatriots on the grass. "Not for all the weed in a Cheech and Chong movie. I may be desperate, but I'm not *that* desperate."

Not only did Sky listen to questionable music, he wrote *even more* questionable music. And his hygiene was even more questionable than both.

At dinner, I filled the guys in on the bizarre details of the afternoon's "sit-in" with Sky.

"Normally," spoke Boone, "I would say you're being too picky. This guy sounds like a complete dork. I'd pass."

Jerry nodded emphatically. "There's no fucking way I'm smoking up with some douche who says 'groovy.' Fuck that."

Instead of hanging out in my room and waiting for Sky's phone call, I went outside to toke up with Jerry and Boone. When I came back to my room, sure enough, Sky had left a message saying he had a "groovy" time. I laughed out loud before realizing that I couldn't dodge the dude's phone calls forever.

Well, this sucks. I wasn't going to let it kill my buzz, however. Taking a bottle of St. Ides Special Brew out of my mini-fridge, I uncapped it and took a huge swig. The cold tang of blue-tinted malt liquor coursed down my throat as I put my headphones in, piping enough Marilyn Manson into my ears to purge the shit tsunami that was Sky's unique brand of tunes from my brain.

The next night, Sky called and remarked how I was less chatty in-person. "You talked a lot more on the phone the other night."

I couldn't hold back any longer. "Well," I hedged. "We don't have much in common."

"What do you mean? We like a lot of the same music."

What planet was this guy from? "I don't know, dude. Mötley Crüe and Dave Matthews are two different worlds."

"You can learn to love Dave," he insisted.

I resisted the urge to shit directly on the phone. Not only was I not a fan of the Dave Matthews Band (okay, I liked one or two songs), I hated when fans referred to the band as "Dave." I could marginally tolerate them being referred to as "D.M.B.," but calling them "Dave" was too much to take.

"Sorry. I'm just not a fan."

"Well," he said. "You seemed to like *my* music."

I was already telling this dude that I wasn't interested, I couldn't deliver the double-whammy of peeing on his songwriting skills, too.

"True," I lied. "You write some good stuff... But that's irrelevant. You and I don't really click. You're a very nice guy, but we have completely different interests with no common ground. It was sweet that you approached me, but I think this would be a waste of your time. There's probably someone out there that will really like listening to your type of music and going to shows with you and all that. That's not really me."

"I'm sorry you feel that way," he snipped before hanging up.

I was relieved to have nipped things in the bud. Maybe I was being too picky, but I had the right to be. I'd rather be alone than have someone try to turn me into something I'm not.

After two (creepy and stinky) guys expressed interest in me that semester, I felt like maybe my luck was changing. I decided that I would test that newfound luck.

There was this tall, heroin-thin Asian metal dude on campus that I saw whenever I was walking to or from the library. He had long, waist-length black hair and wore tight jeans and a leather motorcycle jacket almost exactly like mine.

I would see him around everywhere but didn't know his name. I felt like Charlie Brown in his pursuit of The Little Red Haired Girl, only I had better hair than Charlie Brown and The Little Red Headed Girl was a Tall Asian Metal Dude.

I had Yellow Fever and I had it bad.

One day, after two semesters of seeing him on campus, I resolved to make conversation with him. I was wearing jeans and a thermal that day but decided to head back to my dorm to change into something more appropriate before I approached Hunan Delight.

I rummaged through my closet to find my black mini skirt, black crushed velvet top, and a pair of black tights that didn't have a run in them. I threw on my own black leather jacket and hauled ass out the door, hoping to catch a glimpse of Tall Asian Metal Dude

There he was: walking down the hall, leaving class as I walked towards my next class. I decided it was the time to spring from my Crouching Tiger, Hidden Dragon post and make my move.

I had to think fast. I had to say something witty. Something cool. Something that would grab his attention.

"Hey," I smirked, a gleam in my eye. I looked at him and then I looked down at my own similar attire and blurted: "Nice jacket!"

Wow, that sucked!

My Asian Sensation cocked his head and smiled. I could feel my heart beating in my chest as he opened his mouth to speak.

I don't know what the translation was for what he said, but he laughed and muttered something in Japanese. Probably something to the effect of "Little American Round Eye! You're so silly!"

Then he walked past me in a mad rush to clomp across campus in his tight black pants and tall black boots.

Thus ending any further attempts on my part to try to bridge East with West.

CHAPTER SIXTEEN
BEWARE OF GUYS WEARING DRESSES

Although I struck out with the hot, Asian metal dude who no speakee Engrish, my friend Nicole offered to fix me up on a blind date. Nicole was a cool, funny punk chick I worked with at the library. She was a senior and we got along really well.

Nicole and her new boyfriend were heading to a local club that was having a goth / '80s night. She mentioned her boyfriend had a friend who recently broke up with his girlfriend and they wanted to take him out and show him a good time.

"You should come with us," she said. "You'd like the music. Plus it's a date without being an official date. Even if you don't hit it off, it'll be cool to meet someone new and get out and dance at a club."

"Alright," I said, liking the idea. I trusted her judgment that this would be a fun night out.

Before going out that evening, I dolled myself up in a floor length black dress with a black-and-red choker. After applying a layer of pale foundation, I slicked on a coat of deep burgundy lipstick and midnight blue eyeshadow before giving my long, black hair a fluff. I swung on my leather motorcycle jacket made a beeline for the subway.

I got off at Spring Garden and walked a few blocks to the club. After ponying up the $5 cover charge, the attendant stamped my hand, marking me as under 21.

Having never been to a club before, I hung back against the wall to take it all in – including the weird dance moves some of the older goths were doing – a cross between Vogue-ing and swimming. No sooner than I turned around than Nicole and her boyfriend were standing in front of me.

"You made it!" Nicole exclaimed, giving me a big hug. "I'd like you to meet my boyfriend Dan."

"Nice to meet you," I said, shaking Dan's hand firmly. The three of us stood silent for a few seconds before I saw the guy standing behind Nicole and Dan.

"Hey, back there!" I said cheerily. "Sorry, but I didn't catch your name."

"Hi. I'm Alex," he replied shyly, coming forward and allowing me a better look at him. He was short and slight of build with large brown eyes and long, shoulder-length hair streaked with purple. He wore a long-sleeved mesh shirt with a black beater over it, fishnets and a black, vinyl, zip-front miniskirt over them.

"Nice to meet you, Alex." I shook his hand. "I like your skirt."

"Really?"

"Yeah," I replied sincerely. "It's a brave man who can pull off the skirt look."

"Thank you." He offered a small smile. "It was my ex-girlfriend's."

"Well, it works for you!"

"Dan and I are going downstairs to the '80s party." Nicole leaned in closer to whisper with a wink. "That should give you and Alex some more time to chat."

"Maybe we'll join you downstairs soon."

"I don't think you can. It's 21 and over downstairs. Sorry."

"No big. I think I might have a good time up here."

"We'll be back up to check on you in a bit. Have fun!"

That left Alex and I alone in a dimly lit corner of the club. "So, Alex, I'm not really familiar with this place. You look like you know your way around here."

"A little," he spoke, his voice barely a whisper. "My ex-girlfriend and I used to come here a lot."

"Cool," I masked my uneasiness. This was the second time in under five minutes he had mentioned his ex. "Maybe you could show me around?"

"I'd like that," he said softly, walking ahead of me. "Would you like to sit down and talk first?" He motioned to a plush purple velvet chaise lounge that resembled the interior of a coffin.

"Sure!" I sat down first, leaning my elbow on one of the overstuffed armrests of the chair as Alex sat down next to me. Three feet away.

"Your makeup looks really nice." He looked into my eyes. "It makes your eyes look very striking."

"Thank you. I like playing around with makeup."

"My ex had very blue eyes like yours, too."

I nodded politely. I figured I'd take the bait and ask Alex about her since he seemed so hung up on his former flame.

"How long ago did you two break up?"

"About a month ago." His tone was beyond morose. Even for a goth.

"Did you date very long?"

"About eight months."

"That's a long time." I tried to be consoling.

"I know. It's been a month since we've been apart and I just don't feel that hole in my heart healing."

Alex seemed like a nice guy, but he was clearly in need of some tough love.

"Are you allowing yourself to heal?" I asked, feeling like Oprah. "Don't get me wrong. I'm not judging you, but you seem to be surrounding yourself with a lot of things that remind you of her. You go to the same places you used to go together. You wear her clothes. You seek out things in new people that remind you of her. Sure, the breakup is still fresh, but I get the impression you're torturing yourself by dredging up all these memories."

"No," he replied. "You're right. I *am* torturing myself. I feel like I didn't deserve her."

"If you don't mind my asking, what happened?"

"She dumped me. Just told me that we were done after eight months. Right before we were going to move in together. She said she found someone else and that it was over. She didn't want to see me again."

"Did you know the guy she dumped you for?"

"I think I know who she might be with now, but I'm not sure."

"So, you're coming to the club you two used to go to together to see if you can spot her with this guy?"

"I don't know if I really want to know who he is, or if seeing her with someone else will give me closure."

"I can understand that," I nodded. "You know, it would probably be pretty awesome if you saw her with a guy and he was butt ugly."

"Huh?"

"I call it 'The Inner Snicker.' When you see someone who turned you down and – even though you hate yourself – you still know you look better than the freakshow they're walking around with now. It's like a consolation prize and ego boost all in one."

"My ex was beautiful," he said. "She could get any guy she wanted. I know that I couldn't measure up to who she's with now."

"Alright, dude." I was losing patience. "You can feel that way, but you're not giving yourself much credit. You're a good looking guy..."

"Thank you," he said, still in full-on mope mode.

"You're welcome. But," I continued. "If she was going to come back, she would. Trust me. I wasted four years waiting for a guy to take a romantic interest in me and it never happened. Seriously, dude. Living well is the best revenge."

"I don't feel like living well."

"Yeah, you do," I chided. "Otherwise, you wouldn't have gotten yourself all dressed up to go out." The operative word here being "dress."

He leaned his head against the back of the couch and sighed forlornly. I was half-expecting Alex to lay his hand across his head and start doing Greta Garbo impersonations.

Surveying my surroundings – the mirrored wall, the backlit bar illuminated a strange shade of blue-green, the velvet-clad revelers on the dance floor, and Alex draped over the coffin-like purple couch – I felt like I'd stumbled onto the set of a low-budget music video.

Alex may have been miserable, but I was determined to bring him out of his mope coma and have a good time that night.

"How about I grab us a couple drinks? They'll have to be Shirley Temples, but I've got a couple mini bottles of rum in my purse to get the party started."

"No, that's ok," he sighed. "Thank you for the offer."

"Well, *I'm* going to go get something to drink." I definitely needed a shot of something to maintain my sanity. "I'll be right back."

"Please don't go," he whimpered. "Could you just sit here with me for a few more minutes?"

"Sure." I was befuddled. It wasn't like I was offering any sort of comfort on the couch. He was parked three feet away from me. I interpreted his request that maybe I should try to sit closer to him. I inched myself nearer to Alex, who responded by inching himself further back down the couch, maintaining a silent, sullen, three-foot distance.

Alex was still sprawled across the couch, leaning back in repose like an overly made-up psychiatric patient. Fitting, since this was when Dr. Nova decided to "self-medicate." I reached into my purse and uncapped one of the travel-sized mini bottles of Jack Daniels I had stashed in my evening bag.

Slugging nearly the entire mini bottle, I tossed its empty, plastic carcass beneath the purple couch and felt a burst of energy.

"Alright. I think we've sat long enough. How about we get out on the dance floor."

"I don't feel like dancing."

"Well," I replied, attempting to add a flirtatious edge to my voice. "You still have yet to make good on your promise to show me around the club. How about we go for a walk?"

"Okay." He stood up, smoothing his ex-girlfriend's pleather skirt around his slender thighs. "Do you want to take a look upstairs?"

"Sure!" I followed his lead up the red-carpeted spiral stairwell. It was dark and drafty but it afforded a great view of the entire club from overhead.

"It's a really cool view up here," I remarked conversationally.

"It is," sighed Alex. And before I could even think it, he spouted the words I knew were a-coming: "My ex-girlfriend and I used to come up here and dance all the time."

I halted myself from rolling my eyes and tried to give the situation a positive spin. "Do you want to dance with me up here? Maybe it would help exorcize the old girlfriend demons?"

"I appreciate the offer. But it just wouldn't feel right."

"I understand." I said through gritted teeth. This date was a dud. "How about we go back downstairs?"

"Okay," Alex agreed, following me down the stairwell. As I reached the foot of the stairs, I spotted Nicole and Dan.

"I've been looking for you!" said Nicole bouncily. She leaned in closer and asked, "So, how are things going with you and Alex."

"Dude," I said gravely. "It's awful. All he does is talk about his ex-girlfriend. Everything reminds him of his ex. The upstairs balcony, my eye makeup, the shit stain in the men's pee trough... Everything. I know he's Dan's friend and all, and I really don't want to be rude, but Alex is boring the hell out of me."

"Huh?" Nicole's face registered confusion. "Alex isn't Dan's friend."

"I thought you said Dan was bringing a friend with him that just broke up with his girlfriend?"

"He was. But at the last minute, something came up and his friend couldn't make it."

"Then who the hell is this Alex dude?"

"He was just some guy that was here when we got here. You two just kind of made eye contact and you complimented him on his skirt before Dan and I could tell you that his friend couldn't make it. We thought you'd already hit it off with this Alex guy, so we didn't get a chance to tell you."

"Oh, my God," I said quietly. "You mean, I've been listening to this dork whine the entire night about his ex-girlfriend and I didn't have to? Holy shit."

"Wow." Is he that bad?"

"Oh, yeah. I couldn't get him to drink or dance or do anything. He just sat there on the couch moping for about 20 minutes. When I tried to get up to grab a drink, he was like 'Please don't go.' Jesus! No wonder why his ex dumped him."

"I am *so* sorry," said Nicole sincerely. "If I'd have known he was such a whack job, we'd have come up and rescued you sooner."

"It's not your fault. You and Dan have a good time. I'm going to go back to the dorms and call it a night."

"You're not mad, are you?"

"Of course not!" I was being honest. It wasn't her fault that Alex was a flake.

"Cool. Be safe. I'll see you at work tomorrow."

Just then, Alex the One Man Party came up to me. For a split second, I thought maybe the tide was going to turn. That he might have drummed up enough spunk to dance or do something other than make his mascara run.

"I was wondering where you were."

"Just chatting with my friend, Nicole," I said. "Too bad we're not 21. I hear the '80s party downstairs is pretty awesome."

Alex nodded before speaking again. "Would you like to sit down and talk more?"

"Sure," I said, wondering where this was headed and following him to the couch. He sat down in his familiar position, reclining at the opposite end of the couch and unleashing yet another pathetic sigh.

"So," I said, attempting conversation. "What's on your mind?"

"Nothing much."

I inched closer towards him, trying to close the gap. He moved back even further.

"That girl over there looks almost exactly like my ex," he said, his voice quavering. "Same height. Same hair. It's uncanny. This is so hard for me to deal with."

"Yeah. Me, too," I muttered under my breath. I had enough of this drip mooning over his ex and stood up.

"Where are you going?" he asked pathetically. "Please stay."

"I'm going to get a drink," I lied. "I'll be right back."

"Okay," he replied, flopping back down in a heap of purple and pleather.

Fuck this, I thought to myself. *I'm out of here.*

Taking one last look around, I was hit with a wave of understanding about the cautious loners and emotional wrecks that Bob Seger sang about – the desperate denizens of nightclub scenes the world over.

The irony was, I was surrounded by a room full of people who merely wore the outward façade of being miserable – the costume of doom and gloom. Yet, despite outward appearances, each of them were having a great time.

I wasn't. (Okay, neither was Alex, but that was his choice.)

I couldn't be polite to someone who was so unwilling to give up their misery and let go of the past. I was trying to let go of my own past and here was this doof holding onto his with every man-made fiber of his being.

Suddenly, every horrible memory of every guy who had ever rejected me flooded my brain. It was like being felled by a giant dose of Kryptonite.

Shit, maybe I should have shared some of my miserable experiences with Alex. At least *he* dated someone.

Feeling like a damn fool, I fled the club. The cold night air mingled with my warm tears. I looked fucking ridiculous. My attempt at goth chic was a step or two above clown makeup and was now cascading down my face in ribbons of black, white, and blue. I looked like the bastard offspring of Elvira and Tammy Faye.

It was a long walk back to the subway. I turned down a dark alley so I could scream or cry or do *something* to let out everything I had bottled up for so long.

The booze and the weed I'd been plying myself with for months were just a temporary panacea to push back the emptiness I was feeling. All I wanted was a boyfriend or someone who liked me for who I was. I stopped being "picky" and gave up on chasing after guys who couldn't give a shit about me. I thought maybe I could open myself up to guys who weren't of my choosing but who I might hit it off with anyway. Instead, all I got were stalkers or guys who wanted to mold me into the type of girlfriend *they* wanted, figuring that my physical package wasn't completely hideous, but my personality was something that could be altered to their specifications.

I didn't care that I was in a dark alley in a shitty part of town. I didn't give a fuck if someone knifed or mugged me. Physical pain would be a step up from the emotional agony I was feeling at that moment. I slumped down, sobbing my eyes out, surrounded by concrete and garbage cans.

"Miss," called a female voice. "Are you okay?"

I looked up to see a tall, thin black woman with dreads that reached to nearly the backs of her knees. "Are you alright? You're not hurt, are you?"

I shook my head. "No. I'm okay. It's just been a shitty night."

"Don't I know that," she laughed. "You might want to get up. You're going to get dirt all over yourself sitting down there."

"It's cool," I said, standing up and brushing myself off. "Not like I'm going anywhere."

"This isn't a good place for a girl to be at this hour. Even if you are dressed up to scare people. Halloween was a few months ago. Why're you dressed up?"

I laughed. "I was just coming from this stupid club. I got all dressed up for a blind date. Turns out, he never showed and the guy I thought was my date was just some loser who wanted to talk about his ex-girlfriend all night."

The woman laughed, amused at the absurdity of my story. "That *does* sound like a shitty night! You need to get back home and get some sleep. Get your drink on. Get your pajamas on. Just pass out and relax. Tomorrow's a new day. That's what I said after my first divorce."

It was my turn to laugh. This chick was pretty cool.

"Come on," she said. "I'll walk you to the bus to make sure no one fucks with you."

"Thank you," I said, slightly shocked. "My name's Nova. What's yours?"

"Miriam," she replied. "Nice to meet you, Nova."

"Same here. You have really cool hair. How long did it take you to grow it?"

"About 8 years. It's all tangled and ratty. I gotta do something with it."

"No," I replied seriously. "It's awesome! I wish mine would grow that long."

"Takes patience," she replied as we walked along Spring Garden. "That's what you need. Patience. Good things'll happen. Good guys will come along. There's worse things than being single."

She was right. I didn't have the courage to ask her what her story was. She could have been homeless or a prostitute or both. Here I was, some college kid on scholarship to a great school in a major metropolitan city and thinking it was the end of the world because I couldn't get a date. This woman probably had *real* problems I couldn't even begin to fathom. Yet, she had the kindness and selflessness to approach me in an alley to make sure I was okay. I was embarrassed by how stupid and short-sighted I'd been.

We talked until we reached our destination. It was just small talk, but nice to have the company. When I reached the subway, I thanked Miriam for everything.

"You don't happen to have an extra dollar or two, do you?" she asked.

I took out the $20 I had in my purse. It was all I had, but maybe she needed it more than I did. It was the least I could do to thank her for listening to me and being kind enough to pluck me out of that dark alley where I could have landed myself in some serious shit.

"Thank you," she said, stuffing the money in her boot. "And you be safe, Missy!"

"Thank you," I replied. "I hope things get better for you, Miriam."

"Everything comes in cycles," she said. "Some good. Some bad. You just gotta roll with it. Now get your ass on that bus!"

I never ran into Miriam again, but I hoped that her life ended up better than what I imagined it was. She seemed to be a really upbeat, positive, good-hearted person and it broke my heart that she was out there on the street. I didn't know her whole story and wish I'd have asked her, but was too afraid to. For all I know, she could have thought I was some drunk in an alley and planned on rolling me... Or she could have been an angel.

Regardless of who she was, she probably saved me from my own stupidity that night.

CHAPTER SEVENTEEN
BLIND DATE

My epiphany still didn't deter me from continuing down a slightly safer path of stupidity.

I decided to take a different avenue towards meeting guys. Thumbing through a weekly Philadelphia nightlife paper, I came to the personals section tucked away in the back.

Recalling the grand stories of "Wild" Will Olsen, the thirty-something dancer who had imparted his dating wisdom to me and Orion years back, I decided that I might be able to get a real date through a personals ad. Sure, Will Olsen dated some doozies in his day (counting an amputee among the ranks), and I, too, could wind up with a few winners. But it couldn't be any worse than what I'd already run into.

One ad in particular stood out:

"SWM. Athletically built with long hair. 30s. Divorced. Likes rock music and lives alone. Looking to have a good time. If interested, give me a call."

I analyzed the ad. First off, he had long hair and liked rock music. That was a huge check in the "plus" column. I dug dudes with long hair and the fact that he felt it necessary to list that he enjoyed rock music. Not indie. Not folk. Not shit. But good ol' rock.

He also said that he was "athletically built," which meant he took care of himself and wasn't a lard ass. Yet another check in the "plus" column!

He was in his 30s, which meant he would (hopefully) be more mature than the usual gang of idiots my own age I dealt with. The divorced thing freaked me out, however. That meant he probably had some sort of baggage. Then again, my own father had been married and divorced four times and he was a pretty cool, issue-free guy.

Hey! This divorced thing might not be so bad!

Moving down the list, I noticed that my prospect lived alone. I interpreted it as him being lonely and looking for fun and companionship. However, the last part of his ad – "looking to have a good time" – indicated that he might not have been lonely, per se, but more DTF. It was a tough one to interpret, but I figured either or couldn't be too bad.

I called the number in the back of the paper and reached his voicemail. John – the name of the guy from the ad – was soft-spoken with a masculine edge to his tone. I detected a down-to-earth, yet calming quality to his voice. Now, I was even more hopeful and intrigued about chatting with him.

I sucked at leaving voicemail messages and never knew what to say. At the sound of the beep, my mouth was off and running:

"Hi," I said trying to add a slightly more feminine edge to my relatively deep voice. "My name is Nova. I'm 18, almost 19 and am 5'1" with long, black hair, blue eyes and 36C breasts. I go to college here in the city and love rock, metal, and all sorts of movies – mostly comedy and horror. I'm also a virgin and am looking for someone to date. I'm not a nutcase or a weirdo, just a little shy around guys. Anyway, your ad seemed interesting and I like the sound of your voice. If you could give me a call back, I would love to hear from you."

I hung up the phone, satisfied with my message.

For a second.

Then the voice of reason crept into my head screaming: *What the hell did you just do?!*

I gave the dude my measurements!? I told him I was a virgin?! What sort of dumb slut was this guy going to think I was?!

If I had omitted those things, *maybe* I would have sounded like a halfway decent dating prospect. Instead, I came off as I usually did: desperate and trying too hard.

Oh, well. Worst case scenario, the guy won't call back. This bummed me out since I had already built John up to be a cool, attractive guy that I just might click with. On the flipside, dating via personals ads seemed like my last hope.

As always, I hoped for the best, but expected the worst.

Which was why I was surprised the next night when one of my roommates said that a guy named "John" had called and left me a message.

I snatched the pink Post-It note from her hand like I was Grasshopper and she was Master Po.

Holy shit! He actually called me back! I did an internal version of the Happy Dance. I was elated that this guy didn't find me weird, creepy, or off-putting. *I knew it was smart to go after a divorced guy! I knew it! These guys have ex-wives! Weird chicks like me are a piece of cake to deal with compared to ex-wives!*

Gradually, reality set in and I brought my self-congratulatory moment of joy to a finish. I wanted to tell my friends, but figured they might yell at me for using the personals.

I paced the room for a few minutes, contemplating what I might say to John. Needing more privacy and fearing a lack of judgment if my roommates or friends heard my conversation, I lurched towards the dorm's pay phone to call John back.

I dropped my quarter into the slot and dialed. A man picked up. The ad said he lived alone, so I assumed it was him.

"Hello? Is this John?"

"Yes, this is. Is this Nova?"

"Yep," I replied. "Nice to finally speak with you."

"Honestly," John spoke. "I'm not looking for a girlfriend. I placed the ad because I'm looking for a casual relationship. I think you're a little young to be answering these types of ads. Especially if you really are a virgin."

I felt a sick feeling in the pit of my stomach. I wasn't going to get a date. I was going to get a lecture.

"I just wanted to make sure you're not going to get hurt. You really need to be careful. You never know what lunatics are out there."

"So, you're not judging me?"

"Not my place to judge. I'm just saying you should be careful with who you give your details to. There are people out there waiting to take advantage of you."

"Thank you," I said, considering John's words. "It's nice that you were looking out for me." I decided that maybe I should change the subject and ask him more about himself, just to make sure he knew I was still interested.

We talked for a long time on the phone. It could have been an awkward "getting to know you" conversation, but John and I chatted like old friends. I learned we liked a lot of the same bands and that he had married young. He and his wife were together for ten years before they divorced. He lived alone in an apartment in the city and was still friendly with his ex, who lived with her long-term boyfriend.

"Can I call you tomorrow?" he asked

"I would like that a lot. Or I could call you, too?"

"I will be looking forward to your call tomorrow, then," he said before saying goodnight and hanging up.

I hung up the pay phone and danced giddily, almost skipping back to my room.

The next night, I gave John a call again. He picked up and we had yet another great conversation, this time talking about politics, history, and our hobbies. I mentioned I liked writing and he told me about his involvement in the martial arts and the various disciplines he studied.

We chatted a while longer before wishing one another a good night and hanging up. John said he would call my room around 8 P.M. the next night.

Meanwhile, my friends had been looking for me and wondered where I went, unaware that I was hanging out in the hallway on the dorm's pay phone talking to my personals pal.

I didn't want to tell anyone just yet. I followed the normal pattern and went to smoke up with Jerry and Boone as part of our normal Wednesday night ritual.

My evening phone chats with John had become a ritual of their own for the better part of a week. We had been speaking to each other for about a week and a half and I was anxious to finally meet him. One night, I broached the subject of meeting and John seemed hesitant.

"Are you sure you want to meet up? How do you know I'm not an axe murderer?"

"Real homicidal maniacs don't go around telling people that they're axe murderers. Besides, I'd like to be able to put a face to the voice of the person I've been talking to."

"I'd like to meet you, too. I think you're intelligent and mature in some ways – but I also think you're a little naïve in others. I just don't want you to get hurt."

"I don't think seeing you and going out for a slice of pizza or something is going to scar me for life."

There was a long pause on the other end as I wondered if maybe I had said too much. "Just think about it," I said. "It doesn't have to be anything major. No movies. No fancy dinner. Maybe we could meet up at a record shop on South Street.

Check out some music and get a bite to eat at a local pizza joint or something."

"Okay. How about next Thursday at around 7 P.M.?"

"Awesome!" I exclaimed, not really hiding my enthusiasm. "Looking forward to it."

"Me, too," he replied before bidding me a good evening and hanging up.

I had to tell someone that I would soon be going on a real date in less than a week! I knocked on Carla and Liz's door. Boone and Jerry were already paying them a visit, sprawled out on the girls' floor.

"Guys! I have *huge* news! I have a date next week!"

"Are you serious?" Liz sat up. "That's great!"

"With who? Where did you meet him?" said Carla happily.

"I didn't meet him yet." Seeing the confused looks on the faces of my friends, I clarified that I had answered a personals ad and had been talking to John for over a week now.

"That's a bad move." Jerry raised a barely-there platinum eyebrow. "You shouldn't go around answering personals ads. You never know what nuts are out there."

"Actually, that's what John said, too."

"John? Not our boss John, right?" asked Boone, referring to our library supervisor. "Because I'm going to be really pissed if you told him about this first."

"No way! 'John' is the name of the guy that I've been talking to."

"So that's why you've been missing every night! Holy shit! You fucking sneak!" laughed Boone.

"I'd have told you guys sooner, but would have been embarrassed if nothing happened. And I was worried you would think I was getting myself into deep shit by answering a personals ad."

"Aww!" sighed Carla. "I understand! I think it's great. Tell us a bit more about him!"

"He seems like a really good dude," I said. He's a bit older – early 30s. Divorced. Lives by himself. Been working at the same job for over ten years."

"Okay. I can see you dating older," said Liz approvingly. "Plus, he has a stable job. That's a good sign."

"The catch is, he seems hesitant to meet me and is worried I might be too young."

"That's bullshit," said Boone. "You're pretty mature for your age."

"Does he smoke up?" asked Jerry.

"I'm not sure," I answered. "I know he likes rock and metal. He has long hair. He probably does smoke up."

"Yes!" said Jerry, pumping his fist in the air, eager to add another member to our circle.

"Did you tell your parents or your brother yet?" asked Carla.

"No way. My brother would totally rat me out to Mom. Dad's cool about everything. Not sure how he'd feel about the whole personals ad thing, but... Mom, on the other hand, would hit the roof."

"Really?" asked Boone. "I always got the impression your parents were cool."

"They are. I mean, Mom wouldn't *kill* me... But she would make fun of me constantly. And there's no way I would do that to myself even before I went out on a date with someone."

Finally, Thursday arrived. I put on a long-sleeved black knee-length dress, heels and my black leather jacket. I straightened my hair and put on a bit of makeup before heading to Liz and Carla for inspection.

"Do I look okay?" I asked nervously. "I don't look slutty?"

"You look fine!" exclaimed Liz. "Really! Now go have a good time! And come back here the second you get back from your date so you can tell us all about it!"

"Good luck!" called Carla as I hurried out the door. "Have fun and call us if you run into any trouble."

"I will!" I yelled back over my shoulder. "See you in a few!"

I hurried down the hall, pounding a path to the elevators before walking into the crisp, early spring air. I could feel butterflies in my stomach as I dropped my token into the subway turnstile.

Running as fast as my high heels would carry me, I hauled ass to South Street. John and I agreed to meet up at Tower Records and then hit the South Street Diner for dinner. It was low-key and casual. And there were a lot of people around in case he turned out to be a whack job.

I glanced around before looking at my watch. It was 6:45. I took a once-over of the store, seeing if anyone matched John's description. Not getting a vibe, I parked myself near the window, perusing the new releases. Whenever I heard the store's front door open, I would turn around to see if it was John.

Finally, at almost exactly 7 P.M. on the dot, I turned around to see a tall man with long, wavy brown hair pulled into a ponytail who looked like a young Iggy Pop. He wore jeans and a grey thermal Henley that hinted at his musculature beneath a well-worn, black leather bomber jacket.

"Are you John?" I asked hopefully.

"Some people call me that sometimes."

I recognized his voice instantly and put out my hand. "Nice to finally meet you! I'm Nova."

He took my hand and shook it warmly. "It's very nice to meet you, too, Nova. Would you like to go for a walk around the store?"

We walked around, looking at albums and chatting until I asked John if he wanted to grab something to eat. "You've been at work all day. You're probably starving."

"Actually, I am," he replied. "Which way is the South Street Diner?"

"Follow me," I said, scurrying down the sidewalk.

"Slow down!" John laughed. "Are you trying to lose me?"

"Not at all. I just walk fast. Everyone else I know is tall, so I'm used to walking fast to try to keep up with them. My friends call me 'The Squirrel'." No sooner than the word "squirrel" passed from my lips did I regret saying it.

"The Squirrel?"

"Yeah," I replied, embarrassed by how stupid I must have come across. "It's because I'm short, I walk fast, and my hair kind of looks like a big, fluffy squirrel tail behind me when I walk."

Inner facepalm.

It wasn't long before we arrived at the diner. Not taking much time to look at the menu, John made his decision almost instantly. "I'll have the Chicken Parm, please."

I, on the other hand, was so nervous that I wasn't able to eat anything really heavy. I ordered the fruit plate with cottage cheese, hoping John didn't think I was one of those annoying chicks who only order the salad so their dates don't think they have a fat person hiding inside.

"That's all you're going to eat?"

"I'm nervous. Otherwise, I would probably be wolfing down some Chicken Parm with you right now."

John laughed. "You don't have to be nervous. I'm very glad we met."

"Me, too."

"I haven't been completely honest with you, though."

Uh-oh. This can't be good.

Seeing the expression on my face, John clarified. "John isn't my real name. I didn't want to give anyone who answered the ad my real name in case they were crazy."

"Okay. I can understand that."

"My real name is 'Max.' 'Max Kuznetsov.'" He handed me a neatly printed business card.

I was grateful he handed me his card, otherwise I wouldn't have been able to pronounce his last name.

"So," said The-Blind-Date-Formerly-Known-As-John. "What's your real name? 'Nova' can't be your real name."

"Nope. It is," I said, taking out my student I.D. as proof.

"You really shouldn't have used your real name answering these ads. You have to be careful." He laughed so as to not make it seem like a lecture. "I like it, though. Nova is a very pretty name."

"Thank you. Truthfully, like the name 'Max' better than I do 'John.' It suits you better."

"Well, it's the name my parents gave me. I'm stuck with it."

"Me, too. My parents were big on handing out weird names. My brother is named 'Orion.' We used to beat the crap out of each other growing up, but now we're best friends. He's a good kid."

"How old is he?"

"Almost 15."

"Does he play video games?"

"Nah. He's not really into that. Mom wouldn't let us have video games when we were kids. Or a microwave. She thinks that microwaves give you cancer. My brother digs sports, though. Football, basketball, baseball. He watches ESPN constantly."

"Does he play any sports?" Max asked.

"He used to play Little League, but now he's focused fully on dance. He does everything. Ballet, tap, jazz, hip hop. He's really an awesome dancer." I switched gears. "Do you play any sports?"

"I played football and ran track in high school. I went to a Catholic all-boys high school."

"That had to be interesting. I imagine a lot less drama with no girls around."

"Yeah. Bullies weren't tolerated. Once you went to North, you were a brother for life. You looked out for one another."

"Lucky," I said. "Not like my school at all. Bullying was practically encouraged. You had to fend for yourself. I got bullied for years until I fought back."

"Why would anyone want to bully you?" he said, being completely sincere. "You're too nice and you're too pretty."

"Dude. I was a dog in my high school. I got made fun of constantly because I was different. Being a metalhead was something of an oddity. I had acne, glasses that could burn ants, and bad hair. I was made fun of all the time."

"I don't understand why. You seem pretty great to me."

This was too good to be true. A nice, cool, good looking guy actually thought I was attractive? I had to make sure this was real and not something I was imagining.

"I have a mole on my nose. See? And my right earlobe is torn. That doesn't bother you, does it?" I thought that by blurting out my physical flaws, Max could decide if he was repulsed by me *now*, as opposed to later when I *really* may have liked him

"No." Max was greatly amused by this. "There's nothing wrong with that. How did you tear your earlobe anyway? A fight?"

"No." I laughed and shook my head. "I pierced my own ears when I was 12 years old. My mom wouldn't take me to get them done, so I did them myself. I pierced one ear too low and used to wear really heavy earrings. My earlobe just split right near the bottom. It's not really noticeable since I have a piercing right over it and always wear my hair down... But I can play Pac-Man with my earlobe if I turn my head sideways."

Max seemed to get a kick out of my prattling. He must have really liked me because, looking back, most guys would have turned and ran after hearing the awkward blather that fell out of my mouth.

After we finished dinner, Max picked up the check. I was not expecting that. Nor was I expecting it when he asked if I would still like to walk around South Street for a bit.

He held my hand while we walked. "Now you don't have to walk so fast."

It was sweet. For the first time, I was out with a guy that really liked me and who I liked back. The two and a half weeks it took to finally meet Max were worth the wait.

We stopped in a few stores and talked a bit more until it was time to head home.

"I can drop you off at your dorm, if you'd like?"

Not wanting to say goodbye so soon, I gratefully accepted a ride home.

"I hope you're not put off when you see what my car looks like. I call it 'The Shitbox.'"

"I like shitty cars," I said. "They have personality. Besides, I come from a family of used car owners. My dad is the king of used cars. He gets them from this local guy named Sputty, drives them around for five years and totally runs them into the ground."

Max found his car almost immediately. Standing apart from the shiny cars on the lot, "The Shitbox" was primer grey with a variety of lighter grey splotches covering the side doors and hood.

"It's a good thing my car looks like this," he said, unlocking the passenger side door and opening it for me. "Otherwise I would never find it. It reminds me of a big cloud."

Reaching across the seat and opening the door for Max, he slid in behind the steering wheel and closed the door.

Max got lost, insisting he knew how to get to my dorm. He didn't, but I didn't mind. It meant I got to spend that much longer with him in the car.

We reached the dorms a half hour later. Max parked his car in front of the building and turned the car off.

"I guess this is your stop."

"Yep," I replied. "I had a really nice time. It was so good finally meeting you."

Max leaned towards me as I prepared to make my exit. I leaned in closer, wanting to kiss him but not knowing what the hell to do.

Do I go full on the lips? Will he think I'm a total whore? What if he tries to slip me the tongue and I have no idea what to do?

I leaned in and gave him a quick hug and a kiss on the cheek. "I'll call you to make sure you get home alright, okay?" I opened the door to get out, yet again not realizing how stupid that sounded until I actually said it.

"I'll see you soon?" Max asked hopefully.

"Definitely! Very soon!"

I ran up the stairs to Liz and Carla's room. Sure enough, the boys were there, too.

I didn't even have to knock. Liz had already pounced up and opened the door, anticipating my arrival.

"Well?! How did it go?!" asked Carla excitedly as Boone, Jerry, Liz and her boyfriend Matt peered anxiously at me.

"It was so nice," I said, sounding completely and unexpectedly girly. I recounted the details of my date to the gang. I also informed them of the crucial detail that my date's name wasn't "John," but rather "Max," explaining he had given a fake name when answering the personals ad.

Boone punched Jerry's arm. "I told you it was a fake name. You're buying the next dimebag."

"Did he open the door for you?" asked Jerry.

"Yes."

"And did you open the door for him in the car when he let you in?" asked Carla, her eyes glittering.

"Yes," I answered again.

"Good job!" said Liz. "Guys know that's how a girl is one of the good ones. It was in *A Bronx Tale*. Never go out with a girl who doesn't open the car door for you after you open the door for her."

"Did he kiss you?" asked Boone, on pins and needles.

I took a deep breath. "Sort of. I didn't know what to do when he leaned in at the end of our date. I thought he'd think I was a power slut if I kissed him and I have no clue what to do with a tongue in my mouth. So, I just kissed him on the cheek."

"Dude," said Jerry slowly. "That's bad. He's going to think you don't like him."

"What?! I told him I would see him soon and call him to make sure he got in okay. I think that says 'I like you.'"

"No," Liz and Matt shook their heads before Matt answered this round. "He wouldn't have thought you were skanky if you kissed him. It's a goodnight kiss. You kissed him on the cheek – which was nice. But he's going to think you like him like a brother or something."

Everyone nodded in unison.

"You better call him now to work some damage control," said Boone.

I looked at my watch. Nearly 40 minutes had elapsed since I last saw Max. I figured he should be home by now.

Smiling, Carla handed me the phone.

"You want me to call him now? Here?!"

"Yes!" everyone shouted.

Taking the phone and rolling my eyes, I dialed the number. I had it memorized by now. As if I wasn't putting enough pressure on myself, now I had an audience.

After a few rings, Max picked up.

"Hi, Max," I said, full of cheer. "I promised I'd call you to make sure you got in alright."

"I don't want to keep you long. I know you have to get to bed soon, but I just wanted to thank you. I had a great time tonight and would really like to see you again."

"I had a nice time, too. Would you like to go see a movie or something Sunday?"

"Sunday sounds cool. Is there any movie you'd like to see?"

Carla mouthed the words *"The Wedding Singer"* as Jerry and Boone actually blurted out the movie title themselves.

"Knock it off, you guys!" I hissed with my hand over the receiver.

"I'm fine with anything you want to pick. I have the newspaper right here, so let me know what movie and we'll pick a time."

"How about *The Wedding Singer*?" I asked. "The one with Adam Sandler and Drew Barrymore?"

"That looks pretty good. How about the 5:15 showing? I can pick you up, if you'd like."

I maintained composure. Sort of. "That would be great," I gushed. "Looking forward to seeing you then. Give me a call tomorrow night if you can."

"I certainly will," he said before wishing me a good night and hanging up.

I hung up the phone and felt an overwhelming sense of relief. I *finally* had my first date and was going on a second. Holy shit!

"Now we gotta get you your first real kiss, Cinderella," said Boone with a smirk.

"And we are so meeting him when he comes to pick you up on Sunday, just so you know," kidded Liz.

They got no argument from me.

Sunday couldn't come soon enough. I agonized over picking the right outfit. The girls gave my choice of attire their seal of approval before Max called to let me know he was downstairs.

The entire gang accompanied me to the lobby outside the dorms. Max was sitting on one of the benches, his cloud car parked only a few feet away. I introduced him to my friends and he promised them he'd take good care of me before we pulled away.

As I looked out the window behind me, I saw Jerry and Carla flash me a thumbs up. I settled back into my seat and relaxed, chatting with Max just enough to spark a conversation, but not too much that he would get lost on the way to the Cineplex.

At the movie theater, I was prepared to pay for myself, but Max insisted on paying and getting us some popcorn and soda.

I was hoping he would make a move as we shared the medium-sized bag of popcorn. I kept leaning my hand on the arm rest, hoping he would hold my hand at some point during the film. Finally, he got the hint as I inched closer towards him – arm rest, be damned – and put his arm around me. I wrapped my arm around him and pulled myself closer against him in a long, continuous hug.

He didn't scream. He didn't try to run away. Score!

It was close to 8 P.M. when the movie let out.

"You're sure you're not embarrassed to be seen riding around with me in this car?" Max's eyes were hopeful.

"Not at all. I like it. It's got personality." I smiled back at him across the seat, hoping he would move in for a kiss. I was ready this time. Max moved in and very gently kissed me on the mouth. I put my arms around his neck and moved in a little closer, kissing him back. I hoped I wasn't coming across as completely inept as he slid the tip of his tongue inside my mouth. I could feel my heart pounding like Ron Jeremy in a three-way.

This was it. It was my first *real* kiss. It wasn't a peck on the cheek and it wasn't an obscene amount of tongue. It was sweet and wonderful and memorable. Everything a first kiss should be.

After 19 years, it was worth the wait.

One month later, Max and I exchanged "I love you"s. After years of beating my head against a wall to get a guy to like me, I finally found someone who, with very little effort, loved me. And I loved him back. I felt a bit sappy and girly, but it was good to have someone with whom I had a lot in common and whose company I really enjoyed – and above all, felt the same about me.

CHAPTER EIGHTEEN
EMO HAM

Fast-forward seven years later. I graduated from college and had been working with an ad agency for a few years. Max and I lived together in an apartment in Philadelphia. Like any couple, we argued occasionally (stay with someone over seven years and it's bound to happen), but we were still really happy.

I would still head home to Fletcher to hang out with Orion, my parents, and friends every other weekend.

I had a tight circle of friends and, thanks to the Internet, managed to make several new friends who shared common interests and was also able to track down old friends that I had lost touch with through the years.

The downside to the Internet, however, is that a lot of old "friends" can find *you* just as easily as you can find them.

Social media brought me back in contact with the one and only Wendell from my ballet days. I didn't recognize him at first, considering he had put on about 60 pounds – and it wasn't muscle mass, either. His long, red hair was now cut into a short style that could best be described as Leprechaun Guido. I recognized him by his beady eyes – and what had to be a new, albeit significantly larger version of his grim reaper shirt – captured in all its glory on his profile pic.

What the hell! It couldn't hurt to say "hi" and see how he's doing!

I had long since forgiven any transgressions – namely, turning me down and never returning the RHCP and Butt Trumpet cassettes I loaned him. (When MP3s are the preferred music-listening medium of choice, any offense involving a cassette tape is ancient history.) I hoped Wendell had grown as a person and had found some measure of happiness in his life.

I thought, *Hey, wouldn't it be cool to be friends with this person from the past and clear the air?!*

Boy, was I wrong!

Wendell had other plans. It started out innocently enough, catching up on where life had taken one another. I told him about Max and my life in Philly after graduating.

Wendell had finished his degree and became an in-house IT guy for a small t-shirt company in Fletcher. (Maybe they gave him a discount on his new grim reaper shirt?)

He had a rough break-up two years prior with a girlfriend who got married and pregnant mere months after dumping him. In lieu of dating, he turned his interests towards an obsession with *Grand Theft Auto* and spending time with his sister, her boyfriend, and his niece.

At first, he seemed normal enough. Normal for Wendell. He was always a bit of a layabout so his admission of calling out sick from work play *GTA* online and catch up on *Sopranos* episodes did not come as a surprise.

Wendell displayed classic signs of the bizarre disorder that plagues so many insecure, yet incongruously narcissistic males between the ages of 24 and 33 in which they engage in fervent worship of any form of media that pertains to the Mob or Mafia – regardless of whether they can claim even a drop of Italian heritage.

What was surprising, however, was that Wendell constantly wanted to talk about relationships – my relationship with Max and his own last relationship. I figured I was being a friend and lending an ear to someone who wanted to gauge what a normal, long-term, functioning relationship was compared to one that had fizzled and then blown up like an elementary school science project.

Wendell did not hesitate to give me the gory details of his last few failed romances, although he harped on his last one quite a bit.

"Dude," I said. "You're still hung up on this chick. You've got to let it go and move on. Do something besides play *GTA* and get out there."

"I'm not hung up on her." His voice crackled with protest. "But if she wanted me back, I'd be there with her in a second. Kid and all. I spend a lot of time with my niece and it really makes me want to start a family of my own."

"That's cool, dude," I said, attempting to be reassuring. "But it won't happen if you don't get up off your ass and get over it. Objective observer here. Just sayin'!"

"No. I understand." I detected a note of pissy-ness. "But it's hard to get back in the dating scene. I've put on weight since you've last seen me."

No shit, Sherlock. I restrained myself against criticizing and opted for constructive discourse instead. "So? You can always hit the gym and drop a few. Just get up off the couch. It'll be better for you in the long run."

"I don't have the time," he complained.

"If you've got time for mass amounts of *GTA* and call out of work, you've got time for an hour a day, three times a week to go for a run or lift weights."

Not much had changed in the ten years that had passed. I was actually buying into Wendell's decade-long pity party again, hoping that maybe "tough love" and a pep talk could help the guy out. I recalled he hadn't been dealt the easiest hand early on, his mother throwing him out of the house and all of the problems he had with staying in school. And I remembered that, at one time, both my brother and I called him a friend. Remembering that, I wanted him to beat the odds and do well for himself.

That same weekend, I posted on Facebook that I would be making the trek back to Fletcher and that Mom, Orion, and I were going to a local arts festival. Max wouldn't be visiting my folks with me because A.) he hated traveling and B.) had work that weekend. Wendell commented that he was also going to the same festival and perhaps we would run into each other.

How often do people really mean it when they say, "Hey! We'll hang out next time I'm in town!" It's just one of those polite-yet-hollow things people say.

Wendell, however, made it a point to run into us. Orion knew I had friended the guy online. Like me, he was wary, but still stoked to see a blast from the past.

Wendell walked around with my brother, my mother, and me the entire time at the festival. Both Orion and I thought it was a little fishy but brushed it off. This was Wendell we were talking about: Fat, out of shape, slightly nerdy, formerly-homeless Wendell. He was harmless.

Wendell chatted with Mom quite a bit, turning on the charm. Mom, with her own background in the arts, loved having someone to talk with about dance and acting. I began to get the sneaking suspicion that Wendell had an agenda.

Trying to be nice, Mom invited Wendell over to have some of her famous lasagna, prompting him to unleash a flurry of quotes from *The Godfather* along with a terrible Al Pacino impersonation.

Mom ate it up.

Orion and I exchanged plaintive "What the fuck?" looks.

When Wendell followed Mom through the door, Dad shot me and Orion a similar "What the fuck?" look.

"Jesus," said Dad. "He got fat. What the hell is this bum doing here?"

"Mom invited him." I wrinkled my nose.

Dad looked as if someone just farted in the refrigerator and shut the door.

This was quite a role reversal. Normally, Mom hated my friends. Dad was usually the one who treated total strangers like family. For some unknown reason, Mom had taken a shine to Wendell, who was trying his damnedest to impress Mom.

It wasn't long before Wendell reiterated his sob story of girl-friend- and weight-woes to Mom at dinner. He also spotted a couple of my comic books and graphic novels on the coffee table.

I picked up my copy of *Earth X*. "I just got done reading this one. Great story."

"Really? Can I borrow it?"

I wanted to say no, recalling the last time Wendell "bor-rowed" my RHCP and Butt Trumpet albums, never to return them. Yet, the words "Sure! You can borrow it" dropped out of my mouth.

Wendell took it as an invite to paw through the rest of the pile, helping himself to some of my other books. I was not liking this.

After desert, coffee, and more tableside chat, Wendell was on his merry way along with a tinfoil bundle of Mom's home-made lasagna.

I thought nothing of it until that Monday when I got an email from Wendell saying that he had been fired. They cited "lack of attendance" as one of the causes for his dismissal.

I wanted to say, "I told you no good could come of mara-thoning episodes of *The Sopranos*."

Instead, I tried to be a sympathetic friend, telling him to prep his resume and get back out there.

"How am I going to pay my rent? They're trying to deny me unemployment benefits."

"I don't know, dude. You can try to fight them on it and write a letter stating your case to the unemployment office."

Some things never change. I'd only been reacquainted with Wendell for two weeks and he was already on the verge of homelessness.

"I need to talk to someone," he sighed dramatically.

I didn't know just who the "someone" was until later that night when I got a call from Orion.

"So, I hear Wendell is unemployed again?"

"Yeah," I said, confused. "How did you find out?"

"Because he drove over here right before Mom took me to my dentist appointment. When I told him we couldn't talk that long, he took it as an invitation to go to the fucking dentist's office with us!"

"Are you fucking kidding me?"

"Nope. He just sat there in the waiting room, going on and on about his problems. It was so embarrassing. Especially when he started crying and making a scene about how he didn't know what he was going to do with his life. How he turned his life around, then this happens. He even threw in a completely un-ironic, 'Just when I thought I was out, they pull me back in again.' Thank God Dad showed up and scared him off."

"Holy fucking shit. This is bad."

"Oh," Orion replied. "And just a heads up, but Wendell was asking a lot of questions about Max. Like why doesn't he come up to visit your family with you and what's your relationship with him like."

"You've got to be kidding me."

"Nope. Please tell me you're not thinking of dumping Max for this sack of shit."

"Are you fucking joking?! It hasn't even crossed my mind! I would never dump Max, much less for a chump like this! Why the hell would I do that?!"

"Just checking. Wendell is under the impression that he's going to make you his."

I wanted to vomit on the spot. "Seriously?"

"Yep." I could hear the smirk in my brother's voice. "He kept bragging that 'I talk to your sister every day online. We send each other emails all the time.'"

"Dude! I only reply to his emails because he sends so god-damn many of them! He has no life! He's either complaining that there are no 'mature' gamers online for him to play with. Or, he's getting fired or pining over his ex-girlfriend who dumped his chunky ass two years ago!"

Normally, this would be the part where my brother would bust my balls and make a crack about me becoming Wendell's future girlfriend. Realizing that there was something much more sinister afoot, Orion lapsed into action mode.

"You better set the record straight before he takes this shit further. I think he's trying to make a play for you so you can take care of his unemployed ass."

"Not gonna fucking happen."

I hopped online and went through some of the emails I had traded with Wendell to see if there were any warning signs. No sooner than had logged into my account than I saw a new message from Wendell. Curiosity got the better of me and I opened it, temporarily diverted from my mission.

His email mentioned that he had a wonderful chat with Mom and Orion who invited him to go to the dentist's office with them. According to Wendell, they – and my Dad – were sooooo supportive and gave him good advice that he would soon implement.

Wow. Talk about revisionist history. Wendell's take on his waiting room meltdown was completely different than the account Orion had given me.

I decided not to respond to the email until the following morning, remembering that Wendell made it a point to tell my brother about how often he and I emailed.

In the meantime, I looked over the emails Wendell had sent me before, combing them for anything that looked suspicious. I wanted to get someone else's take on the situation, but I didn't want to tell Max. Max had a jealous streak and never liked that I had several male friends. I doubted he would be too thrilled that some dude I used to have a thing for back in the day was trying to make a play for me. It wouldn't have mattered that I wasn't interested in the guy or that he looked like a tub of margarine with legs, Max would be livid.

To avoid an "I told you so" lecture, I decided to consult an outside source for his take. I was perfectly capable of handling this situation myself, but wanted to be sure I wasn't being paranoid or misreading things.

I sent Wendell's emails to Rick Sanders.

Yes. *That* Rick Sanders.

After I hung up my crush on him, Rick became one of my most trusted friends. He was my go-to guy who gave me the straight dope on all things male.

He pointed out that Wendell's constant mentions of his niece and himself as the doting uncle was supposed to tug at my heartstrings, utilizing the "Guys Who Love Kids Are Just As Precious As The Children Themselves" platform.

"He probably has no clue that you don't want kids," he laughed, knowing my stance on spawning. Which was why I took it seriously when Rick said, "This guy wants to get in your pants. He's trying to pull a scam on you. Look at this line here." He quoted the block of text that read, "I just want to make sure that your boyfriend is treating you right. Every girl should have that sort of 'Ross and Rachel' relationship from *Friends*."

"That right there, is him trying to plant seeds of doubt in your relationship. Fuck this guy! *Friends*? Ross and Rachel? What a pussy!"

I couldn't believe I didn't catch that one myself. Rick continued to point out more of Wendell's greatest hits. "Look at this line here in another email: *'If you wake up in the middle of the night after a nightmare, do you think your boyfriend would go out and pick you up a pint of your favorite ice cream to try to cheer you up?'*"

"Yeah. That was where I started to think maybe something was up."

"Graduated top of your class, eh, Nova?" Rick had honed his sarcasm over the years. "Ice cream? In the middle of the night? Get the hell out of here! This guy is way too emo."

"Oh, you should see him." My own sense of snark was reignited by the revelations that were now coming fast and furious. "Häagen-Dazs is a way of life for this tool."

"Pure and simple, this guy is a piece of shit," Rick said. "He was a piece of shit when we were in high school. He just got sloppy about hiding it now. He's using all the tricks in the book to try to weasel his way into your life and make you feel sorry for him. He's got to go."

"Absolutely. I mean, what the hell was that shit about *'if you wake up in the middle of the night from a nightmare,'*" I replied, imitating Wendell's nasal tone. "Fuck you! I *am* the nightmare!"

"Damn right!" said Rick, the Mickey to my Rocky. "Remember what an evil bitch you were back in high school?"

I nodded and winced at the memory. "Yeah."

"You need that bitch back. Destroy him."

He was right. I was about to make it abundantly clear to Wendell that I was not now, nor would I ever be, interested in him. That ship had sailed over ten years ago.

While I planned on channeling my high school-era inner bitch, I wouldn't make the same mistakes I did when I was 16. I was going to make sure Wendell gave me back my comics that I had stupidly loaned him.

But first, I had to satisfy my curiosity. Why was it that after ten years, Wendell now wanted to capitalize on the feelings I once had for him?

Sending him a friendly email in response to his latest installment regarding how "supportive" my family was during his disastrous dental office display, I didn't let on that I knew the real story and that my family was now onto his game.

I offered a few bullshit words of "support" and asked him why he turned me down all those years ago.

He responded. "It was because I thought your parents were really nice people. Your Mom would always ask me if I wanted anything to eat or would invite me for pizza with you guys."

I recalled that out of all the dudes I used to crush on, Wendell was the only one who bore Mom's Seal of Approval. She felt sorry for him and thought he would eventually make something of himself. Plus, he had an interest in the performing arts.

The rest of his email outlined his rationale: "I figured that if I dated you, your parents wouldn't have been as nice to me. If I needed a place to stay, they probably wouldn't have liked the idea of their daughter's boyfriend living under the same roof. So, that's why I chose Melissa over you."

There it was in black and white. I realized what I had always suspected: Wendell was an opportunist and master manipulator. If I had heard this revelation when I was 16, I would have been really hurt by it. Now, learning the truth only fanned the fires of my hatred. Wendell had blown his chance years ago and decided I was now a viable option. The fact that I had a (nicer, much better looking, gainfully employed, and significantly long-term) boyfriend did nothing to deter him.

Wendell's standard sob story routine may have cut the mustard when he was young and cute, but that strategy doesn't work quite as well when you're fat, out of shape, unemployed, and over thirty.

The next day I rattled off an IM to Wendell telling him that I would be visiting my family again the following weekend. "Maybe you, me, and Orion can grab coffee?"

His response: "Don't have money for coffee."

"Don't worry," I typed back. "I got it this time. By the way, did you get a chance to finish those comics I loaned you?"

"Will definitely be done with them before I see you."

"Perfect." I smiled maliciously at my computer screen. "See ya then!"

That week, I minimized my online contact with Wendell, trying to drive home the point that I was not interested in him. When I failed to answer one of his long, self-pitying emails with some shred of reassurance, he sent me another email, followed by a text message, both slightly miffed in tone:

"Is there some reason why you haven't responded to my emails?"

Rolling my eyes and promptly shooting a copy of it to both Orion and Rick, I replied: "Just busy! Crazy week at work." Lying via email was so easy! All you had to do to sell your point was add a passive-aggressive "smiley face" emoticon at the end of your statement and it diffused any tension.

Meanwhile, I had clued my brother in on the plan for that weekend. It was like old times, Orion and I putting our heads together to concoct a scheme.

It was a good thing, too. Wendell had attempted to hang around my family's house like a stray cat. Mom fed him once and he was trying to become a permanent resident. Screw looking for a job! Hitting my parents up for leftovers was much easier!

"I hate this guy," Orion said on the phone one night. "Really. I can't wait until we get rid of him for good."

The weekend of my visit home, Orion and I prepared to leave the house, heading to the book store to get my comics back and get Wendell out of our lives.

"Where are you kids headed?" asked Mom.

I told her we were headed to Greenfield's, the local bookstore / coffee house.

"Yeah. We're going to teach that bitch Wendell a lesson," replied my brother with all the vitriol of Patton on the eve of the Battle of the Bulge. Although in Wendell's case, this was the Battle of the Bulging.

"Good!" shouted Dad from the kitchen. "I hate that asshole!"

"That's not nice, kids," Mom chided.

"Are you crazy, woman?!" My brother and I exchanged looks. Dad rarely raised his voice, but when he did, you knew shit was about to go down.

"*That's not nice!*" Dad raised his voice higher to mimic Mom's pitch. "Who are you fooling? You can't stand that freeloader, either. Always coming around. Looking for food. Trying to bust up Nova and Max."

Dad was on to Wendell's game. Hell, he had been onto his game ten years ago. Furthermore, Wendell had done the unforgiveable by trying to insinuate a wedge between me and Max. That did not fly with my Pops. Dad and my boyfriend had a mutual man-love bond between them.

"Go give it to that fat asshole, kids." Dad grinned mischievously, waving me and Orion out the door. Given our father's blessing, we sped to Greenfield's.

It was time to take Fredo fishing.

"I bet you any money, he's standing around by the magazines. Because if he was sitting down in the actual cafe, that would mean he would have to order something."

As predicted, Wendell was hovering near the magazine racks. Orion cast a withering glance. "There he is. *The Biggest Loser.*"

Without exchanging a word, our steely expressions plainly declared that this was war and we had to make the first strike.

We caught Wendell in mid-flip of some online gaming magazine. He desperately tried to cover his tracks.

"I was looking through these computer trade magazines and I can't find the one I'm looking for. I need to brush up on my knowledge of computer information systems if I want to get a new job."

"Yeah. So you decided to settle on the fascinating world of *Online Gaming Monthly*. Lots of computer information system info in there."

His non-verbal response was to shoot me the stink eye.

Orion and I decided beforehand that we'd take turns playing Good Cop / Bad Cop. Orion made small talk with Wendell, asking him what he planned to do with his car. Wendell bought a brand new Nissan six months ago. You'd never guess because the car was already dinged to hell with scratches and dents.

"You should really think about selling your car, paying off the remainder of the loan, and using the rest of the money to coast until you get a job."

"Orion, you just don't understand," Wendell kvetched. "I was living paycheck to paycheck."

"If you don't mind my asking," I interjected. "How much did you make?"

"I made $50,000 a year. I was there seven years."

"Wait a minute. You mean, you made $50,000 a year and didn't sock away any savings whatsoever? The cost of living in

Fletcher's nowhere near what it is in Philly and even I had a safety net of cash." What a fucking bone head.

"Look," said Wendell defiantly. "I just don't want to talk about that right now. Capiche?" He folded his arms over his chest, turned on his heels, and began to walk towards the baristas.

"*Capiche*?!" I hissed at my brother. "He *does* realize his last name is 'McGinty,' right?"

Wendell sighed loud enough for the entire café to hear him. "Can we just get a drink and something to eat?"

I noticed Orion rolling his eyes as he stood behind Wendell. "Sure, thing!" I was trying my damnedest to conceal my contempt. *Of course he wanted to get some food.* "Let's get something and sit down."

"Are you paying?" Wendell wasn't even trying to be subtle.

"My treat." I was already prepared to pony up for a coffee. I weighed my options and decided that picking up a four-dollar tab for this clown would be much easier to swallow than taking a forty-dollar hit with him absconding with my comics.

Orion walked up to the counter. My brother and I decided to pick up a couple sodas, hoping Wendell would follow suit. Instead, he took his time browsing the pastry and sandwich cases before ordering a chicken club and a large hot chocolate. "With whipped cream," he added, smiling at the barista behind the counter. "Oh! And two bear claws."

"That mother fucker," I mouthed to my brother, my left eye twitching with anger.

"Dude," he muttered under his breath. "That is such balls."

Wendell happily took his tray full of food and drink and parked himself near the window. We had to make him think everything was cool and that everyone was friends. I wanted my shit back. Especially after Wendell just rooked me for $15.00 dollars on his meal.

Orion and I forced ourselves to smile as Wendell launched into a story about his niece. He was obsessed with the toddler since she was the closest thing to his DNA being replicated considering no woman in her right mind would mate with him.

"I babysat my niece last night." He smiled as he chomped at his triple-decker sandwich. "Ugh. I just felt so bad because my sister and her boyfriend were arguing all weekend. I hate for her to have to see them fight. It just tears my heart up!"

I decided to play along, pretending to be the type of girl Wendell anticipated this sensitive, child-worshipping schtick would work on even though I desperately wanted to vomit on his big, stupid face.

I leaned my head on my hand, propping my elbow on the table and smiled sweetly, allowing Orion to take over the role of Bad Cop.

"Awwww... Were you crying in your pudding today over that?"

I almost spit out my drink.

"That's not funny, you guys! My niece shouldn't have to see them argue! It's not good for her."

On the subject of things that aren't good for you, Wendell had already wolfed down his sandwich and both pastries. Now he was nursing his hot chocolate (with extra whipped cream).

"Hey!" said Orion cheerily. "Let's take a walk around the store. I want to check out a few albums."

Good call! Let's keep him moving and keep him away from the café counter. I don't want him getting any bright ideas and foot a take-out bill.

As we migrated to the back of the store where the CDs were, Wendell continued to prattle about his niece. "You know, even *she* knows that I don't have a job. I called up the house and said 'Hi, sweetie! It's Uncle Wendy,'" adding "That's what she calls me," with a dopey smile.

Orion sensed I was resisting the urge to make a wiseass comment and stepped on my foot as Wendell continued. "She said, 'Uncle Wendy! You're calling a lot! Is it because you don't have a job?' It was so cute!"

"It wasn't cute," I deadpanned. "That kid cut you cold, dude. And she's only four."

Full of pout and vinegar, Wendell plunked all 5'4" inches and 250 pounds of his bulk down at one of the store's listening stations and clapped the oversized headphones over his ears. He dialed through the music choices, declaring loudly, "I need to find some good music... Some good music to kill myself to! My life sucks!"

This wasn't so much a blatant cry for help as it was a ploy for sympathy. I had already gotten wise to the fact that, despite his considerable flaws, Wendell loved himself like no other.

Encouraging Wendell's delusions that the big, bad employer fired him for no real reason wasn't too high on the list of priorities. Neither Orion nor I felt like coddling a 30-year-old. Granted, Orion and I weren't exhibiting a whole helluva lot of maturity at this point, but we were still light years ahead of Cake Ass.

"Music to kill yourself to? Really? That's so fucking stupid."

"No it's not," argued Wendell. "I'd do it the right way, too. I'd slit my wrists vertically, not horizontally. I'd be dead in minutes."

"Wow," I snarled. "This sounds like an episode of *Degrassi*. Only you're like the 30-year-old that got held back a shit ton of times."

"You guys are *not* making me feel any better," whined Wendell, confirming that this wasn't a friendly get-together (or a drop-off for my comics), but actually an intervention he had staged for himself.

"Saying that you're going to kill yourself isn't going to better your situation. *You* have to do that." Switching gears seamlessly,

Orion reverted back to the question Wendell most feared: "So how about your car? Did you decide to sell it yet?"

I was quite familiar with the game Orion was playing. He just flipped the script on Wendell, throwing him off balance.

"I told you I don't want to talk about my car. My life sucks enough as it is. Do you realize I haven't been with a woman in almost two years?"

Jackpot!

"Have you made any attempt at trying to get one?" asked my brother.

"No. Not really. I haven't been interested in too many girls. And besides, I have my Fleshlight. I used it last night."

I looked over at my brother, his face mirroring my own disgust when met with the image of the Emo Ham playing hide the sausage with his pocket pussy.

Wendell began to laugh hysterically. "I knew that would make you guys sooooo embarrassed!"

"No. Not embarrassed," I confessed. "I just want to puke on your shoes is all."

Wendell threw an immediate snit fit. "That's it! I'm soooo tuning you guys out!" He slapped his headphones back on and cued up more emo, wrist-slitting jams

"Yo, dude! Chill!" exclaimed Orion. "We're just trying to help! We're showing you tough love! Step one is to stop being such a fucking woman."

"His tits are almost as big as mine," I said under my breath.

"But I can't," Wendell bleated. "I'm not like you guys. I could never have the attitude that either of you have about relationships." What the hell was he talking about? Did he have any clue as to how many times I had been turned down by dudes before I landed a long-term relationship?!

"You've said yourself that you haven't hooked up with many chicks. Maybe it's because they don't like the way you operate?"

Now Orion was playing Good Cop. "And for the love of all that's holy, listening to better music might improve your game!"

Wendell sat in a state of confusion until Orion cued up Jay-Z's "99 Problems" on the listening booth and forced Wendell to listen, holding the headphones over his ears as J-Hova dropped some knowledge on his ass.

Orion upped the ante by cranking the volume level so loud that you could hear it leaking from the headphones. Wendell frantically tried to turn the song off as my brother and I started rapping along right in the middle of the store, dancing around and high fiving one another like the painfully white jackasses we were.

Wendell was mortified but we were entertaining the hell out of ourselves. That's we took the party to the front of the store, away from the listening stations.

Orion decided to further amuse himself by eyeing up the ladies walking around Greenfield's. He and Wendell found themselves commenting on chicks walking by – and there *were* some hot chicks out and about. I'm comfortable in my sexuality and have no problem scoping out girls, delivering a "hot or not" verdict. However, I preferred to check out dudes, and Greenfield's was sorely lacking in saucy sausage specimens.

"Damn. At least you guys have some eye candy to look at. There is *not one* hot guy in this place for me to ogle."

I honestly didn't mean for my off-handed comment to come off as a jab at Wendell. I was merely stating the obvious.

"Ugh," Wendell piped-up sarcastically. "Thanks, Nova."

I guess I was supposed to retract my comment and say "Present company excluded! You're one spicy meatball, Wendell!" Instead, I took the ball and ran with it.

"No. Really. There are absolutely *no* hot guys here whatsoever. Damn!"

While Wendell seethed, Orion looked at his watch and feigned an excuse that we were meeting up with one of his friends for drinks. This was also a prime opportunity for me to get my stuff back and put the final nail in the coffin.

As we walked through the parking lot, we passed a Dumpster. Still in full-on self-pitying mode, Wendell remarked, "That's probably where I'll be living next."

Unable to resist, Orion took one last opportunity to tell Wendell to trade in his car. Apparently, Wendell *really* didn't want to talk about that option and kicked my brother with all of the power his saggy, out-of-shape frame could muster.

Instead of folding up as Wendell expected him to, Orion just laughed. "Wow! That was like being hit with 250 pounds of ham! You're such a girl!"

He tried to play it off that he was just kidding around, pretending to fight Orion, but my brother knew better. He had gotten under his skin and Wendell was already agitated since his afternoon did not go the way he had probably planned.

In a race to the Nissan, Orion out-distanced Wendell who was now completely winded and sweating profusely as he fumbled for his keys. The scent of hair gel, capicola, and dick cheese hung in the air.

It was pretty bad. I could have kicked Wendell's ass – and was prepared to if he tried to stage a legitimate throw-down with my brother. Hell, I probably had twenty-times the testosterone this dude had.

Wendell reached under the seat of his Nissan, handing me back my stack of comics. I hoped like hell that they hadn't been a resting place for his Fleshlight.

Orion looked down at his watch again. "We gotta boogie, man! We'll have to hang out again soon! Good seeing you!"

Yeah, right.

Orion and I rushed towards our car. I looked through each of my comics, making sure they were all there and mentally communicating with them the trouble I went through to make sure they made their way back to me.

As we pulled out of the parking lot, merging into mall traffic, we saw Emo Ham three cars ahead of us in the opposite lane, stewing inside his Shitmobile and looking fit to be tied. His hand dangled outside the window and he slammed it down on the outside of his car door in a desperate, *I'm so mad I could just cry*! gesture. Judging by all the scratches and dings on his car, he probably did that a lot.

Orion and I saw Wendell, but he couldn't see us. We cracked up laughing. It was well worth the $15 I spent on lunch for this goof. I had my comics back and Wendell got the hint to never email me again.

Sometimes, I wonder what happened to Wendell. Then I remember how much I like knowing that my comic book collection isn't a resting pad for some creepy Guido Leprechaun's pocket pussy and that curiosity passes.

EPILOGUE

Eventually, I told Max the entire story of Wendell's nefarious scheme to lure me in with Fleshlights and pints of midnight ice cream – and how my brother and I valiantly thwarted his insidious plot, restoring honor and dignity to our clan.

Max was more amused by it than I thought he would be. Then again, I waited until a decent cushion of time had elapsed so he wouldn't track down Wendell himself and sully his hands, putting that dolt out of his misery and dumping his carcass in the Pinelands.

"Please," Max said dismissing the ordeal. "Look at me! I'm a god! Did he really think my girl would go for a fat sack of shit? Really."

He was only half joking as he flexed his pectoral muscles to punctuate his statement. Max had no shortage of self-esteem. Consequentially, my years with him had helped improve my self-perception. Not because I finally had a man. Okay, maybe a little, considering my Quixote-like quest for a boyfriend was such a huge part of my identity for so long that it was one of the things that defined me.

I haven't completely banished my inner demons of self-doubt as fully as I'd like. I've come a long way, but total self-love is a hard thing to achieve. I don't tie my identity to my boyfriend or any guy that I had pursued in the past – but they have helped shape who I am.

We all want to play the hero of our story. And it's easy to vilify those who won't give us what we want. I'm no hero. I've lashed out at people for not wanting me back. I've been hurt, but it doesn't give me the right to hurt someone else for making a choice of their own free will that affects them just as much as it does me. For better or worse, my experiences define the person I am today. Thankfully, I can say I like the person I see in the mirror today – at least most days.

I've come to realize that life is a string of odd coincidences. The passage of time doesn't necessarily bring wisdom; it just removes the rose-tinted glasses so you make fewer stupid decisions.

Truth be told, I've had a fool's luck and wound up better than I had any right to.

I'll admit that sometimes I feel cheated that I never got little notes passed to me in class saying that so-and-so liked me and wanted to walk around the mall together. Those moments of innocent, young love – or "young like" – that I missed out on, devoid of any sexual overtones. That time when liking someone just meant wanting to hold hands with them and the most banal thing that ever came to mind involved the dubious prospect of whether or not you'd swap spit.

Yeah. I got screwed out of that innocent strain of young love. And going to the prom. (Who? Me? Bitter? Nah!)

In the end, I got something better. I have a 15-year relationship with someone who loves me and the realization that when the sexual fireworks of an adult relationship dim (because even the Energizer Bunny can only go for so long), when you're truly compatible with someone, the relationship takes on a similar quality as "young love" where you appreciate that person for who they are at their core and are grateful to share your life with them. Simply being in their presence is enough.

When those shades of self-doubt and bitterness come creeping in, I get angry with myself for placing so much weight on things that happened a lifetime ago.

Do we ever leave high school? I don't think so. Hell, I don't think we ever leave elementary school. We all still carry that emotional baggage we picked up all those years ago. Every act of kindness and every hurtful blow we receive shapes who we are.

And while the Internet brought me back into contact with a sideshow like Wendell, it also helped me to clear the air, get some closure, or pave new beginnings with people who were an important part of my life.

Whorin' Hank moved out of Fletcher and doesn't live too far from my current neck of the woods. He's still a fixture on the music scene in the tri-state area. His sense of humor remains intact – as does his whopping sense of confidence and good looks. And yes, ladies, Hank is still single and hasn't found his "tag team partner" just yet.

I haven't hung out with Boone in years, although we still stay in contact via Facebook. I'd have liked to have remained closer than I did with him and the rest of the gang from college, but everyone splintered off to do their own thing. I still feel honored for the walk-on role I played in Boone coming out. I respect him so much for seizing the moment to change his life for the better, to be honest and take that first step towards that elusive thing called happiness. And I'll always be grateful for his kindness in how he handled my crush on him.

Frankie Gilroy and I have made peace since our bitter, Catholic school feud eons ago. Actually, the subject has never been addressed since, and quite frankly, there's no need to. We all do some pretty stupid shit when we're younger. In hindsight, I think came on too strong and failed to consider how being liked by "the ugly girl" or the "tough girl" made him feel. It's impossible to understand men, let alone the inner workings of prepubescent boys. Nevertheless, Frankie Gilroy and I are definitely cool with one another. He's come a long way towards self-realization, too, as evidenced by his own happy, healthy, long-term relationship with an awesome girl. He's also plied his penchant for pop culture, music, and word-smithery into a career writing commercial jingles. We even ended up collaborating on some agency work at one point. Frankie's a talented guy and a damn good dude. I wish him a lot of continued happiness and success. I've learned a lot from him in terms of balancing life with work – and putting family and happiness first. If I held onto a stupid, grade school grudge, that's something I would have completely missed out on.

That said, my story wouldn't be complete without mentioning Rick Sanders.

The week before I went to college, I came to the realization that Rick and I would never be "a thing," but the fact that our friendship had managed to overcome four years of us intermittently putting each other through the ringer spoke volumes.

Even though Rick never had any romantic feelings for me and my feelings for him had long since dissipated, we had a long history as friends, having found ourselves thrown together in several different circles of friends through the years. In some form or another, we were a fixture in each other's lives for decades.

In the years that passed, Rick put himself through college, got married and had two of the coolest, most well-behaved kids ever. I'm proud to call him a friend and that I can trade barbs with Rick without any animosity or tension. That's pretty damn cool.

Even cooler, Rick's next-door neighbor is none other than our old friend Sammi. In the years since we last saw her, she traveled the country, cleaned up her act, got help for her addiction, and has been sober for almost a decade. Sammi is still as good-hearted, fun, and funny as ever. Despite living 100 miles away, we text and talk almost every day. I'm so proud of how far she's come. Don't let the punk Shirley Temple exterior fool you: they come no tougher than Sammi.

Her husband is a great guy and their son is as kind, outgoing, and funny as his mom was when she was his age. He also shares her impeccable taste in music.

And like their parents before them, Rick's kids and Sammi's son are friends that attend the same school. That's some *Lion King* / "Circle of Life" shit right there.

As for me, I'm still with Max. We'll be celebrating 15 years together in March of next year, although it doesn't seem that long. We moved in together during my senior year of college and have been "shacking up" (as Mom likes to say) ever since. Apart from my brother Orion – who just got married to an awesome girl – Max is my best friend and we make each other laugh. He's been there for me through countless ups and downs, has seen me at my worst, and helped to make me a better person. I hope I make him as happy as he makes me.

Folks come in and out of your life for a reason. You lose touch with people, but it doesn't mean that you don't think about them every so often and root for them to do well. And sometimes, you're pleasantly surprised to see who comes back into your life or who sticks around for the long haul. I'm glad the ones who have, did.

###

ACKNOWLEDGEMENTS

The "Acknowledgements" page of a book is a writer's equivalent to making an Academy Awards' acceptance speech – only the writer doesn't have to worry about the orchestra cutting them off, or whether Adrian Brody might try to French them in front of a live national audience.

Seeing as though I'm not famous, I don't light cigars with hundred dollar bills, and there's little chance of me ever accepting a gold statuette, I want to seize the rare opportunity to suck up a couple pages of this book to offer my heartfelt thanks to a lot of great people for all of their support through the years.

Thank you, Mom, for instilling a love of reading, writing, and humor in me from an early age. Thank you for pushing me to write, punishing me when I got a B in English back in 3rd grade, and for always offering honest praise and criticism. I miss you so much.

Thank you, Dad, for teaching me the art of storytelling. While Mom had the grammar market cornered, you gave me the gift of a genuine love for bringing people together to listen to a crazy tale. Not a day goes by that I don't miss you. Here's hoping I can entertain and make as many people laugh as you have.

To my boyfriend of (cough) many years, Emil: Thank you for sharing my life through good times and bad, and for believing in me when I didn't believe in myself. Thanks for telling me when my shit sucked, was too long-winded, and especially for all the times you told me to "stop dicking around on the Internet and start writing."

To my brother and partner-in-crime, Raphael: Thank you for always having my back, being my biggest fan, and your constant encouragement. It means so much, considering all you've accomplished and all the great things I know you will still do in the future. I'm so proud to be your sister. (Except for the time you threw a snit fit at Value City. Oh, and that other time when you thought Steve Stevens was Nikki Sixx.)

To my sister-in-law, Lauren. You're awesome and you're family. I lucked out getting you for a sister-in-law, but Raph lucked out even more.

Thank you to my friend Chrisy Wanner, who was one of the first people to read my book in its entirety. That means so much to me. Thank you!

I'd also like to thank my friend, mentor, and brother-in-arms Adam Williams for all of his valuable insight and encouragement. Thank you for pushing me to write for PopMatters all those years ago. You were the best damn editor a writer could ever hope to work with. And a big thank you to your beautiful and unbelievably sweet wife Mindy for all the good times, miles on the road, and concerts we've been to together. I couldn't ask for two better friends.

Heartfelt thanks are also due to two teachers who had a major influence on me:

To Mr. Howard Rice, for being a great teacher and friend. I'm just one of hundreds of students you've encouraged to write. You have a gift for fostering creativity in others and are a beacon that radiates kindness wherever you go. Thank you for being you.

To Mr. Robert DeFreitas. You epitomize the phrase "a scholar and a gentleman." Thank you for standing as a shining example of the strength it takes to live, thrive, learn, teach, and excel – even when others refuse to recognize you. I never would have made it out of high school in one piece without your guidance and friendship. Thank you so much.

I'm fortunate to have had and to have so many awesome people in my life. I wish I could thank them all here, but there's not enough paper and not enough words. Still, they've made my life a much better place just by being in it. They know who they are and I promise to give each of them personal shout-outs in upcoming books. Thank you for all the good times. I love you guys.

Last, but certainly not least... Thank YOU, dear reader, for taking the time to read this book. (And if you've actually paid for your copy of this book, I owe you a beverage of your choosing and a cookie if our paths ever cross. Seriously. I'm not kidding.) I hope you've enjoyed this ride with Nova Porter, her family, friends, and the dudes she dug who didn't always dig her back.

A writer lives to give life to the stories inside them by spilling them out onto the printed (or electronic) page. While it's gratifying to string those words together and see a story come to life, it's even more gratifying when someone actually reads your words and allows you to momentarily cart them off to spend time in the world you built. To know that someone out there may be touched by what you've written. That maybe some person out there is reading your story and saying, "Fuck yeah!" because they may be feeling the same way as one of your characters or may be going through something similar. It's a damn good feeling to know that your words may have helped eradicate that feeling of loneliness or alienation for someone for just a little while. More than the actual act of writing, I live for being able to connect with and entertain anyone who reads my work. Thank you for letting me do that and thank you for reading this book.

ABOUT THE AUTHOR

Lana Cooper was born and raised in Scranton, PA and currently resides in Philadelphia. She graduated from Temple University with a BA in Communications. Cooper currently holds it down 9-to-5 as a copywriter and editor for a Philly-based Internet marketing agency. She doesn't usually talk about herself in the first person, but makes an exception when writing an author bio.

A writer, critic, and journalist, Cooper has written extensively on a variety of pop culture topics for such sites as PopMatters and Ghouls On Film. She's also written full-length news stories for EDGE Media, a leading nationwide network of sites devoted to LGBT news and issues.

In her spare time, Cooper enjoys spending time with her family, reading comic books, books with lots of words and no pictures, and talking to strangers on public transportation. *Bad Taste In Men* is her first full-length novel.

Cooper is currently working on her next book and a buttload of short stories. Find out what crap she's up to and check out her blog over at www.lanacooper.com.